CURVEBALL

AN EXTRA INNINGS NOVEL

AK LANDOW

CURVEBALL: An Extra Innings Novel

Copyright © 2024 by AK Landow

All rights reserved.

Published by Author AK Landow, LLC

ISBN: 978-1-962575-13-3

Edited and Proofread By: Chrisandra's Corrections

Cover Design & Illustration By: K.B. Designs

 Created with Vellum

DEDICATION

To the sport of softball for uniquely having a place for girls and women of all shapes and sizes.

"Girls of all kinds can be beautiful - from the thin, plus-sized, short, very tall, ebony to porcelain-skinned; the quirky, clumsy, shy, outgoing and all in between. It's not easy though because many people still put beauty into a confining, narrow box... Think outside of the box..."
-Tyra Banks

BASEBALL/ SOFTBALL GLOSSARY

WORD/PHRASE	DEFINITION
RiseBall	Pitch thrown at upward trajectory
The Zone	The strike zone
Starting Rotation	The rotation of starting pitchers
Bomb	A home run
Bang-Bang Play	When the runner & ball arrive simultneously
Seeing-Eye Single	A soft ground ball the goes between infielders
Humpback Liner	A batted ball that sinks.
Sacrifice Bunt	Bunt intended to advance a baserunner, not be a hit
Sacrifice Fly	Batter hits a fly-ball that allows the runner to tag & score
Paydirt	Success; victory

PROLOGUE

PHILADELPHIA – PRESENT DAY

RIPLEY - AGE 28 {QUINCY - AGE 33}

No, no, no, no. It can't be true. I close my eyes and then look at the pregnancy test again, hoping for a different result. Peeling them open, I find that it still has two lines.

Deep breaths, Rip. Deep breaths. Mom did it alone, you can too.

Maybe it's a false positive. Yes! That's it. It happens all the time, right?

I grab the second test I bought and place it by the sink next to my toilet. Downing a large glass of water, I wait. It's not like I can pee on demand six minutes after I last went to the bathroom.

I look at myself in the mirror. My long, curly, red hair is down and looking good, but my skin appears unusually pasty.

This is my first northeast winter. It's not actually winter quite yet, but it feels like it to this California-raised girl.

Needing a distraction, I walk into Arizona's room. It's empty without her. I miss her so much. My best friend is shooting a bathing suit ad campaign in Fiji right now, only one week into her two-month worldwide shoot.

She's going to look amazing. She has the perfect body for it. I doubt I'd ever be asked to do a skimpy bikini campaign. I'm what you'd consider, "curvy" or "big boned." Of course, those are the nice words. I've had plenty of the nasty ones slung at me throughout the years.

Nonetheless, I'm doing a bit of modeling for plus-size lingerie right now. It's been very empowering, and the company called me back this week asking if I'm available to work with them again.

The younger me laughs at that fact. I was incredibly insecure about my body for a long time. Now I do my best to embrace it.

A smile finds my lips, knowing the boost in my confidence is in large part thanks to one special man who made me feel sexy. Because of him, I eventually learned to accept my own body.

My daydreaming is broken by the ringing of my text tone. Looking down at my phone, I notice that it's my teammate, friend, and neighbor, Kamryn Hart.

> Kam: Get your sweet tits next door. I want to pregame, and my sister is MIA. Again!

Kam's identical twin sister, Bailey, is her roommate. She nannies for a single father and has recently been needed many more evenings than in the past.

Kam and Bailey live in the apartment next door to us. It's been fun having our entire college crew back together again.

We've all played on separate professional softball teams since we graduated six years ago. A few months ago, we were all signed by the new team in Philadelphia, the Philly Anacondas.

Arizona, our catcher, is dating Layton Lancaster, the star of the local professional baseball team, the Philadelphia Cougars. Layton has been Arizona's dream man for as long as I can remember. I'm so happy for her that they found each other and fell in love. She's had a bumpy road and deserves all good things.

Her brother, Quincy, the longtime object of my affection, is on the Cougars too. In fact, he and Layton are best friends.

Our group has become close with several of the Cougars players, including Layton and Quincy. We're meeting them for drinks at a bar, Screwballs, tonight.

> Me: How do you know that my tits are sweet?

> Kam: Don't all gingers have sweet tits? It's practically the law.

> Me: LOL. I think you're right. Give me a few. I just got out of the shower.

Not true. I'm dressed and ready to go, but I need to find out if I'm pregnant. This will change everything. I realized several weeks ago that my period was late, but it took me until now to work up the courage to buy the test and take it.

> Kam: Hurry the fuck up.

I let out a laugh. She's so impatient. And direct.

I think the water is finally doing its job on my bladder. Time to walk the plank.

Seven minutes later, I stand there in shock. I'm. Fucking. Pregnant.

I know what this means. I just officially lost the man I love. Forever.

An hour later, we walk into Screwballs. I'm doing my best to smile and act like everything is okay, despite knowing I'm going to have to do something that makes me physically ill.

In our regular booth, I notice my newer friends, Cougars players Ezra Decker and Cruz "Cheetah" Gonzales. Ezra has a girl with him who I've never seen before. Quincy is seated at the end, chatting and smiling, making my heart flutter.

He's the man who gives me whiplash. The man who I've been forced to love from afar and in the shadows my whole life. The man who's mine, but only in my dreams. I know what I'm about to do will be the final nail in the coffin of those dreams ever becoming my reality.

My hands start to shake. I need another minute to compose myself. "Kam, I'm running to the bathroom. I'll meet you in the booth. Try not to screw with Cheetah too much in my absence." Kam loves to mess with his head. She flirts and then usually, though not always, leaves him high and dry. Or they make bets as to who can score with a specific woman. Kam casually indulges in both men and women, and she *always* wins their bets.

I go to the bathroom, mostly to collect myself, but in part because I drank too much water. I'm sitting on the toilet when I hear two women chatting by the sinks.

A whiny voice coos, "I hear Layton Lancaster is on the

prowl again. I hope he's here tonight. Best lay I've ever had. I'm definitely going home with him if he shows up."

Oh Christ.

The other woman responds, "Have you been seeing him on the down-low this whole time?"

Please don't let it be true. Arizona doesn't deserve this. Layton seems so in love with her. I refuse to believe it's anything other than the real deal between them.

"No, he hasn't reached out since *she* came into the picture, but now that they broke up, I'll be getting *#laidbylayton* again."

No you won't, bitch.

The other girl responds, "I didn't hear about any breakup. Are you sure?"

"There are pictures everywhere of his girlfriend making out with Butch McVey. Obviously they're over."

"Oh, I think you're right. I saw them on TMZ. I've been trying to get with Quincy Abbott for ages. He's so hot."

My head starts spinning. I want to yell that he's mine, but I can't. He's not mine. And I'm about to lose him forever.

The bitch who wants Layton scoffs. "Sorry, but you don't have a chance. You have a hot body. Everyone knows he likes fat girls."

I can't help the small smile that finds my lips at that revelation.

She continues, "He takes home a different fat girl every single night."

My face drops. It's not like I don't know he sleeps with countless women but hearing it doesn't feel great.

Before I know it, they're gone, and I'm headed back toward the booth. Quincy is sitting there drinking his beer. I stop to stare at him. He's so gorgeous. He always has been. I remember the first time I saw him as a little girl, when my crush first began.

He's a pitcher, like me. He's tall and lean, with dirty blond hair that's always a little too long and curls in the back. I have visions of running my fingers through that hair as his blue eyes look into mine. His body moving inside me. I ache for those times.

Sadness blankets me knowing I'll never have it again once I tell him that I'm pregnant.

He notices me approaching and cordially stands for me to move into the booth. I give him a small smile of gratitude as I slide in.

Before sitting back down, he asks, "What do you want to drink? I'll go to the bar and get it for you. The waitress is slammed tonight."

I shake my head. "I'm not up for a drink right now. Thanks anyway."

He shrugs and sits back down next to me.

The door to Screwballs opens, and Layton walks in. All heads turn when Layton Lancaster walks into a room. He's one of the most famous people in Philly, and he's obscenely attractive, with dark brown hair, blue-green eyes, and the most chiseled chin I've ever seen.

He slowly makes his way to the table due to his broken leg. It happened in a horrific collision at home plate in their World Series game nearly a month ago. He's in a cast with crutches. He was supposed to be in the bathing suit ads with Arizona but had to cancel after the injury. They were both devastated by it. Unfortunately, she was contractually obligated to go, so she left, and he's here in Philly, brokenhearted without her.

He plops down on the other side of the booth, his cast-covered leg sticking out.

Cheetah turns to Layton. "You're last to arrive, buddy. Pay the piper."

When Arizona and Quincy were kids, their mom started this rule that whoever was last to the dinner table had to tell everyone a random fact. It spread to our friends and teammates. Quincy brought it to the Cougars team, so now they all love to make the person who arrives last give a random fact. It's a fun little game.

Layton sighs. "Seriously? Have you seen how slow I am these days? I'll be last to everything."

Cheetah shrugs. "Sorry, man. You know the rules."

Layton thinks for a moment and then gives us a hopeful smile. "It's a proven fact that cuddling can relieve physical pain."

Aww. He misses Arizona. The guys said he's been miserable all week since she left. He won't even leave his penthouse. This is his first time venturing out.

I smile at him. "I like that one. It's sweet. Have you spoken with Arizona today?"

His face falls. "Yep. I got to watch Butch grope her via FaceTime for my benefit for what feels like the hundredth day in a row."

They replaced Layton on the shoot with Butch McVey, the most popular baseball player in the world. He's attractive, and photos are leaking every day of them in bathing suits with his hands all over Arizona. I'm sure it's hard for Layton to have to see that online each morning when he wakes up.

I take his hand and squeeze it. "It's not like she's enjoying it. She loves you and misses you."

She's just as miserable as him. She tried desperately to get out of this contract, not wanting to go without Layton. But the company wouldn't budge.

He lets out a long breath. "I hope so. This whole thing is fucked. I should have paid her way out of the contract."

Suddenly, we hear, "Hey, Layton." I recognize that ear-piercing voice. It's the whorebag from the bathroom who mentioned wanting to go home with Layton.

He rolls his eyes as he looks up at her and grits out, "Hi, Delta. Long time, no see. How are you?"

She bats her long, dark, fake as fuck eyelashes at him. "I'm well. I hear you're on the market again. We should hang out."

Layton shakes his head. "You heard wrong."

She holds out her phone for him. He stares at it with disgust before practically throwing it at her. "It's just a photo shoot. They're playing it up for the cameras. It's their job."

The slut won't take the hint that she's unwanted. "It doesn't look like an act to me. There have been photos of them on dates too."

I've had enough of this bitch encroaching on my best friend's man. I straighten my back and cross my arms. "He's not interested. Hit the road. No skanks welcome here."

She snaps her head toward me and looks me up and down. "What are you going to do, fat ass? Sit on m..."

Before she can finish spewing her nastiness, Quincy jumps out of his seat and gets right into the woman's face. "If you ever talk to her like that again, it will be the last words you utter."

Her eyes practically pop out of her fake eyelashes in fear.

Quincy then enlists the owner and has the woman thrown out of the bar.

Ezra tugs on Quincy's shirt. "Have a seat, Q. Relax, big bear."

Everyone at the table has shocked looks on their faces. They've never seen this side of Quincy. I have. Many times.

They know Quincy Abbott as the laid back, West Coast, happy guy. I know the animal within. My cheeks flush just thinking about what that animal is capable of doing to my body.

He sits back down next to me and looks at me with a tenderness that threatens to break me in half. "Are you okay?"

I give my best brave face. "I'm fine. It doesn't bother me. I've had comments like that my whole life. I'm used to it."

He lovingly rubs my face and I nearly moan. "It's not fine. No one should talk to you like that. You're beautiful. You're perfect."

My heart sinks. Him saying that to me in front of people is a big deal. Why now? Why does it have to be on the day that I realized I'll never have him?

I need to put an end to this. I lean in and whisper to him, "Don't touch me. We're over."

His face turns from caring to angry as he stands and nearly pulls my arm out of the socket. "I need to talk to you. Now!"

He pulls me until we're out of sight and out of earshot. He immediately puts his face in mine and snarls, "What are you talking about?"

I gently push him away, needing some physical distance. "Quincy, this hot and cold, back and forth thing we do is over. I'm done with it."

He shakes his head in disgust. "You can't just decide we're over. You're my wife."

Tears find my eyes. "I'm not your wife."

"The hell you're not. Check our marriage certificate, Shortcake, you're mine. My. Wife."

"On paper. Not in any of the ways that truly matter. I want a divorce. It's long overdue."

He shakes his head. "No. I won't give it to you."

"Quincy, it's time for us both to move on. We're not really married. We don't live as husband and wife. We both see other people and lead separate lives. No one else except a random justice of the peace even knows we're married. Not our families. Not our friends. No one." I steel myself, knowing I need to be strong right now. "It's time."

He crosses his arms in defiance. "Nope. Not happening."

"When you hear what I have to say, I promise that you'll want the divorce too."

"Over my dead body will I give you that divorce. Until death do us part."

Tears begin streaming down my cheeks as I say the one thing that will forever push him away. He'll want nothing to do with me when he finds out.

With sobs threatening to break through, knowing what this will mean, I manage to croak out, "I'm pregnant."

His eyes widen as what I've said registers. We stare at each other for several long beats.

Taking one deep breath, he does what I knew he'd do. Without another word, he turns and walks out the front door.

CALIFORNIA

THE EARLY YEARS

CHAPTER ONE

RIPLEY - AGE 5 {QUINCY - AGE 10}

"A re you ready for your first day of kindergarten, sweetie?"

I nod my head, trying to hide my fear of starting a new school in the middle of the year. Will everyone already have friends? Will there be room for me? What if I have to sit alone at lunch?

Mommy looks me up and down. "Are you sure you don't want to wear something...prettier?"

I glance at my leggings and oversized Team Canada Olympic softball sweatshirt. It's about as fancy as I get. "No. I'm good. Where's my glove?" I don't go anywhere without my softball glove.

She smiles as she hands it to me. "I can't believe how warm the weather is here in January. We can throw outside after school today if you want."

She's right. We'd be under ten feet of snow right now if we still lived in Toronto.

We eventually make our way into the school. I try not to let my nerves get the best of me.

My mommy walks next to me with all the confidence in the world. She's a beautiful, tall, skinny redhead. Her makeup and hair are always perfect. She dresses nicely too. Grown-up boys always stop to talk to her.

After my mommy fills out paperwork, we walk toward my new classroom. I hope the girls are nice. Sometimes girls are mean to me because of my size or because I don't like to wear pretty dresses like they do.

I'm introduced to my new teacher, Mrs. Sandwick, who sends my mother on her way. Mommy starts her job teaching and coaching at the high school tomorrow, but today she's supposed to be unpacking. Having moved about ten times in my five years in and around Toronto, I know it means that she'll leave everything in boxes for months. I'll end up unpacking everything because I hate when things are messy.

Mrs. Sandwick takes my hand as she calls the other students to come sit in a circle. "Class, this is Ripley St. James. She just moved here from Canada. Do you know where Canada is?"

A boy raises his hand, and Mrs. Sandwick calls on him. "Yes, Nathaniel."

"It's on top, right?"

The class laughs, and Mrs. Stanwick smiles. "Yes, it's north of the US. It's a different country."

He turns to me and asks, "Do you speak English?"

I nod. "Yes. A little French too, but mostly English."

Mrs. Stanwick looks around. "Can I have a volunteer to be Ripley's buddy for today? To show her how we do things here?"

A pretty blonde girl immediately raises her hand. She's the

only other girl not in a dress. In fact, she's in sweatpants and a T-shirt. "I will."

"Wonderful, Arizona. Thank you. Boys and girls, don't forget about the father-daughter and mother-son picnic on Saturday. It's going to be so much fun."

Oh no.

She continues, "You all have about fifteen more minutes of playtime before we begin our day. Arizona, please show Ripley around the classroom and where to store her lunch."

Everyone runs off except Arizona, who stands. Oh, she's tall like me. I've always been the tallest girl my age, but we're about the same height. She approaches me and smiles. "Hi. I'm Arizona Abbott. I love your glove and your sweatshirt. Do you play softball?"

I nod. "Thanks. I do. My mommy was in the Olympics for softball."

Her eyes widen. "Wow. That's awesome. What position did she play?"

"Pitcher. I'm a pitcher like her. She's been training me."

"Cool. My brother is a pitcher. I was thinking about pitching too, but maybe I'll learn to be a catcher instead so we can throw together. Maybe *we'll* be in the Olympics one day like your mom was."

I can't help but smile as I'm immediately put at ease. I have my first friend. And she's awesome.

"I'd like that. All of it. I have a ball in my bag and an extra glove. Maybe we can throw at recess."

She shrugs. "I'm a lefty. Your extra glove is probably for righties."

My face falls. "Oh. Yes, it is."

She smiles. "But I have a glove in my bag too. I never leave home without it. We can definitely throw. I'm so excited to have another girl to throw with. I've never thrown with other girls, only boys."

I go on to have the most amazing first day. Arizona and I spend every minute together. We play catch at recess. She has the best arm I've ever seen on a girl our age. We're already talking about playing on the same team this spring.

At some point, one girl came over to me and made fun of my size. I know I'm very big for my age, but it always hurts. Before I could respond, Arizona pushed the girl to the ground and made her cry.

When no one was looking, she poured a cup of water into the girl's lunchbox and soaked her sandwich. We giggled as we watched the girl open it with water and sandwich bits pouring all over her dress.

At the end of the day, we walk out toward the school buses, and that's when I see him. The cutest boy I've ever seen in my life. He's got blond hair and blue eyes I can clearly see from a hundred feet away. He must be at least thirteen years old. So old.

He's got a red backpack hanging off his shoulder and is staring at Arizona. I understand. She's very pretty.

I lean over. "That cute boy is looking at you. I think he likes you."

She starts giggling uncontrollably. "That's my brother, silly. He's not cute at all. He's gross. He farts all the time. Yuck."

"Oh. How old is he? Is he a teenager?"

"He's ten. He's just tall for his age, like us. Come on. I'll introduce you to him. He waits for me every day to make sure I get home."

I quickly look around and don't see my mommy. She said she'd pick me up right after school. It's of no surprise to me that she forgot. She's been doing that for five straight years.

We walk over toward her brother. My palms are sweating. I

take deep breaths as I feel my heart racing. He gets cuter and cuter with every step we take.

Arizona punches him in the arm. "Hey, Q. This is my new best friend, Ripley. Ripley, this is my nose-picking, loud-farting brother, Quincy. You can call him Q if you want."

Quincy is a dream name. I'd rather call him that.

He nods my way, unfazed by her digs. "What's up, Shortcake?"

I pinch my eyebrows together. Shortcake? I'm not short. Just the opposite.

He motions his head toward my lunchbox. It has Strawberry Shortcake on it. My face flushes with embarrassment at my babyish lunchbox. "Oh. My mom got it for me. I hate it."

He chuckles. "I think it's perfect for you. Her red, curly hair matches yours."

I touch my hair, suddenly feeling self-conscious. Does he like it? Does he hate it?

He answers with a smile. "I've never seen anyone with that color. It's super cool."

Phew.

He leans over and sniffs. "You smell like strawberries too."

I did have some for lunch. I try to smell myself, but I don't smell strawberries.

Arizona links her arm through mine. "Ripley is awesome at softball. She's a pitcher like you, Q. Her mom pitched in the Olympics. Can she play with us after school? Please?" She turns to me. "Quincy lets me play with him and his friends at the park near our house." She straightens her shoulders with pride. "I'm the only girl they allow on the field with them."

He shrugs. "Can she *really* throw? You know how those guys are about new people joining us, especially a girl."

Arizona nods enthusiastically "As good as me. Maybe better."

I'm not sure that's true, but it's nice of her to say.

His eyes widen. "Z throws harder than most of my friends. If you're as good as her, you can play with us."

He smiles at me again, and my heart sputters. His smile is a little crooked, but it's so darn perfect on him.

I stare at the emptying carpool line, still not seeing my mommy. "I think my mom forgot to pick me up." I look down, embarrassed. "It happens a lot." Usually the school has to call her.

Arizona points toward the school buses, which are lined up. "Our mom never picks us up. She works super late. Where do you live? I'm sure there's a bus."

I shrug my shoulders. "I don't know. We just moved here."

"Do you know the street name?"

"Hmm, Maple-something."

Quincy asks, "Maplewood?"

I nod. "Yes! That's it."

He points toward the bus right behind him. "You're only two streets over from our house. You must be on our bus. If your mom won't get mad, you should come with us."

Mad? No.

"Okay."

It turns out I do only live two streets from the Abbotts. Arizona said we can walk to each other's houses. I tell them that I'll walk to their house after I stop at mine, but Quincy insists that they get off at my stop. He said since it's my first time on the bus, he wants to make sure I get home, and then they can show me the path to their house.

He's so nice.

When we get to my house, my mother is standing outside talking to a man. I roll my eyes. She's always talking to men.

As soon as she sees me, her face falls. "Oh crap. I was running late. I'm so sorry, sweetie."

"It's okay. My new friends showed me how to use the bus. And they live nearby. I can ride with them every day." I'd *much* rather do that anyway.

She smiles. "Wonderful."

I introduce them, and then I grab what I need to go to the park to play baseball. I walk with them to their house. It's super close. There's even a path that cuts through a few backyards.

As soon as they open their door, an enormous, golden-colored dog sprints through it and jumps into Quincy's arms, knocking him over and then licking all over his face. *Lucky dog.*

I suck in a breath. "Oh my god, that dog is huge. What is it? What's his name?"

Arizona smiles down at Quincy and the dog's loving interaction. "Her name is Diamond, as in the ball field."

"What kind of dog is she?"

"A Great Dane. She looks scary but she's a big softie, especially for Quincy." Arizona pets her head and in a playful voice, says, "Aren't you, girl? Nothing but a big teddy bear."

She looks up at me. "She sleeps with Quincy. He feeds her and walks her." She whispers, "He really loves the dog."

Loves? Once again, I think *lucky dog.*

When we step inside, the house is nice. It's similar to mine, but they have a lot of furniture and things hanging on the walls. "Your house is pretty."

Quincy shakes his head. "When I'm a famous baseball player, I'm going to buy the biggest and best house in the world, with a gigantic yard so I can have a million dogs like Diamond."

The house is quiet. "Are your mom and dad here?"

Arizona shakes her head. "No, they're working. They're not usually here when we get home from school."

For the first time since we met, Quincy frowns. "Never. Not once in my life."

"Is it scary?" I've never been home without an adult.

He puffs out his chest. "No. I take care of my sister. I always protect her."

If I wasn't already, I think I'm now officially in love with him.

Arizona gathers some equipment while Quincy walks the dog. About twenty minutes later, we're on our way to the park, which I'm also realizing is only a short walk from our houses. Diamond is with us. She's not on a leash, but she stays near us the whole walk, never straying too far away.

When we arrive, there are three boys around Quincy's age waiting for us. They roll their eyes when they see me. One of them whines, "Ugh, another little girl. What the hell, Abbott?"

Quincy narrows his eyes and spits on the boy's shoe. "My little sister is better than you, Jay, and Wyatt all put together. You know it's true. She said her friend can hang. If Arizona says so, consider it the law."

The boy's shoulders slump. "Fine, she can stay, but she better not suck."

"She won't."

Quincy removes his shirt, and my stomach feels weird. It's like butterflies are flying around in there.

Arizona notices me staring. "Don't mind him. He never wears a shirt. He gets into trouble at school all the time for it. He's a weirdo. A smelly weirdo with flippers for feet."

No, he's beautiful and perfect. And not at all smelly. I look down. He does have big feet though. Wow, I've never seen a kid with such big feet.

He flexes his muscles. "I'm not weird. I'm buff. If I'm going to play professional baseball one day, I need muscles."

He gives an overexaggerated grunt as he flexes again. Arizona simply giggles. I watch him in complete and total awe.

We finally start to throw the ball around. They know a ton of fun games we can play without a full team.

While I'm definitely not fast like Arizona is, I have a great arm and the boys are in shock. It takes all of two minutes for me to blend in with them. I'm having the best time. I can't believe they do this every day.

When we're walking home, Arizona stops to tie her shoe, and Diamond waits by her side, leaving Quincy and me alone for the first time. "Thanks for inviting me. It was fun."

He shrugs. "You're a good ballplayer. Despite your lunchbox, Shortcake, I knew you'd be able to hang if my sister said so. She's never allowed another girl to come with us to the park before. *Ever.*"

I smile, feeling so proud right now.

"You have a pretty smile. It makes your eyes look extra blue."

"Thank you." I think that was a compliment. "Today is the first time a boy has ever stuck up for me. It's the first time I've ever played ball with boys."

He smiles. It's lopsided and cute. His blue eyes sparkle. "First time, huh?"

I nod. "Yep."

He throws his arm around me. I'm in heaven. "I think I'll take all your firsts, Shortcake. Okay?"

I don't know what that means, but he can have them. Whatever they are, they're his. "Okay."

"Are you going to the picnic on Saturday?"

I hang my head. "I can't. I don't have a dad."

"Oh, he doesn't live with you?"

"I...umm...I've never met him before."

Quincy slowly nods, like he's thinking about something.

"Well, our dad never comes to stuff for Z. I have to be her dad sometimes. I can be yours too. We can all go to the picnic together."

I smile. "Really?"

"Sure thing, Shortcake."

That picnic was the first of many events Quincy attended with me when I didn't have anyone else. It was rarely discussed. It was just assumed he would take me to father-daughter picnics, dances, and other school events.

We spent years going to the park after school and playing ball with the older boys. Even when new boys complained about Arizona and me tagging along, Quincy always stood up for us. As soon as they saw us play, they usually shut up pretty quickly.

I'll never forget that first day though. It's the day that I met my best friend, Arizona Abbott, and the day I think I fell in love with Quincy Abbott. The day I promised him all my firsts.

CHAPTER TWO

QUINCY - AGE 21 {RIPLEY - AGE 16}

Caleb bro hugs me. "Good luck, buddy. Bring some of that West Coast fun to the pros."

I chuckle. "Thanks, man. Let's hope it actually happens. If not, I'll be back sharing a bathroom with your smelly ass."

"Nah, man, you're the real deal. This is happening for you. Today is the day dreams are made of. Live it for all of us."

I slap his back. "Your time will come. Thanks for waking up so early to say goodbye. Wherever I end up, you'll come visit, right?"

"You know it. Now put on a fucking shirt and get out of here. You know you have to wear a shirt to play pro ball, right? There are no topless leagues."

I wink. If I'm not playing ball, I'm usually shirtless. I'm always so hot. The guys make fun of me for it, but

I'm more comfortable that way, and now I do it half the time just to get a rise out of them.

After slipping on my T-shirt, I get in my car, which is packed to the gills, and pull out for the last time. *I hope.*

I'm on my way home from college. It's a several hours long drive from Southern California to Northern California, so I left early this morning. *Very* early.

Even though I only just completed my junior year at UCLA, I've cleared out my apartment on campus. The Major League Baseball draft is today and, according to my new sports agent, Tad, I'm going to be selected either late in the first round or early in the second. If that happens, I won't go back for my senior year of college. I'll head straight to fulfill my lifetime dream of becoming a professional baseball player. A pitcher in the big leagues. It's hard to believe.

My sister, Arizona, has organized a huge draft day party at our house. Yes, my sixteen-year-old sister had to do it because my parents can't be bothered. They own a furniture business that they eat, sleep, and breathe. It's their favorite child. I can count on one hand how many baseball games of mine my father has attended. My mother came to a few more games than him throughout my life, but not many. Neither have been to a single college game of mine, claiming that they can't leave the store unattended.

I haven't been home in a long time. I visited for one day over Thanksgiving and another day for Christmas, but I otherwise haven't spent time in my hometown in at least a year and a half. If it wasn't for my sister, I'd never go back.

Arizona visits me at school when she can get away, which isn't often enough. She's the one I miss the most.

She's a phenomenal softball player, which keeps her busy, but she sits in the stands for as many of my college games as she can get away with.

It's late morning on a warm July day as I pull into the driveway. I see balloons and banners everywhere. I knew my sister would go all out. That's the kind of person she is. My success is her success. I feel the same way about hers. I have zero doubt that Arizona Abbott will light the world on fire one day. She's a superstar through and through.

I walk toward the front door and am immediately flooded with memories of Diamond greeting me. She died my junior year in high school. My parents refused to get another dog because they said I was leaving for college and wouldn't be here to take care of it. All I want is to have my own house so I can get another dog just like Diamond.

As soon as I walk through the door, I'm greeted by a big, round ass up on a ladder, hanging another banner. It's definitely not Arizona. She's not that round. My sister is a true leggy California blonde. Unfortunately, she's stunningly beautiful. Despite the five year age gap, I've been hearing it from my friends for years. I have to play bodyguard every time my college teammates see her, threatening bodily harm to anyone who goes near her. She always laughs it off. I think she's used to the attention.

My eyes move up from that plush ass until they meet the gorgeous red hair of Ripley St. James, my sister's best friend. She's in jean shorts and a T-shirt.

She startles at the noise I make and begins to wobble. I quickly rush to her to make sure she doesn't fall.

She turns and slips off the ladder just as I catch her.

Our bodies are now pressed together. I can't help but look down at her chest. Last time I saw her, she was still a girl. Not anymore. She's a woman now. *All* woman. I look back up at her face. She's fucking gorgeous. What the hell?

I can't help but inhale her aroma. She still smells like strawberries. Yum. So many fun memories are immediately triggered by her scent.

I smile down at her in my arms, "You're clumsy, Shortcake."

She blushes at the nickname I've called her for over ten years. She always has.

I suddenly hear a voice. "Is there a reason you're groping my bestie?"

I quickly release Ripley and step back, realizing our close proximity. I playfully narrow my eyes at my sister. "I just saved her life."

Ripley lets out a laugh. "I was two feet in the air. I think I would have survived the fall."

I shrug. "Next time I'll be sure to drop your ass." A fucking phenomenal ass.

My sister smiles as she jumps into my arms for a hug. "I'm happy you're home and so excited about today. I'm proud of you, Q."

I squeeze her in return. "Thanks, Z. I can't believe this day is finally here."

"Me too." She rubs her hand over my hair. "It's getting long. You look like a girl."

I smirk. "Chicks dig it."

I see Ripley nodding in agreement. "I *love* it. The curls in the back are amazing. I didn't even know you had curly hair." She starts to run her fingers through it but then catches herself and quickly pulls away. "Sorry."

"Don't be. It doesn't bother me." In fact, I think I like it.

I take the opportunity to really look Ripley up and down, head to toe. She's truly blossomed into a full-blown sexpot. When did that happen? She's never been petite, but now it's just sexy curves for miles. I can't fathom how many guys must chase after her.

I turn to Arizona. "Are Mom and Dad here?"

Her face falls, and she subtly shakes her head. "They're working. Mom said she'd try to make it in time."

I let out a long breath. "Their son might get drafted to play pro ball, and they can't take a few hours off? Typical. I should have known."

She scrunches her nose. "Sorry, Q. Forget them. Half the town is coming. Everyone is excited for you. I'm just praying that you get drafted by a team close to home so I can watch you play."

I'm filled with warmth for my amazing sister. She's the only reason I'm doing this here instead of at school with my teammates.

"I have no idea if, when, and by whom I'll get drafted. I hope I don't let you down."

Her face softens. "Not a chance. My fucking brother is about to become a major leaguer. You're living both our dreams. I wish there was pro softball so I could play after college."

"I think there will be someday soon."

Ripley nods in agreement. "My mom thinks so too. She said there's a lot of chatter about it in the softball world."

While Ripley's mother is a little nutty—well, a lot nutty—she does coach at the high school and coaches

Arizona and Ripley's club team. They travel all over in the summer playing against the best teams in the country. They're both undoubtedly going to get college scholarships for softball.

I smile. "See, it's going to happen. Plus, the two of you are shoo-ins for the Olympic team one day. I have no doubt."

They have been talking about being in the Olympics together for as long as I can remember. Crazily enough, it's not unrealistic. They're among the top players in the country for their age.

The front door opens and a tall guy with short, dark hair walks in like he owns the place. He looks my sister up and down as he makes a beeline straight for her and kisses her. Hard.

I grab him by the shirt, pull him off her, and shove him into the wall. "Who the fuck are you? Keep your hands off her."

Arizona slaps my hand. "Cut it out, caveman. This is my boyfriend, Noah."

I scowl at Noah. "How old are you?" He looks like a grown man.

With a fucking smug look on his face, he responds, "Eighteen."

I turn to Arizona. "He's too old for you. And he's a dipshit." Looking back at him, I growl, "Get the fuck out of my house."

Arizona grabs his hand and pulls him toward the kitchen. "Ignore him, babe. Come help me put the beer on ice."

I shout after them, "Beer? You're sixteen."

She shouts back, "Did you drink beer at sixteen?"

Hmm. She's got me there.

Ripley gives me a small smile. "Noah isn't a bad guy. He worships the ground she walks on. They practically run the school. They were the prom king and queen."

"Prom queen? She was only a sophomore this year."

Ripley raises an eyebrow. "She looks like a model and is the most popular girl at the school. You must know that."

I run my hands through my hair. "When did my sister grow up so much? I can't believe she's dating a grown man."

Ripley lets out a laugh. "We're growing up. Like it or not."

I nod as I unashamedly move my eyes up and down her body again. "You look good, Shortcake."

Her cheeks redden and she bites her lip. "Thank you."

And then it occurs to me. Does she have a boyfriend? And why does the thought of that make me...angry?

"Do...do you have a boyfriend too?"

She shakes her head. "No, I don't."

I mumble. "Good."

We're both silent, staring at each other. She bites her lip again, and I feel it in my cock. I suddenly want to bite that lip too. It's red and full and...Ah, stop it. It's Ripley. Arizona's ever-present sidekick. I bandaged her knee when she fell off a bike, and I took her to her first father-daughter dance.

She fidgets with the bottom of her shirt. "Congrats on your success. I'm happy for you, Quincy. You deserve it."

I can only manage a nod as I come to terms with the fact that I'm suddenly having this intense attraction to my sister's best friend. After a few awkward moments, I say, "I'm nervous for today. I hope it goes well. I don't want to disappoint anyone, especially Z."

She smiles. "It will go fine. Any team would be lucky to have you. I've...umm...seen a few of your games on TV. Your curveball has gotten really good. Your changeup too. I see you moved from a two-seam fastball to a four-seam. It's given you a little extra pop. I told you so."

I can't help but smile. I nearly forgot what it was like to be around girls who know baseball. Arizona and Ripley are as knowledgeable as any of my teammates.

I let out a laugh. "You're right. You did, in fact, mention it when I was in high school. I should have listened then. You certainly know pitching grips."

If eyes could smile, hers do at the compliment. Were they always this sparkly blue? How have I never noticed how pretty her eyes are?

Before I know it, my house is full of people. Most faces are familiar, but some aren't. We're all downing beers, crowded in front of the television as pick after pick is made without my name being called. I can feel the intensity of the glares from people each time my name isn't called. Looks of pity. Maybe it's all a mistake. Maybe I'm not getting drafted.

My agent, Tad, the only person here in a business suit, has been on the phone the whole time. He's trying to figure out who will draft me and when.

At some point, my mother runs into the house with a frantic look on her face. "Did I miss it?"

Arizona clears out a spot for her on the sofa. "No, Mom. Not yet. Any minute now. I can feel it."

Arizona nods at me in reassurance. I'm doing my best to look confident. I don't want to disappoint her.

My mother walks over and hugs me. "I'm so proud of you."

I kiss her cheek. "Is Dad coming?"

She gives me a sad smile. "He can't leave the store, sweetie. He said to call him as soon as it happens."

"Yep. Your son getting drafted to play professional baseball happens every day. I'm sure the end table he'll sell this afternoon will be worth missing it."

My mother gives me a disapproving look. "He's doing his best. We have Arizona's college tuition coming up. We need the money."

I roll my eyes. They're clueless. "She's one of the best softball players in the country. She'll be going to college for free. If you bothered to watch her play, you'd know that."

Arizona elbows me. "Leave her alone. It's a good day. Let's focus on that."

The first round ends, and I haven't been drafted. I'm disappointed and feeling anxious. What if it doesn't happen at all? All these people came to see me get drafted. I can feel the sweat dripping down my back. Would it be in poor taste to remove my shirt? I'm guessing it would be.

There are a few picks in the second round before Tad gets off the phone with a huge smile. "Turn the television up. It's showtime, buddy."

I look at him, wide-eyed. He winks and gives me a small nod of encouragement. The baseball commissioner stands at the podium. "With the tenth pick in the second round, the Houston Hurricanes select Quincy Abbott, right-handed pitcher from UCLA."

The whole room stands and erupts in loud cheers. Everyone pats my back and hugs me. I look toward the front door, willing my father to have snuck in and saw the moment, but he didn't. He never does.

Arizona leaps into my arms with tears streaming down her face. "You did it! Ahh. I'm so happy right now."

"*We* did it. Most teenage boys pitch to their dads in the backyard for hours. I'm probably the only one who pitched to his little sister. The only one whose little sister could actually catch for him. Thanks for all you did, Z. All the early mornings. All the late nights. All the bruises from targets I missed. I wouldn't be here without you."

She humbly nods as she continues to cry tears of joy for me.

The next few hours are a blur of elation and celebration. My father eventually came home and congratulated me. Too little, too late. I ignored him.

As the daylight bleeds into night, most people have left, but there are a handful still here, and we're sitting in the hot tub in the backyard. My sister has had too much to drink. I've been watching Noah like a hawk. His fingers are all over her bikini-clad body, making my blood pressure skyrocket.

His hands suddenly disappear well below the waterline. I'm about to reach my breaking point and kick him out when Ripley notices and intervenes. She has a towel wrapped around her, only sticking her feet in the water, but she grabs Noah's arm. "She's had a lot to drink, Noah. Why don't you head out? I'm going to put her to bed."

He smirks. "I'll put her to bed."

I shove him. "Get the fuck out. Stay away from her."

After retrieving a towel for Arizona, Ripley pulls her out and guides her into the house. Once they disappear, I grab Noah by the back of the neck. "I'm not fucking around. Stay away from my sister. She's too good for you."

His eyes practically bug out of his head before he wiggles away and finally leaves.

My remaining friends eventually say goodbye, and I'm left alone to reflect on the day.

Surrounded by the steam of the hot tub, I tilt my head back and take another gulp of my beer. Holy shit. I can't believe I'm going to get to play professional baseball. I'm living my dream. I'm living the dream of every little boy in this country. In the world. I'm still finding it hard to believe.

A few minutes later, Ripley walks back out. "Arizona is asleep. I'm going to head home. Congrats again, Quincy. I wish you all the luck in the world."

"No need to rush. Get in. We barely got to speak today. Let's catch up, Shortcake." For some reason, I don't want her to leave.

She hesitates briefly before sitting back on the ledge, still with her towel wrapped around her, and places her feet in the water. I wonder why she won't get in.

"Get in. It feels great."

She squeezes her towel even tighter and looks down. "Not right now. Maybe in a bit."

Suddenly it occurs to me. She doesn't want to show me her body. She's insecure. I can't imagine why. Yes, she's bigger than most girls, but not in a bad way. Women are supposed to have curves, and she's got them in spades.

I turn around to get another beer from the cooler behind me, pretending to be searching for the one I want so my back is turned for an extended time. When I turn back, she's in the water, mostly covered by the darkness of the evening. Though I can see the tops of her breasts just above the water. So fucking hot.

I snap out of my thoughts and make eye contact with her. "Catch me up on all things Ripley St. James."

She smiles as she gathers her flowy red hair into a messy bun and ties it in place. A few stray curls fall out. Her blue eyes are shining extra bright in the water. She's so beautiful. My heart is suddenly beating too fast.

"It was a fun year. Lots of parties. As you know, we won the state championship for softball. Your sister had a great season."

I let out a laugh. "I followed the season, Shortcake. You only let up three runs the entire year. It sounds like it was *you* who had the great season."

The corners of her mouth rise in amusement. "We both did."

"How's your mom?" June St. James is a character, to say the least.

Ripley rolls her eyes. "If you're asking if she still loves to bring home random guys and publicly embarrass me, the answer is yes."

I chuckle. It's all true. "You're starting to look like her." June is an attractive redhead.

"I don't see it."

"That's because you have a much better body." My jaw drops. I can't believe I said that out loud. June is tall, like Ripley, but doesn't have the sexy curves.

Every inch of Ripley blushes at the compliment. It's adorable.

I need a subject change. "What's with Noah? I hate him. He's a douche."

She giggles. "You'd hate anyone she dated. Noah isn't bad. He's whipped. She's not. He leaves for college next month. At her suggestion, they're breaking up before he leaves. They have an expiration date."

"Good. What about you? You mentioned not having a boyfriend right now, but what about this year?" For some reason, I need to know.

She shakes her head. "No."

"Why not?"

She looks down again. "I'm not exactly high school desirable. Guys aren't into me. I think I outweigh most of them. At least the guys my age."

"High school boys are idiots. A real woman should have curves, and real men appreciate them. You've grown up a lot since I last saw you." I reach over and tilt her chin up so I can look her in the eyes. "Ripley, you're stunning. I thought it the second I walked in this morning. Don't ever think otherwise."

She blushes and then visibly swallows. "Thank you. I'd rather not waste my time on guys my age anyway. I've always had my eye on a slightly older guy, but he doesn't see me that way." She briefly pauses. "At least he hasn't in the past. I've saved myself for him. I've saved my firsts for him."

I try to muster a smile, both hating and feeling jealous of this ignorant dickhead. "He's a lucky guy. There's no shame in saving your virtue until this meathead opens his eyes."

"I've saved everything for him. *Every*thing."

"Not even a kiss?"

She slowly shakes her head.

"Does he know?"

She shrugs. "I don't think so."

"You should tell him. I bet he's crazy about you too. How could he not be?" *Or don't tell him at all.*

"Do you really think so?"

I nod. "Yes." *No. Why am I jealous of this loser?*

"I'm dying for him to be my first kiss."

"Talk to him. I'll bet he wants it too. Any guy would be crazy for you."

She slowly moves across the hot tub until she's only inches from me. My eyes widen at the surprise move. "Ripley, what are you doing?"

She tilts her head to the side. "You never knew?"

"Knew what?"

She's silent as she drags her lower lip through her teeth. When it pops back out, along with a sudden stirring in my pants, she breathes, "It's you, Quincy. It's always been you. I promised you all my firsts. I've saved them for you. For years, I've wanted it to be you."

I'm in shock. I had no idea. I've never considered her a woman until tonight. Today.

She looks so gorgeous and innocent right now. Her cheeks are red though not as red as her parted, lush lips. Her hair is messy in the sexiest way possible. Her generous chest is moving up and down at a gradually increasing pace.

I know I shouldn't, but I can't seem to help myself. Running my hand along her soft face, I rub my thumb over her lips. She shuts her eyes and leans into my hand as if she's savoring it.

How have I missed her feelings for me? In fairness, she was never the woman standing in front of me. She was Ripley, Arizona's best friend, who always hung around. But that's not how I'm seeing her right now.

I breathe, "You're so beautiful," as I close the distance between us and softly bring my lips to hers.

The kiss starts off tender, our lips joining together

for the first time. She smells and tastes so familiar. It's old and comfortable, yet new and exciting at the same time.

She moves a little closer so that our chests meet. My fingers graze her waist while hers gently touch the backs of my shoulders.

I genuinely intend to simply give her the sweet first kiss she deserves, but she takes things up a notch. She takes them up several notches.

Her tongue gently coaxes my mouth open at the same time she moves to straddle my lap. Crashing down on my suddenly severely hardened dick, she gasps into my mouth.

It seems to embolden her because she begins gyrating over me. The kiss that started tender is no longer that. Not at all.

She grabs onto the back of my hair as our tongues taste each other. The kiss is deep and nearing erotic. It's hard to believe this is her first.

As if having a life of their own, my hands grab onto her ass, encouraging her movements over me. Her ass is soft and fits naturally in my large hands. I don't know that I've ever been an ass man, but noticing hers earlier today and now touching the supple flesh has got me so fucking turned on.

She circles her hips as her moans into my mouth escalate. I think she might have an orgasm from this.

I begin thrusting my own hips up a bit, so my covered cock is pushing through her covered pussy. She breaks the kiss and tilts her head back. "Oh god, I think I'm coming."

Not able to help myself, I pull down the left side of the top of her bathing suit, taking in her rosy, pebbled nipple. I mumble, "So fucking perfect," as I take it into my mouth. As soon as I apply suction, she starts shaking and moans out my name.

Seeing her like this sets me off, and, for the first time since I was probably about thirteen, I come in my pants.

She breathlessly tilts her head back toward me. Her eyes are wide. I think she's in shock too. "Wow. What... what can I do for you? What do you need?"

She has no idea that I came in my pants. She has no idea because she's fucking sixteen and inexperienced. What the hell have I done? She's a kid. The same age as my little sister. My sister's best friend. I've known her since she was five years old.

Shame washes over me as I pull back. "I...I'm so sorry, Ripley. I shouldn't have let it get that far."

She grabs my face, so I'm forced to stare into her shimmering, lust-filled blue eyes. "Don't be. It was worth the wait." She softly smiles. "Best first kiss ever. And...it's the first time I've ever come. Thank you."

CHAPTER THREE

RIPLEY - AGE 18 {QUINCY - AGE 23}

"Mom! I'm going to Arizona's hou..." I open her bedroom door and there's a topless man in her bed with the sheets pooled at his waist, clearly naked. My mother is nowhere to be found. Without an ounce of surprise, I mumble. "Shit. Sorry. Where's my mother?"

She sings, "In here, sweetie." I turn and hear her voice coming from her bathroom.

She continues, "I'll be right out," as if a random man in her bed is normal. For her, I suppose it is.

She emerges from the bathroom in a tiny silk robe with a shameless smile and doesn't bother to acknowledge the naked man ten feet away from us. "Good morning. Are you ready for the big game?"

Tonight is the California high school state softball championship. We've won it the previous three years. It's a little anticlimactic at this point. It's barely even a challenge, but this is our senior year. We want to go out on top.

Arizona and I were both offered full softball scholarships to play at UCLA next year. We're so excited to be continuing our softball journey together. My heart is already onto the next phase of our lives in Los Angeles, not here for this easy-to-win game.

With minimal enthusiasm, I respond, "Yes. Thrilled. I'm heading over to Arizona's. I'll drive there with her and meet you." Mom is the coach of our team. "There's a big party tonight, so I'm sleeping at her house."

With her always cheery demeanor, she says, "Sounds good. Oh, meet my friend, Bill."

He corrects, "Phil."

"Riiight. Meet Phil."

I give him a fake smile. "Hi, Phil." I'll never see him again. No need to bother with any more pleasantries.

Mom holds up her finger for me to wait a minute and chirps, "I need to talk with you about something. Are you planning to have intercourse with Jack tonight?"

I gasp in horror at her asking this in front of her latest bedfellow. "Mom!"

"What? Bill doesn't care."

He reminds her, "Phil."

"Oh, right. Phil doesn't care. I left you a box of condoms in your bathroom. I know you have the IUD, but I want you to double up."

I grit out, "I saw the box. We don't need to discuss this right now."

"Okay, but if you're *finally* going to visit the flower shop, be safe."

Please tell me she did *not* just refer to me losing my virginity as visiting the flower shop. In front of a strange man, nonetheless. Just when I think she couldn't possibly embarrass me anymore, she never ceases to disappoint.

"Mom!"

She pulls me into the hallway and closes her bedroom door. "I'm not kidding. I want you to be safe. Trust me, an unplanned pregnancy is no walk in the park."

"I'm sorry having me was so terrible for you."

Her face softens as she softly grabs me by my shoulders and looks me in the eyes. "Having you is the single best thing I've ever done in my life. Seeing the incredible woman you've become makes up for all the mistakes I've made. But it wasn't easy. Especially those first few years. I sacrificed and worked hard for this life we have. I just don't want you to struggle like me. In life or in love."

She's never once in my life mentioned the word love in a romantic context, only that she loves me. I want to ask questions about my father. I have so many, but I know now isn't the time with Bill/Phil in the other room.

I nod. "I'll be safe. I promise."

She hugs me. "I'm so proud of you. I know you're over high school ball and ready for life at UCLA, but winning four straight state championships is something to be proud of. It's a rarity. You're a once-in-a-generation talent, my love. You're going to be in the Olympics one day. I just don't want anything or anyone to stand in your way."

I can't help but smile at that thought. It's all Arizona and I have talked about since we were little girls. "Do you really think I'm good enough to be on the Olympic team one day?"

She nods. "I know you are. You're a chip off the old block. I'll be there in the front row cheering for you." She winks. "This Canadian might even consider wearing Team USA apparel."

We giggle as she heads back to her bedroom, and I make my way out the front door.

I walk the short few blocks to Arizona's house and let

myself in, as I've done for the past thirteen years. Per always, her parents don't seem to be home. I don't see her downstairs, so I make my way upstairs to her bedroom.

When I open the door to her bedroom and walk in, I see her lying in bed, dressed for the day. She's staring at the poster of superstar baseball player, Layton Lancaster, on her ceiling.

I shake my head. "You need to stop drooling over him."

She sighs. "Have you ever seen a hotter man in your life?"

Hmm, yes. Your brother, but I don't think I'll say that out loud. I lay down next to her, looking at Layton in his dark blue pinstriped Philly Cougars uniform. "He's definitely a hottie."

"I wish my brother was drafted by Philly instead of Houston. They're close in age. I bet they'd be friends." She tilts her head to the side. "I've been studying Layton's face. His chin is so square that it almost looks fake. I wonder if it's photoshopped."

"Maybe one day you'll find out by getting to sit on that square chin."

She giggles. "A girl can dream. I think I now have a square chin fetish from staring at this poster every day for the past few years."

I sigh. "I just met another Barney." Barney is the universal name Arizona and I have given to the revolving door of men in my mother's bed.

"Your mother gets more action than Layton Lancaster. Speaking of action, are you finally going to give it up to Jack? We graduate tomorrow. You said you didn't want to finish high school a virgin."

Jack and I have been dating for the past few months. We planned to have sex at prom last week, but something held me back. *Someone.*

I groan. "He's so sweet, but I just don't have this all-consuming need for him. He's like a teddy bear. I want to cuddle with him, not fuck him. He's too nice. It annoys me."

She lets out a laugh. "Too nice? Most women would kill for a guy like Jack to dote on them the way he dotes on you. You gave yourself this deadline, not me. Do what feels right. You shouldn't feel pressured by an arbitrary date."

She sits up. "Oh, I have good news. My brother got permission from his coach to have today and tomorrow off. He's on an airplane right now. He'll be able to see the game tonight and our graduation tomorrow before flying back tomorrow night."

"That's great. I saw he wasn't scheduled to pitch tonight or tomorrow night. I was hopeful." After two seasons in the minor leagues, Quincy is now in the majors. It's so exciting to see him play. I rarely miss a game he pitches on television. I love watching him. I secretly have his jersey and wear it to bed when I'm alone...and doing other things by myself. To myself.

Knowing Quincy could be under the same roof as me means I definitely won't be having sex with Jack. My night in the hot tub with Quincy plays over and over in my head. I know what it's like to want someone with every fiber of my being. That's exactly how I felt with Quincy that night. I wish I had sex with him, but he was freaked out after our kiss and abruptly ended the evening. I'm thankful for what we did. Saving my first kiss and orgasm for him was worth it.

I haven't seen him since. He only does daytrip visits for the holidays, never spending any real time here. Part of me thinks he's avoiding me, but the other part knows he didn't spend time here before that night. There's another reason he doesn't spend time at home. I don't know what it is.

He and Arizona talk all the time though. He flies her to Houston as much as her schedule permits but never their parents. I envy their close sibling relationship. I wish I had siblings of my own, but Arizona is like a sister to me, and our friendship means everything.

We're up two runs going into the last inning of the state championship. I haven't given up two runs in a game throughout my entire high school career, let alone one inning. I think it's safe to assume that we're about to win another title.

I look over in the stands. Jack is cheering for me like a madman. Quincy is sitting with his mother, smiling politely as they chat. Their dad is nowhere to be found. He misses everything. At least they have a dad. He makes sporadic appearances, but they eat dinner as a family before he heads back to his woodshop. Still, I would kill to have that kind of family life.

Instead, I only have a mother who teaches at my school in tight tops and short skirts. The number of jokes I've had to endure throughout my high school life is mind-boggling. I'm more than happy to put it in the past.

Quincy arrived just after the game started. If possible, he's gotten even more attractive. My heart still beats erratically when he's nearby. It always has.

Part of me hopes that if I do have sex with Quincy Abbott, I can finally move past him. He occupies too many of my thoughts. I want to have a normal, physical relationship with someone without being consumed by this need to give Quincy my firsts.

Mom grabs my arm before I head out onto the field. "Stick with the rise and the curveball."

I shake my head. "I can simply throw fastballs. These girls can't catch up to my speed."

Her face falls. "That's lazy, Ripley. You should always be working on things. Never be content. Fastballs won't work for you at UCLA next year."

She's right. I know she is. If there's one thing in this world my mother knows, it's softball, especially pitching. She might have been a bit unconventional as a caregiver, but as a coach, she's the best. "Okay, Mom."

"Don't fuck around. Stay in the zone. No free rides."

"I got it."

We head out onto the field, and I take the mound. The first two pitches I throw are called balls. Shit. Nothing drives my mother nuts more than me falling behind in a count.

I hear her yell, "Pound the zone, Ripley."

Even behind her catcher's mask, I see Arizona smile. My mom has been saying, *pound the zone*, for as long as I can remember. The second we were old enough to understand the double entendre, Arizona and I began giggling every time she said it. It's our running joke.

I smile back at her, which relaxes me enough to get the job done. Nine pitches later, we win the state championship. *Again*.

I'm excited, I truly am, but I can't get my mind off my dream man sitting in the stands. I won't have another opportunity like tonight. I'm not letting it go to waste. I've already got a plan forming in my mind.

When the team celebration on the field dies down, the fans come to embrace us. Jack, who's a linebacker on the school football team, engulfs me in a huge hug. "You were great, babe." He kisses my cheek. "I'm so proud of you."

I give him a small smile of gratitude as I look at Quincy, who seems to be scowling at us. Jack notices my line of sight. With his arm still wrapped around me, he smiles. "Wow. Quincy Abbott. It's an honor to meet you."

Quincy runs his fingers through his sexy scruff without giving Jack so much as a hint of a smile. "And who are you?"

"I'm Jack. Ripley's boyfriend."

I see Quincy's jaw tic. Is he jealous? I love that. I snuggle a little more into Jack just to see how Quincy reacts. Seeing his fists balling gives me the last bit of courage I need to push my plan forward. There's something electric between us. I know he feels it too.

Arizona shoves Quincy's arm. "You were the last fan to arrive at the game. You know what that means."

He scrunches his nose and then smiles. "I came all this way and you're making me play our silly game?"

"Absolutely. You know the rules."

"Hmm. Let me think. Ooh, I've got one for you. Flamingos aren't born pink. They're born gray and white." He stares at me with nothing but intensity in his eyes. "Their beauty slowly develops over time until they turn into one of the most stunning creatures on earth. Clearly, they're worth the wait."

Despite the warm, California summer night, I get chills all over my body. I look around to see if anyone else realizes that he was talking to me. They don't. Everyone seems to contemplate what he said.

Arizona shrugs. "That's a good one. I've never heard it before."

I see my mother walking over to our group. Oh hell. This is guaranteed to be embarrassing.

She smiles. "Quincy, how wonderful to see you."

He kisses her cheek. "You as well, June. You look great."

That's true. My mother is undoubtedly a beautiful woman. People say we look alike, but I don't see it. I have her hair color, her height, and some of her facial features, but she's way skinnier than I am. She tells me that I get my larger size from my father, but I've never met him, and I'm not convinced she even knows who he is. Considering the number of men she beds, I can't imagine her having a clue who my real father is. Anytime I broach the subject, she attempts to divert the topic. I've stopped trying.

I barely remember our time in Canada. My earliest memories are from the time I met Arizona and Quincy when I was in kindergarten. The day I promised Quincy all my firsts.

"Thank you." She turns to Jack and hands him something. "If you're going to tear off my daughter's maiden tag tonight, make sure you wrap it before you tap it."

Oh. My. God. She just handed my boyfriend a condom. In public.

Arizona bursts out into her unique snort-laugh. Jack looks like he wants to crawl into a hole. Quincy looks like he's going to murder someone.

A FEW HOURS LATER, Arizona and I are in her room, lying in her bed. I blow out a long breath. "I broke up with Jack at the party tonight."

She snaps her head to me. "What? When you guys disappeared, I thought you were having sex. I wanted to ask you about it." She grins. "I wanted to know if you used the condom your mother handed him at the game to *rip off your maiden tag.*"

She starts giggling.

I shake my head. "No. He's not the right one."

"Well then, I guess you're graduating a virgin."

"I suppose."

"You have to admit what your mom did tonight was epic."

"Epically embarrassing, per always."

"She means well, Rip. She just lacks the normal mom gene."

"I know. Sometimes I'm the only adult in the house. I want a mom, not a friend or even a child that I often have to take care of. Ugh, and she's such a slob. I can't go to bed at night without cleaning the house and picking up her shit."

Arizona smiles. "I love when you clean my room for me."

"You're a slob too. I'm moving from one slob to another."

"I'm so excited for UCLA. We're going to have the best four years."

"I hope so. I'm ready to get away from June St. James and her bevy of Barneys. I want to meet new people."

"Those twins from Florida seem nice. Kamryn was really funny on the phone. She's definitely a party girl."

I nod. "For sure. I'm glad we're rooming with them." I take a long breath. "Arizona?"

"Yes."

"We'll always be best friends, right?"

"Obviously. Why?"

"If I did something you didn't approve of, you wouldn't hate me forever, right?"

"Where is this coming from?" She gasps. "You're not thinking of bailing on UCLA, are you?"

"No, of course not. I'm so excited. But, if I did bail, would you hate me?"

"I could never hate you. You're family to me. I love you like a sister. But you're not bailing, right?"

We both had a lot of offers from several colleges before landing on UCLA. Some pursued me a little harder and some pursued her a little harder. We chose UCLA, in part, because they equally wanted both of us.

"I promise, I'm not bailing."

"Good. I'm not tired. Let's watch a movie."

She smiles as we both yell, "*Top Gun*," at the same time and then giggle. We've watched it no less than a thousand times throughout the years.

The movie plays, and I watch her eyelids grow heavy. With Quincy right down the hallway, there's no chance of me falling asleep.

I wait a few hours. Once I'm confident Arizona is in a deep slumber and everything is quiet in their parents' bedroom, I quietly slip out of her room.

I tiptoe down the hallway and slowly open Quincy's door. Despite the darkness, I can see him in his bed, on his back, wide awake. His blue eyes take me in as the blankets sit just below his waist. He's not wearing a shirt and his hands are under his head. He's the most gorgeous man in existence.

He's bulked up since he was drafted two years ago. His biceps are bulging, and his abs don't seem to have an ounce of fat. His sexy hair is messy, hanging over his forehead, and now he has chest hair too. Quincy Abbott is a god among men.

In his deep voice, he grumbles, "I knew you'd come to me. I could feel it in my bones."

I wordlessly nod as I close the door and make my way to his bed.

He stares at me. "Saving your firsts for me. You mentioned it that night in the hot tub. I didn't think much of it at the time, but I've thought of it often since. It goes back to the day we met, right? When I told you that you owed me all your firsts."

I nod again. "Yes."

"This isn't exactly what I meant though I frankly don't know what I intended at the time. I was ten."

"It doesn't matter. I've saved them all for you because that's what I wanted to do. I want you to have them. No one else."

"What about Jack? Arizona said you've been dating for months. Your mother certainly seemed onboard."

I shake my head. "No. Not tonight. Not ever. I broke up with him a few hours ago. I need it to be you, Quincy. That's what I want. What I've always wanted."

He gives one small nod of acknowledgment.

I start to lift the blankets to get into the bed, but he instructs me to stop. I get self-conscious, thinking he doesn't want me, but then he quickly instructs, "Take your clothes off. I want to see you. *All* of you."

I freeze in place. That's my worst nightmare. Exposing my body to him. I want to get undressed under the safety and cover of the blankets, where I can't be seen.

He sits up, his bottom half still mostly covered. Looking up at me, he demands, "If we're going to do this, I want to see you. I *need* to see you. It's all of you or nothing at all. I won't settle for anything less than every glorious inch."

His gaze is so intense. I have to look away. "I...I don't know if I can."

He takes my hand in his and waits until my eyes find his again. He gives me a reassuring nod. "I know you can. I'll go first."

He pulls the blanket off his body, revealing himself as completely naked with nothing but a very hard and exceedingly large penis. Quincy Abbott is a big man. He's a long man, standing at six feet, five inches. He wears size sixteen shoes. I suppose I was expecting a larger-than-average penis, but I wasn't expecting this much. I'm suddenly terrified.

I visibly swallow and he gives me a cocky smirk. "You'll be fine. I promise to take care of you. It's your turn, Shortcake."

My hands shake as I slowly move to place my thumbs into the waistband of my sleep shorts. Before I can muster the courage to remove them, he grabs my wrist. "May I?"

I nod. "Please." I honestly can't bear to do it myself.

He reaches into my waistband. The mere act of his fingers touching my body sends an electric current through me. He pulls down my shorts and panties together, in one slow motion. Once they're on the floor, he runs his hands up my thighs. My thighs are big, but I love that they momentarily don't seem that way in his enormous hands.

I see his breathing becoming more labored. The tip of his cock begins to glisten.

He's turned on by what he sees. I was afraid he'd be repulsed, but he's turned on by me.

That emboldens me to grab the bottom of my T-shirt and lift it over my head. I'm now standing in front of him completely naked.

No one has ever seen me completely naked before. No man, no saleswoman, not Arizona, no one. Another first belonging to him.

His eyes and hands continue the slow path up my body until his fingers stop at my breasts, cupping them and teasing my nipples with his thumbs in the process. His eyes then meet mine. "You're the most beautiful woman I've ever seen."

I don't know if he means it or not, but right now, I want to believe him, so I do. The lust I see in his eyes tells me that he means it.

I bend my head until our lips meet, craving that connection. We've only kissed once, and it was two years ago, but it's somehow immediately familiar and comfortable.

His lips, his tongue, his taste. They both soothe and excite me at the same time.

I smile into his mouth and mumble, "I nearly forgot what a good kisser you are."

He smiles back into mine. "You're about to learn that I'm good at everything."

Our lips lock again as he kisses me voraciously. He continues moving his fingers all over my body, lighting me up in a way I've never felt. His hands immediately find my ass, again bringing me back to our first kiss when he practically worshiped it. My fingers dive into his sexy hair, running through his long curls.

If I only have this one night, I want everything. Every first I've saved for this perfect man.

I break the kiss and run my lips down his gorgeous body until I fall to my knees in front of him, between his legs.

I look up at him. "Tell me what to do. What you like."

He nods. "Grab the base."

I tentatively move my fingers until they're wrapped around him. It's so smooth, thick, and hard. I can feel the veins popping out like they're ready to burst.

Holy shit. I'm touching Quincy Abbott's penis. It's shameful how much I've thought about it throughout the years.

He runs the backs of his fingers lovingly over my cheek. "Explore me with your tongue. Lick your way around until you're ready to slip him between your lips. Take your time. We're in no rush. There's nothing you can do with your mouth that I won't like."

I nod eagerly as my tongue slides out, and I lick the tip first, tasting the saltiness leaking out. That tastes better than I had imagined. And it's so warm. I wasn't expecting that.

I then glide my tongue up and down a few times until I work my way to his balls. Am I supposed to do something with these things?

As if reading my mind, he says, "It's up to you. Everything you're doing feels good."

I want to give him everything. Wetting them with my

tongue swirling around them at first, I eventually suck them into my mouth. They taste so...manly.

He hisses and fists the sheets as if he's trying to control himself. I think those are good things.

After giving them a bit of attention, I move back up to the tip. I look up at him as I wrap my lips around him and lower my mouth onto his length.

His jaw slackens. "Good. Now move your hand and mouth in unison. Take it as deep as you can into your throat. You'll have to relax. There's no better sound than that of a woman choking on my cock."

I do as he instructed until I feel him hit the back of my throat. I gag a bit but keep going, desperate to be good at this. If he wants me to choke on him, I will.

He grabs me by the hair and begins to thrust his hips. I've seen men do that to women in porn. I'm doing everything I can to imitate what I've watched. He seems like he's enjoying it. I'm loving the look of ecstasy on his face right now as he pushes himself into my mouth over and over. I'm shockingly loving him pulling my hair while I do this.

After just a few minutes he suddenly pulls me off him. For a moment I'm afraid I did something wrong, but that's clearly not the case.

He lifts me by the arms until I'm standing. "I don't want this to end too quickly. Get into bed. On your back. Spread your legs so I can see what sucking my cock did to your pussy. I want to taste you too."

Is this dirty talk? If it is, I think I'm into it.

I swallow hard as I lay down on the bed and slightly spread my knees apart. He climbs over me until he's situated between my legs. I can feel his long hardness lying heavily on my stomach, but I'm more focused on the fact that our bodies are touching skin to skin for the first time. I have no words for the way it feels to finally have Quincy's body on mine with nothing between us. I could lie like this forever.

We stare at each other, savoring the moment. He slowly runs his hands up the side of my body, as if he's committing it to memory. As if this moment means nearly as much to him as it does to me. I know it doesn't, but I'm going to pretend for the briefest of moments that Quincy Abbott feels for me the way I feel for him.

He peppers kisses down my throat, chest, and stomach until he eventually slides down enough so his face is staring directly between my legs. He spreads them as wide as they can go, pinning my thighs to the bed. I feel so exposed like this, but the look on his face is pure bliss. It sends a ripple of heat up my body and a shot of liquid lust to my core.

He runs his nose through my pubic hair several times before, finally, loudly inhaling me. "I've been dreaming about what your pussy looks and smells like for two years. So pink. Strawberry Shortcake through and through." He then licks where no man has ever licked before. "Hmm. And now I know all of you tastes like strawberries too."

Holy hell. That might be the greatest sensation in existence. I pray he does it again. And again.

He looks back up at me. "I know the first time you came was with me. What about since then?"

I bite my lip, a bit embarrassed as I admit, "Only by myself."

He smiles before pulling my lips apart and sinking his long, thick tongue back into me. My eyes flutter. Oh. My. God. This is the best thing I've ever felt in my life.

He licks through me several times before settling on my clit, circling his tongue around it over and over. He's like a viper with the speed of his tongue on me. I have to grip the sheets and bury my mouth in my shoulder to keep the moans at bay.

My nerve endings are being brought to life in a way I never knew existed. I've lost complete control over my sense of awareness. The world could stop right now, and I wouldn't notice. This house could burn down around us, and I'd still beg him to keep his tongue in place.

The pleasure he's giving my body is unimaginable. But when he sinks his fingers inside of me, I start to float. Or, at least, that's what it feels like.

I moan, "Oh god, Quincy. So good."

He looks up. His lips are glistening with my arousal. "Shhh. Grab a pillow and yell into that when I make you come harder than you've ever come in your life."

As soon as his tongue touches me again, I know I'm seconds away from learning the truth of his statement. I've made myself come countless times in the past two years, mostly to thoughts of him doing this very thing to me, but none have felt like this. The buildup is otherworldly.

His fingers curl inside me. I quickly grab a pillow and cover my face with it as my whole body goes numb and then detonates. I yell into it as my back arches, writhing uncontrollably. He does his best to keep me pinned to the bed, but every inch of me shakes and convulses.

After several long minutes, the best minutes of my life, the pleasure begins to fade away. I wish I could feel like that forever.

I'm so...so...satisfied. My body is limp. Every single part of me. I could die happy right now.

Quincy licks up my body until his mouth reaches mine for a deep, hard kiss. I can taste myself on him. Is that what most people do? I have no idea. There's not a lot of this in porn, but I don't care. I want this kiss to last forever. I run my tongue over his. There's something so erotic about tasting me in his mouth. I might be addicted to this.

He breaks the kiss, sits up on his knees, reaches into the drawer in the table next to his bed, and grabs a condom. Oh shit. In my euphoric state, I completely forgot about that. I'm glad he has one.

I watch as he tears the wrapper open and rolls the condom on his length. It doesn't even go all the way down on his long dick. How is that sucker going to fit inside me? I'm doing the physics in my head, and the math is not adding up.

He must notice the fear in my eyes. He rubs my face with his hand. "Don't worry. I'll go slow. It's going to burn at first, but you're wet and ready. I'll get it in and then wait until the pain is gone and the pleasure sets in. I promise. Do you trust me?"

I swallow as I nod. "I trust you. I want it. It has to be you. Do it."

He smiles as he lays back down on top of me. I love the way he feels and smells. He's so dominating like this.

I can feel his tip teasing my entrance. Even though I just came, I'm suddenly so turned on again. It's like my body is calling to his, begging him to enter me. Reaching for him.

Just as he pushes in the first bit, his lips take mine again. I love the way he kisses. It's wet but not too wet. There's suction but passion too. And his taste? It's everything.

I wrap my arms and legs around him. At first, I return his kiss, but then I break it so I can lock my eyes with his for this momentous occasion in my life.

His blue eyes pierce through me, straight to my soul. I've dreamed countless times of looking into them while I gave him my virtue. It's hard to believe this is my reality. I'm not dreaming. For a brief moment in time, Quincy Abbott is mine and I'm his.

His gaze lingers as he surges forward. I wince, feeling the burn. Ooh, that hurts.

"Are you okay?"

Trying to be strong, I grit out, "Keep going."

He reaches his hand down and rubs my clit with his fingers. I involuntarily convulse, still sensitive from my orgasm moments ago. It distracts me enough for him to push in a little bit more.

He squeezes his eyes shut and I grab his face, worried that I've done something to hurt him. "What's wrong?"

"Nothing. You're so tight. I'm trying to maintain control. I don't want this to be over before it even starts."

The idea of him losing control excites me. I'm so happy that I waited for him. I don't want to do this with anyone else.

After a few minutes of gradually pushing inside me and a pain-pleasure push and pull, he's in. I did it. I gave Quincy Abbott all my firsts. Now I want to enjoy myself for what I know will be the only time we're together like this. This beautiful, perfect man is inside my body. It's a moment I'll never forget.

He looks down at me with lust in his eyes. He breathes, "Ripley," as if he's trying to maintain control. Trying to contain his emotions. I must misread it because it almost appears as if he's going to cry.

I can't do anything but breathe back, "Quincy," as tears fill my own eyes.

He sinks his nose into my neck and whispers, "Thank you for giving this to me. Thank you for waiting for me."

He worships my body in a way I won't come to appreciate until the next few years as different boyfriends come in and out of my life. I don't know if he felt it too, but the connection we shared was an out-of-body experience that would be near impossible to ever replicate.

TEXAS

THE HOUSTON YEARS

CHAPTER FOUR

QUINCY - AGE 27 {RIPLEY - AGE 22}

> Arizona: Ripley doesn't know anyone in Houston. Please look out for her.

> Me: Ripley doesn't need a babysitter. She'll make friends.

I can be such a dick sometimes. Arizona and Ripley graduated from college last month. They were both drafted into the new women's professional softball league. Arizona was drafted by the team in Anaheim, California. Ripley was drafted by the team out of Houston, Texas. What are the chances that she'd end up in the same town as me?

> Arizona: Just because your hair is styled
> like a girl doesn't mean you get to act like a
> little bitch. Invite her out with your friends.
> Or stop by her new apartment. Don't big
> time me, Abbott, I knew you when you shit
> your pants at the Barson's haunted
> mansion. I had to run all the way home to
> get you clean clothes. You owe me.

I can't help but let out a laugh at the pants-shitting incident reminder. She brings it up at least once a year.

She proceeds to give me the address. It's not far from me, but I'm in no rush to do anything about it. Opening that can of worms might be a mistake.

Ripley St. James has become the woman I measure all others against. The problem? None of them come remotely close to the real thing.

I can't explain the connection or the feelings evoked in me the evening we spent together, but they're there. I've never felt anything like it with anyone before or since. She was an inexperienced virgin before our one night together, yet I would give anything to feel half of what I felt that night with another woman.

WE HAD a day game today so a bunch of us are at Blast Off, a trendy nightclub with a name that's a nod to the nearby Kennedy Space Center. We're all drinking, surrounded by women, having a great time.

My teammate, Drew, smiles at me. "Yo, California, you heading out soon?"

Admittedly, I don't stick around these evenings very

long. I find a woman of interest and leave with her relatively early. What's the point in all the *get-to-know-you* crap? I'm in and out for a one-night good time only.

I lean back and smile, as I often do. "Soon. Maybe I'll have one more drink."

I notice a new group of women walk in through the front door. Despite the crowd, I immediately see Ripley among them. She stands out, having that sexy, red, curly hair, and by usually being a lot taller than most other women.

I was a minute away from leaving with the groupie standing at our table talking to me. I'm not sure I remember her name. Now that I see Ripley, I know there's no chance of me leaving with Ms. No Name.

I look Ripley up and down. Suddenly, the only thing I want tonight are those red curls bouncing on top of me. I want to bury my face between those thick thighs and take in that unique strawberry scent of hers. I have to adjust myself simply thinking of it.

I ignore the woman I've been talking to and watch Ripley for the next thirty minutes. She doesn't see me, but I can't stop staring at her. I notice that she's different than she was four years ago, having a bit more confidence and swagger.

She's in a skirt. I've rarely, if ever, seen her dressed up. It's definitely more form-fitting than anything she's worn in front of me in the past. Her curves are on display for every creepy fucker in here. My mouth is watering.

Her curls are down and wild. She's got on makeup and looks every bit the twenty-two-year-old temptress she now is.

She and her friends are at the bar, having a good time. My teammate Drew eventually notices them. I see him walking their way. I grind my teeth. He better not go near her.

Fortunately, I see him approach one of her friends. I almost feel bad for the girl. I might not ever be into relationships, but I don't pretend otherwise. I'm very clear up front with women that there is zero chance of anything beyond sex happening. Drew makes them feel like they're going to get married when of course they're not. It's a sleazeball way to be. He's my teammate, so I tolerate his antics, but I don't care for him at all.

While Drew is busy chatting with Ripley's friend, some guy I don't recognize walks up to Ripley and starts talking. Within seconds, she's laughing at something he said to her. Ugh, I hate that. Now he's laughing at something she said. I think I hate that even more.

Admittedly, even if not with me, I'm happy to see that she's clearly become more confident. She no longer looks like the insecure teenager I remember. She's a woman who seems more comfortable in her own skin. I'm proud of her for that.

After a few minutes, she stands. I have a glimmer of hope, thinking that maybe she's walking away from him. Nope, he's holding her hand, leading her to the dance floor. I feel my jaw tighten.

I watch his hands on her body while they dance for about half a song before I can't take it anymore.

I practically jump out of my seat and glide toward the dance floor. Without her noticing me, I sneak up behind her, push my body against her back, and whisper in her ear, "Don't forget, all your firsts are mine, including your first dance."

I feel her immediately stiffen before she turns around, wide-eyed. "Quincy?"

I fix an errant curl of hers while brushing my thumb along her soft face. "Shortcake."

The other guy tries to place his hand on her shoulder, but I slap it away and growl, "Get lost. She's mine."

I have five inches and sixty pounds on the guy. His brief moment of hesitancy quickly gives way to logic as he turns and walks away.

She tilts her head to the side like she's shocked by what I just did. "What's your problem? Don't be a cockblock. He was cute."

I pull her hips to mine and start moving us both to the beat of the music. "I thought you wanted me."

"I wanted you as my firsts. Mission accomplished. I haven't seen or heard from you in over four years, Quincy. Not since that night."

"What a night it was. Have you thought of me?"

She's quiet.

I give a satisfied smile. "I thought so."

"I'm not the same girl you once knew."

I look her body up and down in an outfit the Ripley I knew would never wear. "I can see that you're no longer a girl. You're a woman. A sexy woman. Let's have a drink so I can get to know the new Ripley St. James. I promised my sister I'd welcome you to Houston."

She quirks an eyebrow. "I've been here for over a month." *Yes, I'm a dick.* "An accidental run-in is quite the welcome, Quincy. I hope you didn't hurt yourself rolling out the red carpet for me."

Her words are biting, but her blue eyes are playful. She's not mad. She had no expectations of me reaching out to her.

"How about I make it up to you while we revisit all your firsts? Am I still the only?"

She lets out a laugh. It's belly-deep and so...so...Ripley. "You wish, Abbott. Four years is a *long* time, and I'm no longer an inexperienced, shy, eager girl willing to take whatever it is you'll throw my way."

I can't help but smile. "I like confident Ripley. It's sexy."

She smirks. "I like her too." She runs her fingers through the long curls at the back of my head. "I see you've kept these around."

"You said you liked them."

"When did I say that?"

"About six years ago."

"Are you telling me you've kept your hair long because of me?"

"What if I were to say yes?"

"I'd say you're full of shit. You haven't given me a second thought in years. I was one of many for you."

That's not true, but I'm not getting into this with her.

We continue to dance, our bodies pressed together, neither of us moving to break apart. We stare at each other. Ripley and I undoubtedly share a strong connection. There's no denying that. I didn't imagine it all those years ago.

Because I can't help myself, I bend and sink my face into her neck, inhaling deeply. She has such a distinct scent. Strawberries. It draws me to her. It's just so... comforting. It's like a warm blanket around me. One I crave.

She breathes, "What are you doing?"

"Taking you in. I love the way you smell. *Everywhere.*"

She gives me a small shove, enough to put some space

between us. "This is a mistake. Go back to wherever you came from."

I grab her hand. "Come on. Let's have that drink. We need to catch up, old friend."

She attempts to pull out of my hold, but I overpower her, not letting go.

She rolls her eyes at me. "Fine. One drink. Then I'm getting back to the hottie I was dancing with before you cut in."

"No problem." *Fat chance.*

I bring her to our table and introduce her to my teammates. I simply say her name, not that she's my little sister's best friend. It occurs to me that I don't think I've ever introduced her to anyone as anything other than Arizona's friend before.

The waitress approaches and we order drinks. Fortunately, a table of professional baseball players garners top-notch service.

There's only one available chair at the table. I sit and start to pull Ripley onto my lap, but she pulls back. "Stop. I'm too big for that."

I'm stronger than she is, so I overpower her and pull her to sit on my lap, whispering in her ear, "I seem to remember a time when you very much enjoyed sitting on my lap."

She bites her lip as her cheeks flush at the memory. There's that lip bite I remember well. It's more of a lip-dragging. It stirs something in me. I want to suck on that lip.

I squeeze her close and maneuver her so that my leg is snugly between hers. It's under the table and very dark in here, so no one else can see it, but she looks back at me with a look of warning. I smile innocently.

Our drinks arrive, and we're chatting with my friends. Her friend Emily is sitting with Drew as they shamelessly make out at the table.

I'm happy to have Ripley in my arms again as I take liberties with my hands. I love her curvy, womanly body. She's so voluptuous.

I inhale her hair. Her smell is intoxicating to me.

"Tell me about college."

She smiles as if remembering. "We had the best four years. Arizona and I lived with two other girls on the team, twins Bailey and Kamryn Hart. Kamryn is the craziest person I've ever met."

I let out a laugh. "I've heard about her antics. Arizona talks about them all the time."

She nods. "Crazy but amazing. I miss all of them, especially your sister. This month is the longest she and I have ever been apart since the day we met."

"I love your friendship. I envied it at times. It's not easy to find truly trustworthy people. You two have that."

"We do. I love her like a sister. I'd do anything in the world for her."

I can't help but smile at the sincerity with which she loves Arizona.

She continues, "As you know, we won two national championships. It should have been three. I'm sorry you missed them. I know Arizona wished you could have been there."

"I couldn't come with my schedule. Your games were on the same days as ours. I watched most of them on television though. Sometimes I snuck my phone into the bullpen to watch during our games. You've had a great career. I love seeing you play. Both of you. I feel, in part, responsible."

She aimlessly runs her fingers through my hair. "You were. You always let us play with the older boys. It made both of us better."

Countless women love playing with my hair, but for some reason, when Ripley does it, it drives me wild. It's worth the harassment I've endured from teammates through the years about it just to have her fingers in it again. Her touch sends electricity running through my body, and she doesn't even realize it. Though I'm hard as a rock under her. She must feel that.

"What about you, Quincy? How are things? She worries about you. You're so tight-lipped. You never come home. It's always her flying here for visits. Why not the other way around?"

I shrug. "I fly in and out for a holiday now and then. Besides her, I have nothing to come home to."

"What about your parents?"

"They're busy. They never made time for us. Why should I make time for them?"

"That's not totally true."

"They've never once come to watch me play. With my first big contract, I offered to help them retire. They said no. I then offered to pay for a manager to give them more opportunities to see Arizona and I play. Again, they declined. I'm over it. I'm over them. My sister was the only thing I had tying me to our hometown. She doesn't live there anymore. I have no reason to ever go back."

I see a moment of hurt flash in her face before she steels herself. "They're good, hard-working people. Cut them some slack."

"I don't want to talk about my parents."

"Fine." She sighs. "How do you like it here in Houston?"

"It's not bad. I'm not totally enamored with this city, but the guys are a good group. We have fun. Make sure you go to the rodeo. It's a life experience no one should miss."

"I plan to. Any girlfriends?"

"The only girl, woman, I want sitting on my lap is the one on there right now."

"You're full of crap, Quincy Abbott."

"I'm not. There's something comforting about having you back in my arms again."

She relaxes a bit and smiles. I know she feels it too.

"I saw your game on TV today. Your curveball is wicked this season. It's much better than in the past."

"I love that you watch me, and I love that you notice things like that. We got a new pitching coach. I like him. How's your team looking?"

"Not bad. We've only had practices so far. I've been spoiled having your sister catch for me for my entire career. As you know, a great catcher is invaluable to us pitchers. I need to get used to my new catcher. Our games start in a few weeks. I think I'll be the opening day pitcher. The coach told me he considers me the ace of the staff."

"Wow, that's amazing, though I'm not surprised. Good for you, Shortcake."

She smiles again as she continues playing with my curls. "I've always loved when you called me that."

"I know. Your whole body flushes. You'd think I was saying something dirty."

"You never say it in front of other people. Only when we're alone."

I never noticed that. I suppose it's true.

We continue talking and catching up like old friends. As the evening goes on, she gradually becomes more and more comfortable with my roaming hands until she eventually leans back into me and begins to circle her hips a bit.

I sweep her hair to the side and run my lips up her neck, whispering, "I want you to come on my lap again. I think about that night all the time. Use me. Take what you need. I'll talk you through it."

She turns her head, so our eyes meet, and I nod in encouragement. Hesitating for a moment, she then spreads her legs a little wider, letting me know she's onboard.

Lifting my thigh just a bit more, I run it between her legs with as much friction as I can in this position. She momentarily gasps, but then grinds herself onto me.

She leans her head back onto my shoulder and continues her movements on my leg. I whisper in her ear, "That's it, Shortcake. I remember how wet your pink pussy got for me when I tasted you, when my cock was inside you. Give me all your juices."

I shake my leg a bit. She grabs hold of my jeans and moans, "Oh shit."

"I also remember how sensitive your nipples are." The first time in the hot tub, she came as soon as I sucked on one of her nipples.

I'm able to discreetly slide my hand up her shirt without anyone noticing. I pull the cup of her bra down and tweak her nipple, which is hardened and ready. I wish we were alone so I could tear these clothes off her and take it into my mouth.

She squeezes her legs around my thigh. I can feel her wet warmth against me.

"I want to suck on this nipple and taste your sweetness. I remember how hard it made you come. I remember how rosy and perfect it is. Your big tits. I want them in my face. I want to slide my cock through them."

She turns her head, runs her fingers through my hair, and breathes, "Kiss me."

I hesitate only briefly before my lips find hers. Her strawberry taste takes me back in time to the night she was mine. The two nights she was mine.

I have no doubt my teammates are looking on in shock. They've never seen me kiss a woman like this before because I haven't. I won't. I can't.

She grinds and circles my leg as our tongues dance a perfect tango. I squeeze her nipple hard, and she loses the battle of control. I swallow her moans as she begins quivering over my leg.

I kiss her through it, loving that she came on my lap again, just like that first night. I want to be inside her so badly. I want to do everything with her.

As she comes down, I can feel her smiling into my mouth. "You didn't come in your pants again, did you?"

I smile back. "You knew?"

She giggles. "I figured it out."

"It was the first time that had happened since I was a horny preteen. That was the mark you left on me, Shortcake."

Our faces break apart as reality appears to set in. She looks around in a bit of shock. The guys aren't looking. I'm sure they saw, but ballplayers making out with women in clubs isn't exactly new and exciting for them. They know not to stare, just as I wouldn't stare at them.

Ripley is clearly mortified though. Her smile completely drops. Her playful attitude is gone. She starts to stand but I hold her on my lap. "Relax."

"Let me go. This was a mistake."

"Come home with me. I want to touch you with nothing between us."

"No." When she again tries unsuccessfully to stand, she grits out, "Let me go. Now." Tears begin to sting her eyes.

I relent and she stands, straightening her skirt. "I'm not going down this road. Keeping this secret all these years has been hard enough. Goodbye, Quincy. I'll see you around."

CHAPTER FIVE

QUINCY - AGE 27 {RIPLEY - AGE 22}

I saw Ripley in the stands at my game last night. She was there the last time I pitched too. She wasn't with anyone. She simply came to watch me play.

It's been two weeks since that night in the club. I've contemplated reaching out to her but seeing her come to my game last night convinced me I should. That, and I can't be bothered with other women. There's only one on my mind.

I have her address and find myself knocking on her door the next morning. She opens it red-faced while wiping tears streaming down her face.

Her shoulders fall when she sees me. "I'm not up for this, Quincy. Not today."

I push my way in and close the door. She throws her hands up in exasperation and sarcastically snipes, "By all means, come in."

"What's wrong?"

"Nothing that impacts you."

I don't like seeing her upset. "Tell me what's happening. I'm not leaving until you tell me who has upset you. If it's a man, just give me a name and an address and I'll take care of it."

She narrows her eyes. "Who *are* you? Everyone sees you as laid-back, carefree, and chill. You're anything but."

I lift my backward baseball hat and run my fingers through my hair before replacing the hat on my head. "I don't give a fuck about anyone else right now. Tell. Me. Now."

She plops down on her couch and leans back, letting her shoulders fall. "Let it go. It's not a man. That's all you need to know."

I have this innate need to look out for her. I'm not leaving until she tells me, even if I have to coax it out of her.

I sit down near her and pull her bare feet to my lap.

She pinches her eyebrows together. "What are you doing?"

"If you won't share it with me, at least I can help you relax. I'll rub your feet."

She skeptically lays back on the pillow before a small smile finds her lips. "Does the great Quincy Abbott have a foot fetish? I didn't know this."

I let out a laugh. "No, not in the least. Your feet are ugly. I'm just being a nice guy."

She feigns shock. "My feet aren't ugly." She grimaces. "Though once a season starts, I can't say they're beautiful."

I chuckle. "At least they're not smelly. As someone

who shares a locker room with a lot of sweaty men, I value feet that aren't smelly." I pull them closer to me. "Let me help you relax."

I start rubbing her feet, and she lets out a moan. "Oh god, that feels good."

"Sex feels good too. That helps with stress." I wiggle my eyebrows at her.

She giggles. "Nice try. Not happening."

I sigh. "Fine, we'll do the small talk thing. You guys start your games this week, right?"

"Yes." She mumbles, "Theoretically."

"It seems like you've made friends."

"I have. I suppose I'm closest to Emily, the girl your friend was with. I think they're still hanging out."

"Heads up, he's a bit of a bullshitter."

"What do you mean?"

"He promises forever to get women into bed. He says the same crap to every woman." In a mock deep voice, I say, "I can really see this becoming something, baby. I've always dreamed of finding a woman like you. You're so special. Blah blah blah."

She cringes. "Ugh. He definitely said those things to her. What a dick."

"It's an asshole move for sure."

"What do you promise women, Quincy?"

"A good time and nothing more. I'm very clear up front."

"What if you meet someone special?"

I continue rubbing her feet. "Not looking. What about you?"

"I dated a few guys my first two years of college but was with the same guy for the last two years. We both knew we had an expiration date though. It was a healthy, good relationship. We're still friends."

"Will you tell me why you're upset? Please. Maybe I can help."

She blows out a breath. "Okay. Just don't stop rubbing. It feels amazing."

"There are other areas I could rub that would feel even better."

She shakes her head. "Not happening, Abbott."

I smile as I continue rubbing her feet. "Tell me what's going on. What made you so upset?"

She lifts her head off the sofa pillow as I see sadness take over. "Just my mom being...my mom. You know how she is."

That could mean one of two things. Ripley's mom was always either flaking out on her or bed-hopping from man to man.

I lift my eyebrows waiting for a real answer.

She sinks her head back down and lets out a breath. "Fine. You know how we moved from Canada when I was five, right?"

"Yes. Of course."

"When I woke up this morning, I had a message from the team owner. Apparently, I'm not a legal citizen of the US. My nutjob of a mother never bothered to file the appropriate paperwork. She did it for herself, but not me. When I called her just now, she said she didn't think she needed to because I was five. So I've lived here illegally for seventeen years. If I'm not here legally, I can't play professional softball."

"What about when you applied to college? No one picked up on it then?"

She shrugs. "I have no idea. I guess illegal aliens can have social security numbers. Who knew? I didn't know anything about this until about an hour ago."

"What about a work visa? I'm sure the team can help make that happen."

"Our games start next week, and that will take months, meaning I can't play this season. And because I've been here illegally for so many years, I might not get it at all." The tears start up again and trickle down her cheeks. "I don't know what to do. I suppose I need an attorney. I can't really afford it, but what else am I supposed to do?"

"I'll pay for an attorney."

She shakes her head. "Absolutely not."

I hate seeing her in pain. I wrack my brain, thinking, until it hits me. The perfect solution. "I've got an...idea."

She pinches her eyebrows together with a hopeful expression. "What is it?"

"Just hear me out. It's a little out of the box. Let's..." I swallow. "Let's get married."

Her chin drops. "What? Are you nuts?"

"I'm not kidding. Let's get married. You'll be legal if you're my wife. That solves all your problems. Immediately."

"I...I...We can't just get married."

I stop massaging her feet and cross my arms. "Why not?"

She sits up on the couch and runs her fingers through her hair before turning her head to me. "I'm not getting married under these circumstances. Why would *you* even want to?"

I shrug. "I'm never *really* getting married or having

kids. If I can help you out, it's not a big deal. It fixes everything for you."

"Why don't you ever want to get married and have kids? I've never heard about this before."

"Because I refuse to turn into my parents who made their kids feel like an afterthought. Who never prioritized us."

"I know your parents weren't around much, but they love you guys."

"Maybe, but they love their business more. My job requires me to travel. I'd rather not have kids than have them and make them feel the way I felt, like I came in second place. So I'm not having any. Same goes for a wife. I can't exactly work with my wife like my father does; therefore, I'm not getting married."

"What about when you retire? You'll change your mind. You'll want a wife and kids then."

"I'm a pitcher. I can play for a long time. I could play until I'm in my forties. Plenty of pitchers have done it. That's a long time away. And what else am I suited for? I'll end up coaching or being an analyst when I retire. I'll still need to travel. Nope. Never getting married for real and *definitely* never having kids. I don't want them."

"That's silly. You'll feel differently one day."

"I promise I won't. I'm serious about this. I've seen several urologists about having a vasectomy. No one will perform the procedure at my age, but in a few years, I'll be getting it done to ensure that it never accidentally happens to me. That's my biggest nightmare."

She opens and closes her mouth several times. "But I want to get married and have kids one day."

"Then we'll get divorced. It's just a paper marriage. People do it all the time."

"The immigration agency would know it's fake."

"We're not strangers. We've known each other for more than fifteen years. No one will question it."

She's silent for a moment before shaking her head. "I don't think I can do that. I want to marry for love. I want something real."

"Do whatever you want, but this solves your problem, and whenever you meet someone, we'll simply end our arrangement."

She quietly contemplates for several long minutes.

"Would we tell anyone?"

"No, of course not. It stays between us."

"I've never kept a secret from Arizona in my life."

I lift my eyebrows. "So you told her that you lost your virginity to me?" I smile. "That you snuck into my bedroom in the middle of the night and seduced me?"

Her mouth opens in shock, and she pokes me in the chest. "What? You seduced me."

"*You* came to *me*. Not the other way around."

She scrunches her nose. "You were naked and waiting."

"Because I know how irresistible I am to you."

She rolls her eyes.

"Regardless, I know you haven't told her because she would tear me a new one if she found out."

She's quiet before admitting, "She thinks I lost my virginity to my first college boyfriend."

I smile in triumph. "I thought so. This isn't a real marriage. We'll fuck when we want to fuck and won't when we don't. We're both obviously free to date other people."

"Who says I want to fuck you?"

"I know you want to fuck me. I felt it all over my leg

the other night." I smirk. "I refuse to wash my jeans. It's a constant reminder."

She lets out a deep breath. "I don't know if there's room for you, me, and your ego in a marriage."

I chuckle. "I think the three of us could get along quite well." I take her hand in mine. "Look, we're friends. We've been friends for a long time. I'm in a position to help you. This is a quick fix to your dilemma. It will be our secret, and when the day comes that you want to get married to someone else, we'll quietly divorce. No one will be the wiser."

She sighs. "It seems so wrong." She nibbles on her lower lip. I'm jealous of that damn lip. "So...a friends with benefits kind of thing?" She's quick to add, "But no benefits."

I twist my face. "More like a marriage with benefits. The benefits of having sex with each other or other people whenever we please. Honestly? It's revolutionary."

"You're a real pioneer in fucked up situations." She shakes her head in disbelief. "I can't believe I'm considering this. If we get married, I'm not suddenly having sex with you. It might be better if we don't cross that line...again. This way when it's time to end it, there won't be any feelings involved."

"My offer has nothing to do with sex and certainly nothing to do with feelings. I'll never catch feelings for anyone, and you can't catch feelings for me. Like I said, we'll have sex if and when we want. We're otherwise free to see other people. The ball is in your court. I'm always willing as long as you can separate the physical from the emotional. Physical is all I'm ever offering."

Tears fill her eyes. "I can't believe it's come to this."

I wrap my arm around her. "Don't cry, Shortcake. I hate it. I'm just trying to help."

She relaxes her head into my chest. "I know. Thank you for offering, I just don't know that I can do it."

After several hours of continued conversation and contemplation, Ripley St. James and I officially get married.

CHAPTER SIX

RIPLEY - AGE 23 {QUINCY - AGE 28}

I t's been a few months since Quincy and I got married.
I'm struggling with having married him under these circumstances. I'm struggling with what he mentioned about marriage and children. I'm struggling to keep this all from my best friend. I wish I had someone to talk to, but I can't exactly tell people that I have a fraudulent marriage.

Arizona and I talk every day, and I feel like the worst friend in the world. I've been out on a handful of dates. One of the men was even around for two months, but it's hard for me to be deceitful. I'm married to one man and dating another. What the fuck happened to my life?

The season went well. I edged out Arizona for the league's Rookie of the Year honors. We had a few good laughs about it. She's genuinely happy for me. That's the kind of friendship we have, which only makes lying to her feel that much more horrible.

It's the off-season, and I'm working at a clothing store.

Professional softball players don't make a fraction of what professional baseball players make. I have to work to help make ends meet.

Quincy's new season just started back up. Ours doesn't start again for a few months. Not until mid-summer.

I couldn't help but go watch his first game pitching this season. Seeing him play makes me happy. It always has. And he's sexy as hell in his uniform, taking charge on the mound.

When I arrive back home from the game, I strip and take a long hot bath. I'm sitting there enjoying a glass of wine when there's a loud knocking at my front door. Crap. Who's at my door this late at night?

I quickly throw on my white silk robe and run to answer it.

Looking through the peephole, I notice that it's Quincy. I wonder why he's here. He hasn't been here since our wedding day. We ran into each other a few times when Drew and Emily were dating, but he broke her heart and that's in the past. It's been a while.

I open the door, and he looks me up and down in my state of undress. I'm quickly realizing that a flimsy silk robe wasn't the best thing to wear while answering the door.

I clutch the top closed as if that'll be better at shielding me. "Quincy? What are you doing here?"

"I saw you at the game."

He gives me a cocky smirk. He's so handsome in jeans, a black T-shirt, and his backward hat with his curls spilling out.

I narrow my eyes at him. "There were probably forty thousand people there. You noticed me?"

He shrugs his shoulders. "What can I say? You stick out to me, Shortcake."

My cheeks redden. I don't know why him calling me that always makes my heart race. It's a special term of endearment for me, and that fact does things to me.

"Is there something you need?"

He looks my body up and down while licking his lips before meeting my eyes. "I...umm...I'm just checking in on you. We haven't spoken in a while." He gives me a boyish grin. "Just trying to be a good husband."

I let out a laugh as I open the door wider in invitation. "Husband of the year, please come in."

He chuckles as he walks through the door, and I close it. We stand there a little awkwardly. I think we're both a little tongue-tied as to how to behave or what to say to the other.

He slides his hands into his pockets and rocks on his feet a bit nervously. "How have you been?"

"I'm good. I'm working at the mall. I feel like a teenager doing that again, but I need the money, and the hours are flexible so I can still get in my workouts."

His face falls. "I didn't realize things were so tough. I can help you out."

I shake my head. "Absolutely not."

"Does my sister have a job?"

"She does a little modeling for a few upstart softball brands. I think it keeps her afloat. I wish being a softball player was half as lucrative as being a baseball player."

He nods in understanding. "It should be. Maybe one day."

I motion toward my sofa. "Have a seat. I'm going to throw on some clothing."

He gently grabs my arm and pulls me toward the sofa. "No need." He winks. "I prefer you this way."

I sigh as I sit. "What are you really doing here? Do you want a divorce already? I'm game for that."

He lets out a laugh. "No. Definitely not. I honestly just stopped by to check on you and maybe hang out. We've been friends most of our lives. Is it so crazy that I want to check in now and then?"

I'm considering his words when he grabs my legs and swivels me so that I have to lay down and my feet are on his lap. He immediately starts kneading them. "I know how much you like this."

My eyes flutter and I think I let out a moan. "Oh god yes."

He freezes. "If you moan like that, I can't be held responsible for my actions."

I swallow hard. It's been a long time for me, and no man's touch has ever lit me up like his.

He continues rubbing. "How's your mom?"

I sigh, as I often do when her name comes up. "She's a handful, as always."

He lets out a laugh. "I get a kick out of her."

"You wouldn't if she was your mother."

"She was always there for you in her own special way. What about your father? I've never heard anything about him."

"Honestly, Quincy, I'm not convinced she knows who it is. You saw how she was always sleeping around. I tried for years to pry information from her, but I've never once had any question answered." I look down at my body. "I assume he was a big guy. That's about all I know. I don't even have a name."

"You could do a little investigatory work. There are professionals who could probably get you all the answers."

"That shit isn't cheap. I can't afford it."

"I'll pay for it."

"No. I don't want your money. Stop offering it. It makes me uncomfortable."

"Half of mine is yours, wife."

I smile. "You should have had me sign a prenup, Abbott. I could take your ass to the cleaners."

He lets out a laugh. "But you won't. Feel free though. I'd happily give it to you. It's stupid how much they pay us."

I nod. "Consider yourself lucky."

"I do. I should send Arizona money."

"Ask her first. She's a prideful person. She might not want a handout."

"We'll see about that." He nods toward the television. "Let's watch a movie."

"How about T—"

"Don't even think about saying *Top Gun*. Anything else. I have nightmares about that movie. You and Arizona must have watched it ten thousand times as kids."

I giggle. "When he makes a fool of himself singing 'You've Lost That Loving Feeling,' it's the most romantic thing I've ever seen in my life." I clutch my heart. "He has a terrible voice but did it for her."

He rolls his eyes. "Pick. Something. Else. Anything. Else. That scene gives me a nervous tic."

"Fine, Mr. Bossy Pants. *Field of Dreams*?" I remember that was his favorite movie as a kid.

He enthusiastically nods. "Deal."

I fiddle with the remote and turn on the sweet baseball movie.

At some point he turns to me. "Did you know that Ben Affleck and Matt Damon are in this movie as extras? They were kids when it was filmed."

"I didn't know that. Is that one of your random, fun facts?"

He smiles. "It is. I brought our random fact thing to my team. One of the guys told us that one. I had no idea."

"I learned a lot at your family dinners."

"Tell me some of your favorites?"

"Hmm. Oh, I think it was Arizona who researched this fact. One in eighteen people have a third nipple. Every time I'm on a new team or start a new class, I look around and wonder which person there has a third nipple." I giggle. "Arizona and I used to make a game of it during classes we had together. Trying to guess who it was."

He gives me a knowing smirk. "I do the same thing."

We both laugh. It's so easy between us. He makes me smile.

We're only about half an hour into the movie when his hands start to travel higher up my legs.

"Quincy," I warn.

He gives me a mischievous grin. "Let's play the firetruck game. I'll run my hand up your leg and you say *red light* when you want me to stop."

"Red light."

He shrugs. "Sorry, firetrucks don't stop at red lights."

I let out a mock laugh. "Oh my god. That's horrible."

He winks as he moves his hands back to my feet. Admittedly, it feels nice.

The movie continues, as does the upward trajectory of his hands. I should stop him, but I don't. I love the feel of his hands on my body. His hands on my legs do more for me than *anything* other men have done to me in a long while, if ever.

It's not long before his hand slides under my robe and to my breast. He begins aimlessly running his fingers over my nipples. I can feel the pace of my breathing speed up. The throb between my legs builds.

He turns his face to me. "I remember how sensitive your nipples are."

I close my eyes and nod as I squirm on the sofa. My nipples are extremely sensitive.

His other hand is now on my inner thigh. I can't help but spread my legs a bit. I'm only human.

As soon as I do, he runs a finger through me. My hips buck of their own volition.

For a long time, he simply teases me, moving his fingers through me over and over, but never inside me until I'm panting for it. He knows exactly what he's doing, and I'm putty in his hands.

I shift my body down toward him, hoping he'll slide them in, but he doesn't.

When I've reached my boiling point, I breathe, "Quincy, do it."

He nods as he slowly slides a finger inside me. I can feel my walls tighten around him.

I hear him whisper, "Time to consummate this marriage, wife."

I must be fucked up because I want it too. Desperately.

His fingers that were on my breast move and begin to tug on the sash of my robe, but I clutch the top and hold it closed, not wanting to bare myself in the brightness of the room. "Let's turn off the lights."

He immediately withdraws his fingers from inside me. His face turns angry. "Why do we need to turn them off?"

My shoulders fall and I lower my head in shame. "Because I'm not comfortable with you seeing me under these bright lights. I don't look like the other women you sleep with."

"How do you know what the women who I sleep with are like?"

I suppose I don't. "I assume."

"Well, you assume wrong. They all pale in comparison to you."

I let out a long breath. I don't know if I can handle him saying things like that to me.

He stands, and I'm suddenly fearful he'll leave, but instead he grabs my hand and pulls me up. "Come with me."

As if I have a choice; he forcefully drags me toward my bedroom. His eyes search the room until they land on my full-length mirror. Pushing me until I stand in front of it, he immediately removes my robe before I can stop him.

As it falls to the floor, I look down and try to cover myself, but he grabs me by the wrists, pinning them to my sides. "Lift your head and look at yourself in the mirror, Ripley. Now."

Tears sting my eyes as I do, hating the reflection staring back at me. While Quincy made me feel good about myself the night we spent together and gave me a little more confidence with men, I still don't care for being seen in a well-lit room or in the harsh reflection of a mirror.

His eyes slowly drink my body in before they meet mine again. "Tell me, what do you see?"

"An overweight woman. One who, no matter how much she diets or works out, can never seem to have the body she wants."

He pulls his front flush to my back and thrusts his hips. His rock-hard boner pushes into my ass. "Can you feel what your body does to me?"

I nod.

"I've been hard since you opened that door in your little robe with your nipples taunting me, imagining all the things I want to do to you."

He slowly runs his fingertips over my hips. "Real women should have hips. Why would I ever want a woman to be built like a man with small, narrow hips? The day I first started to look at you as a woman, it was these hips," he squeezes them, "and this ass," he squeezes it, "that made my mouth water. It was the day I got drafted. Getting to fulfill my lifetime dream of playing professional ball should have been the subject of my obsession that day, but instead, it was your body I couldn't get out of my mind. The girl I watched grow up suddenly became a full-fledged woman. A stunning, sexy woman."

His hands move over my stomach. I try not to flinch. "Your skin is an unmatched shade of peaches and cream. I dream of the way it looks. How much it flushes when I

89

touch you, like it is right now. How it smells like strawberries." He sinks his nose into my neck and audibly inhales. "You've always smelled like strawberries, Shortcake, since day one."

He cups my breasts and gives them both a hard squeeze. "These full tits star in my dreams. I ache to suck them again while watching you come undone. I bet I can give you an orgasm from simply playing with them the way I know you like it."

I think he might be right about that.

His hands move down to my thighs. I cringe at their thickness. There's nothing positive he could say about them.

"Men are solid and hardened. Why in the world would I want a woman to feel like that against my body? Real women should be smooth and soft like you. I love having something to grab onto when I move inside your body. It gets me off. *You* get me off."

I attempt to turn around, dying to kiss him, but he stops me. "Don't move until I tell you it's time. We're not done appreciating your body. I'll give you what you want when you give me what I want."

He tosses his hat to the side before he reaches back with one hand and removes his T-shirt. I can feel his warm, hard chest pressed to my back. I can smell his delicious aftershave. Power emanates from his every pore. He's so masculine and domineering.

Running his hands up my sides, he peppers kisses on my neck, causing my entire body to break out in goosebumps, and my nipples to harden to a near painful point. "I love your height." I'm about six feet tall, leaving him a few inches taller than me. "I hate the logistics of being with a small woman. It feels unnatural, but everything about being with you feels right."

That's true. It feels right being with him. Nothing has ever felt more right for me.

I can both hear and feel him unfastening his belt. Before I know it, he's completely naked, pressed against the back of my body.

Our eyes meet in the mirror. "I have the most beautiful wife."

My eyes flutter. I wish this was real. I wish I was his and he was mine.

He rubs his thumb over my face and then my lips, all without breaking eye contact in the mirror. "Tell me you understand how beautiful you are."

"Quincy—"

Before I can finish protesting, he spanks me hard.

I gasp. I've never been spanked before but can feel the unexpected enjoyment pooling between my legs.

As if he can read my body, his fingers move down and through my folds. He then brings those fingers up and sucks them into his mouth. "Hmm. You liked that, didn't you, wife? My wife likes it when I spank her." The corners of his mouth raise slightly. "I liked it too."

I feel him move around and then slide down my body until he's on his knees in front of me. I can see his muscular back and sexy ass in the mirror.

He grabs the back of my thighs and licks once through my center. It feels so good, but he lifts his head and looks up at me.

"Do you want more of that?"

I enthusiastically nod.

"Tell me. Tell me what I want to hear."

I close my eyes.

"Open them and really look at yourself. I need you to see the beauty I see in you. My stunning wife."

I slowly peel them open and take in the scene before me.

I'm standing naked with my legs spread ever so slightly. The most perfect, gorgeous man is equally naked, physically on his knees in front of me. Worshiping me and my body. The evidence of what my being naked does to him is as clear as day with his massive, engorged, leaking cock pointing at me.

I nod and barely whisper, "I'm...I'm beautiful."

"Louder."

I take a deep breath. In a regular voice, I confidently declare, "I'm beautiful."

"And perfect."

I let out another breath.

"Say it."

"And perfect."

A much bigger smile finds his lips before he buries his face between my legs and begins to lick up and down through me. When he did this to me over four years ago, it was the greatest pleasure I'd ever known. What I've learned since is that finding a man who does it well isn't easy. I've never come harder than I did the one and only other time Quincy Abbott did this to me.

He grabs onto my ass and starts to go to town, eating me like a starved man. He moans like I'm doing this to him. I have to grip his sexy curls, as I'm barely able to remain upright.

My legs feel wobbly. I breathe, "I can't stand anymore. It's too good."

Without removing his tongue from me, he crawls until I feel the backs of my legs brush against my bed. He places his hand on my stomach and pushes me down onto the bed.

Still without removing his tongue, he remains on the ground, spreads my legs as wide as they can go, and grabs my thighs for leverage as he drives me into a frenzy with his tongue magically working over my clit.

He moves one hand until I feel his fingers prod my

entrance. Teasing me for a moment, he eventually slides two then three fingers into me.

His fingers start to fuck me hard. "Ah, Quincy, it's too much."

He mumbles, "You'll take it."

And I do. The combination of his thick, long fingers and his tongue has me screaming out. Fuck, he's deep.

Before I know it, a tidal wave of an orgasm begins to build. Oh my god, it's big. I'm climbing fast to reach its crest. As if sensing it, he simultaneously pushes in deeper, curls his fingers, and sucks on my clit.

That's it for me. I have to grip the sheets as my back arches. The bright room goes temporarily dark as I come so fucking hard and long. There's nothing in the world that could stifle my screams of ecstasy right now.

As I start to drift down off the high, I feel his hand move up my body until it reaches my throat. He only then breaks the contact of his mouth on me and licks up my body.

Now he's got both hands on my throat as he gets situated between my legs. After applying a slight squeeze, he grits, "Can you take it a little harder than last time?"

I nod eagerly.

"Do you like my hands on your throat?"

I can't believe I do; I've never contemplated it before, but I can't deny that I get off on his dominance over me in the bedroom.

I nod again.

"Good girl. I knew you would. You like submitting to me." I catch his crooked smirk just before he brings his lips to mine. Quincy Abbott kisses are my everything. My first, my best, the one I've never been able to erase from my mind. In every other aspect, he's domineering, but his kisses are always so tender and sweet. Any woman who's blessed with his lips must find it hard to ever kiss another man. I know I do. His slow tongue, his soft lips. There's something emotional about it. I know he doesn't love me or have some deep, meaningful affection for me, but he kisses me like he does.

I run my fingers through his curls and latch on, trying to mirror his movements and kiss him back as perfectly as he kisses me.

His thumbs gently massage my neck as his tongue sweeps through my mouth. I feel his cock rubbing through my wetness. Every hard ridge and vein causes tremors to vibrate through my body.

I want him so badly. I mumble, "Quincy, I need you."

One of his hands moves off me and feels around the bed. He suddenly breaks our lips apart. I hate it. I could kiss him forever.

He lifts his body and tears open a condom, rolling it down his massive length. I obviously knew Quincy was big the first time we were together, but I don't think I appreciated it until I started seeing other men. Quincy Abbott is a man among boys. A god among men. Perfection in an imperfect world.

He sits back on his knees, raking his gaze over my body with lust-hooded eyes. I'm making Quincy Abbott feel this way. Me. Ripley St. James. An imperfect woman.

I breathe, "Please. I want you."

He places his elbows on either side of me. We're finally chest to chest again. It feels like both yesterday and a hundred years since I felt him this close.

He begins to push into me. I don't recognize the sounds coming out of my mouth as he slides in. My walls stretch and form to his girth. Everything that is right in this world opens inside me. Is this how it was our first time? I was too scared to remember the feeling when he entered me. But this? This is bliss.

"You're so warm and snug, Shortcake."

He pulls back out a few inches. I hate it. I immediately want him back inside me. Before I can process another thought, he slams back in, and husky moans escape both of our mouths. His jaw is slack as he pulls out and then back in again. I can barely catch my breath, paralyzed by pleasure.

He begins to establish a rhythm. At times my legs are wrapped around his body, but at others I feel the need to spread them as wide as they can go, wanting him as deep inside my body as physically possible.

The heat building inside me is euphoric, but when one of his hands reaches my throat, the sensations head into orbit. Watching Quincy control my body, taking and giving, exerting his pure masculine dominance, is something I know I'll forever need.

He moves his lips back to mine, first nibbling on my lower lip and then latching on while his tongue plunges into my mouth.

He's fucking me hard, squeezing my throat, but kissing me with all the reverence in the world. What he's really doing is blowing my mind.

Every nerve ending is worked to the max until I feel my orgasm teasing me. I'm working my way up a huge mountain, knowing I'm about to reach the highest of heights. The peak.

He lifts his lips from mine while his scorching eyes find mine. He squeezes my throat a drop harder and mouths, "Come for me."

And I do. I can feel my walls clench around him. I cry out his name as I lose all control and ride into a starry sea of bliss.

He groans out, "Oh fuck, that's good," as he roars into his own orgasm, emptying himself into the condom.

In the aftermath, we lay tangled in a sweaty, breathless, sated embrace. My top leg is wrapped around him.

We're quiet for several minutes as we gather our breath and process the unimaginable sex we just had.

I eventually attempt to move my leg off him, but he holds it in place. "Not yet. I don't want to come down off this high." I feel him smile into my neck as he blesses the spot behind my ear with delicate kisses. "We've consummated our marriage. It's now official."

I giggle. "I guess we're stuck with each other now." I playfully shrug my shoulders. "You *really* should have insisted on a prenup. I've got you right where I want you, Abbott."

He chuckles. "I suppose I'm now your sex slave. I can live with that."

"Hmm." I nuzzle into his sexy chest and allow myself for the briefest of moments to think about what it would be like to really be his wife. To be able to lay in bed with him like this every morning and every night.

What's crazy is that he seems just as content as me. This is too intimate. It's dangerous for me. I need to say something to break it.

"What do you do in your spare time here?"

I feel him shrug his shoulders. "Normal stuff. Hang with friends, work out, and practice. Oh, and sometimes I volunteer at the Great Dane Rescue League. Those dogs need exercise. They're always happy to have volunteers take them to the park for long walks."

I smile. "That's so sweet. Do any of them look like Diamond?"

"A few. It's so tempting to adopt one, but my lifestyle isn't right for a dog. One day when I have a house, maybe it will happen."

"I remember you always wanting a house. Why don't you buy one?"

"I'm not sure Houston is a permanent situation for me."

"How come?"

He scrunches his nose. "I like it, but I don't love it here. I'll buy a house when I love somewhere. A place I can see myself forever."

I reach over and run my fingers through his hair. "God, I love your hair."

He smiles. It's genuine and carefree. "I know you do."

"Women must go crazy for it."

His face falls. "I don't want to talk about other women."

"It's not like I don't know that you date."

"They're faceless and nameless."

I start thinking about him in high school. I've never known him to have a girlfriend.

"Why didn't you ever have girlfriends when we were growing up? I don't remember any hanging around your house. Arizona thought you were gay for the longest time. I told her you definitely weren't."

He lifts his head before raising an eyebrow. "How did you know I wasn't?"

"Well, I pined after you, and that didn't really play into my fantasy."

He nods. "I had girlfriends, but I was never serious with anyone. I just didn't bring them home with me. Perhaps in part because I was embarrassed by my absentee parents, and in part I just wanted my own, private, untainted space. I've never once invited a woman to my apartment."

"Never?"

He shakes his head. "No. It's always her place. My place is sacred. I don't bring home random hookups ever."

I tap his chest over his heart. "You're twenty-eight years old. You've never let *anyone* in?"

"No."

"I think it's unhealthy."

"I never claimed to be healthy."

I wiggle my hips. "You felt *very* healthy to me."

He smiles. "We have a physical connection that I can't explain. Something I've never shared with anyone else."

Part of me is happy that he feels it too, but then there's another part of me that's sad knowing we can never be anything more than what we are right now.

CHAPTER SEVEN

QUINCY - AGE 31 {RIPLEY - AGE 26}

"I'm engaged! Ahh!"

My face falls. "To whom?"

I can hear Arizona sigh in disappointment at my question. "To Marc, asshole. My boyfriend. The man I've been dating for over two years."

Ripley and I are in bed. She pinches her eyebrows at my sour expression. I point at the phone and mouth, "It's Arizona."

I put the phone on speaker so she can hear but motion for her to be quiet. She nods.

I grumble, "Oh. How about a long engagement? Maybe ten years or so?"

Ripley's eyes widen and she mouths, "They're engaged?"

I nod.

Arizona barks, "Quincy, cut it out. Marc is a good guy."

"No, he's not. And he's not good enough for you."
Actually, he's a pompous asshole, and I can't stand him.
There's no way he's not running around on her.

"You don't like him because you know he's sleeping
with your sister. He's going to be your brother soon, so
snap out of it. We're planning to get married within the
year."

I can't pretend to be happy for her. Marc Whittaker is
a douchebag. He's a pro baseball player too. I've only met
him a handful of times, but I don't like him at all. I
certainly don't like the way he treats her. She deserves
better.

"Hmm. We'll see. Don't rush into anything. Make
sure he's the one."

"Q, I accepted his proposal. I'm sure. I need you to be
happy for me."

"I'll try my best. Have you told Ripley yet?"

"No, silly, I called my big brother first. She's my next
call."

"Why don't you do that, and we'll chat later?"

"Okay. Talk soon. Love you, shit stain."

I roll my eyes at the never-ending references to that
unfortunate incident. "Love you too."

I end the call and look at Ripley in my bed. The sheets
are just barely covering her naked breasts. In the
morning light, her skin glows bright like an angel. And
her hair is so sexy. It's wild, more wild than usual. Likely
from the hours and hours we went at it last night.

She bites her lip. "I didn't see this coming, did you?"

I shake my head. "No. I hate him. He's not the right
man for her. He doesn't treat her properly."

"Normally I think you're an overprotective ogre when it

comes to the men she dates, but this time you're right on the money. I can't believe they're engaged. She was talking about breaking up with him last week. What is she thinking?"

Before I can agree, her phone rings. Ripley reaches for it and nods at me, confirming it's Arizona.

"Put it on speaker."

She accepts the call, places it on speaker, and happily says, "Good morning, babe."

"Rip! I have huge news! Marc proposed! We're getting married! Can you believe it?"

Ripley St. James doesn't have a fake bone in her body. In fact, I'm shocked that she's been able to keep our marriage and sporadic sexual relationship a secret for the past few years.

With enthusiasm I can tell is hard for her to muster, she replies, "Oh wow. Congrats. How did he propose?"

"After he fucked my brains out in bed last night."

My face falls and Ripley giggles. "That sounds... romantic."

"It was spontaneous. He didn't have a ring or anything. I think I'm just so good in bed that he felt compelled to lock me down in the moment. We're ring shopping this week sometime."

I'm sick to my stomach but Ripley has a huge smile. I know it's not from the engagement news, so it's clearly at me having to suffer through this conversation. She looks at me with mischief on her face. "Give me some more details about the sex." She covers her mouth to hold in her laugh.

I narrow my eyes at her.

"Later, I need to give you wedding details first."

Perhaps it's time for me to have a little fun of my

own. I quickly pull the sheets down and away from her, exposing her body to me.

Her eyes widen but she doesn't otherwise flinch. Ripley has changed in the past three years. We're only together once or twice a month, but she's no longer shy about her body. She embraces her sexiness. Us showering together in the mornings after spending a night together has become the norm. She walks around naked all the time without a care. I love that I played some small part in making her feel that way.

As Arizona rambles on and on about bridal details, I stop listening, instead focusing on the beautiful woman in the bed. The one I don't have often enough but know I can't be greedy and take any more of it than I do.

I press the button, turning the phone off speakerphone. I don't need to hear my sister when I'm naked with her best friend.

She eyes me warily as I spread and then kneel between her legs.

I bend my head down and circle her taut nipple with my tongue before sucking it into my mouth.

Her eyes flutter as she attempts to remain present in her conversation.

I slide my fingers down to find her nice and wet. Ripley is *always* turned on. I love taking my time to get her ready for me, but I don't need to. The woman is permanently horny, ready, and willing.

I slip two fingers inside her as I increase the suction on her nipple.

She moans, "Yes."

Even with the phone off speaker, I hear Arizona squeal. "Yay. You're officially my maid of honor."

Ripley's back arches as she manages, "Umm hmm."

She pushes my head down her body until my mouth is exactly where she wants it. I pull my fingers out and slide my tongue inside her.

I hear Arizona talking, but I can't make out her words.

Ripley replies, "Yes, I'm seeing someone casually. That's all I'm interested in. Just a random Barney." She makes eye contact with me. "He's really good in bed. I'm using him for that. It's not like I'm going to marry the guy."

She gives me a cheeky smile.

"Yep, his dick is huge. It's so freaking long. He fucks me deep. I'm learning that I need that. *Really* need that. So I'll stay with him until I find someone with a bigger, longer dick."

Her chest shakes as she attempts to contain her giggles, loving to fuck with me.

She's going to pay for that comment though.

I slide up her body until just my tip breaches her entrance. She reaches over for a condom, but I shake my head and mouth, "Just the tip," as I move it in and out of her over and over again.

"Great. Let's talk about the bridal shower details tomorrow. I have to take care of something right now. I'll call you then."

She ends the call and throws her phone across the bed. "Get a condom on and fuck me deep."

I lift my eyebrow. "Until someone who can fuck you deeper comes along?"

"Exactly."

"You know, scientifically speaking, most women's g-spots are very shallow. You might enjoy a little tip action."

I continue to move my tip in and out of her, loving the feeling of being bare inside her, something I've certainly never considered with anyone else. She gives me an unimpressed look. "*This* woman's g-spot isn't shallow. It's very deep. Mariana Trench deep."

I chuckle. "The deepest trench in the ocean? That's what you're comparing yourself to?"

She smiles. "Yep. Now get that condom on and find my Mariana Trench."

"Hmm. Did you know that I was a marine biology major before I left college?"

She bites her lip as she nods. Of course she knows. She's so smart. This woman misses nothing.

"I'm very well versed on the ocean, and I'm feeling a bit like Jacques Cousteau right now. I need to do some investigative exploring before my *long* submarine can enter these *deep*, wet waters. Trenches are dangerous, especially one as deep as the Mariana Trench."

She giggles as she widens her legs. "Explore away, Mr. Cousteau."

I start with two fingers and slide them in. "We're entering at the sunlight zone. You might know it as the continental shelf. It's the warmest part of the ocean, but I would argue that for your trench, it only gets warmer as we get deeper. It's what makes you a wonder of the world."

Her face lights up, enjoying this little game.

I add a third finger and push in a drop deeper. "And now we hit the twilight zone. There's little to no sunlight here."

Her hips start to gyrate. She breathes, "More. Give me more."

A fourth finger enters her, and I push just a little deeper. She moans loudly.

"Now we're getting close to the abyss. It's very dark here. We're below the *Titanic*, Shortcake."

Her eyes flutter. "Oh god, Quincy. So good. Keep going."

With some maneuvering, I'm able to get my whole hand inside her. I pump her hard and deep. "Ahh. We've arrived at our final destination. Mr. Cousteau finally gets to his target where he's now laid claim to the deepest part of the St. James Trench, my personal favorite. Very few things can live here, but I sure want to."

I pump her ferociously. She's writhing and screaming my name. Every inch of her flushes. Her toes start to curl, her tell that she's about to come. One of many tells. She's so responsive to me.

I thrust my hand in and out as fast as I can. The bed is smacking against the wall. She's gripping the sheets, enjoying the hard ride. I pound and pound until she yells out into her orgasm, her body squeezing my fist like I'll never get it back out again.

As she begins to come down from the high, she lifts her head and looks at my hand buried in her. "Holy shit. You really did get the whole thing in there."

"I'm an excellent marine biologist." I pull my hand out and lather my cock with her juices, giving it several long pumps. "Now it's time for some missile submarine exploration."

She grabs the condom and pushes me until I'm lying down. Crawling over me, she says, "I think I'd like to control this submarine expedition. I don't want him going rogue."

I happily let her take the reins. She rolls the condom

on, positions me at her entrance, and sinks down onto me.

I suck in a breath. "Fuck, Shortcake. That feels good. These are my favorite waters to explore."

She smiles as her nipples rub against my chest. I do love the feeling of her soft body on my hard one.

She starts off with slow, purposeful movements, but quickly begins bouncing ferociously on top of me. Ripley hated being on top when we first started having sex, but now she loves it. As much as I like to control things in the bedroom, I get off on seeing her like this. Powerful, confident, taking charge.

I watch her full tits bounce up and down as she takes what she needs from me, grinding her clit on me every time she comes down.

"Play with your perfect tits."

Without hesitation, she listens as she continues to ride me. I love the sight of her squeezing her own sensitive nipples. It's so hot.

As her orgasm approaches, her movements become more erratic. I sit up and grab her ass to take control, thrusting deep inside her where she likes it.

She wraps her arms around my shoulders and joins her lips to mine. Her tongue is everywhere, doing some deep-sea exploring of its own.

I love her kisses. I crave them. They're so heartfelt. It's like she can't taste enough of me.

I feel her walls constrict around me. "Your pussy is milking me."

She throws her head back.

"Ah, Quincy."

"That's right. Be loud. Show me what my cock does to you."

Keeping one hand on her ass, I reach the other up to her throat and give it a squeeze. As soon as I do, her eyes flutter.

I can feel her coming, so I begin to let go and give into my own pleasure.

Just as we're both reaching that peak, she sinks her face into my neck and mumbles, "I love you," as we both moan into our respective orgasms.

For a few long awkward moments, there are no sounds but our heavy breathing.

Her face is still buried in my neck, our sweaty chests stuck together. I start to pull away, but she tightens her hold on me and whispers, "I know what this means. Let me have one more minute."

I keep my arms wrapped around her and pretend for the entire sixty seconds that I'm a normal man and am capable of giving her normal things. That a woman like Ripley St. James telling me she loves me is the best day of my life, not the beginning of the end.

I take deep breaths to inhale her scent, knowing I likely won't get to do it again.

When we eventually pull away, I see that her face is covered in tears. "I didn't mean to say it, but I can't lie and tell you that I don't mean it." She nervously licks her lips. "I'm in love with you, Quincy. I won't pretend otherwise anymore."

I pull away from her. I can't say this while her body is touching mine. While I'm still inside her.

I place her on the bed, stand, and run my fingers through my hair. "Why couldn't you leave it be? We had a good thing going."

She pulls her knees to her chest and looks up at me with sad eyes. "Because I want more. I love you. I can't be with anyone else because of my feelings for you. I don't want to. Why can't we just be together? For real."

"Because we don't want the same things in life. I was never unclear on this arrangement, Ripley."

She slowly nods. "I know, but I suppose I was hoping you loved me too, and that it would change things for you." She swallows. "I see that it hasn't."

"If we can just go back—"

She shakes her head and takes a deep breath. "No, we can't. I'm happy this happened. Maybe it will help me finally break free. I can't keep doing this to myself. I've spent more than three years being your dial-a-fuck and nothing more. You go out and do god knows what with all these women, while I can't bring myself to go near another man. It makes me sick to my stomach to have to pretend like I don't love you. It makes me sick to my stomach to lie to my best friend. I need to love you in the open or not at all. I need you to love me back or let me go."

Opening and closing my mouth a few times, I start to feel tears well in my eyes as I whisper, "I'm so sorry."

Her chin sinks to her chest. "Are you embarrassed to be seen with me? Is that what this is? Handsome, perfect, superstar Quincy Abbott, who can have any woman he wants, saddled with an overweight, mediocre woman."

My heart sinks. "Is that really what you think?"

She stands and wraps herself in a robe before gathering my clothes from the floor. Handing them to me, she croaks out, "It's what I know. I need you to leave. I need you to stop calling me every few weeks when you need someone to fall into bed with her legs wide open for you. Obviously you'll always be in my life to some extent. I love Arizona too much to walk away from you completely, but we'll be cordial when we need to be, nothing more." She steels her shoulders, being the strong woman I know her to be. "Let me go. It's time."

"Short—"

"Don't call me that. It's special to me. It's our secret name, but now it's tainted, and I can't hear it again. You only call me that in private because you won't love me in public." She begins to walk into her bathroom. "Goodbye, Quincy. Don't be here when I come back out. Lose my number."

She closes the bathroom door behind her. My heart fucking hurts, which is exactly how I know she's right. It's time to end this.

I hear her sobbing behind the door. Desperate to go to her, but knowing it's a mistake, I get dressed and walk out of her life.

PENNSYLVANIA
THE PHILADELPHIA YEARS

CHAPTER EIGHT

QUINCY - AGE 32 {RIPLEY - AGE 27}

I was traded to the Philadelphia Cougars a few days ago. Frankly, it's a welcome change. My team in Houston was young and in a rebuilding phase. The Cougars are a little older and contenders for the World Series this season. There's a lot of talent on the team.

Harold Greene, the longtime owner, said I'll slot right into their starting rotation. The season doesn't start for a few months. I moved early so that I have time to acclimate to my new team and my new city. Arizona plays professional softball for a team out of Southern California. I certainly have no need to go to my parents' house, so I find myself in Philly well ahead of our start date.

I grew to love the city of Houston, but it was time to leave. Running into Ripley became harder and harder. She's barely spoken to me since that day well over a year ago in her bedroom. The pain in her face when she sees me is unbearable.

Even while we both were there for Arizona when Marc left her at the altar, she maintained a cold distance from me. Now I don't have any reason to see her at all. She's in Houston, I'm in Philadelphia, and Arizona is single, in Southern California. I think it's all for the best.

Philly is now my home, and I'm excited about this fresh start.

I'm in athletic shorts and no top as I begin the daunting task of unpacking and getting settled into my new apartment when there's a knock at the door. I open it to see an adorable elderly lady holding a huge golden-colored Great Dane. He reminds me of Diamond.

She's tiny, with short gray hair styled like a football helmet and bright blue eyes. She's wearing one of those sweatsuits that you can hear swishing when the person walks.

The woman looks at my shirtless chest and fans her face. "You shouldn't answer your door like that. You'll give this old crow a heart attack."

I can't help but let out a laugh. "I'll keep that in mind. Can I help you?"

"Oh yes, I'm sorry, I was distracted by your beefcake body. It looks like our building has a Dr. McDreamy in the house. I'm Blanche, your new neighbor."

I do my best to bite back my smile. "Hi, Blanche. I'm Quincy, Quincy McDreamy."

She giggles as she hands me a basket. "I made you cookies. I could lie and tell you that I made them from scratch, but I didn't. I can't bake but want to be neighborly. Welcome to the building. Thanks for bringing me some eye candy."

I smile as I take them. She's a riot. "Thank you, Blanche. They smell amazing. Just like they're homemade. I'd never know the difference." They don't. They're very obviously store bought.

She giggles.

I nod toward the dog. "Is he a Great Dane?"

"He is. His name is Thor. I have a thing for muscular men with longer blond hair and broad chests." She winks at me. Blanche is a full-fledged flirt. I inwardly laugh. She must have well over forty years on me.

"I had a Great Dane growing up. It's my favorite breed. One day when I own a house, I hope to have another."

She nods. "Yes, they're hard to have in a building like this, but I had him before I moved here, when we lived in a bigger place. My husband passed two years ago, and I decided just this year that I didn't want to care for a house. The move hasn't been so great for Thor though. There's a teenager in the building who takes him for long walks every day so Thor can get some exercise."

"I'm happy to take him for walks too."

She reaches out and squeezes my hand. "Thank you. I'm getting a little old for those long walks, but I'm not too old for everything." She winks again.

I can't help but chuckle. "That's...umm...good to know."

"I may be getting old, but I'll never grow up."

"You're not old, Blanche. You're perfect just as you are. Prettiest lady I've met in the building yet."

She waves her hand dismissively. "Oh please. I'm so old that when I let out a huge fart last week, it threw out my back for two days."

I can't help but let out a loud laugh at that one.

"You're funny, Blanche. I happen to like my women funny."

She giggles like a schoolgirl. I think I officially love Blanche.

I see a guy walking down the hallway toward us. As he gets closer, I realize it's one of the most famous athletes in all of baseball, Layton Lancaster. He's the catcher on the Cougars. He's a bit older than me, nearing the end of his career, but he's likely a future Hall of Famer, and I'm excited to play with him.

He smiles as he approaches. "Quincy Abbott, right?"

I nod.

He holds out his hand. "I'm Layton. Harold asked me to stop by and welcome you to Philly. We're excited to have you."

I shake his hand in return. "It's an honor to meet you. I'm a huge fan of yours."

"Nonsense. It's me who's a fan of yours." He smiles at Blanche. "I didn't realize you had beautiful company. I can come back later if you're on a hot date."

She blushes at the compliment before fanning herself again. "First Thor and now Captain America? My battery-operated friend will be getting a workout later tonight."

Layton and I look at each other with huge grins on our faces.

"I'll leave you boys to it. You know where to find me for a good time. I've never had a threesome, but YOLO."

"Bye, Blanche. Thanks for the cookies. Don't forget to come by when Thor needs a walk."

"I will. Thank you."

I turn to Layton and open the door wider. "Please,

come in before my eighty-year-old neighbor talks us into her bedroom."

He lets out a loud laugh before looking at my bare chest. "Am I...interrupting you? I can come back another time if you have company."

I shake my head. "Not at all. I'm just unpacking. It was hot."

I wave him inside and he walks through the door. Looking around, he whistles, "This place is great." He points at my severely oversized television. "And that's fucking awesome."

I nod. "I'm a big sports fan. I love basketball and football. I like to watch it on a big screen."

"Nice. Me too. I'll watch with you sometime." He sits on my new sofa and makes himself comfortable like we're old friends. "If you want to work out together, I usually go over to the stadium in the early mornings. The young guys go later in the day, but my old ass likes the quiet of the morning."

I smile. "So do I. I guess it's part of aging. I can't sleep in anymore and I'd rather get my workout in before I start my day. There seems to be a mix of old and young guys on this team. The Hurricanes were so young. I had a hard time keeping up with their late-night antics. The club scene is getting old."

He chuckles. "I hear you. Trust me, I hear you. The young guys on this team hit the clubs until all hours. Us oldies keep it low-key at a local sports bar. The owner saves a private booth for us to kick back. I'm meeting Trey, Cheetah, and Ezra there tonight. You should join us. We're the unofficial oldie Cougars club."

I know all those names. Trey DePaul is the Cougars third baseman. He started his career in New York. I don't remember the exact circumstances, but I remember there was some crazy spectacle over him being traded from New York to Philly a few years ago. It was all over the news at the time.

Cheetah is the nickname for Cruz Gonzales. He's the centerfielder and widely considered the fastest player in the sport, hence the nickname, Cheetah. That leaves Ezra Decker, the longtime Cougars second baseman. He's a solid player. They're all over thirty years old. It's truly nice to have a group like this. I'm feeling very fortunate and very excited for this new opportunity.

"Thanks, man. That sounds fun. I'd love to."

Layton hangs around most of the day. He's an awesome guy, and it's really nice of him to befriend and welcome me.

At the allotted time, I take an Uber to a place called Screwballs. What a great name for a sports bar.

When I walk in, I see the four of them sitting in a corner booth that appears to be roped off from the rest of the patrons.

Layton immediately smiles when he sees me and motions for me to join them, which I do. After shaking all their hands, I decide to bring my family and teammate tradition to this team. It's always been a bonding activity.

"Are you guys game for something a little different?"

They all nod.

"My father loses track of time like no one I've ever met. He's a carpenter, and once he's in his shop, hours go by and he's clueless. When I was growing up, he was always late for everything, including dinner. Fearing my sister and I would turn into him, my mother started this game which I've brought to all the teams I've ever been on. Whoever is last to arrive has to offer up a random fact. It's just a small incentive to be on time and, frankly, you learn a lot from it. It's kind of fun and always a conversation starter. It keeps you on your toes."

Layton looks confused. "Like what?"

"I was last to arrive tonight, so I have to give you all some obscure fact. Let me think for a moment. Hmm. Baby elephants suck their trunks for comfort. It's like thumb-sucking to them."

Cheetah scoffs. "If I could suck my own *trunk*, I'd never leave the house."

We all laugh. I nod. "I think we all can agree with that statement."

Layton asks, "Do you research this stuff? Give us another example."

"I always have a bunch on hand at any moment just in case. You guys will like this one. A hippo's jaw opens wide enough to fit a sports car inside."

They all start playing with their jaws, as do most people when I give them that random fact.

Cheetah wiggles his. "I knew a girl like that once. Her name was Carissa." He shivers. "Hmm. She could open that mouth so damn wide."

Layton nods. "I remember her. That's the girl who we —"

Cheetah interrupts, "That's her."

I look at them in question and Layton shrugs. "Sometimes Cheetah and I share women. Or watch each other with women. We have similar tastes."

They fist-bump each other.

I look around. Even though it's a sports bar, there's a band playing cover music and dancing on a small dance floor. Most of the women are dancing for the benefit of our table. "I assume you all catch a lot of tail here?"

Layton smirks. "We sure do. All of us except Trey."

Trey lifts an eyebrow. "When you have the most perfect diamond at home, there's no need to go for these rough, unpolished stones. Enjoy your canned sardines. I'll be feasting on lobster later tonight."

Cheetah nods enthusiastically. "Gemma DePaul is most definitely a diamond and a lobster. She's the reason I'm currently obsessed with dark-haired beauties. And her tits..." Cheetah bites his lip and shivers again.

What the hell?

Trey scowls at him. "Stay away from my wife."

Cheetah winks at Trey. "I can't do that. We have book club together. The book she recommended this month has a couple that does it on a rowboat in the middle of a lake on their kids' overnight field trip. Holy crap. Best book scene ever."

Layton rolls his eyes. "Cheetah loves romance novels. And porn. He's obsessed with porn. The worst thing in the world is getting stuck with him as a roommate on a road trip. He watches that shit all night."

Cheetah proudly smiles. "I do, but none of those women are as hot as Gemma DePaul."

Trey practically growls at him, but I can tell that Cheetah is just having fun with him. These guys are a riot.

Cheetah turns to me. "Trey is a Neanderthal about Gemma. He rarely leaves her side. We like to bust his balls. She's in her third trimester with their first child or she'd be here tonight. She may always look fancy, but she likes hanging with the boys."

Layton sips his beer and nods. "Gemma is cool. We all love her...like a sister." He grins at Trey and then mock whispers, "A crazy hot sister with a bangin' body."

I mumble, "I know all about that."

Cheetah wiggles his eyebrows up and down. "What was that, Abbott? Did I just hear you admit that you have a hot sister? Perhaps she should join us one night."

I make a look of disgust. "Unfortunately, yes, I do. I've been chasing my friends away from her for as long as I can remember. I'm just happy she lives far away from you guys. She's a pro softball player. Her team is based out of Southern California."

He looks impressed. "Pro softball? That's cool. Too bad they don't have a team here in Philly. Then we could hang with your hot sister all the time."

I sarcastically reply, "Yes, it's truly a shame your womanizing self can't hang with my baby sister."

We spend the next hour chatting and getting to know each other. This is a good group of guys.

At some point, I notice an attractive brunette on the dance floor staring at Layton. I whistle. "Wow, she's kind of obvious. She's not even bothering to hide it."

Layton twists his lips. "That's Delta. She's a sure thing. A good lay though. She certainly likes sucking on elephant trunks. If nothing else piques my interest, I always have her ready, wet, and willing. If you want her, go ahead. I don't give a shit. Or we can tag team her. She's down for anything."

I shake my head. "Not my type. I like a little meat on the bones."

Cheetah's eyes widen. "Are you a chubby chaser?"

The corner of my mouth raises. My teammates have been calling me that for years. "Maybe by your standards. I just like a woman with real curves on her body. I don't like skin and bones. I need something I can grab onto when I fuck her. Big tits, thick thighs, and a big booty do it for me."

Though none have ever done it for me as much as Ripley St. James. Fuck, I love her body. I miss her, but I also know she's better off without me in her life. Part of me hopes she finds what she's looking for, and part of me can't stand the thought of her with someone else.

They all look around. There's a full-figured woman dancing with her friends. They nod her way. Cheetah asks, "Like her?"

I nod. "Yep, she'll do. I can have her on her back within the hour. In fact, I think it's time."

Layton's eyes widen. "Already?"

"Why not?" I stand. "I'll see you guys at the gym tomorrow morning, right?"

They all nod and catcall as I walk away.

I head over to the woman and ask her to dance. She immediately agrees. It takes all of half a song for her to agree to take me back to her place. I grab her hand and we exit the bar. As we get into the Uber, I tell her, "I promise you'll come several times tonight, but no kissing." I stare out the window and think, *I save my kisses for one special woman. My wife.*

AT EIGHT O'CLOCK THE next morning, we're in the team gym at the stadium. It's a beautiful, state-of-the-art facility. It's empty except for the five of us.

I can't help but smile. "You guys weren't kidding. The young guns don't work out early."

Layton nods. "They'll trickle in at some point. Half

will be hungover. Coach will bust their balls about it, and they'll straighten out for a few weeks until the cycle begins all over again. Eventually they learn. Or get old like us where it takes two days to recover."

I nod. "Well, Cheetah, that means technically you were the last to arrive." He walked in just after me. "You're going to have to give us a random fact."

He rubs his hands in excitement. "I was up half the night looking things up. There's some crazy shit out there, but I found my favorite. Snakes can smell with their tongues." He makes a V with his fingers and suggestively flicks his tongue through it. "Luckiest fuckers on the planet."

The guys all laugh while my mind flashes to Ripley's strawberry smell and taste. It feels like forever since I've had it on my tongue.

My daydream is broken by Layton asking me to spot him for squats, which I do. His leg muscles are huge. I suppose that's normal for a catcher. "Dude, do you walk around with a bag of bricks on your back every day?"

He shrugs. "A job hazard, I guess."

"I get it. My sister is a catcher too. Her quads are strong."

"That's cool. She any good?"

I can't help but smile. These guys are clueless about softball, as are many baseball players. "Honestly? She's probably the best in the country. I think she'll be on the next Olympic team."

His eyes widen. "Wow. I guess she must have a pretty good arm too?"

I smirk. "Like you wouldn't believe. She probably throws about as hard as most major leaguers."

"I need to check her out."

"Their season starts later than ours. Usually around July first."

"Cool. Maybe we can catch a game if it works with our schedule."

"I would love that. I haven't been able to see her play in person in a long time."

We spend the next hour spotting and cheering each other on as we lift. At some point, the loud metal door to the gym opens. Cougars' manager Dutton Steel walks in. Admittedly, I'm a little starstruck. Dutton was widely considered one of the best baseball players ever with a certain path to the Hall of Fame. At least until his life took a turn for the worse. When he was in the prime of his career, his wife was diagnosed with an aggressive form of breast cancer. He notoriously walked away from the game to care for her, and then when she eventually passed, to care for their young children. About five years ago, when his youngest left for college, he re-entered the baseball world as the manager of the Cougars.

The other guys all fist-bump him. Their affection for Dutton is immediately apparent to me. That's refreshing. In Houston, we had a revolving door of managers, which is often the case when a team underperforms.

Dutton, who's also in workout clothes, is still in great shape. He's got darker hair, which I can see is just starting to gray a bit. I'm guessing that he's about fifty years old.

He holds out his hand to me. "Quincy Abbott. So fucking happy to have you here. You're the missing piece to our pitching puzzle." He looks around at the other guys. "Though I'm already skeptical of your judgment considering the company you're keeping."

All the guys chuckle and Dutton smiles. I like that they have a jovial relationship with him.

I shake his hand in return. "It's an honor to meet you, Coach Steel. I'm beyond excited to be here."

He waves his hand dismissively. "Call me Dutton." He motions for me to follow him. "Come spot me so we can chat."

I follow him to a few benches in the corner, out of earshot of the rest of the gang, where he proceeds to add more weight to a bar than I'm capable of bench pressing. I'm about to tell him that I can't lift that much weight when he lays down on the bench and starts lifting it himself.

I stand behind him and do my job as a spotter. "Damn, you're strong."

He shrugs. "Exercise has always been an outlet for me. Tell me, how are you acclimating to Philly?"

"I only just got here, but those guys have been welcoming. More than welcoming. I appreciate it."

He nods. "Good. It must be hard at your age to pack up and move across the country. You got a family?"

"I'm not married with children if that's what you're asking."

"Leaving anyone behind?"

I shake my head. "No. My only real family is my sister, and she lives in Southern California."

"Oh, I didn't realize you had lost your parents. I suppose you and Layton have that in common."

"I didn't. I'm just not close with them. I see them now and then. It's usually my sister who forces it on me."

He nods in acknowledgment as he continues to lift the weights as if they weigh nothing. "No lady friends?"

"No one of note." There's no need for me to mention

to him that the only one I care about is a fiery redhead who isn't even talking to me right now. Oh, and she's my wife.

He lifts one of his thick eyebrows. "I'm sensing there's more to it."

"What makes you say that?"

"I've been living with a broken heart for a very long time. Let's just say it increases your radar for others suffering a similar fate."

"Oh, I'm not brokenhearted."

"If you say so. Well, like I said, we're happy to add you to our rotation. This is a solid team. Your new buddies are great leaders to the younger guys. I think the young guys see the brotherhood they've formed throughout the years. They genuinely care for each other. We don't have selfish players on this team. I won't stand for it, and neither will the owner, Harold Greene." He says that as a bit more of a command than purely informational.

"It's refreshing. That wasn't the team culture in Houston. I welcome the change."

He nods. "I know it wasn't. That's why I'm mentioning it. This team is a family. We support each other on *and* off the field."

"Yes, sir. I'm all in. I've never played for a contender. I'm thrilled about the opportunity."

"Glad to hear it." I help him set the weights in place before he sits up and wipes his brow with a towel. "I'm here for you for whatever you need."

He says that in almost a fatherly way. Not that I would know what it looks like. I barely speak to my father.

"Thanks, Dutton. I genuinely appreciate it."

CHAPTER NINE

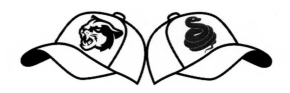

QUINCY - AGE 33 {RIPLEY - AGE 28}

"Can you believe it, Q?"

I look at her smiling, emotional face on our FaceTime call. "I have no words right now, Z."

"We're going to be living in the same city for the first time in fifteen years."

"They're really starting a pro softball team in Philly?"

"Yep, and they want me as their marquee player. Q, they're paying me more than double my current salary and are covering all my moving expenses."

"That's not surprising. You're the best player in the league. You're worth ten times what you're being paid right now. It's such bullshit that you ladies make so much less than us. You're every bit as talented, if not more."

"Thanks." She pauses. "Do you watch many of my games?"

"Fuck yes. I try not to miss any. I subscribe to the

streaming service. That shit should be on national television."

"I didn't know that you watched. Thank you."

"Of course." I don't tell her I also watch Ripley play. She's easily become the best pitcher in the league. She throws heat. "My little sister is going to make the Olympic team in four years. Do you know how excited I am about that?"

"Don't fucking jinx it. Rip and I have been dreaming of this forever." Her eyes light up. "I haven't even told you the best part yet."

"I can't imagine it getting better than you living nearby."

Her eyes sparkle. "They're signing Ripley, Kamryn, and Bailey too. Our whole fucking UCLA gang is going to play together again."

I'm speechless. Ripley St. James is moving to Philly? Holy. Fucking. Shit.

"Q? Are you okay?"

Oh shit. I didn't respond. "Sorry, I'm just shocked. Wow. Just, wow."

"Yep. It's amazing. Obviously I'll get an apartment with Rip. Kam and Bailey mentioned trying to find one in the same building. Q, I think this is just what I need to break out of this post-Marc funk."

My whole body tightens just thinking about what he did to her. Marc Whittaker didn't just break her heart. He shattered her special Arizona spirit. She's been a shell of the free-spirited, confident woman I've always known her to be.

She does need this fresh start. And as hard as it might be for me to have Ripley around, Arizona needs her. She needs both of us to be there for her.

I nod. "I think this could be great for you. Put that piece of shit in your past. Permanently."

She lifts her eyebrows. "Stop fucking beaning him every time you face him."

I smirk. When I pitch against his team, I throw the ball right at his fucking head every damn time. I don't care about getting ejected from the game. That fucker has it coming, and I'll never stop. Though after the last time, the league threatened a suspension if I do it again.

She rolls her eyes. "I see you smiling."

I chuckle. "It's funny watching him wince when he gets nailed with a hundred-mile-per-hour pitch. I put a little something extra into it just for him."

She sighs. "Don't let him keep getting to you. You're going to get suspended if you do it again."

"It's fine. We only have one more series against them this season, and it's not for a while."

"I'm staying away from that game, but I'm psyched I'll get to catch you in action when it doesn't interfere with my playing schedule. Maybe Mom and Dad will come out for a few days. They can see both of us play."

I let out a laugh. "Yeah right. Don't hold your breath. They'll never leave that precious shop of theirs to fly across the country."

"Ugh. You're so hard on them."

"Z, I've played pro ball for a dozen years, and they've never once come to a game."

She sighs. She's so defensive of them. "That's not true. They go to your games in Oakland and San Fran every year."

"They arrive in the fucking seventh or eighth inning every time. They don't see shit."

"They do the best they can."

"Do they?"

Her face falls. "I'll admit it's kind of crazy. I'll never be that kind of parent. I won't miss anything for my kids."

"That's why I'm never having any kids. No one to disappoint."

She rolls her eyes as she always does when I mention my lack of desire to be a parent. She thinks I'm kidding.

"Whatever. You'll change your tune one day."

"Unlikely. When are you moving?"

"My flight is a week from Monday. Ripley is coming on the same day. Kam and Bailey arrive a few days later."

I scrunch my face. "Shit. We have a weeklong road trip leading into the all-star break. I won't be in town to help when you get here, but then I'll have a few days off."

"It's cool. It's such bullshit that you didn't make the all-star team. This is the best season of your career."

I smile with a bit of pride at that. It's true. I've never thrown better. "It's not a big deal. They gave it to the younger guys. It means more to them. Frankly, I welcome a few days off. I want my team to win the World Series this year. I don't give a shit about individual, meaningless accolades. I want to rest up for the second half of our season. We have a real chance at going far. I assume with the four of you reunited, your team will be immediate contenders."

"You're right. Maybe we'll both win championships this year. That would be amazing."

"Sure would."

She smiles nervously. "Are you seriously besties with Layton Lancaster?"

I point at her. "Stay away from him. Yes, he's my best friend here, but he's a womanizing manwhore. He has no respect for women at all. He's the last thing you need after the Marc disaster."

Arizona had a damn shrine to him in her bedroom when she was a teenager. Something I most definitely will not ever share with Lancaster.

"I know. I'm *never* dating a baseball player again. Guaranteed."

"Good. I'm sick of beating teammates off with a stick to keep them away from you. I spent all of my college years doing that."

She giggles. It's music to my ears. She's been a mess since the Marc debacle. I miss my happy, sassy, nutty, little sister.

She looks closely into the phone. "Are you topless? Why don't you ever wear shirts? It's weird."

"It's fucking hot here. East Coast summers are no joke. Are you jealous of my abs?"

"More like flabs. You're getting old. You have a dadbod now."

I look down, examining myself, and hear her unique Arizona snort-laugh. She's fucking with me. I have a good body.

"Z, I love hearing you laugh, even if it's at my expense."

She gives me a small smile as she nods in agreement. "Me too."

I'M WALKING out on the tarmac toward our plane to board it for a long road trip before the all-star break. I can't stop thinking about Ripley moving to Philly and what it will mean. I feel like it's a car crash you observe unfolding but can't do anything about it. I hope we all come out of this unscathed; Arizona, Ripley, and me.

It looks like everyone else has made their way onto the plane. I see Layton walk out of a different exit from me, an equal distance from the steps of the plane. We stare at each other, smile, and then both take off in a dead sprint, not wanting to be last.

I make it to the steps just a hair ahead of him and laugh. "I can't believe you let a pitcher kick your ass."

He grimaces. "I'm a catcher. Our knees are always fucked. Damn it. Now I need to come up with something."

We both walk on the plane. Cheetah, who's taken to my little random fact game quite well, immediately yells out, "You're up, Lancaster. Give us a good one."

Layton smiles. He's clearly got something in mind. "Everyone's tongue print is different. It's like a fingerprint that way. There are lots of ladies who have a very unique #laidbylayton tongue print on them." He flicks his tongue suggestively and then thrusts his hips.

Everyone starts laughing. #laidbylayton is always trending. Women he sleeps with, women he doesn't sleep with, and basically any woman in her twenties in the city of Philadelphia and any town we visit love to pose for photos with him and include that hashtag. It doesn't bother him at all. In fact, he embraces it.

I head toward the back of the plane, needing a little alone time away from the crazies for this trip. I elect to sit next to Dutton.

He looks up at me from his seated position. "How's it going, Q?"

I blow out a long breath. "I have a few things on my mind. I need a little peace and quiet for this trip."

He nods in understanding. "You want to talk about it, or no?"

I'm quiet for a moment. "My sister is moving to Philly."

"Is that a good or bad thing?"

I chuckle. "A very good thing. We're extremely close. We haven't lived in the same city since I left for college. It's more than welcome."

"Then what's weighing on you?"

I'm silent.

"Ah, the broken heart. What does it have to do with your sister?" He narrows his eyes. "Oh shit. Have you been reading Cheetah's books? Stepsister shit is cool in porn and romance novels, not in real life."

I can't help but start laughing. "No. She's not my stepsister, and it only relates to my real sister because the woman is her best friend and she's moving here too."

He breathes a sigh of relief. "Thank fuck for that. I don't need a PR nightmare. What's the problem? Did it end badly?"

"It did."

"You don't have to give me details if you don't want to, but you're thirty-three. Put on your big boy pants and have a real conversation with this woman. Is she one of the crazies?"

I shake my head. "No. She's perfect. Too perfect for my fucked-up ass."

"There ya go. Talk to her. Talking is very underrated in your generation. Don't text, don't email, don't fucking SnapShit or whatever it's called. Pull her aside and have a real adult conversation. Put this shit to bed. You're the ace of our staff right now. I need you focused, not involved in childish drama."

I nod. "You're right. Thanks for the advice."

He places his hand on my shoulder. "I told you, my door is always open. I'm here for you on and off the field."

"Thanks, Dutton. What about you? Do you date at all?"

He sighs. "I didn't for a very long time after my wife passed. It was hard to fathom being with someone else. She was the only woman I ever loved. I'm on a few dating websites. It's more of a hassle having to sift through profiles and play stupid games. I haven't met anyone who truly interests me. I'm not sure I ever will."

"Do you want to get married again?"

He shrugs. "I'm not against it. I loved being married." He stares at me for a few long beats. "Don't overthink. When the situation is right, you'll know. I promise."

Not what I was thinking at all. It will never be right for me.

CHAPTER TEN

RIPLEY - AGE 28 {QUINCY - AGE 33}

Three weeks ago, I was signed by the Philadelphia Anacondas, as were Arizona, Kamryn, and Bailey. It's a dream come true. I get to live and play with Arizona again. It's been six long years apart. We'll get to finish the last few years of our careers just as we started them. Together. And we can practice as we try to make the Olympic team in four years. I'm busting with excitement.

We all moved across the country. Arizona and I rented an apartment together in Philly. Kamryn and Bailey rented the apartment next door. It's like being in college again.

I have mixed emotions over being in the same town as Quincy. He moved here nearly eight months ago, and we hadn't spoken since the aftermath of Arizona's wedding that never was. I saw him when we all went out a few nights ago. It was awkward, but I think we masked it well. It's both painful and soothing to see him. Painful in that I loved him, soothing in that I've missed him. He was my friend in addition to being my lover. I miss all aspects of Quincy in my life.

I worked hard to get over him. It took a long time before I could go on any dates, but I eventually did. His leaving Houston was the best thing for me. I no longer ran the risk of running into him. It was the time I needed to heal. I think I have.

As for Arizona, she's definitely not healed after having her heart broken. I know she's better off without him, but everything that happened has extinguished the light inside my best friend. Admittedly, I was on the fence about moving here because of Quincy, but I know Arizona needs me, and this opportunity was too good to pass on.

Our first two weeks here have been a little crazy. The Cougars were sold to a group of billionaires. The Daulton, Windsor, and Bouvier families are now the owners. They also own our new team, the Anacondas.

In what might be the craziest thing I've ever heard, the new owners asked Arizona to pretend to date Layton Lancaster for public relations reasons. Yes, *that* Layton Lancaster. The same one she pined after as a teen. They think Layton's notoriety will be good for our team.

Arizona was flipping out when they asked but eventually realized that it might genuinely help our team and sport flourish. She's sworn off the possibility of it being anything more, but I know my best friend. She's wanted him for as long as I can remember, and he seems awfully into her. Most men are.

We have a short practice this morning ahead of our opening game tonight. Our coach just wanted to talk about things and do an abbreviated warm-up.

We're on the field practicing, but I'm off to the side pitching to Arizona when I see Coach Billie walking my way.

Wilhelmina "Billie" Kramer is a little ball of fire. She's got lighter hair and pretty blue eyes. She had a nice softball career herself about fifteen to twenty years ago.

She approaches me. "How are you feeling?"

"Great, Coach Billie. Arizona caught for me for the first seventeen years that I played, all the way through college. Throwing to her again is like coming home. She spoiled me. I had the best in the business for so long. I'm just happy to have her back."

Arizona rolls her eyes as she approaches. "I just catch the ball. You're the one who throws the unhittable pitches."

Coach Billie slowly nods. "You guys have chemistry, don't you?"

I nod enthusiastically. "We sure do. You can't manufacture what we have together."

Her eyes toggle between us. "I'm not an ego coach, and I'm not a control freak. I know almost all coaches call pitch signals, but I doubt there's anyone who could call your games better than Arizona."

I shrug. "Yep. No one knows my game better than her and my mom."

She smiles. "Right. You're June St. James's daughter. I watched your mom play. She was one of the best ever and then she kind of fell off the map after the Olympics. What happened to her?"

"I happened."

She lets out a laugh. "I suppose pitching and pregnancy don't mix."

"Nope. She coached us for a long time and still coaches at our old high school. I learned everything I know from her."

"I bet." She turns to Arizona. "I'm going to let you call her games."

Arizona's face lights up. Every catcher in the world wants

to call pitches, but few are ever given that vote of confidence by their coaches. You have to have a special mind for the game to be able to do that. It's the right decision given our history together, but most coaches wouldn't give up that control.

Arizona pumps her fist. "Thanks, Coach Billie."

"We'll see how it goes."

"I won't let you down."

Coach Billie walks away. Arizona and I practically jump up and down in excitement. "Rip, can you believe this?"

Before I can answer, one of the team owners, Reagan Daulton, approaches us. She's dressed like a fancy businesswoman in a navy-blue pantsuit and expensive shoes, though she doesn't let it bother her as she walks through the dusty field.

Arizona has already met her, but I haven't. She smiles at Arizona. "How are practices going?"

Arizona responds, "Great. Have you met Ripley St. James?"

She shakes her head and holds out her hand with a genuine smile on her pretty face. "I'm Reagan Daulton. Welcome to Philly. We're ecstatic to have you here."

I hesitate, looking at my dirty hand, but she grabs it anyway. "I'm not prissy. I don't mind getting my hands a little dirty." She winks at me.

"It's nice to meet you, Mrs. Daulton—"

"Reagan."

"It's nice to meet you, Reagan. Thank you for the opportunity." I'm not only playing with my besties, but she's paying me double my previous salary.

"It's me who should thank you. You're the best pitcher around, and we're lucky to have you here." She turns to Arizona. "Can we chat for a minute?"

Arizona nods in my direction. "I know I wasn't supposed

to tell anyone, but Ripley knows about my PR relationship with Layton. She's been my ride-or-die since we were five years old. You can trust her."

I make a show of zipping my lips and throwing away the key.

Reagan sighs. "We can't let this get out. A PR dream can turn into a PR nightmare faster than my ex-boyfriend's premature ejaculation."

Arizona and I giggle.

Nodding, I assure her, "I understand. No one will hear it from me. For what it's worth, I know my best friend. She's a sister to me. I would have figured it out."

She nods in understanding before turning back to Arizona. "You and Layton are doing a great job being seen in public. Is everything okay between you two?"

Arizona blushes, and I think Reagan catches it. I knew she'd be into him. Who wouldn't be? He's gorgeous, and she's always had a thing for him.

"It's fine. We've gone on a few dates and have been photographed. Honestly, Layton has been a perfect gentleman. It's not as bad as I thought it was going to be."

Reagan nods. I can see her wheels turning. "I'm glad to hear it. I'll let you two get back to work. I'm excited for your first game."

I smile. "Us too."

She walks away. I look at Arizona. "She's gorgeous. You two could be sisters." Both have blonde hair, blue eyes, and are tall.

She lets out a laugh. "You should see her husband. He's so hot. He's got a beard you want to sit on and never get up. Layton and I were with them at that party in New York last week. They couldn't keep their hands or eyes off each other."

I blow out a long breath. "I haven't had sex in months. I miss intimacy."

She lifts her eyebrow. "I don't want to hear it. I haven't had sex in over a year."

"You're dating sex on legs. You should fuck him."

"Not happening. No more baseball players. Ever."

She'll be fucking him within a month. I'd bet on it.

IT'S OPENING NIGHT. The stands are about half full. That's not terrible for a new team. Philly isn't a softball town. Yet.

The fans all cheer for Layton as he walks out onto the field in an Anacondas jersey with Arizona's number. It reads *Arizona's Admirer* on the back.

He turns and shows it to her as she laughs. She's already gone for this guy. She just doesn't realize it yet. I'm pretty sure he's gone for her too.

He throws out the ceremonial first-ever pitch for the Philadelphia Anacondas. I'll be throwing the real first pitch. It's exciting to be pitching the franchise's first game—hopefully the first of many.

The game is about to start when we hear a huge ruckus in the stands. We all step out of the dugout and look up to see Quincy, Cheetah, and Ezra all making their way to join Layton in the stands. It's sweet of them to be here.

The fans are eating up, taking selfies and asking for autographs. Having them here will help our future attendance.

Cheetah lost a bet with Kam the other night so now he's dancing topless with her name written across his chest, per the terms of their bet. We all laugh at that vision.

I can't help but look at Quincy as he laughs at Cheetah's

antics. He's so handsome and looks so happy. I see my number on the front of his Anacondas jersey. I get choked up that he's wearing my jersey and not his sister's.

He cares. I know he does. But it's not enough. It never will be.

In between innings, I sit next to Arizona in the dugout. I nudge her shoulder. "Did you see Layton's jersey?"

She smiles. "I did."

"Is that what you guys are wearing to the *Sports Illustrated* shoot?"

Reagan Daulton arranged for Layton and Arizona to be in the body image issue of *Sports Illustrated*. I remember the last time that issue was published. The athletes were practically naked.

She shrugs. "I have no idea what we're wearing. I'm nervous about being half-naked with him all day."

"Nervous or excited?"

"Definitely nervous."

"I think it's awesome. I doubt I could ever do something like that, especially with a man. You're so brave."

She blows out a breath. "Or stupid."

"No, babe, you're going to be awesome. It's going to be hot as hell, guaranteed."

CHAPTER ELEVEN

RIPLEY

W e won our opening game last night, and tonight we're going to the Cougars' game. Afterward, we'll go to a bar called Screwballs where the boys like to hang out.

I'm doing my makeup in my bathroom when Arizona walks in. Her eyes meet mine in the mirror. "Wow, you look good. We're just going to a ballgame."

I shrug. "We don't all have hot fake boyfriends. I'm officially on the prowl. I told you, I miss intimacy."

She looks at my oversized T-shirt that I'm only wearing while I put on my makeup, the one I took from an ex-boyfriend in college, Aaron, and smiles. "That shirt always makes me laugh." It reads, *I Love to Eat Out*, and it has a stick figure woman sitting on the face of a stick figure man.

I do a little curtsy in the well-worn shirt that I wear to bed most nights. "Are you ready to play the doting girlfriend tonight?" I bat my eyelashes.

She turns around in her tight-as-sin Lancaster jersey. The

back reads, *Layton's Lady*. "You know it. Layton's fake lady is always ready. I'm heading next door to Kam and Bailey's for a drink. Come over when you're done."

Just after she leaves, my phone rings. I see that it's my mother and I reluctantly answer. "Hi, Mom. What's wrong?"

"Does something have to be wrong for me to call you?"

"You called me on my first day of college to tell me that you thought you might be pregnant and you had no clue who the father was. Fortunately, that was a false alarm. You called me on the first day of my senior year to tell me you didn't think you could afford the house and were selling it. You called me just after I got to Houston to tell me that I had been an illegal alien in this country for seventeen years. Need I go on?"

"Well, Miss Sassy Pants, I called to see how you're settling in and when I can come for a visit."

Oh hell. She's the last thing I need. "It's really hot here right now. July in Philly is no joke. Come for a visit when it cools off. I think Paul and Pamela are doing the same." Paul and Pamela are Arizona and Quincy's parents.

"Okay. I'll wait. I ran into Pamela last week. She showed me a picture from the tabloids of Arizona and Layton Lancaster. He's a hunk of man meat."

"Mom, no one says *man meat*. They're friends. Layton is Quincy's best friend."

"How's Quincy? Do you still have a crush on him?"

"That was like fifteen years ago, Mom."

"We both know it was more than that. You wore his jersey to bed every night, and he popped your cherry."

Why did I ever tell her that? I couldn't tell Arizona, and I needed to talk to someone about it. I had the only mother on the planet who reverse slut shamed their child. It drove her nuts that I was a virgin for so long. She wanted me playing the field or, as she used to say, *trying on as many shoes as possible before finding the one that fits.* She practically had a party when I told her about Quincy when I was eighteen.

"That was also a long time ago. We're just friends now."

"Find someone. Make sure you're coming on the regular. It relaxes you. You're a better pitcher when you're relaxed."

In my most sarcastic tone, I reassure her, "I promise to come at least once or twice a day."

"Don't forget, an orgasm a day keeps home run hitters away."

"Words to live by, Mom."

"They certainly are."

"I'm pretty sure the saying is an apple a day keeps the doctors away, not an orgasm a day keeps home run hitters away."

"It should be an orgasm. They're better than apples."

I sigh. "Can we change the topic of conversation?"

"I need to run anyway. I have a date tonight, and I want to get a Brazilian wax, so my goodies are looking their best."

"Have fun with that."

"Love you."

"Love you too."

I throw on my new Philly Cougars Quincy Abbott jersey and head next door. I hear uncontrollable laughter coming from Kamryn's room.

I walk in and see her straddling a pillow on her new waterbed, humping it. I look at all three of them. "What is happening right now?"

Bailey tosses her long brown hair to the side and giggles. "Kam is showing us how sex worked on her waterbed the other night."

Kam fulfilled her lifetime dream of owning a waterbed when we moved to Philly. She's been anxious to see how sex on the waterbed feels.

Kam nods. "I was riding her face, and I got into a good motion with the flow of the water. It was like riding a bull, but the bull's tongue was inside me, so it was even better. Unfortunately, I got a little carried away, and I came down too hard on her face because of the motion of the water. She was whining. I think I can only ride a man's face on this thing. Maybe I'll find some guy tonight and give it a go. I'm guessing an orgasm could be explosive on the waterbed under the right circumstances."

Arizona shakes her head. "With the amount of sex you have, I'm convinced this thing is going to pop one day."

Kam unashamedly sleeps around, rarely repeating a bedfellow.

I nod in agreement. "This thing is the Titanic waiting to happen."

Kam smiles proudly. "But what a way to go down. I mean that in every sense."

An hour later, we're at the baseball game. Because of Arizona's status as Layton Lancaster's girlfriend, we have front-row seats right behind the Cougars' dugout. The cameras love to find us. We play it up, dancing for them. It's bringing attention to our team and league. Plus, we're having fun all being back together again.

Quincy pitches a gem. He's having the best season of his career. He seems happier on this team than he ever did in Houston. I wonder why.

When it's over, we all head to Screwballs where our roped-off booth is waiting for us. It's technically waiting for the guys, but now that we're with them all the time, it's ours for the taking too.

Cheetah is last to arrive and Quincy smiles at him. "Finally! You're last, sucker. You owe us a fun fact."

Cheetah chuckles and says, "Human beings, especially me,

are most creative in the shower. Warm water increases the flow of dopamine, which stimulates creativity." He winks at Kam. "I'm *very* creative and *very* stimulated in my showers, what about you?"

Without any shame, she responds, "I'm always up for a little creativity and stimulation in the shower. In fact, I had some last week. With a lion. I believe lions trump cheetahs in the animal kingdom."

Cheetah scowls at her. He's dying to get into her pants. He then turns to Bailey, "Why don't you hookup like your sister does?"

Bailey responds, "Because I don't separate the emotional and physical like she does. I need to feel something before the physical kicks in for me. I'm not an *any big dick will do* woman, like my beloved little sister. Or *any sweet vajayjay*, for that matter. No vajayjay for me. I'm a magic wand only kind of girl. *One* magic wand at a time, and only if I'm genuinely interested. I'd rather be celibate than be with someone I'm not genuinely into."

Kam nods. "She's a serial masturdater."

Cheetah lifts an eyebrow. "You mean, masturbater?"

Kam shakes her head. "No, I meant masturdater. She dates herself. She'll happily go out to a meal alone, see a movie by herself, buy herself flowers, and yes, get off on her own, before being with someone she doesn't share an emotional connection with. She can't ever just give in to physical needs."

Bailey sighs. "Your ability to make up words is unmatched. Just because I don't fall for lines like," In a deep voice, she mocks, "*you're so hot my zipper is falling for you*, to get me on my back doesn't mean I don't hookup."

I giggle. "That's a good line."

Cheetah leans over toward Kam, staring at her intensely. "How about this line? Your legs are like an Oreo cookie. I want to split them down the middle and eat all the good creamy stuff in the middle."

She playfully looks at Cheetah. "Is that the best you've got, kitten?"

She started calling him kitten the night they met as a takeoff on his nickname, Cheetah.

"You got something better, Kam bam?" And he started calling her that.

She nods as her eyes light up with mischief. "Want to play Barbie? You can be Ken and I'll be the box you come in."

The whole table erupts in laughter. While they're distracted, Quincy gently tugs on my arm. "Come to the bar with me to grab drinks?"

I reluctantly nod. This will be our first time alone together since I've moved here. Actually, it's our first time alone together in nearly two years.

We walk up to the bar. He places our large order before turning his head to me and touching my arm. My heart races at his touch. I thought I was past this. Why does this man affect me so much?

He squeezes me. "I'm truly sorry for how things ended between us in Houston. I handled myself poorly, and I regret it. You deserved better. And then it only got worse with the wedding debacle. I had a lot of anger during that time period. My head was a mess, and my heart was breaking for my sister. I should have spoken to you about everything that happened."

I do my best to play it cool. Like what happened isn't a big deal. Like it didn't take me over a year to even consider letting another man touch me.

I straighten my back. "Our relationship, or whatever it was, ran its course. It was time for us both to let go. I see that now. Please don't feel guilty. The clean break was good for me. As for the wedding time period, we were all hurting for her, me included. She's better off without him, even if she's damaged from how it went down."

He blows out a breath like this has been weighing on him. "Thank you for being so gracious. I don't deserve it."

His fingers run through his hair. He unwittingly does that when he gets nervous. I bite my lip. I miss running my fingers through his hair. It was my favorite thing to do.

He briefly stares at my lips before continuing, "And she's *definitely* better off without him, but I agree, she hasn't been herself. What do you make of this whole Lancaster PR relationship thing? I'm not a fool. I know he was her teen crush. I remember the posters."

"She's adamant that it's all business. She doesn't want it to be anything more."

I don't think I'll share with him that I think her words are hollow.

He nods. "I'm glad to hear that. I really do love the guy. He immediately took me in when I arrived and made me feel more at home in just a few days than any of my teammates ever made me feel in Houston. He's my best friend, but he's also the biggest womanizer I've ever met. A different woman each night. I don't want her to start catching feelings only to be crushed again."

"Neither do I. I'm hoping this move will heal her."

"Good. We're on the same page. I need you to keep an eye on her. She'd never share anything with me, only you."

"I'll always have her back, Quincy. You know that."

He mumbles, "I do," as he aimlessly tucks a stray curl of mine behind my ear. I quickly glance over at the table to see if anyone is looking at us. They're not.

Realization hits and he quickly pulls his hand back. "Sorry. Habit." He briefly squeezes his eyes shut. "I...I miss you, Shortcake." He gives me his crooked smile. "I miss my wife."

I shake my head and do my best to hold off from cracking. "Don't call me that." I nervously chew on my bottom lip before admitting, "I miss you too, but we're truly better off this way. Can we return to what we always were, Quincy? Friends. I miss our friendship."

He visibly swallows. "Is that what you want?"

"Yes. I think it's for the best. I can't constantly fall into your bed and expect to find someone who wants the same things as me. I'm twenty-eight. I want to fall in love, get married, for real, and have kids one day. I know you want none of those things." I briefly pause before admitting, "You have this hold over me, Quincy. I've loved you from the shadows my whole life. I need someone who lets me love them in the light. Someone who wants to love me in that same light. Please, if you care about me, let me go."

He pinches his lips together. "I hate the thought of you with other men. Kissing you, touching you, being inside you."

I hold up my hand. "Stop. You know it happens, just as I know that you're with other women. *A lot* of other women. You haven't been celibate the past two years and neither have I. It took me a while to get there, a long while, but I did. I know sex is purely physical for you, and that's all you want, but I want and need more."

He looks like he wants to say something but then thinks better of it and simply nods.

I rub his arm. "Be my friend and help me get there. My citizenship is secure. We can get our divorce and put this crazy chapter of our lives behind us for good."

His eyes widen. "No rush. We can wait until you meet someone. I'll do my best to support you. You deserve to have what you want." He hangs his head. "We both know I'm not the man to give it to you."

I rub his arm. "Thank you." I give him a small smile. "Now

let's talk about the season you're having. I've never seen you throw this hard or with this many spins on your pitches. And the team is good. *Really* good."

He smiles. It's the type of carefree smile from him that I've missed seeing. "I know. I can't explain it. This team and this organization are incredible. I've never felt stronger or healthier in my career. Maybe it's the fact that we're contenders that has my juices flowing."

"Whatever it is, it's definitely working for you. I love watching you throw. I always have, but you're in a zone right now I've never seen before."

"Thank you. You seem on top of your game too, though you always are."

"The Anacondas' games are the first you've seen me throw since we were kids."

He gives me a guilty smile. "I came to a few games in Houston too."

"I didn't know that." I'm surprised to hear it.

He shrugs. "When I could. I sat in the back with a hat, so I wasn't noticed. I enjoy watching you pitch. Now it's twice as exciting since I'll get to watch both you and Z play."

I smile. "I saw you in my jersey at our game."

His gorgeous blue eyes sparkle. "I saw you in mine."

I giggle. "Old habits die hard. I guess we'll always be friends who cheer for each other." Holding out my hand, I swallow down my feelings and offer, "Friends?"

He nods as he takes it in his. "Friends."

CHAPTER TWELVE

QUINCY

I'm sitting at the Anacondas game with Layton, Ezra, Cheetah, and Blanche, who I invited to tag along. She and I have struck up a friendship. I walk Thor a few times a week, and she makes me a home-cooked meal a few times a month.

She likes to prod me about my love life. Assuming she'd never meet Ripley, I did confide in her about our time in Houston. I don't know if she's connected the dots just yet.

She and Cheetah are getting along well. He's flirting with her, and she's eating it up.

He winks at her. "Blanche, is it true that women only get better with age?"

She smiles. "There's only one way to find out. Did I ever tell you that my husband was Latino?" She wiggles her eyebrows. "I've always had a thing for Latino men. Especially those who talk dirty in Spanish."

"He sido un chico malo. Necesito una nalgada." *I've been a bad boy. I might need a spanking.*

I have no idea what he just said, but Blanche lets out a loud laugh and says that she's game for whatever he said.

She loops her arm through mine. "Your friends are fun. Thanks for bringing me."

"I'm happy to. Stay away from Cheetah though. He's trouble. I don't want him breaking your heart."

She smiles. "I could use a little trouble. My neighbor won't put out."

I chuckle. "Blanche, you have a one-track mind."

"Umm hmm. That's what my husband always said." She leans over so the others can't hear her. "I'm guessing that adorable redheaded pitcher is the woman you once mentioned to me."

I raise an eyebrow. "Isn't memory supposed to fade with age?"

"I have a memory like an elephant."

I sigh. "Apparently. Yes, it's her. We've agreed to be friends."

"Is that what you want?"

I blow out a breath. "I can't give her what she needs, so a friendship will have to do."

She leans her head on my shoulder. "Things change. We'll see."

"Cotton-Eyed Joe" starts playing on the speakers between innings. Cheetah, who loves to make a spectacle of himself, pulls Blanche up by her hand and dances with her. She obliges with some impressive moves of her own. The cameras immediately find them, and they appear on the big screen, much to the delight of the fans.

I can't help but smile. Cheetah is a jokester, but he's a

good guy underneath it all. He's gone out of his way tonight to give Blanche a good time.

The Anacondas take the field and my eye catches Layton simply staring at my sister. He wants her. I can tell. He promised me he wouldn't go there, but I know what a man in lust looks like.

What's worse is that I see her looking over at him every now and then. Something either has or is about to happen between them. It's driving me nuts. I don't want to see her get hurt again.

We're now a few innings into the game, and Ripley is throwing a no-hitter. She's so fucking good. So dominant in her sport. I'm mesmerized watching her play.

At some point I see Cheetah looking Ripley up and down. He leans over and mutters, "I wonder if she's a real redhead. Do you think the carpet matches the drapes?"

Without thinking, I picture her naked body, smile, and say, "It does."

Shit.

He stares at me with his mouth wide open. I quickly look around to see if anyone else heard me. Layton's gazing at my sister like a lost puppy. He didn't hear me. I don't think Ezra did either, though I catch Blanche trying to hide her smile. That old bat has bat ears.

Cheetah grabs my arm. "Q, why don't you and I go get a beer?"

He practically drags me up to the concourse. "Are you sneaky linking Ripley?"

"No, I'm not."

He crosses his arms and smirks. "How do you know about her carpet?"

"I've...umm...known her since she was a kid. She's

always had red hair. I was simply stating that it's not fake."

I can physically see him thinking and then I see the moment it hits him. "Ho-lee-fuck. She's why you like bigger chicks. You want Ripley, so you find women who have similar figures to hers." His face lights up. "Now it all makes sense."

I roll my eyes. "That's not true. I've always been into bigger women."

"And you've always known Ripley."

"Unrelated."

"You're clapping cheeks with her, aren't you?"

"Nope."

"You two are playing hide the sausage, aren't you?"

"No."

"I know you're shaking the sheets with her."

"Stop it."

"Does Arizona know? Maybe I should chat with her about it."

I put my finger in his face. "Don't you fucking dare. She doesn't know anything."

He smiles. "Ah, but there's something there. I know I'm right. She's smokin' hot. What's the big deal?"

I blow out a breath. "I need you to keep this between us." I fix my hat and run my fingers through my hair nervously. "We used to hook up. It was casual. Always on the down-low. When she caught feelings, we ended things. It's been a long time since we were together. We've agreed to remain friends. That's the truth."

"Dude, a blind man can see that you're hung up on her. Have you hooked up with random chicks since she came to town?"

I reluctantly shake my head.

"You're still into her." He doesn't ask it as a question. He says it as a statement. "Is she still into you?"

"She used to be. She says she's over me."

"She's not. She's always staring at you when you're not looking. Same way you do with her. Why aren't you together? She's an awesome chick."

"Because she wants marriage and kids. I don't."

"Never?"

"Never."

"I think you're fucking nuts. She's hot, funny, nice, and has the exact kind of body you're into." He holds out his hands. "She has a huge rack."

I roll my eyes. "I'm well aware of her rack. She deserves better than me though."

He shrugs. "You may get what you want. When we were out the other night, I was sitting next to her. Some dude was texting her. They were making plans to go out."

"Are you fucking with me?"

"No, but your reaction tells me all I need to know."

RIPLEY

Thanks to Arizona and Layton's fake, I'm not sure it's that fake anymore, relationship, the Anacondas are getting so much attention in the press. And our team is truly putting on a show. We're the best team in the league. Our fanbase grows each and every day.

Several of us are now fielding calls for sponsorship opportunities. Unbelievably, I had an offer today to model plus-sized lingerie.

I'm mulling it over as I stand in front of the mirror looking at myself in a bra and panties. I turn to Arizona. "I don't know if I can do this."

"Why not? It's so much money. You won't have to work at all this off-season if you don't want to."

"I'll feel so...exposed."

"Rip, you're gorgeous. I thought you finally understood that. I love how much more confident you've become since college."

"There's a difference between feeling more confident around people you know and having millions of strangers seeing your body, judging you. I know the type of society we live in. The bodies we do and don't find appealing."

"Fuck society. Your body is society. Not everyone looks like Kam and Bailey. They're the ones who aren't normal."

They have ridiculously good figures.

She continues. "I'm not as skinny as them. I'm a professional catcher with huge thighs. You know what? I don't care. I'm gonna rock that *Sports Illustrated* shoot. I'm not a size zero, and I'm confident about it. Young girls need to see women like us, not reality stars with chefs and trainers, who have nothing else to do all day but work on being skinny. It's not real life."

"You're all muscle. You don't have fat like I do."

She rolls her eyes. "Rip, we all have insecurities about our own bodies. You're beautiful and perfect, both inside and out. Show those fuckers that not everyone eats lettuce and keto gummies all day. Not if you want to be the best damn pitcher in the world. When you win a gold medal in four years, you can shove those keto gummies up all the skinny bitches' asses."

I smile. "I wonder if they're as effective when you take them up the ass."

She laughs. "There's only one way to find out."

We're in a fit of giggles when we hear our door open and the ever-present bickering between Kam and Bailey. "Bay, you need to do this. It's so much money."

"No fucking way. I swore I'd never model again."

They walk into my bedroom. Kam's eyes light up when she looks at me. "Is that the lingerie they want you to wear?"

I nod. "They sent it over so I can check it out before I sign my contract."

She squeals with excitement. "You look so fucking hot. Your ass and tits are going to be the wet dreams of every man and woman in America. I might even Jill-off to you."

I pinch my eyebrows. "Jill off?"

She nods. "I'm not a dude. I don't jack off. I'm a woman. I Jill off."

I giggle while Bailey rolls her eyes. "You seriously make up words and assume all of us will know what you're talking about."

"Google it. I didn't even make this one up. I swear. It's as common a phrase for female masturbation as dialing the rotary phone or a ménage à moi."

I laugh again while Arizona gives me an *I told you so* look. "I've been telling her for an hour how hot she looks."

Bailey nods. "Oh, Rip, you look like a porcelain doll, babe. Don't doubt yourself."

I place my hands on my hips, offering a bit of attitude. "Why aren't you accepting the makeup company's offer?"

Kamryn accepted a deal to model in ads for a skincare line, but Bailey refuses to accept any modeling offers, including a lucrative offer from a makeup company.

"Kam and I did a ton of twin modeling as kids. It was excessive. I swore to myself I'd never do it again. It doesn't appeal to me."

Kam sighs. "Bails, if we don't have to work this off-season, we can travel. We've always wanted to do that."

"*You've* always wanted to do that." Bailey shakes her head. "It's not happening. I like working with kids in the off-season. It makes me happy. I'll find a job along those lines."

Kamryn's face drops. Bailey touches her shoulder. "We're making more playing in Philly. I'll be able to travel with you a little, just not the whole time. It's not what I want. Modeling never made me happy. I need to do something I like. Working with kids feeds my soul."

I nod in agreement. "You should always do what makes you happy, Bails."

She smiles. She doesn't love the limelight like Kam does. Half the time I think she only plays softball because of Kam. I'm pretty sure that if it was up to Bailey, she'd be a kindergarten teacher.

Arizona looks at Bailey. "That reminds me. I met with Layton's agent today, Tanner Montgomery. His nanny quit. His seven-year-old daughter was with him at work. He's looking for help and I left him your number. I meant to tell you earlier."

Bailey's eyes light up. "Really? How many kids do they have?"

"It's just him. He's divorced. He only has Harper half the time. I thought that might work for you since we're still in season and you can't offer too much time just yet."

"Definitely. Thanks."

"And Harper is a huge softball fan. Apparently they come to a lot of games. Tanner knew who you were right away."

"This could be perfect." She turns to Kam. "See, things work out. I don't need to model again. Ever."

Kam sighs in resignation before looking at me. "What about you, Rip? You're gonna do it, right?"

I nod. "I think so. I've never had financial freedom in the off-season. It's kind of hard to pass up."

She pulls open the drawer in my nightstand and narrows her eyes. "Why is your vibrator so fucking long? Do you have a deep tunnel of love?"

I walk over and slam the small drawer shut. "You can't just walk into someone's room and check out their vibrator."

Arizona interrupts, "She likes it super deep. She has for years. Apparently she was fucking some guy in Houston with a long dong, and he ruined her for all other men."

Before I can dispute anything, Arizona's phone rings, as it has been all day. She's fielding modeling offers left and right. That was why she met with Tanner Montgomery, sports agent to the biggest stars. He's helping her negotiate the best deals. I'm so happy for my friend that she's getting the recognition she deserves. It's an added bonus that she's helping to get our team and our sport the attention needed to stay in business.

Kam gets a call and walks out too, leaving just Bailey and me.

I look at my friend. Something is clearly weighing on her.

"Bails, is everything okay?"

She plops down on my bed. "I suppose. Why do you ask?"

"Did something happen to you when you modeled as a kid?" Her being adamant about not modeling has me concerned.

"Not what you're thinking. I just need something away from my sister. I live in her shadow, and it's a big fucking shadow. She's the better ballplayer, she's the bigger personality, she's smarter, she's prettier—"

"Prettier? You two are identical."

She lets out a long breath. "Her outgoing, funny personality makes her prettier. Most people can tell the difference between us because they're just something extra about her. Only strangers can't tell the difference."

"I can't answer that because you two look different to me. Neither being better than the other, and both drop-dead gorgeous." I bite my lip. "Do you enjoy softball, Bails?"

"Honestly? Not like her. We both know I never would have been given a scholarship to play at a top softball school like UCLA if it wasn't for Kam telling coaches she wouldn't come without me. Don't get me wrong. I love my sister. She has always stood up for me and looked out for me, but she's the star."

I start to speak but she holds up her hands. "I know I'm a good softball player now. Maybe even a great one—"

"You *are* great."

She gives me a small smile in gratitude before that smile turns almost Kam-like. "Do you know what she sucks at?"

"What?"

"Being around kids. It's painful, yet equally amusing, to watch her struggle with little ones. You know what I'm really good at?"

"Being around kids?"

She nods. "Yep. I love it. I know it's my true calling. It's something I have that she doesn't. Maybe I'll stick things out with softball a little longer because being in the Olympics with you guys would be awesome, but I'm equally okay if that doesn't happen for me. The three of you practically live for it. It's your dream. It's not mine. Softball is something I do, it's not something I am."

I'm considering her words when my phone buzzes with a text notification. The phone is on my bed, closer to Bailey. I nod at it. "Can you hand that to me?"

"Sure." She briefly looks down at the phone as she hands it to me.

"It's Quincy."

Oh shit. I hope he didn't say anything incriminating. I look down.

> Quincy: Can you help me with something tomorrow?

That's not so bad.

"Let me see what he needs. He's probably been trying to get in touch with Arizona. She's been on the phone all day."

I begin typing.

> Me: Sure. What is it?

> Quincy: Get your sexy ass here at ten tomorrow morning. I have to be at the ballpark for our game by about three.

> Me: Can you give me some details?

> Quincy: Wear shoes that can get dirty.

> Me: Please define dirty.

> Quincy: Your mind is always in the gutter. Actual dirt.

> Me: What the hell are we doing?

> Quincy: You'll see, Shortcake. Wear something tight.

> Me: Why do I need to wear something tight if we're getting dirty?

Quincy: You don't. I just want to see you in it.

Me: You're a dick. See you at ten. I'll be in baggy clothes.

Quincy: You're no fun.

I can't help but smile as I place my phone down. Bailey is staring at me. "Is something going on between you and Quincy?"

"No. We've been friends for over twenty years."

She tilts her head to the side. "I see the way you look at him. I also see how protective he is over you."

"He's the same with Arizona."

"Yes, but she's his sister. You're not."

"Perhaps he sees me that way. Sisterly."

She lifts an eyebrow. "Your entire body is flushing just talking about him. You're practically naked right now. I can see it. It's not very sibling-like."

I brush her away with my hand. "You're overreading this situation." I head toward my bathroom to avoid any further inquisition. "I'm jumping in the shower. I'll see you later."

CHAPTER THIRTEEN

RIPLEY

I knock on Quincy's door at ten in the morning. He opens it in board shorts and no top. Holy fuck, he's hot. It's been a long time since I've seen his naked body, and I'm suddenly feeling a bit of an ache for it. I have to bite my lip in an attempt to maintain a cool demeanor.

Quincy Abbott is just so...manly. Every inch of him. In an era where men think women want waxed chests, Quincy is all man with a healthy dose of blond chest hair a little darker than that on his head. He's broad and sexy as hell. I love sinking my nose into him and taking in his scent. And the trail that leads down from his belly button into his shorts. The one I've traced with my tongue many times.

I know my cheeks must be flushing. I can feel them heating up at the memories of our time together.

He quirks an eyebrow. "You're not looking at me in a very *friendly* manner, Shortcake."

Shit. I bring my eyes up to his. "Sorry."

Christ, I need to get laid. I haven't had a non-self-induced orgasm in several long months.

He smirks. "Anytime you want to take advantage of your husband, you just let me know. Our bodies work quite well together." He rubs the back of his hand along my face. "More than well."

My mouth and panties are pooling. He does make a compelling case. It's been a little while for me. No one makes me come like Quincy Abbott.

No, no, no. I can't go there. My feelings for him are too strong. I know where he stands. I can't do this to myself all over again. I'm not trashing the small amount of progress I've made.

I narrow my eyes at him. "I'm all set, thanks. Did you answer the door topless on purpose?"

He winks at me. "You know I never wear a top. Summer in Philly is hot as hell."

"You live in what must be a two-million-dollar condo. I imagine you have ample air conditioning."

He chuckles. "I'm always a little extra hot when I'm around my wife." He looks my body up and down. "So sexy."

I roll my eyes. "Stop calling me that."

"Sexy? Can't help it. That's what you are."

I sigh. "You know what I meant. Stop calling me your wife."

He mouths, "Never."

I swear he does it just to fuck with me. At least we're back to a playful place. I prefer that to awkward, forced polite conversation.

"What is it you need help with, Abbott? If it's to clean your apartment, I'm leaving."

He lets out a laugh. "No, but I do miss your clean freak ways. You kept my place in Houston spick and span. You're still the only woman I've ever allowed in my space."

I nod, unable to otherwise form words.

"Let me grab a shirt, and we'll head out."

"Where are we going?"

"You'll see."

We walk out the door just as a little old lady and an enormous dog walk by. I think I saw her with Quincy at our game the other night.

The dog immediately pulls away from the woman and jumps up on his hind legs into Quincy's arms, licking his face. Quincy smiles just like he did when Diamond used to kiss him. I have a brief moment of nostalgia remembering their loving relationship. I also remember how devastated he was when Diamond died. Inconsolable for weeks. Arizona and I kept bringing him his favorite candy, hoping it would make him feel better.

Quincy rubs the dog's tummy. "Relax, Thor. I'll walk you later, buddy."

Thor drops down and walks over to me. With a huge smile, I pet his head and rub behind his ear. "Ahh. So gorgeous."

Quincy nods. "I know. And he's a gentle giant." He wiggles his eyebrows. "And this stunner is my girlfriend, Blanche."

Blanche blushes. Is there any woman immune to Quincy Abbott? She swats his chest playfully. "Oh stop it. I'm not your girlfriend. I have no interest in that type of commitment. I'm your side action."

I can't help but let out a laugh. Quincy grins from ear to ear.

She turns to me. "You must be Ripley."

I pinch my eyebrows together. "You've heard of me?"

Quincy quickly responds, "I brought Blanche to one of your games. Cheetah was hitting on her all day."

She nods. "He reminds me of my husband, God rest his soul. He wants me to be a cougar to his Cheetah." She rubs

Quincy's arm. "He means nothing, darling. I'm still holding out hope that you will come around."

I smile. "It's nice to meet you, Blanche, though you have questionable taste in men."

She giggles. "It's hard to resist a beefcake who never wears a shirt."

I nod. "He's been refusing shirts since he was a little kid."

She winks. "Lucky us."

Quincy clears his throat. "Blanche allows me the honor of walking Thor a few times each week. He's my best buddy."

I internally laugh at his name, considering Quincy actually looks like Thor, and I may have a thing for that particular character because of it.

I continue rubbing Thor's ear, which he seems to like. "I assume Quincy told you about his dog growing up. Thor looks just like her."

She nods. "He has. Quincy's been a godsend to me. When I moved from our big house to an apartment, I hadn't considered how much exercise Thor would need. I'm so thankful for Quincy."

He shrugs. "It's how I'm worming my way into your heart."

"I'd rather you wormed your way into other parts of my body."

I can't help the very loud cackle that comes from my mouth. I feel like Blanche is Kam in fifty years. I sort of want the two of them to meet.

Ten minutes later, we're in his car. We seem to be heading away from the city, toward the suburbs.

"What's my sister up to today?"

"She and Layton went for a jog around the river."

His jaw clenches. "Those two are getting mighty chummy."

I shrug. "I think they realized being friends is easier. That's all it is."

"It better be."

"Why do you care? She's a big girl. Layton seems like a good guy."

"He's a womanizer."

"So are you, Abbott."

He adjusts himself. "Stop calling me Abbott. It makes me think of the Mariana Trench, which, incidentally, has been in my dreams a lot lately."

I sigh. I'd be lying if I said that little interaction doesn't play in my mind from time to time as well. Both the good, he made me come so hard, and the bad, it was our last time together before I ruined it by telling him that I love him.

Without thinking, I look down at his dick. The bulge is, in fact, becoming a bit more prominent. I have flashes of what he feels like inside me. What he tastes like. I had many nights taking that monster deep into my mouth and driving him crazy. And the one time I did it to him in the car...

"Are you thinking about that time on the way to Lake Jackson when you sucked my dick in the car?"

I turn my head toward the window. "No." Shit. Busted. I went down on him while he was driving, and then we parked overlooking the lake where he bent me over the hood of the car and gave me three orgasms.

He squeezes my leg. "I was thinking of it too."

I close my eyes. It's a mistake to spend time alone with him. I hate how attracted I am to him. When will it finally go away? Why can't I feel this with other men?

The drive starts to get bumpy. I look around and realize we're on a gravelly, dirt road. "Where are we?"

As we reach a clearing to a big, empty piece of land, I see a man with shoulder-length hair in jeans and a blue button-down shirt, waiting by a big pickup truck.

"I bought this lot. I'm having a house built on it."

"A house? How come?"

"I've never owned one. I think I want to stay here in Philly even after I'm done playing, but I'm sick of city living. I've been doing it for twelve years. I want space with a big yard. I want a giant media room, a pool for parties, and that kind of crap."

I point to the man. "Is he the architect?"

"No, he's the builder, but he offers design-build services. The team owners recommended him."

"Oh, I met one of them. Reagan Daulton."

He nods. "Yes, she and her husband, Carter, recommended this guy. Apparently he built their house, which is supposed to be the nicest in Philly. You have great taste. I thought you could help. I don't know about paint colors and shit."

"A pre-design meeting with a builder has nothing to do with paint colors."

"You know what I mean. I want a woman's touch. I don't want the house to be a bachelor pad cliché."

"You want me to help you design your new house?"

He nods. "I do."

"You could have asked your sister."

"Hmm. I prefer the taste of redheads, and I mean that in *every* way possible." He wiggles his eyebrows up and down and I roll my eyes.

We pull up next to the truck and get out of his car. The man, about forty years old, who incidentally is ridiculously attractive, smiles and holds out his hand to us. "I'm Collin Fitz. It's nice to meet you both."

Quincy shakes Collin's hand. "I'm Quincy Abbott. This is my wife, Ripley."

Collin pinches his eyebrow together in obvious confusion. Quincy Abbott is well known in this town as a bachelor.

I sigh. "He's joking. I'm not his wife." I hold out my hand. "I'm Ripley St. James. I'm just a friend helping make sure this house doesn't turn into a bachelor pad whorehouse." I turn to Quincy. "Though I could see you as the Hugh Hefner of the East Coast."

I bat my eyelashes and Collin laughs. "I know who you both are. I didn't think you were married."

We hear his passenger car door open and a woman, a little younger than me, who's dressed to the nines in a business pantsuit, exits and stands.

She's a stunning blonde who's as tall as me and about seventy pounds lighter. Collin points to her. "This is my baby mama, Jade. When I'm a good boy, she helps me out with the design aspect of things. She does virtual modeling."

She smiles at him. It's neither sweet nor innocent. "I prefer you be a bad boy, but whatever." Jade turns to us. "Yep, designer, baby mama, and sex goddess. I'm a full-service woman."

Collin starts laughing before nodding. "It's true, she's all those things."

I study her. There's something very familiar about her. Maybe I've met her before.

She notices and apparently can read my mind. "No, we haven't met. Reagan Daulton is my cousin. We look alike."

I let out an audible breath. "Yes! That's why you're familiar. You two really do look alike."

"Yep. I know. And your team co-owner, Beckett Windsor, is my stepfather. Well, soon-to-be stepfather. My mom won't make an honest man of him just yet."

"Got it. I've met Beckett's daughter. She comes to our games."

"Yes, my soon-to-be stepsister loves softball. She plays. She even has a poster of Arizona in her bedroom."

Quincy sighs. "At least she's not a teenage boy. Unfortunately, I have a lot of them telling me they have her poster in their bedrooms too."

Jade and I both giggle at that.

Collin leads the way as he lays out some general thoughts to Quincy. They seem to be getting along well. Jade loops her arm through mine as we walk a few feet behind them. She looks me up and down. "I love having a woman who's my height. I always tower over people."

I smile. "I know the feeling. I always feel like a giant. At least my softball friends are all tall too."

"Right. Arizona is tall. And you and her grew up together, right? I think I read that somewhere."

"We did. We've been best friends our whole lives."

"So...does she know you're sleeping with her brother?"

I stop dead in my tracks. "What makes you say that?"

"Hmm. I heard him call you his wife, he brought you to this meeting, and every time you talk, he looks at you like he's about to devour you. I know what a man in lust looks like. He's lusting hardcore for you."

"I don't think that's true. We're not together."

"That's not what I asked, but I think I have my answer."

"You're kind of nosy, Jade."

She lets out a laugh. "You don't know the half of it. Why aren't you together? You're obviously equally into him."

I let out a breath of exasperation. Man, I need to do a better job hiding things. First Bailey, and now a stranger.

She squeezes my arm. "It's clear to me that something has or is going on with you two. It's also clear to me that Arizona doesn't know. You must need to unload on someone."

She's kind of right. I wouldn't mind someone to talk to.

She's the only person I know without any real connection to Arizona.

"We've known each other most of our lives. I pined for him from afar for years until the day he noticed. We've been secretly on and off for years, but that ended nearly two years ago. We want different things in life. I want marriage and family. He wants none of those things."

"Why?"

"In his mind, he had a less than ideal upbringing and doesn't want to duplicate it."

"Ever?"

"Ever."

She nods as she appears to think for a moment. "You know, I used to feel similarly. My father was absent from my life for a long time. My mom might be marrying a billionaire now, but she and I struggled throughout nearly my entire childhood. I was dead set against ever committing to one man or having a child. Now I have both."

"What changed your mind?"

She turns her head and looks lovingly at Collin before looking back at me. "I found my soulmate. I want to be with him and no one else."

"Maybe I'm not his soulmate."

"Maybe not. If that's the case, you need to stop hanging onto him and start looking elsewhere."

I consider her words for a moment. "We met ten minutes ago. I love that you feel it's appropriate to offer me life advice."

She gives me a mischievous smile. "No need to thank me now. You'll thank me later. I promise."

Collin turns back. "Jade, you're supposed to be helping me. I need you to focus on Quincy's vision so you can make it come alive in your designs. You're not listening."

She places her hands on her hips and lifts an eyebrow.

"Quincy wants a non-bachelor pad bachelor pad. A classy frat house vibe. He wants the amenities of a bachelor pad, like a stupid-big media room, unnecessarily oversized bars, and both indoor and outdoor party spaces, but he doesn't want stripper poles, dance floors, and disco balls. I'm guessing leather couches and animal print rugs are out too. He's from California, so we'll add a touch of that by having a lot of big windows and other modern amenities. Obviously everything will revolve around this amazing view of the skyline." She crosses her arms. "How's that for not listening?"

Quincy mumbles, "Holy shit, she must have dog ears."

Collin winks at her. "Let's hope Tyson has your brains, baby girl."

Jade blows him a kiss. "Agree. And for his sake, let's hope he's hung like you, big daddy."

Quincy cough-laughs at the same time Collin nods and replies, "A perfect combo."

These two are a riot. Though Collin's right, Jade is smart. Maybe I need to start actively looking elsewhere so I can finally put Quincy in my past. As much as he can be while I'm still married to him.

A cute guy from my gym asked for my number and has texted me a few times. He's asked me out, but I put him off. Maybe I should give it a go.

My thoughts are interrupted by Quincy. "What do you think?"

I look around. It truly is an impressive piece of land. "It's a gorgeous space." I look at Collin. "Quincy likes a lot of natural light, so the windows Jade mentioned make a lot of sense. He's a big man, so everything should be a little oversized. The shower, bathtub, ceilings, doorways. Make sure the kitchen is gourmet, complete with a wood-burning pizza oven. Quincy can cook, and pizza is his specialty. He's always wanted his own pizza oven. Not a high-tech one but an old-school pizza oven."

Collin scribbles away on his notepad but Quincy turns to me. I think I catch tears welling in his eyes.

The drive home is met with silence at first. Eventually he turns to me and whispers, "You remembered."

One day, when I was only six or seven years old, Arizona wasn't at school and Quincy wasn't on our bus. I didn't know why, so I went straight to their house when the school day was over. I found Quincy in the kitchen. I asked him where she was. He said she was sick and that he stayed home to take care of her because their parents had to work.

He was making a pizza from scratch. Flour was all over the kitchen, which, of course, I immediately cleaned. I asked him about it. Normally, people eat soup when they're sick. He said pizza was his specialty and that it always made Arizona feel better. And boy, was he right. It was the best pizza I ever had. He told me that when he was a rich baseball player, his dream was to have a house with one of the real, old-school pizza ovens.

I nod. "I remember everything you've ever said to me," I mumble, "the good and the bad."

He grabs my hand and squeezes it. "I've missed you."

I don't respond. I can't.

Sensing a topic change is needed, he says, "I found this hole-in-the-wall pizza joint. They have one of those brick ovens you rarely see anymore. You have to order your dough in advance. Maybe we can go sometime."

"You sure you want to be seen in public with me?"

He pulls his hand away, clearly annoyed by my comment. "I hate when you say stuff like that."

"Quincy, I don't think I can spend any more time alone with you. It's confusing for me. I'm moving on. I have a date coming up, and I need to see it through."

I don't officially have the date yet, but that's semantics.

I see his jaw stiffen.

"You can't have it both ways. You don't want to be with me —"

"I'd happily be with you."

"You want to have sporadic booty call sex with me. Not date me. I'm twenty-eight. That's not what I'm looking for."

"I know. I'm sorry. Let's talk about something I know we can agree on. I assume you realize who we play tonight, right?"

I nod. "Of course." They're playing the team Marc Whittaker, Arizona's ex-fiancé, is on. "Arizona doesn't want to go to the game even though you're pitching. We're gonna chill at our place and watch a movie."

"I don't blame her. She should stay away from him."

"Don't bean him again. It's enough with that."

A small smile finds his lips. "We'll see. Sometimes the ball just...slips out of my hand." He shrugs. "I can't help it."

"You're going to throw at him, aren't you?"

"You bet your sexy ass I am."

"You'll probably get suspended."

"Worth it."

"She doesn't want you to."

"Too bad. He has it coming."

CHAPTER FOURTEEN

QUINCY

Today was Arizona and Layton's big *Sports Illustrated* body image photo shoot. I wonder how they dealt with Layton's bruised cheek after our bench-clearing brawl with Whittaker and his team last night. I smile at the memory of Layton and I both pounding Whittaker with our fists over and over until our teammates and coaches pulled us away.

If nothing else, I know Lancaster cares about my sister. He was a man possessed last night. I got choked up with emotion over him taking the brunt of things so I didn't get suspended, though we both got ejected from the game.

Then my mind drifts to the photo shoot. I cringe at the thought of them half-naked together all day. I know she was nervous about it, so I want to check on her.

I dial her number, and she answers after one ring, completely out of breath. She pants, "Hello."

What the hell! "Where the fuck are you?"

"You're cheery as ever, grumpy. I'm out on the river jogging." *Phew*. "What's up?"

"Oh, I just wanted to see how today went."

"It...it was fine."

"Did something happen? Did he try to touch you inappropriately?"

"Ugh, no. Cut it out. Layton was fine. It was just a long day. I'm beat."

"Then why are you jogging?"

"It helps me think. I've got a lot going on right now, Q."

"I know you do. I'm sorry. What are you and Rip up to tonight? Do you want to hang out?"

"Honestly, I just want to take a long bath and go to bed. Ripley has a date. She's not around."

I grind my molars and try to sound calm. "Who with?"

"I don't know. She wouldn't give me any details, but she was excited about it. She bought a new dress and looked gorgeous in it."

Calm. Stay calm. "Any clue where they went?"

"I think she said Zahav. Whoever it is must have money."

Zahav is one of the nicest restaurants in Philly. It sounds like this sleazeball wants to get into her pants.

"Cool. Are you okay from yesterday? Everything with Whittaker?"

"I've been watching GIFs of him getting laid out by Layton all day. It was pretty fucking awesome."

I smile. "It was. Layton was brilliant. It was all his idea."

"I know. Thanks, Q. Love you, stinky pants."

"Love you too, Z. Have a good night."

"You too."

I pull up the Uber app on my phone. Where to? Zahav.

RIPLEY

This date is going really well. The best I've had in a long time.

Brandon is sweet and attentive. And so cute, with thick brown hair and a sexy beard. He's asking me a lot of questions and seems genuinely interested. We've been texting on and off for a few weeks. Yesterday with Quincy was the push I needed to finally say yes to Brandon about having dinner. He was thrilled and asked to do so immediately.

I'm glad I did this. I need it to move on from the hold Quincy has over me.

My date is the opposite of Quincy, being so mellow and easy-going. Though Quincy is outwardly like that with others. Just not always with me.

Brandon has a job in finance but was a former college football player. An offensive lineman. I need a big man, and he more than fits the bill.

"How was it playing football in college?"

"A huge time commitment. You know all about that though." He smiles. "I googled you. Wow. You're incredible. A few national championships, player of the year finalist, and you're considered a shoo-in for the 2028 Olympic team."

I bat my eyelashes. "Not bad for the awkward, chunky kid, right?"

He picks up my hand and kisses it. "I think you're the most stunning woman I've ever seen."

He pulls his hand away and sits up straight. "Sorry. I don't mean to come on so strong."

I smile softly. "It's okay. I don't mind."

"I was trying to learn the differences between softball and baseball. I know it's a bigger ball and a smaller field. What about pitching? Are there differences there too?"

"The biggest difference in pitching is our motion. In baseball, they pitch overhand from a raised mound. In softball, we pitch underhand from a flat surface."

He nods. "Is it all the same kinds of pitches?"

"Mostly, except we can throw a rise ball in softball. There's nothing like it in baseball. A rise ball looks like it's coming into the strike zone but because of the spin, it rises at the last second. It's a wicked pitch. If thrown correctly, it's hard to hit."

"How well do you throw it?"

I try to remain humble. "Pretty darn well...most of the time."

"Wow. That's so cool. I want to see you play. Your family must be so proud."

"I have a small family. I was raised by a single mother, and I never knew my father."

"Oh, did he pass?"

"Honestly, I know nothing about him. My mother has always been reluctant to talk about it."

"That must have been hard growing up. Things fathers do with their daughters. Father-daughter dances and the like."

I consider his words as Quincy pops into my mind. He always took me to that kind of stuff. Come to think of it, we never discussed anything. It was assumed every time I needed a surrogate male in my life, Quincy would be there. Always there for me in his own special way.

Brandon clears his throat. "I lost you. Where did you go?"

"Nowhere. I'm sorry."

"We're all settled up. It's a nice summer night. Would you like to go for a walk?" He gives me a boyish grin. "I don't want the date to end."

I nod. "I'd love to."

We walk a few blocks hand in hand. He makes it clear that we're near his apartment, even pointing to the building. I think he's feeling me out to see if I'm willing to come to his apartment tonight.

At some point, he stops and pulls me into his arms. His body is tight to mine. Smiling down at me, he admits, "I really like you."

I run my fingertips through his thick beard. "I like you too."

I do like him. It's the best non-Quincy date I've been on in years. Maybe there is life after Quincy Abbott after all.

He begins to lower his lips toward mine. I close my eyes and tilt my head to the side, anticipating his kiss. Just as his lips touch mine, he's gone. His lips, his arms, his body, all of it.

I blink my eyes open to see Quincy shoving Brandon. He barks out, "Keep your hands off my wife."

Brandon's eyes widen in horror as he looks my way. "You're married?"

I sigh. "Yes and no. I can expla—"

Brandon holds up his hands in surrender. "Please don't. I like you, Ripley. I like you a lot, but I want no part of this. You two work out your shit. Call me if and when you're truly available." He turns and walks away.

Tears fill my eyes as I ball my fists in anger. I'm so mad right now. I shout, "What are you doing here?"

"I don't want my wife kissing other men." He runs his fingers through his hair over and over. "I can't watch it."

"No one asked you to come here and watch it. Are you fucking crazy? What's wrong with you? I'm not your wife."

"Yes, you are. He can't have you. You belong to me."

"You can fuck anyone you want in our little arrangement, but I can't?"

"I haven't fucked anyone since you got to town."

"Get the man a medal." I throw my hands up in the air. "God, Quincy! This whole thing is so messed up. I can't have you holding me back anymore. I want a divorce. I'm not kidding. I need to rid myself of you."

"No."

"Why? Just let me go. You don't love me. We want different things. We're no good for each other. I want my happily ever after. You're incapable. Don't you want me to be happy?"

He looks pained but says nothing.

I hold my hand up for a cab and one stops. As I'm getting in, I say, "It's time. I'm getting an attorney. I can't do this fucked up dance with you anymore."

I shut the door. Just as I'm about to give the cab driver my address, the other door opens, and Quincy gets in. He immediately gives the cab driver his address.

"Quincy, I'm not going home with you."

"We need to talk."

"Quincy, we're friends. We started as friends. I want to stay that way, but you're making it increasingly difficult. Your sister is the most important person in the world to me. I don't want problems. I just need to move on from you. It's time. You need to accept it."

"Please. Let's talk."

I throw my head back on the seat. Why am I so weak for this man? I hate feeling weak. I've spent my whole fucking life trying to be strong. I had no father. I had a mother who was a child herself. There were more times than not that I had to be the adult in my house.

This man is my fucking kryptonite.

A few minutes later, we arrive at his luxury building in the most upscale neighborhood in Philly.

We quietly make our way up to his condo. As soon as he opens the front door, I bark out, "Five minutes. You have five minutes, and then I'm leaving you. For good. I mean it."

We walk in and I get about a half a step past the door before he shuts it and has me caged in. His body is pressed to mine.

My anger resurfaces.

I look into his eyes, which are mere inches from my own. "How dare you screw up my date. The first man I've had any interest in for a long time."

"I can't stomach the thought of another man touching you."

I need to hit him where it hurts. "You do realize that I've fucked other men, right?"

His jaw tics.

"They've touched me, kissed me, tasted me, been inside me. *Deep* inside me. I don't belong to you. I never will."

He rubs his thumb over my lower lip. "We both know that's not true. If I snapped my fingers, you'd get on your knees for me right here and now and suck my cock with a big fucking smile on your face."

Without thinking, I rear my hand back and slap him in the face. Hard.

The shock of it has him frozen for all of two seconds before his hand is on my throat. It's not intended to hurt me. Just the opposite. He applies the pressure he knows gets me off. Shit.

His forehead meets mine. We're breathing heavily, not from physical exertion, from emotional.

I whisper, "Let me go." I don't mean his hand on my throat, and he knows it.

He whispers back, "I can't."

I can smell his breath. It's so...so Quincy, and I need it like I need oxygen.

"Please, Shortcake, one last time. If you're really leaving me, let me have you one more time."

"And then you promise you'll let me go?"

He gives me a small nod.

Because I'm weak and in love with him, I make the worst possible decision. I slide my tongue out and lick across the seam of his lips.

He starts to run his hands up and under my dress, but I shove him away and walk him backward toward the sofa. "You know what? I'm sick of always doing this your way."

He smiles as he continues moving backward. "Always? We haven't been together in two years."

"Well, we always did it your way." I shove him again. "Tonight, I'm in charge."

His eyes practically glaze over with lust. "Yes, have your wicked way with me."

I push him down on the sofa. "Lay down."

He immediately listens. I'm loving bossing his normally bossy ass around. If the giant bulge in his jeans and the shit-eating grin on his face are any indication, he's loving it too.

I reach under my dress and pull down my panties. After kicking them to the side, I climb on top of him, approaching his face.

I straddle it with my bare pussy to his mouth. "I need a good orgasm. Make me come. Hard."

He mumbles into me, "Yes, ma'am," as he spreads my lips, and his long tongue enters me.

Admittedly, no one I've ever been with does this as well as Quincy. The speed at which he can make me come is unparalleled.

I run my fingers through his hair because I've missed doing that. I love his hair.

My hips take on a life of their own as I basically fuck his tongue.

His fingers work my clit over like a man who knows my body inside and out. It's mere minutes before I feel my orgasm rising to the surface.

"Oh fuck, Quincy, that's good."

I need this so badly. So much pent-up energy and frustration. Sadness and anger.

His long tongue slides in and out of me. I can feel my walls squeezing him.

He mumbles something about strawberries. I'm too lost in pleasure to comprehend.

It builds and builds until I have no choice but to let go. My vision goes blank for a moment, and I see stars. I can feel my juices pour out of me. He slurps up every last ounce.

Fucking hell, I needed that.

I take a deep breath and start to move off his face. I know what he thinks is going to happen, but it's not.

Standing, I grab my panties and start to slide back into them. His eyes narrow in anger. "What are you doing? Sit on my cock!"

After pulling up my panties and fixing my dress, I lean over and lick across the seam of his mouth again. This time, I can taste myself.

I run my hands through his curls and whisper into his mouth, "You owed me that goodbye. Thanks for the orgasm."

Giving him one last soft kiss, I breathe, "We're over. For the last time, I want a divorce. If you don't call an attorney, I will. I mean it."

At that, I turn and walk straight out of his condo and close the door behind me.

I'm filled with pride. I've let Quincy dictate every aspect of our relationship since day one. It's time for me to take a little control back. Maybe I'll be physical with him again sometime and maybe I won't, but it's not coming from manipulation. Not when he crashes my date and scares the poor guy away. How dare Quincy do that to me after all he's put me through.

When I reach his lobby, it occurs to me I shouldn't go home. When Arizona was out jogging, Layton stopped by. He wants her. She wants him. I let him inside to wait for her. They need a night alone without me interrupting them.

Tears begin to sting my eyes as I meander toward the front door of the building. Before I approach it, Blanche and Thor walk through. She's clearly struggling to control the giant beast. She's going to break a hip if she keeps this up.

I wipe my eyes, which she notices. "Ripley, sweetheart, are you okay?"

"I'm fine." I hold out my hand for the leash. "Let me help you take him to your apartment."

"You don't have to, dear."

I try to smile. "I'm happy to."

I take the leash, and we head back up. I'm careful to be quiet as we pass Quincy's door, feeling better once we're inside Blanche's apartment.

I release Thor, and he flops over to his water bowl, downing about a gallon per lick and spilling just as much on the ground.

Blanche gives me a compassionate smile. "I'm going to make some tea for both of us."

I nod, unable to form words right now, simply grateful for her compassion in my time of need.

She fiddles around in the kitchen before coming back out and pouring us both cups of tea. She motions for me to sit on her sofa as she does the same.

"Do you want to tell me what, or who, has you so upset? Perhaps a certain neighbor of mine?"

I'm quiet.

"You're in love with him."

I close my eyes and tears stream out of them as I croak out, "But I don't want to be."

She lovingly rubs my hand. "Tell me the story of you and Quincy. I've heard tidbits from him, but I got the feeling yesterday that it's a longer one."

"What makes you so sure?"

She gives me a small smile. "Eighty-plus years of on-the-job training. Tell me everything. Don't leave anything out. These old ears can handle it."

So I do. I unload everything on this poor woman. For nearly an hour, I get all of it off my chest. Every feeling, every insecurity, every rejection. She listens. She holds my hand. She lets me cry. It's a purging that I didn't realize I needed.

By the end, she's crying too. "Oh, Ripley, you're so deeply in love with him."

I close my eyes and whisper, "I know. I hate myself for it."

"Why?"

"I want to be a strong woman, not a weak one. Loving him makes me weak."

"No, it doesn't. From what you've told me about your life, you're incredibly strong." She squeezes my hand. "I never had a daughter. I have one son who I rarely see. If I ever had a daughter or granddaughter, I'd want her to be exactly like you."

"A mess over a man she'll never have?"

"No, one who loves with her whole heart. Flaws and all."

I take a tissue from the box she offers and blow my nose. "I can't go on like this."

"Don't give up on him. Can I tell you what I think?"

"Please."

"I think he loves you too. He'd be crazy not to. It's just unexpected for him, and he doesn't know how to handle it. Look at his actions. He can't bear to see you with another man. If he didn't care, he wouldn't feel that way. Give him time. He'll get there eventually. Sometimes men don't see what's right in front of them. It takes them longer than us to see the truth in things. I think he has some demons that have nothing to do with you. Give him space to work on those before you completely write him off."

I nod, not in agreement, simply in understanding. Quincy never has and never will love me, but I'm not arguing with her over it. "Can I stay a little longer? My roommate needs the place to herself. Unlike me, she has a man who's making his intentions clear."

She sets her tea down and stands. "You'll stay here tonight. I'll make up the guest bedroom for you."

"Are you sure? I don't want to impose."

She smiles. "I haven't had a girly sleepover in seventy years." She rubs her hands together in excitement. "I'll make popcorn, and we'll watch a movie. What's your favorite movie?"

"I've always loved *Top Gun*."

"You like the scene where he sings to her, don't you?"

"How did you know?"

"You're a romantic, like me. My husband used to sing to me all the time. He had the best voice."

"Will you tell me about him?"

"I'd be happy to."

CHAPTER FIFTEEN

RIPLEY

I'm glad I stayed away from my apartment the other night. I walked in that morning to Arizona and Layton sound asleep, *very* satisfied, *very* naked, *very* tangled in each other in her bed. For the past few days, they've been going at it every free second they can find. Both teams have had busy game schedules, but they capture stolen moments when they're able to. I've never seen Arizona happier, and I'm truly happy for her. She deserves this.

We're leaving for a short road trip tomorrow, which is followed by a long one for the Cougars. I imagine Arizona and Layton will be fucking their brains out all night. I need to get out of dodge. I'm about to call Kam and Bailey to see if they want to hang out when Arizona walks into my room.

She sits on my bed and rubs my arm. "Do you want to talk about where you were the other night?"

I shake my head. "It's nothing."

"Rip, you don't sleep around. If you stayed with someone, he means something to you. Why won't you share it?"

I hate lying to her, but there's no part of this story I can share with my best friend. It's better for her to think that I'm having casual sex.

"We haven't lived together for six years. I've changed. I can separate the physical and the emotional like Kam does. Trust me, there's nothing and no one to report."

"I don't believe you, and I wish you'd share it with me. Something is going on with you. Maybe I haven't lived with you for a long time, but you're my best friend in the whole world. I know you better than anyone. Whenever you're ready, I'm here for you. No judgment. No matter what, I love you, and I support you."

At least one Abbott outwardly loves me. I smile at her warmth and support. "I love you too. I'm fine though."

She sighs. "Okay. The Daultons asked Layton and me to show face at the pro basketball game tonight."

I shrug. "I figured you would be with him. No biggie. I'll hang with Kam and Bailey."

"They gave us a bunch of tickets. I want you to join us. The seats are courtside. It could be fun."

That perks me up. "Ooh. I'd love that. Thanks."

"Cool. Quincy is coming too."

Shit. I feign a smile and grit out, "Sounds good."

A little while later, I'm getting ready for the game when my text tone pings.

> Quincy: I'm sorry about the other night. Interrupting your date was wrong. I can't go back to us not talking. I promise to be a good boy from now on. Please. I miss my friend.

Me: Actions speak louder than words. See you in a bit. Behave.

Quincy: I love when you're bossy.

I GASP when we get to our seats. "Holy shit. These are amazing." We're right on the floor at center court. We're technically closer to the action than the players on the bench.

Arizona nods. "Yep. The Daultons are the best."

We take our seats where we receive the full VIP treatment. Waitresses actually bring us food and drinks right to our seats. It's amazing.

The announcers pay us a ton of attention. Not just Quincy and Layton, but Arizona and me too, calling us the best ballplayers in the city. It feels nice to have so much hometown support. It wasn't like this in Houston. The Daultons have done such a great job promoting us. The whole city is excited for the upcoming playoffs. It looks like both the Cougars and Anacondas are on pace to make the playoffs in our respective leagues. The buzz is electric.

At some point, the crowd and announcers encourage Arizona and Layton to kiss for the cameras. I know their relationship is real, and the crowd assumes it's real, but Quincy is still foolishly hoping it's not.

They kiss, but Arizona, being my crazy best friend, takes it up a notch and opens her mouth. They're fully going at it, mouths open, tongues in mouths, all allegedly for the cameras. The fans all cheer, but Quincy practically tackles Layton. The crowd thinks it's a joke. I know it's not.

Layton plays it off for the cameras, but I can tell he's annoyed with Quincy, who's simmering.

I mouth to him, "Relax."

Eventually they both chill out, and we have a nice time. We have a few beers and laughs. Quincy is watching Arizona and Layton like a hawk, but he's otherwise being his fun self.

When the game is over, several of the professional basketball players walk over to shake Layton and Quincy's hands. They all tell Arizona and me how much they love watching us and ask for photos. This level of notoriety is something Arizona and I have never known.

Quincy offers to take us home, encouraging Layton to go back to his place. That's Quincy's way of protecting Arizona.

The three of us walk into our apartment. Quincy looks at Arizona. "Can we talk?"

She nods. "Sure."

I take the hint. "I'm going to get changed for bed. Have a good night, Quincy."

He nods. "You too."

I change into my usual oversized T-shirt that I wear to bed, wash my face, and brush my teeth. I listen at my bedroom door, and it's quiet. He must have left.

I walk out to get some water knowing Layton must be on his way soon. I need to get out of their way. But it's Quincy who I see sitting on the sofa running his hands through his hair.

"Oh, sorry. I assumed you left. Where's Arizona?"

"She's in the shower."

"Is everything okay?"

With his elbows on his knees, he turns his head to me. "Please tell me the truth. What exactly is going on with them?"

I take a breath. "It's not my business to discuss. She's my

best friend. My loyalty lies with her. I would never in a million years break her confidence."

His lips turn down. His face is pained. "What about me? I'm your husband. Shouldn't you be loyal to me?"

"Not for long. I called an attorney today."

"You what?"

"I told you I was. He's drafting the paperwork so I can file for divorce."

He takes a few deep breaths, eventually gritting out, "I don't have the mental energy for this. Just tell me about Arizona and Layton. Was it ever fake? Have they been lying to me for months?"

"No, I will not discuss this further with you. I'm not your spy. If you want to know something about Arizona, ask Arizona, not me."

"I tried. She said it's nothing."

"Then I suppose you'll have to believe her."

He stands, takes three long strides, and gets in my face. So close I can smell his aftershave. His blue eyes meet mine. "I need you to be my wife right now."

I look up at him, refusing to back down. "I guess we don't all get our needs met, Quincy."

He looks my body up and down, landing on the silly wording of my T-shirt. "What the hell kind of shirt is that?"

I giggle, falsely assuming he's breaking the tension. "I think it's funny. It belonged to my college boyfriend. I wear it to bed." In a purposefully antagonizing fashion, I add, "When I'm alone."

Before I can even process anything, he grabs the collar of the shirt and tears it in half. Straight down the middle.

I gasp in shock.

He growls, "How dare you wear another's man shirt. You're. My. Wife."

I'm standing there completely exposed. I have nothing on underneath. His eyes penetrate mine as he presses himself against me, his leg pushing between mine.

Our noses are so close they nearly touch. He runs his thumb over my lower lip as he looks my naked body up and down. "You're so beautiful. One day soon, you'll be back in my bed where you belong, but I need you to want it." He increases the pressure of his leg between mine. "I'll wait until you're ravenous for me. Frothing at the mouth."

My body heats and my core throbs. Tears pool in my eyes at both loving and hating the effect he has on me.

He visibly swallows. "Do you feel this? Do you feel what's happening between our bodies? The ever-present pull? I know I'm not alone in this."

I squeeze my eyes shut, wishing I could say that I don't feel it. Wishing I wasn't in love with this enigmatic man who gives me nothing but whiplash. Tears begin to spill out.

In an unexpected move, he presses his lips tenderly to my forehead. It's such a contrast to the animal that just tore my shirt in half and pressed his body against mine without invitation. "Don't give up on me, Shortcake. Not yet."

He then turns and walks out, leaving me sliding down the wall in tears.

CHAPTER SIXTEEN

RIPLEY

After a few long weeks of travel, we're finally back home. We were off today, but the guys have a game tonight, and we're all going.

I'm lying in Bailey's bed while Arizona is in our apartment showering. "How is it going at Tanner Montgomery's house with his daughter?"

She gives me a huge smile. "It's amazing. Harper is a doll. I adore her. The house is like nothing you've ever imagined. I know Tanner Montgomery is the biggest sports agent around, but I don't think I appreciated it until I saw that house. It's the biggest and nicest I've ever seen. He just had a batting cage built in the backyard, so Harper and I hit every time I'm there. He said he was sick of taking her to the crappy cages all the time. He put in a whole state-of-the-art system for her. He's such a good dad."

She says it with a dreamy look on her face.

Kam was making fun of Bailey earlier for possibly having a

crush on Tanner. I wasn't sure it was true, but now I'm thinking it is.

"Are you crushing on him?"

Before she can answer, Kam walks in and answers, "Fuck yes, she is. She's always been into older guys."

Bailey rolls her eyes. "Cut it out. I've been into guys five or six years older. Tanner is *a lot* older."

Kam shrugs. "Fifteen years isn't a big deal. You just barely make it into the age gap rulebook."

Bailey sighs. "I'm afraid to ask what that means. What age gap rulebook?"

"Half your age plus seven is acceptable. You said Tanner is forty-three. Half his age is roughly twenty-one, plus seven is twenty-eight, your exact age. And before you ask, I didn't make it up. That's definitely a real thing."

Bailey shakes her head. "I don't think that's a real thing, but it doesn't matter. There's nothing going on between us."

"Yet." Kam smiles. "I bet you can say *yes daddy* with your mouth full."

I burst out laughing. Bailey is trying to hold in hers.

Kam places her hand on Bailey's shoulder. "Just remember, you can't pick your father, but you *can* pick your daddy."

Even Bailey can't help but laugh at that one. "You're ducking nuts."

Kam raises an eyebrow. "Ducking? If you're ducking and not fucking, you're doing it wrong."

Bailey smiles. "My biggest issue is watching my mouth around Harper." She narrows her eyes at Kam. "Living with you my whole life has given me a foul mouth and a dirty mind. I need to work on censoring myself, even when Harper and her friends aren't around."

Kam shrugs. "Well, I'm jumping in the shower so I can

make sure my bussy is nice and ready for whoever enters her tonight."

WE'RE AT THE GAME. It's tied at one going into the seventh inning. Quincy is pitching a gem. Every time he takes the mound each inning, he looks my way.

Kam leans over and whispers, "You can't possibly tell me there's nothing going on between you two. He eye fucks you every damn inning."

She's not wrong. He's never been this obvious before. I look at Arizona to see if she's noticing it too, but fortunately she's staring at Layton when they run onto the field every inning. Not Quincy.

I ignore Kam and whisper to Arizona. "You should tell your brother about you and Layton. It's not fair to keep lying to him."

She nods. "Soon. I'm just terrified that if something goes wrong with Layton, it will impact his relationship with Quincy. They're such good friends. And teammates. You see how Quincy is with Marc. I can't have that happen between him and Layton."

"It doesn't look like you and Layton are splitting anytime soon. And they're friends. Quincy and Marc weren't. Quincy always hated him."

She nods, knowing I'm right. "I guess we should tell him. Soon. Maybe after the season. They're about to start the playoffs. I don't want to mess with that."

"That's still a few weeks off. You guys are so obvious."

She takes a deep breath. "Okay. We'll tone it down until the

season is over." She bites her lip. "Well, we'll try to. He's just so
—"

"In love with you."

She looks at me with uncertainty.

I wrap my arm around her. "He's in love with you, babe."

She blows out a breath. "It's all happening so fast."

I can't help but look at Quincy. "When you know, you know. It's an unstoppable force of nature."

QUINCY GAVE up a two-run home run in the top of the eighth inning. I could tell he was beating himself up when it happened. Instead of celebrating the fact that he's ascended to the top spot in the pitching rotation of one of the best teams in baseball, he's carrying the burden of the team's success on his shoulders. I can physically see it weighing on him. I've never seen him more stressed than he is right now.

Fortunately for him, Layton hit a three-run bomb at the bottom of the eighth inning, and the Cougars won the game by one run. Layton is on the best hitting streak of his career. We're all headed to Screwballs after the game to celebrate the important late-season victory.

Layton walks in without Arizona. I look at him. "Where's our girl?"

"She's outside talking to Quincy. I'll order her favorite beer."

"She likes the—"

He holds up his hand and gives me a sweet smile. "I know what my girl drinks."

Yep, he's in love with her.

The whole crew is here, even Trey and Gemma, who don't

always join us due to having a new baby at home. Trey goes to the bar and Gemma quickly turns to the table. In a bit of a panicked, low voice, she says, "His birthday is next week. Do you guys have any ideas for gifts? I'm drawing a blank. He honestly has everything."

Cheetah raises his eyebrow. "You know what all men want for their birthdays?"

She narrows her eyes. "I'm afraid to ask. What?"

"We all wear blow jobs. Size? Your mouth."

Gemma starts laughing. "Oh shit, that's a good one. I'm gonna use that in one of my books."

She gasps, quickly covers her mouth, and mumbles, "Shit."

I look at her. "I thought you were a lawyer. Are you an author too?"

Cheetah smirks. He knows something we don't know.

She scrunches her face. "I...umm...I actually write romance novels under a pen name. Not many people know about it. I would appreciate you keeping it between us. Trey says he's proud of me, but I'm sure judgmental assholes would have a field day with him if they found out. And I don't want to use his notoriety."

I stand there in shock. We're all usually very casual, but not Gemma. She's always got on designer clothes. She's not snobby at all, she's just always perfectly made up and classy. I didn't expect this from her.

I ask, "What have you written?"

She shrugs as if it's no big deal. "A handful of books. It's just a fun hobby. I can send you a link to my website if you want to check them out."

Kam seems intrigued. "Are they super spicy?"

Gemma gives a guilty look. "It's all relative, I suppose. Nothing too dark and depraved, but I think most people think of them as super spicy."

Kam nods. "Give us an example of something dirty you've recently written. Be very specific."

"Hmm." She gives a sly smile as something occurs to her. "I just wrote a scene where the man eats cherries directly from the woman's—"

Cheetah interrupts, "Love tunnel?"

Gemma giggles. "Yes, love tunnel. That's a good name. I might use that too. Cheetah, you're a gold mine for my books."

He winks at her like they have a secret but then turns back to the rest of us. "I think my new food fetish is growing." He turns to Kam. "Kam bam, I'm in the mood for Japanese tonight. Maybe your bento box will do."

She shakes her head. "I'm not an all-you-can-eat buffet, kitten."

"In my mind you are." He thumps his head. "I dream every night about your long legs wrapped around my face. They're like peanut butter. Smooth and easy to spread."

Kam licks her lips suggestively. "That's *very* presumptuous of you. What makes you think they're smooth?"

Cheetah smiles at her as something passes between them. "I would kill to eat your muffin for breakfast."

Kam's eyes sparkle. "Why do you get to have all the fun? Maybe I want a meal for two with a hairy view?"

Man, these two never let up. They've each met their match.

Arizona finally walks in, followed shortly thereafter by Quincy. She looks annoyed, and he looks unhappy.

After some fun banter among this crazy crew, Trey holds up his drink. "To Layton, for another career night. It's great to see you playing this way again, brother."

We all lift our glasses, but Layton stares at Arizona with pure lust in his eyes. "It's all thanks to my beautiful muse." And then he kisses her. Deeply.

In true Arizona fashion, she gives it right back to him.

It just got very hot in here. So much for toning it down.

Everyone starts hooting and hollering, but I look at Quincy, and he seems pained as he turns his head to me and mouths, "Is it real?"

Unwilling to betray Arizona, I remain stoic and simply shrug my shoulders.

He appears hurt. Not by the kiss in front of him, but that I'm choosing her over him.

He stands abruptly, causing his chair to screech, and walks straight out of Screwballs.

Arizona assumes he's pissed about the kiss and starts to go after him, but I grab her arm. "I've got it. I'll talk to him. You stay and have fun with your man."

She lets out a breath. "Fine by me. I'm sick of him treating me like a child when he's the *real* child. He just had a temper tantrum."

I don't think that's what just happened, but I'm certainly not saying anything. "I know, sweetie. He worries about you. I'll talk to him."

I get up and leave in search of Quincy, quickly finding him around the corner of the building in an alleyway. He's leaning up against the brick wall, looking tormented.

He turns his head when he hears me coming. "Why do you always choose her over me?"

"She's my best friend. The most important person in the world to me. I love her."

He gives me a small, crooked smile. "I thought you loved me too."

"You don't want my love."

He takes a few breaths and tightens his jaw. "What if I do?"

"A knee-jerk reaction from seeing me with another man isn't a reason for you to accept my love. I told you. I won't be kept in the dark anymore. I have needs too and, unlike yours, they're not just physical."

He nods. He knows I'm right. "I'm sorry I can't be what you need. I wish more than anything that I could be."

"Me too, Quincy. Me too."

Before I can stop him, he pulls me into his arms. I try to pull away, but he overpowers me. "Please. Let me hold you for a minute. Let me take you in. It calms the chaos in my head."

I can't help but relax into him and wrap my arms around his waist. My head rests on his chest as we stand there embracing silently for several long minutes.

He's hurting so much. It breaks my heart.

He sinks his nose into my neck, inhaling me as he often used to do. His voice cracks as he admits, "I miss this. I miss us."

"You miss sex."

He pulls his head back. Tears sting his eyes. "Don't you understand? It has nothing to do with sex. I miss you. I'm empty without you. Nothing has meaning to me without you."

I want to confront him about messing with my head. About telling me not to love him, telling me we can't be together long term, but then also telling me he's missing me and that he's empty without me. But as it has so many times in the past, my desire to help him, to please him, trumps everything else right now, even my own sanity.

I reach down for his belt buckle and unfasten it. He pinches his eyebrows together. "What are you doing?"

"Let me help you relax. I know what you need. I'll take care of you." I mumble, "Like always."

He watches on as I unzip his pants, slide my hand inside his boxers, and pull out his rapidly growing cock.

Cheez, that fucker is big. It always shocks me. Did it get

bigger in the past two years? Maybe seeing other men has me forgetting that he practically has a third arm.

I'm suddenly throbbing, remembering what it does to my body.

I drop down to my knees, and he whispers, "Holy shit."

I give him a few pumps. He briefly closes his eyes. "I've missed your touch. So much."

Without breaking eye contact or my grip on him, I slowly lick around his balls. I learned our first night together how much he enjoys that and have done it many times since. There's nothing better than having him at my mercy for a change.

My tongue eagerly worships every crevice and vein on his perfect cock as I slowly work my way up. He loves the long tease. Seemingly oblivious to our surroundings, that's what I give him.

Swirling my tongue around his crown, I taste the saltiness already oozing from him.

"Fuck, Shortcake. You're so fucking good at this."

I can't help but smile as I eventually take him into my mouth, all the way to the back of my throat. It took me some time to learn how to do that for him, but I did, and I love the pleasure that oozes from him when I do.

I move my head back slowly, sucking as hard as I can along the way. His cock further hardens as I do it.

He looks down at me. "Every other fucking woman goes right for the main event. No one takes better care of me than you. No one makes me come harder."

I'd jump for joy right now if I didn't have a mouth full of Quincy. Is it fucked up that his words of praise turn me on, even while referencing other women? You bet it is, but it also has me squeezing my own legs together to tame the throb.

I open my throat and suck him back in until I find a pace that has him moaning in an animalistic fashion. Knowing what he enjoys, I then raise my hands and intertwine my fingers on my head.

He grabs them along with a fistful of my hair and starts to fuck my mouth hard. My eyes and mouth are watering while my throat tightens around him.

"Oh fuck, baby. Yes."

He thrusts in and out of my mouth with reckless abandon. I happily give him tongue, suction, and moans, all the things he wants and needs.

I feel him swell just a drop more, his tell that he's about to come. He pushes in deep. With a loud groan, he overflows my mouth as he comes long and hard down the back of my throat.

I'm able to swallow most of it, though a little leaks out. I know he's going to scoop it up and feed it to me, which he does. I happily oblige, sucking his semen-covered finger into my mouth.

Breathlessly leaning against the wall, he releases his hold on my hands and hair.

I stand and run my hands up his chest until they slide around his neck. Looking up at him, our eyes meet. His are pleading for more.

I nod and can't help but move my lips toward his. For the first time in two years, our lips meet. His taste is the most comforting, natural thing in the world to me. It takes me back to our first kiss twelve years ago. To the first time he made love to me ten years ago. To every time he's made love to me since. He always kisses me long and hard. Even if we would meet for a quickie, kissing has never been absent. I wonder if other women get lost in his kisses like I do.

He moans into my mouth as he deepens the kiss. His hands immediately move down the back of my leggings and into my panties. Quincy has always been obsessed with my ass. I don't know why, it's big, flabby, and dimpled, but he undoubtedly worships it. When we were sleeping together in Houston, he couldn't keep his hands or anything else off it. He's probably done me from behind as many times as facing each other. And then there's the one night I gave him my ass. Another first belonging to him. I don't think I've ever seen him more turned on than he was that night.

He grinds his quickly forming partial erection against me. I ache for him on a level I'll never truly understand.

He turns us around, so my back is now to the wall, and mumbles into my lips, "I need you, Shortcake."

Because I need him too, I respond, "I know. Take what you need."

Without breaking the kiss, he manages to remove my shoes before dragging my leggings and panties down my legs.

I mumble into his mouth, "Do you have a condom? I don't have the IUD anymore." Not that we didn't always use condoms before, but now I need to be extra diligent.

As he reaches for his wallet, I start to turn around, assuming he'll do me from behind, but he holds me in place. "I want to look into your eyes when I'm back inside you. I miss your eyes."

I don't know if I can handle the intimacy of that, and I'm not sure how the logistics of this are going to work, but I'll go with it for now. Maybe he can lift one of my legs.

He pulls down his pants just a bit more. I grab his cock and start to pump him. He just came a minute ago and will need some coaxing.

He grabs my wrist and pulls my hand away. He then runs his fingers through my folds, which are now practically dripping.

"You're soaked, Shortcake. Does sucking my cock make you wet?"

I breathe, "You know it does."

Looking me square in the eyes, he sticks those fingers into his mouth. I feel and then see his cock harden to full mast in what must be a world record for turnaround time.

There's something so erotic about the fact that my taste did that to him. My pussy is now pulsing, aching to be filled by him in a way only Quincy can.

He sheaths himself in the condom and grabs one of my legs. When he goes to grab the other, I stop him. "What are you doing? You can't lift me. You'll get injured."

"If I want to lift you up and fuck you against this wall, I will."

At that, he lifts my other leg. Newsflash, I'm heavy. *Very* heavy. There's a reason I've never had sex like this. I'm not the kind of woman you can lift and fuck against a shower wall, or any other wall for that matter. I don't know what Quincy's thinking. I'm suddenly terrified that he's going to miss the playoffs because he throws his back out by trying to lift me.

I lock my ankles and try to lean as much of my weight against the wall as I can.

He doesn't seem concerned about any of that. He also doesn't seem to have any trouble with this position. Swiveling his hips until his tip finds my entrance, he then slams it into me.

I throw my head back as much as I can against the hard wall. "Ah, Quincy. Relax."

"Don't tell me how to fuck my wife. I know what she needs."

He starts to drive in and out of me. I can't believe we're having sex like this. And it's good, *really* good. He must be Hercules. Or Popeye, and he ate lots of spinach this morning because it seems effortless for him to hold me and fuck me this way.

He buries his face in my neck as the delicious onslaught

continues. He mumbles into me, "Oh god, I've missed this. You have no idea how much I need you."

Him saying things like that fucks with my head, but I'm not going to focus on it. I know this is purely a physical release for him. I'm focusing on what he's doing to my body, not what he's whispering in my ear. It's what he's always done to my body, electrify it. Why can't I share this kind of passion with anyone else?

He kisses up my neck. "And I miss kissing."

I don't know what that means, but his lips take mine, and all rational thought escapes me. Our tongues work together like they've done it a thousand times before. They *have* done it a thousand times before. And it's perfect. Like always.

I think I'd rather he just fuck me, not kiss me. I know I read too much into his kisses because whenever his lips are sealed over mine, I can't help but be flooded with hope. I can't help but feel like he loves me the way I love him.

He pushes his long cock in so damn deep. It's like he reaches the end of me...and then some. It's not possible for other men to reach the depths Quincy does, both physically and metaphorically.

I'm pulling his gorgeous hair. I tear my lips away and breathe, "So good. Oh, Quincy."

He pushes his tongue back into my mouth as he pants, "More kissing. I need it. I need you."

He pounds into my body like a man possessed, both with his cock and tongue. I open my eyes and stare at him. His face is dripping with desire. If I didn't know better, I'd think he was desperate for me.

At some point, I hear Arizona giggling around the corner. She and Layton must be outside of the bar. They're not very quiet in their flirting and dirty talk. Did they forget we're supposed to be out here talking? He mentions them going to his place.

I quickly look at Quincy. He's so absorbed in what we're doing that he doesn't even hear them. I spend a minute terrified that he'll hear their banter and spend another fearful that they'll find us, but after a few moments, it's quiet again, other than our moans and slapping skin.

He's had both hands on my ass the whole time, but now one of them slides up my shirt, pulls down my bra, and grabs one of my breasts. "God, I miss these tits. You have the best tits."

I run my fingers through his curls while he starts massaging my nipple. I feel the sexy pitching-produced callouses of his fingertips before he pinches my nipple hard, how he knows I like it.

It's a direct line to my clit. I feel fireworks working their way through my body. Inch by inch, making their way to my core until I'm ready to detonate in a way that only Quincy Abbott can bring out of me.

"Fuck yes. I can feel you squeezing my cock so perfectly. Do you have any idea how good your pussy feels? Your wet, tasty pussy. After the other night, I had to lick my lips, tasting you just to get myself off. So fucking sweet."

His dirty talk never ceases to ignite me.

He then moves his hand up to my throat. My Achilles heel. As he applies pressure, he whispers, "I know what my wife needs to get off. I own your pussy, baby, I always will."

That's about all I can handle. My toes curl and I explode in pure bliss. It's more than just an orgasm. It's two years of missing him being inside me physically pouring out. I can hear the sounds of my slickness. I can feel it gushing out of me.

I bite his shoulder to attempt to stifle my unavoidable screams, having no clue whether or not I'm successful because the rest of the world, and the fact that we're in a city alley, ceases to exist right now.

Once he knows that I'm taken care of, he picks up the pace and pistons into me until he finds his own release, grunting loudly, *very* loudly, as he floods the condom with his warm seed.

We don't move for several minutes, both panting heavily. His face is buried in my neck, constantly inhaling me. It's something he's always done. I know he likes the way I smell. He's never been shy about it.

At some point, I pat his back. "Put me down. You're going to get hurt."

He doesn't move. "No. I don't want this to end."

I unlock my ankles and slowly force my legs down. They're a bit numb and wobbly from the mind-blowing orgasm he just gave me. It takes me a moment to get my bearings.

I try to push him away, but he won't budge. "Quincy," I whine.

He mumbles into my neck, "Will you come home with me?"

"It's not a good idea."

He sighs as his shoulders fall and he lifts his head, looking sad. "Then I'll take you back to Arizona, so I know you'll get home safely."

"Umm...she left."

"Without you?"

I look up and give him a look, trying to convey what he must already know.

I see the moment realization hits. "She left with him, didn't she?"

I nod once.

"His place?"

I nod again.

"How long has it been going on?"

"I'm not saying anything else."

He hangs his head. In a resigned tone, he says, "Okay. I'll take you home."

"You don't have to."

"I want to. Can we walk though? It's nice out."

"Sure."

We get dressed and begin the walk toward my apartment. He intertwines his fingers through mine. His thumb lovingly runs over my fingers. I love the animal in Quincy, but tender Quincy threatens my psyche more than anything. Even something as simple as handholding isn't the norm for him, so it hits me extra hard when he does it.

We're silent for a bit until I ask, "I still don't understand why you care so much about Arizona and Layton. It's silly. I know you said he's a womanizer, but she can handle herself."

His jaw tightens. "Like she did with Marc?"

"She was young and naïve. She's different now. Stronger. And Layton isn't Marc. Neither of us liked Marc. We both adore Layton. Don't you see the way he looks at her?"

He rolls his eyes. "Yes, I fucking see it, but I watched him move from woman to woman for eight months. I'm telling you; he was with a different woman every night. I've seen too much. I'd rather die than see her go through that hurt again. I practically lost my sister after Marc left her."

"I know. I felt the same. Honestly, I didn't want to move to Philly knowing I'd see you all the time. I did it for her. She needed me."

He winces. "Ouch."

"It's the truth. This isn't easy for me. Being around you so much. I told you I was in love with you, and you responded by walking out of my life."

"You kicked me out and told me it was over. You're the one who walked away."

"No, Quincy. I told you I was in love with you. You couldn't handle it. You didn't love me back. I wasn't okay. I'm still not okay. I was doing better, but being around you again stifles my progress." I look down and swallow at what I'm going to say. "I've been thinking about it. Arizona is in a good place now. When this season is done, I think I might request a trade."

His eyes widen. "What? Why?"

"You know why, and you know it's for the best. You have a chokehold on me."

He smirks. "I thought you liked my chokehold on you."

I can't help but smile and throw him a soft elbow to the gut.

He mock grunts. "Don't do anything rash. We all love having you around."

We walk into my building. I try to send him home, but he insists on dropping me at my door. As we're walking down the hallway, we hear a woman's scream coming from Kam and Bailey's apartment. Then we hear a man scream too.

I turn to Quincy. He scrunches his face in confusion. "That's Cheetah."

Then we hear another woman's scream followed by laughter. It's actually two women laughing while Cheetah is still screaming. Screaming sort of like a girl.

I shake my head. "You should go. I'm going to see what insanity has gone on in there. God knows what those crazies are up to."

He chuckles. "Do you think Kam and Cheetah finally sealed the deal?"

I shrug. "I have no idea. I'll see you later."

He rubs my face. "Thanks for tonight. It was...it was... perfect."

Not wanting to show any emotion, I kiss his cheek and turn to open Kam and Bailey's door. I'm most definitely not prepared for the scene in front of me.

There is water everywhere, and I mean *everywhere*. Bailey is in pajamas, and Kam is clearly naked but wrapped in a sheet. What truly catches my eye is Cheetah running around like a madman, naked, trying to throw a completely inadequate number of towels on the water pouring from Kam's bedroom.

I look at Kam and Bailey with a huge smile. "The waterbed popped?"

Kam straightens her shoulders and smiles proudly. "We fucked it to death."

I let out a laugh. "We all saw that one coming."

Cheetah is screaming in Spanish while he runs around. I yell, "Cheetah, towels aren't going to work."

"Dios mio! I have to do something."

I look him up and down and then turn to Kam and Bailey. "Is it me or are his balls bizarrely big?"

Kam nods. "They're fucking huge. He said they've always been that way. And they're sensitive. *Really* sensitive. He was practically fucking me and spanking me at the same time. It was kinda cool."

I can't take my eyes off them. "I've never seen anything like it. They're like alien balls."

Bailey giggles. "They're *extrateressticle* for sure."

We all laugh as Cheetah continues to run around naked.

Eventually, the superintendent shows up. It's a long night of cleaning. With Arizona gone, Kam and Bailey sleep in her bed while the cleaning crew continues to work on their apartment and the one below them, both completely flooded.

CHAPTER SEVENTEEN

RIPLEY

Tonight is the *Sports Illustrated* body image issue unveiling party. I can't wait to see Arizona and Layton's picture. I'm sure it's gorgeous. From what Arizona told me about the heat between them at the photo shoot, this picture is going to be crazy hot.

We're all getting dressed up and taking a party bus up to New York City for the big event. It's going to be a fun night celebrating our friends.

One of the team owners, Auburn Bouvier, owns a fashion house. Arizona is wearing one of his dresses, which supposedly is worth tens of thousands of dollars. It's crazy. He's also sending hair and makeup professionals. Arizona insisted that we all get pampered, not just her. She even included Gemma DePaul, so the five of us have been having a girlie afternoon filled with lots of laughs.

The makeup woman is running a few minutes late. Apparently, she also does the makeup for huge pop star, Ella

Ervin, and is running a bit behind schedule getting Ella ready for her concert in Philly later tonight.

We're all in various stages of getting our hair done when Kam admits, "I hooked up with a guy who had a bit of dick jewelry last night."

Arizona asks, "A penis ring?"

Kam shakes her head. "First of all, they're called cock rings, not penis rings, and no, it was more...permanent in nature."

Arizona pinches her eyebrows together. "Cock rings can't be permanent?"

Kam looks around, seeking an answer, but everyone is silent until Gemma matter-of-factly states, "Cock rings are different from piercings. There are many different types of piercings. *Many.* Most names revolve around the spot on the penis that has the piercing. There's the Prince Albert that goes through the urethra and comes out the bottom of the shaft, there's the apadravya that kind of goes across the shaft, there the king's crown that goes vertically through the ridge, there's the deep shafter which is exactly as it sounds, there's the frenum which—"

Bailey holds up her hands. "Okay, okay, we get it. There are a lot of piercings. What about rings?"

Gemma answers as if she's simply rattling off a grocery list. "Again, there are a lot, but they're mostly just for sex, not more permanent like the piercings. A majority of them simply roll on and restrict blood flow, making the erection stronger and longer lasting. Some vibrate too, which is nice for us. Then you've got the metal ones that go in the urethra for urethral sounding, which is inserting objects into the urethra. That's supposed to be pleasurable for guys."

We all stare at Gemma in complete and total shock.

Naturally, Kam asks what we're all thinking. "How the hell do you know all that?"

She smiles. "I needed to know it for...work."

"Are you a hooker?"

She giggles. "Sort of. I'm an attorney, but you now know I write romance novels on the side. I use a lot of this stuff in my books."

I mumble, "I need to start reading these books." Turning to Kam, I ask, "What did the guy last night have?"

"A piercing. I don't know the fucking name. I'm not like the porn queen of the East, Gemma DePaul. It was my first time with one. It was fucking incredible though. It felt so good."

My mouth falls open. "Oh wow." I turn to the rest of the girls. "Have you guys been with any men who have dick piercings?"

Arizona and Bailey shake their heads, but Gemma gives us a small smile. I look at her wide-eyed. "When was this? When you were younger?" Gemma is about five or six years older than the rest of us and seemingly quite experienced.

Her green eyes sparkle. "Would you judge me if I told you the most recent time was this morning?"

The four of us look at each other in shock. Kam crosses her arms. "Are you telling us that Mr. Perfect Hair, doting husband and father, all-American, apple pie, Trey DePaul has a dick piercing?"

"He does," she mock shivers, "and it's incredible. Addicting. Life-altering."

Kam giggles and asks, "When did he get it? It must have hurt like a bitch."

Gemma leans back in her chair. "Let's just say that Trey is into grand romantic gestures as one of the ways he shows his love for me."

Kam scoffs. "If he put extra holes in his dick for you, I'd call that love."

We all laugh, including Gemma.

Just then, an exceedingly attractive woman with dark hair and nearly purple eyes runs in. She's dressed casually in a pink tracksuit but somehow makes it look fashionable with an equally stylish ponytail and sparkly headband. I look like a homeless man when I wear sweatpants. She looks like the company paid her to walk around in their clothing.

Out of breath, she pants, "I'm so sorry I'm late."

We all look at her, having no clue who she is. I ask, "And you are...?"

She slaps the heel of her hand on her forehead. "Sorry. Hi, I'm Bristol. I'll be doing your makeup today."

That makes sense. Her makeup is flawless. In fact, everything about her face and body is flawless.

There's a giant blond man with her who carries her large makeup trunk into the room and gently places it down for her. Who is this woman that she needs a bodyguard? Weird.

We all introduce ourselves as she unpacks her supplies and immediately starts working on Arizona's makeup. "Catch me up. What have you ladies been gossiping about?"

Kam smiles. "Dick piercings. I popped my dick-piercing cherry last night, but Gemma over here is apparently a pro." She points at Gemma who unashamedly winks.

Bristol giggles. "You guys would get along well with my friends down in Texas. That's where I live."

I ask, "Where in Texas? I lived in Houston for nearly six years."

"The Dallas area."

"Oh. I never went quite that far. What brings you all the way to Philly?"

"I used to be Ella Ervin's personal makeup artist, traveling with her all over the world. Now that I'm married with a daughter, I only travel with her for a few big shows a year. My husband had some business up here, so it worked out. I know Auburn Bouvier well. His cousin is one of my girlfriends. When he heard I'd be in town today, he asked me to help out."

"Where's your husband now?"

She motions her thumb toward the door. "He's right outside. He's the big guy that carried my stuff in."

My mouth drops. "I thought he was a bodyguard. He's huge." He must be at least six feet, eight inches.

She smirks. "That's why everyone calls him Tank. That, and because he's packing a giant cannon."

We all start laughing.

She smiles. "Not pierced or anything, but I do like to dress it up in cute hats."

"Your husband?"

"No, his dick."

We hear a deep, authoritative, gravelly voice from the hallway. "Stop telling people about that. It's private."

I whisper. "He's kind of scary."

She shakes her head. "He's nothing but a teddy bear. Maybe a bit of a tongue magician too, but a sweet little teddy bear. *Big* teddy bear."

The deep voice again rings out, "Bris, cut it out. I have a rep to protect."

Her shoulders shake in laughter.

They're adorable.

She looks around at all of us. "I don't even know why we're here. Are you guys models? Do you have an event tonight?"

Arizona lets out a laugh. "Umm, no. Definitely not. We're professional softball players."

Bristol's gorgeous eyes light up. "That's awesome. I played basketball in high school." She mock blows on her fingernails. "All state my senior year."

Bailey nods. "I played basketball too. I preferred it to

softball, but my sister sucked at it and forced me to play softball with her."

I didn't know that.

Kam scrunches her face. "True story. I was so bad, and Bails was amazing. She popped three-pointers like Caitlin Clark. She was better than all the guys at our school too."

Bristol rubs her hands together. "Don't you love when men underestimate you because of the way you look, and then you school them by showing off your athletic prowess?" She shouts a little louder, "Right, honey?"

He shouts back, "You're a basketball queen, sweetness. She hustled my friends like a pro when we first started dating. They never saw it coming given how irresistibly sexy she is. They were busy staring at her ass while she was dribbling around them."

Bristol smiles. "Yep. He loves me for my mad basketball skills."

"I love you because you have no gag reflex."

She lifts a smug eyebrow. "True." Looking around at us, she asks, "Seriously, where are you all headed tonight?"

Arizona answers, "We have a party for *Sports Illustrated*—"

I interrupt, "Arizona and her boyfriend modeled for their body image issue. We're going for moral support."

Bristol gasps. "Omigod, my friend Blaire and her husband did that a few years ago." She fans herself. "It was so fucking hot."

Kam asks, "What sport does Blaire play?"

"She doesn't. She's a doctor. Her husband is Axel Broxton."

Gemma's eyes practically bug out of her head. "He's so hot." She notices our lack of familiarity with his name. "He's the best tight end in football with an ass that lives up to the name of his position."

Bristol smiles. "She's not wrong."

We're all kind of shocked that Gemma knows this. She notices our surprise and shrugs. "I might be married to a baseball player, but I'm a football girl at heart. I can throw a ball pretty well. You ladies aren't the only athletes in the room."

Gemma DePaul is officially the most mysterious, enigmatic, unexpected woman I've ever met.

A few hours later, we're dressed and ready. Admittedly, we look amazing. Bristol is a true artist. I've never had makeup look this perfect, and I'm in the nicest dress I've ever worn. It's emerald green with a plunging neckline. I've never worn anything this revealing.

Trey texts Gemma that the boys will be pulling up in a few minutes in the party bus. We head downstairs and walk out in time to see the bus moving up the street.

Before it even comes to a complete stop, Layton jumps out and practically sprints toward Arizona, kissing her hand and whispering in her ear. She practically melts into him at whatever he just said to her. They're so in love.

Trey also gets off the bus and eye fucks the hell out of Gemma before scooping her up and joking that he's taking her around the corner for a little fun. When I look at him all I can think of is his pierced dick. I wonder if it gets caught in his zipper.

Kam winks at me and smiles. I know she's thinking the same thing.

We step onto the bus, and Quincy's eyes are immediately pinned on me. He looks gorgeous in his tuxedo. He's oozing sex right now and I hear him breathe, "Holy fuck."

QUINCY

The past week has been crazy. I caught Layton and Arizona doing things no brother should ever have to witness. After a long conversation with Arizona and days of ignoring Layton, he finally came to my place and sat down with me. He told me how strongly he feels for her. It was an impassioned speech. He's apparently completely fallen for her and sees her as his endgame. It's still a little hard for me to stomach, but I'm doing my best to let her make decisions for herself. I can only hope he doesn't break her heart. Admittedly, he's completely different with her and hasn't so much as looked at another woman, only having eyes for her.

Tonight is the *Sports Illustrated* reveal party. While a party to celebrate my sister and Layton being half-naked together in a magazine for millions of creepy guys to ogle isn't appealing to me, I know it's a big deal, and I'm trying to be supportive.

We're on a big party bus on the way to pick up the girls. We've all had a bit of whiskey and a fun time along the way.

The bus pulls up to Arizona and Ripley's building. We see the girls walking out and they all look stunning, but it's the redheaded temptress in a green dress that knocks the wind out of my lungs.

I've never seen her in anything like this. I have no words for how beautiful she is.

Fucking Layton sprints off the bus to slobber all over my sister, but I can't be bothered with him right now.

Ripley steps onto the bus and gives me a once-over in my tuxedo. Her neck flushes. As she passes by, she offers me a small smile. I think I curse in awe of her beauty. I can't help but stick out my fingers and discreetly brush them against hers. I catch her eyes flutter ever so subtly.

I expect her to pull her hand away, but she brushes her fingers against mine too. There's a heat between us tonight. Even more than usual.

The entire ride to New York is full of fun despite Layton having his hands all over Arizona. Their coming out party is not for the squeamish.

Why can't I be like Layton? Ripley is on the other side of the bus when I really want her on my lap like Arizona is with Layton. I want to touch her and smell her.

She makes eye contact with me, and I mouth, "You're so beautiful."

She gives me a small smile. I wish I could give her everything she deserves. I wish I was that man.

The ride up to New York City is a blur for me. My desperation to be normal mixed with my inability to do so has me on edge, but I feign a smile and join in on the laughter. It mostly consists of making fun of Cheetah. Apparently, he and Kam broke her waterbed the other night.

When we arrive, the rest of us make our way out of the bus, leaving Layton and Arizona behind to make their grand entrance.

Trey and Gemma pose for paparazzi photos together, and then the rest of us do so as a big group.

I whisper into Ripley's ear, "When we get inside, can I get a minute alone with you?"

She nods.

Everyone else heads to some sort of ballroom while Ripley and I discreetly make our way to an empty hallway.

She looks up at me through her smokey-looking, sexy eye makeup. "What do you want?"

"Just to tell you that you're magnificent. I've never seen anyone more beautiful than you are tonight."

She gives me a soft smile. "Thank you. You're very handsome too. Is...is that all you need?"

"I just couldn't let another minute go by without telling you. I might have to stand behind you all night just to hide my boner."

She giggles. "No problem."

A noise coming from around the corner breaks our concentration. I poke my head around to see an attractive older couple laughing. His hands are all over her. *All* over her. The woman smiles when she notices us.

I assume she's going to say something to me, but it's Ripley who has caught her attention. "Ripley St. James?"

Ripley graciously nods. "Yes."

The brunette beauty holds out her hand. "I'm Darian Knight. My daughter is Reagan Daulton. I'm such a big fan of yours."

Ripley smiles. "Thank you so much. What Reagan has created in such a short time is nothing short of a miracle."

Darian nods. "I'm so proud of her." She points to the tall, dark-haired man standing next to her. "This is my husband, Jackson. We've been to a lot of games. We're excited for the playoffs."

We all shake hands. Jackson eventually grabs Darian's hand. "We'll leave you to your conversation. Good luck to both of you in the playoffs. I need a minute of my wife's time."

He winks at me as he pulls her away with his hand on her ass.

Ripley and I smile at each other. She mumbles, "Jeez, I hope I'm still doing that at their age."

"You're more than welcome to do that tonight. With me."

She sighs as she shakes her head in exasperation. "Let's get back to the party."

A few minutes later, I'm staring at the big screen, which is now displaying the cover for the upcoming *Sports Illustrated* body image issue. I lean over and whisper to Layton, "It's a good thing I know about you two, because I'd certainly know now."

It's *very* provocative. Arizona is in lace panties and a barely there bra. Her legs are wrapped around him, and he's in his boxer briefs. He's got her pinned to the scoreboard with his head buried in her neck. She looks like she's mid-orgasm. A sight I'd prefer to have never seen.

I can't believe the cover is this explicit. Fucking hell. If every man in America wasn't already pining after my sister, they will be now.

CHAPTER EIGHTEEN

RIPLEY

M y chin all but drops to the floor. Without moving my eyes from the near-pornographic yet sexy as fuck cover image, I mumble to Arizona, "Holy shit. I think I just came from that picture."

I turn and look at her. I'm not sure she heard me. She's in shock. I think everyone is in shock except maybe Layton. He's smiling like—

Before I can finish my thought, Kam leans over and whispers, "Layton is smiling like his dick is being sucked right now."

I wordlessly nod. Exactly.

After a few minutes of madness, in which hordes of people congratulate them, Layton and Arizona disappear. Bailey approaches us with a very attractive older man next to her. He's tall and has a beard. He's got dark hair with a little gray mixed in.

Bailey smiles. "Ripley, Kamryn, this is Tanner

Montgomery. Tanner, this is Ripley St. James and my sister, Kamryn Hart."

I see Bailey mouth to Kam, "Behave."

Tanner smiles and shakes my hand.

"It's nice to meet you, Ripley. I've been watching you pitch all season. I have a budding softball player myself. She idolizes you." He looks around. "She idolizes all of you. The Anacondas are the best thing to ever happen to women's sports in Philly."

I return his smile. "Thank you. The support of this town has been amazing. I didn't have this in Houston. The Daultons have done an incredible job promoting us."

He gives me a knowing smirk. I know he's well aware of the Arizona and Layton PR relationship.

Kam takes his hand. "I believe we briefly met by the bar earlier, but it's nice to officially meet you, Daddy Tanner."

Bailey narrows her eyes at Kam. Tanner looks confused for a moment before collecting himself. "Oh, because Bailey babysits my daughter. I get it."

Kam nods. "Riiight. That's it."

I'm pretty sure Tanner catches on, but he continues playing it smoothly. "Bailey mentioned that you two have offers for endorsements. I'm more than happy to assist you with your contracts. Anything to support this team and its continued success."

Kam and I look at each other in shock. Tanner Montgomery is one of the biggest sports agents in the world. We're small potatoes for someone like him.

He continues. "I work with Trey DePaul, Cruz Gonzales, and obviously Layton and Arizona. They all speak highly of you."

Kam smiles. "That would be fan-fucking-tastic, Daddy Tanner."

He looks at me, and I nod. "Agreed. Thank you."

"Great. Let's strike while the iron is hot. Everyone in this town is talking about the upcoming playoffs. Why don't we set up a meeting right away?"

He turns to Bailey. "Are you positive that you're not interested in pursuing these opportunities?"

"A thousand percent. I'm not interested in being in front of the camera again."

I see a small smile find his lips as he gives her one quick nod. I wonder what that's about.

Looking back at us, he says, "I'll have my assistant contact you on Monday morning."

We agree, and he walks away.

Kam is practically bouncing up and down. "Rip! Holy fuck. Tanner *fucking* Montgomery is taking us on as clients. Are you so excited?"

Quincy interrupts, "Excited about what?" as he and Cheetah approach us.

Kam answers, "Tanner Montgomery just offered to represent Ripley and me for endorsements. I already have a skincare campaign coming up, and Rip has the lingerie shoot, but he thinks there could be more."

He snaps his head to me. "You're doing a lingerie shoot?"

"I have the offer. I haven't accepted it yet."

He licks his lips and discreetly adjusts himself. Wide-eyed, I look around to see if anyone else notices. They seem blissfully unaware.

Cheetah wiggles his eyebrows up and down. "You might need a bodyguard, Rip. Perhaps I should accompany you. I can hold your clothes for you while you get naked. Maybe be your oil boy to make sure you're at your shiny best."

I giggle. "I think I'll be okay. Thanks for the offer though."

He turns to Kam. "What about you, Kam bam? Need an emotional support snake?"

She shakes her head in disbelief. "Your cojones are both literally and figuratively enormous."

"Want to gargle with them again?"

The two of them go back and forth, but I lose interest in what they're saying. Quincy is looking me up and down, unashamedly undressing me with his eyes. He's trying to hide it, but I know his body like the back of my hand. He has an erection right now.

The fact that the mere thought of my lingerie shoot turns him on is turning me on. His eyes move down my body to the spot that has grown slick with need. I see a smile find his lips. Yep, he knows my body too.

Cheetah and Kam disappear to the bar, leaving Quincy and me alone. My back is to a wall, and he leans over me, asserting his dominance. With one hand over my head, he slowly runs the fingers of his other hand along the tops of my breasts.

I look around to see if anyone notices before I breathe, "What are you doing?"

"I'm going to fuck you in this dress tonight. It's going to be around your waist before the evening is through. My tongue will slide through your sweetness. My cock will run through your tightness." He moves his hand down to my ass, applying a little pressure along the center. "Maybe I'll take you here again. Another first that belonged to me."

I swallow hard. Holy fuck. He's never publicly done anything like this before. I'm not sure where it's coming from.

He gives me a deep inhale. "I can smell how wet I'm making you. I bet no other man has ever made you this wet."

Damn fucking straight they haven't.

He whispers in my ear, "And if anyone is going to be your

oil boy, it will be me. I know every inch of your body. I look forward to exploring it in a few hours."

He pushes off the wall. "Later, Shortcake. Don't go disappearing on me."

QUINCY

We're on the bus heading back to Philly. Gemma and Trey are full-blown making out in the corner. It's not remotely unusual for those two.

Layton is unashamedly groping my sister throughout the entire ride. I'm trying not to look, but I think his hand is up her dress.

I keep telling myself that she's twenty-eight, smart, and can more than handle herself. It's not easy.

Normally I would say something, but right now I'm focused on Ripley. Seeing her in that dress and knowing she'll be modeling lingerie has given me a never-ending boner. I will absolutely be going to that shoot, no matter what.

We've been glancing at each other all night. She's as turned on as I am. I can tell. She's flushed and has gnawed at that lower lip for over an hour. The sexual tension between us is about to reach a boiling point.

I'm sitting there with a drink. My legs are spread as I mentally stalk my prey, just counting the seconds until I can pounce.

I see her staring at me, rubbing her legs together. She's breathing at an increased rate. She's so beautiful I can barely manage myself.

I pull out my phone.

> Me: How wet is your pussy right now?

She pulls her phone from her purse and looks down at my message. She's still for a few beats, contemplating her response.

Finally, my phone pings.

> Ripley: It's a good thing this dress isn't a loaner.

I look up at her, and she's running that damn lip through her teeth.

I write back.

> Me: I can almost taste you. My Strawberry Shortcake. Where do you want to come first, my tongue or my cock? Both are happening.

Her phone pings and she looks down. She briefly closes her eyes before opening them. Staring at me, she mouths, "Tongue."

I nod at her. I'm so fucking hard right now. This bus couldn't possibly be going any slower.

We drop Trey and Gemma first. He carries her and sprints off the bus. They're followed by Ezra. In a surprise move, Bailey gets off the bus with Ezra to a sea of catcalls.

Cheetah and I look at each other in shock. We know he's been crushing on her, but she's shown no interest.

As we pull up to Layton's building, I offer to escort both Arizona and Ripley home, to which Kam lets out a laugh and says, "Did you even see the cover photo? Did you pick up on any tension at the party or on this bus, or are you simply deaf, dumb, and blind? If you don't realize that they're about to go fuck their brains out all night, you're an idiot."

I cringe at her words but Cheetah bursts into laughter. "Kam bam, you're one of a kind. Q, have another drink. Say good night to Layton and your sister. She's *definitely* not staying on this bus with us."

Arizona waves and gives me an antagonistic smile. "Have a good night. I know I will."

They exit the bus and walk toward his private elevator. I run my fingers through my hair. "Oh god, is he going to hurt her?"

Kam rolls her eyes. "He's the one who should be afraid, not her. My girl knows what she's doing."

She and Ripley both smile.

My chin drops. "That was an unnecessary statement."

Layton and Arizona step into his private elevator. As if on cue, she rips open his shirt as the doors of the elevator close.

I turn my head away and close my eyes. "I really wish I hadn't seen that."

Kam and Ripley giggle and high five. Cheetah is pinching his lips together, trying to hold in the laughter.

Cheetah and Kam begin talking about going out to a club tonight. I quickly whip out my phone again.

Me: They're going to ask us to join them. It's a hard no for you.

Ripley: Don't boss me around. I'll go if I want to.

> Me: Shortcake, your pussy has been screaming for me from the first second you saw me tonight. Don't pretend otherwise. If you want me to make you come like you know only I can, then tell them no. While you're at it, cancel your plans for the week. You won't be able to walk.

I can see her face flush again. She stares at me from across the bus. I nod toward her phone and mouth, "Do it."

Kam looks at her. "Rip, do you want to join us?" She turns. "You too, Quincy."

I shake my head. "I'm traumatized from the evening. I'm heading home. I want to pretend like everything I saw tonight was a nightmare and I'll wake up from it tomorrow."

She laughs and moves her eyes back to Ripley, waiting for an answer.

She's quiet for a few long beats before finally saying, "I'm beat. I think I'm headed to bed."

Kam sighs. "You're totally going home to that bizarrely long vibrator you have, aren't you?"

The amount of pleasure I take in knowing she has a long vibrator should be illegal. I have to bite the inside of my mouth to mask the grin threatening to break through.

Cheetah cough-laughs. "You like a long shlong, Rip?" He subtly turns to me and winks. We've shared a locker room all year. He knows how long I am.

Ripley simply smiles sexily. "What can I say, I need it deep."

I can't help but smirk. "Mariana Trench deep?"

She nods. "Exactly."

Cheetah and Kam instruct the driver to drop them at a club, leaving me and Ripley alone on the bus.

We're sitting on opposite sides. The sexual tension that's been building all night reaches new heights. My fingers physically twitch to touch her. My tongue wets my lips, anticipating her sweet taste being on them soon.

I slowly walk up to the bus driver and hand him a wad of hundred-dollar bills. I quietly instruct, "Keep your eyes on the road and drive around until you hear from me again."

He looks down at the huge payday and grins widely. "Yes, sir. No problem."

I turn around and stare at Ripley. She bites her bottom lip and squirms in her seat. She crooks her finger at me, letting me know it's go time.

I take a few long strides toward her and run my fingertips up her long legs until I'm just under her dress. Even through the material of her dress, I can see her nipples harden. "I'm going to fuck you from behind on this bus with that dress around your waist, as promised. Then I'm going to take you home, tear that dress off you, and fuck you all night in every hole."

"Quincy—"

Before she can finish her sentence, undoubtedly protesting some part of my plan, I slip my hand all the way under her dress and straight to her pussy. She gasps. Even through her panties, I can feel how wet she is. Applying pressure, I grit out, "Let's not play our normal cat-and-mouse game tonight, Shortcake. Your nipples are hard, and your pussy is begging for my cock. Don't even try to deny it."

I move her panties to the side and slide two fingers into her. *Deep* into her. I can already hear the sounds of her arousal, that's how turned on she is. "This pussy has wanted me all night, hasn't it?"

She stills for a moment before nodding.

"Have you been thinking of my cock inside you?"

She breaks eye contact but nods again.

Pulling my fingers out of her, I slip them into my mouth and mumble, "Hmm. So good. Strawberries. I'm going to feast on you tonight."

I begin to slide her dress up her legs. She stares at me with pure heat in her eyes, spreading her legs further and further as her dress moves up. The old Ripley would have been shy about this. The woman before me is anything but. She wants me and is making it known.

I drop to my knees between her legs and lick up her inner thigh. Her whole body immediately shakes. Responsive as ever.

I run my nose over her panties and inhale deeply. "So good."

I then grab them with my teeth and rip her panties from her body.

She gasps. "Oh my god."

I bark, "You'll be shouting that all night," as I bury my face between her legs again and lick through her one slow, long time.

She arches her back and moans, "More. Give me more."

"Put your feet on my shoulders and spread as wide as you can." She does as she's told while I simply rest my mouth on her mound for a second, taking her in. The taste of Ripley St. James is my drug of choice, and I'm addicted.

I love the short, trimmed red hair that surrounds her pussy. I think redheads have pinker pussies than the rest.

I purposefully haven't been with any others, wanting her to be the only one.

I wrap my lips around her swollen clit and suck hard. Her hips buck. "Ah, Quincy."

After a bit of nibbling, I flatten my tongue and methodically circle her clit the way I know she likes it. She enjoys me building her up this way before sliding my fingers deep into her. It doesn't prevent my fingers from teasing her entrance, which I start to do.

She squirms, begging for more. I mumble, "This cunt is so fucking wet. Tell me how much you want me inside you."

She pulls my hair as she whimpers, "Please. I need it."

I slowly slide two fingers into her hot pussy, feeling her walls immediately tighten around them. I'm desperate for that to be my cock again. The way she spasms around me when she comes is the greatest pleasure I've ever known. It usually sets me off right away.

I mumble, "That's right. Squeeze me when you come. Your pussy will be choking on my cock soon."

I look up in time to see her eyes roll back in her head. It's time to move in for the kill. Pushing my fingers in to the knuckles, then past the knuckles, I apply pressure to the spot I know as if it's my own.

She fists the end of the seat cushion to the point where I think she might tear it, arches her back, and screams out, "Oh god. Oh, Quincy. Fuck yes." I can feel her toes curl on my shoulders as she comes in my mouth. Her whole body convulses uncontrollably. I suck on her clit to draw it out for as long as I can.

When she eventually comes down from her high, I lift my head. "You're so fucking sexy when you come."

She looks spent, breathing out, "That was amazing."

I rub her thighs. "I know, baby. You came so perfectly for me. Such a good girl. Let's do it again. Let me see that plush ass of yours. I'm going to watch it bounce as I fuck you."

I see her eyes move toward the driver, who so far seems to be doing as instructed. I draw her attention back to me. "His eyes are on the road. Stay with me."

She smiles, looking satisfied, though she does look around. "I hope there aren't any cameras in here. Cheetah will probably come across it on one of his porn sites."

I chuckle but quickly scan the bus, thankfully not seeing any cameras.

Though still shaking a bit, she manages to flip over. Fucking hell, her ass is straight from heaven. I've missed it so much. I begin to massage it and then rub the precum leaking from my dick all over it. "Feel what this ass does to me." I then spank her hard, and she moans. She loves a little pain with her pleasure, even more so when it's around her neck.

I can't help but bury my face in her ass, licking all around her back entrance, squeezing her round ass with my hands.

"Oh god, Quincy. So good."

I quickly reach for my wallet and grab a condom.

As I sheath myself, she whines and wiggles her ass into me. "Get inside me."

With the tip of my cock just breaching her entrance, I reach around, grab her by the throat, and practically bark into her ear, "You'll get it when I'm ready to give it to you."

Her body starts shaking. For a moment I think I've hurt her, but that's not what's happening. She's coming again...from me grabbing her throat. Only my tip is inside her right now.

She's clawing at the seatback in front of her. Her movements seem involuntary and out of control. It's like she's having a seizure.

I stand there in shock for a moment. I've never seen her do this. Maybe it's just the aftershocks of the last orgasm. It was intense.

I reach down and run my fingers through her pussy. Nope, she's coming again. It's pouring out of her. Holy shit. I need to be inside there.

I quickly thrust my cock into her. She yells out, and I suck in a breath at what I feel. She's convulsing so damn hard, squeezing my dick. "Shit, Shortcake."

I push in all the way, which only serves to make her screams intensify. The poor fucking bus driver must think I'm murdering her.

Reaching down into the top of her dress, I grab her tit. She loves having her nipples pinched. I've got one hand on her throat and the other on her nipple.

She yells out, "Ah, Quincy."

And the orgasm rolls on. The longest I've ever seen.

I begin my thrusts inside her. Long and deep, just where she wants it.

She's got a vice grip on my cock, making it hard for me to focus, but I want to give her everything she needs and more.

I thrust and thrust, doing my best to drag this out for her and also to enjoy what her body is doing to mine.

Her juices are dripping down my balls and onto my pants. I happily welcome them.

She gains a little control and pushes back onto me. We're going at it with reckless abandon. Ripley and I have shared *a lot* of great sex throughout the years, but it has never measured up to this.

I pull out my hand on her nipple and grab her ass again. Despite my rapid thrusts, I manage to slide two fingers into her slickened back entrance. Deep inside her. She practically mewls when I do. Her grip on my cock is like nothing I've ever felt. I don't think her orgasm has ended. If anything, the intensity just went back up.

I feel my orgasm building all over my body. My balls feel so full they might explode. And when I come, it feels like they do. I roar into it. This woman fries my brain.

I fall over to the seat, completely out of breath and covered in sweat. She falls over, sitting in a similar position to me.

I look down. My load was so big that it's spilling out of the condom. She looks over at it and starts giggling. "Hell, Quincy, that was a whale load."

I let out a laugh. "How do you know how much semen whales produce?"

"It's like a few gallons every time, right? I know I read that somewhere. Kam probably made a joke about it."

"It's actually four hundred gallons every time a blue whale ejaculates."

Her mouth opens wide. "Holy shit. That's a lot of fluids. Poor pink whales."

We both smile at the fun post-coital banter we used to have. We're half-dressed in the back of a party bus, her dress is around her waist and my dick is hanging out of my pants, yet this still feels more right than anything ever has with any other woman.

I remove my condom, tuck myself in, and then help her pull her dress down.

I rub her re-covered thighs once her dress is back in place. "Come home with me. I'm not done with you."

She thinks for a moment. I assume she's going to say no, but she surprises me by asking, "Will you come home with me? We both know your sister won't be there tonight."

I wince. "Ugh. Don't remind me of what's going on over there."

Ripley wiggles her eyebrows. "For her sake, I hope it's half as good as what just happened in here."

I look up into her blue eyes. "You want me to stay with you tonight? All night?"

She nods. "I do."

AFTER ANOTHER ROUND of mind-blowing sex, we lay sated in her bed. We're front to front, staring at each other, running our fingertips aimlessly over one another's naked bodies, reacquainting ourselves.

The feelings we share are so strong. There's so much I want to say but know I shouldn't.

She looks up at me. "Penny for your thoughts."

"Just wishing we could have this all the time."

Her face falls as she looks down. "I suppose I gave up wishing for that a long time ago."

"What if I want this?"

"You want sex. You don't want me or marriage and kids. I won't give that up for you."

"We have the marriage."

"No, we have a paper marriage, not a real one. Look at

the way Layton treats your sister. The way he looks at her. He's not embarrassed—"

"I'm not embarrassed. That has nothing to do with it. Stop saying that."

"Whatever. You won't love me the way I want to be loved. We have different visions of our future. I've done my best to accept it. I'm not interested in having the same conversation over and over." She toggles her hand between us. "But this physical connection won't go away. That's why I need to distance myself from you. As long as I'm around you, I'll never truly move on. I'm too drawn to you. You have too much power over me."

"Maybe I want to try being together."

She's quiet for a moment. "Would we tell people?"

"Why don't we wait and see—"

"No."

I sigh. "Give it a chance."

"Do you want to have kids one day?"

I tighten my jaw. "No. Never. That's a hard line for me."

"There you have it. Having children is a hard line for me. Per always, we're at an impasse." She nuzzles her head into my chest. "Let's just enjoy these last moments we have together. Our seasons will be over in a couple of weeks, and then I'm requesting a trade."

She says it so matter-of-factly. As if my heart isn't breaking. She's completely resigned on this issue.

I do the only thing I can right now. I hold her close and wish things were different.

I WAKE in the morning temporarily feeling better than I have in years. It's been so long since I woke up with her in my arms. My eyes aren't even open, but her scent envelops me in happiness.

The front of my naked body is pressed to the back of hers. My hands are on her tits, my hard cock pressed against her ass.

And then I remember our conversation before we fell asleep. She's leaving. She's giving up on us. On me.

Our time together has an expiration date, and that day is coming soon.

I don't know what time it is, but I know she must have to get going, and I have to get out of here before Arizona comes home. But I need her one more time.

She's sound asleep, likely exhausted from the long evening we had. We went at it like we didn't know if we'd ever get to do it again. I know we were both thinking that.

I roll her to her back and look at her naked body. How could she ever have any doubts? She's all woman, in every way possible. Sheer perfection.

I reach my head down and suck her nipple into my mouth. She begins to stir when I hear a female voice getting louder by the second. "Rip, I need to talk to—"

I turn my head in time to see Bailey enter the door. She gasps and covers her mouth. "Holy Red Wedding! What the fudge is this?"

Ripley's eyes startle open. I quickly cover her with the sheet.

Bailey lets out a nervous laugh. "I've...umm...seen her naked a thousand times." She toggles her finger between us. "How long has this been going on? Man, what a plot twist this is. Kam was right. She's gone on and on about how you two were fucking on the down low. I told her she was nuts. Damn it. I hate it when she's right."

Ripley and I look at each other and then her shoulders fall as she turns back to Bailey. "It was just a one-time thing. It's...meaningless. Purely physical. Keep it between us, please. There's no reason to make a whole thing of it. We drank too much, that's all. It will *never* happen again."

That cut deep, though what else should I expect?

Bailey looks skeptical but nods, nonetheless. "O...kay. I wanted to talk to you before we head out to the ballpark. Just text me when you get a minute, please."

Ripley has concern written all over her beautiful face. "Are you okay, Bails? Is this about you leaving with Ezra last night?"

Bailey's eyes widen, and she motions her head toward me. "Can we discuss this later?"

"Sure." Ripley toggles her finger between the two of us. "And can you please keep this quiet?"

Bailey gives her a small smile and replies, "Of course," before she turns and leaves.

When I hear the front door close, I turn to Ripley. "Do you think she's truly into Ezra? I never saw anything before last night."

"Honestly? I think she's into Tanner. I have no idea about last night. I'm sure she was here to talk to me about it."

"Bailey is sleeping with Tanner Montgomery? Doesn't she nanny for his kid? Isn't he way older?"

"Yes, she nannies. Yes, he's way older. I don't know if they're sleeping together. Kam thinks she is, but I'm not sure. It might just be a crush." She pats my chest. "You should get going."

"I will. Thanks for last night. I—"

She holds up her hand. "Don't. Don't say anything that will ruin this. Maybe we both needed this grand finale. I know I sound like a broken record, but it can't happen again. I don't know what you're looking for, Quincy, but I truly hope you find it one day. I hope you overcome whatever it is you're battling and that you find someone who gives you whatever it is that you need." Her eyes tear. "I know it's not me."

I want to tell her that she's the only one who can give me what I need, but I don't because I can't give her what she needs. I have to try to let her go. It's time.

CHAPTER NINETEEN

RIPLEY

I suppose I knew this moment was coming. I prayed to delay it, but it's always been inevitable. It's a force of nature that I'm powerless to stop.

It's time for a June St. James visit.

I love my mom, but she's a handful and lacks a filter. All my friends get a kick out of her, but it's not always easy having a mother like her. She and Kam together are like a nuclear explosion. One time in college, they both ended up dancing topless on a bar. That isn't even one of the top ten most humiliating moments with my mother.

She's taking an Uber from the airport to my apartment. At the expected time, there's a knock at our door. I see Arizona smile. She sings out, "It's tiiiiiiiime."

I take a breath. "Here we go. Let the madness begin."

I open the door to see my exquisite mother not looking like she just traveled all the way across the country. She looks like

Nicole Kidman when she's walking the red carpet. Perfection. People have been saying that for years.

I smile. "Welcome to Philly, Mom."

She immediately drops her bags on the ground and envelops me in a big hug. "I've missed you. You look stunning. Philly agrees with you."

"Thanks, Mom. You look great, as always." I pull away. "Come in."

I close the door as she walks in and notices Arizona, immediately embracing her. "Ahh. I'm so happy you two are together again. It warms my heart." Mom steps back. "But you're not framing her rise ball like I taught you. Lift your body a drop more to create the illusion that it's landing in the middle of your chest."

Arizona smiles widely. "Yes, Coach June. Anything for you."

I playfully swat her arm. "Mom, leave her alone. She's the best player in the league."

Mom waves her hand dismissively. "Nonsense. You're both stars. Best battery in the history of the game. Reunited just in time to train for the Olympics. I'm so proud of you both."

Just then, our door flies open, and Kam is standing there with a huge smile. She jumps up and down with her hands in the air. "Mama June! Mama June!"

Mom laughs and holds her arms open. "Honey Boo Boo!"

They both laugh at the pop culture reference they've been using for a decade and hug.

Kam looks her up and down. "Fucking hell, June, I hope I'm half as hot as you when I grow up."

Mom shakes her head. "You don't have to worry...you'll never grow up."

Kam laughs. "That's true."

Mom looks behind her at the door. "Where's Chickadee?"

Kam raises an eyebrow. "Allegedly babysitting, but I think she's really just fucking the father. He's closer to your age than ours."

"Is he hot?"

Kam nods. "Yep."

"Good for Bailey." She turns to me. "I hope you're getting laid too."

Kam starts giggling, but I simply roll my eyes.

Arizona answers, "I think she is, but she won't talk about it."

Mom lifts an eyebrow. "Interesting." She gives me a look suggesting we'll discuss this later. "Where should I put my bags?"

Arizona answers, "In my room. I'll stay at my boyfriend's place while you're visiting. I put fresh sheets on for you this morning."

Mom smirks. "Thank you. Ah, yes, your boyfriend. I've seen your photos all over with that hunk of man meat. I've pinched the princess to his handsome face on more than one occasion."

Kam and Arizona start laughing hysterically. I shake my head. "You've been here for less than three minutes and you're already discussing your masturbation habits. That's a record, even for you, Mom."

She straightens her shoulders. "I have a rep to protect."

I grab one of her bags. "Let's get you settled."

Arizona kisses Mom's cheek. "It's good to have you here, June. I'm going to drop my stuff at Layton's. I'll see you guys at the ballpark."

We're all heading to a Cougars game tonight.

Kam shakes her head. "What she's really doing is blowing him before his game. That seems to be their M.O."

Arizona simply winks as she leaves, followed shortly thereafter by Kam, leaving Mom and me alone.

After she gets settled in, we sit on the sofa. She rubs my leg. "Tell me what's going on with you."

I shrug. "Same old. Obviously, the team is doing great."

"You guys will win the whole thing, I have no doubt. You have a much better team behind you than you did in Houston."

I nod. "I definitely do. There's a comfort in throwing to Arizona and in having my college teammates at shortstop and second base."

"It shows in your pitching. And what about your love life?"

"Not much to report."

"You haven't started up with Quincy again, have you?"

She knows everything that went on in Houston besides the marriage. She assumed the team took care of my immigration status, and I've never corrected her.

I'm quiet.

"That's why Arizona knows you're getting laid but knows nothing else."

I blow out a breath. "I've tried to stay away—"

"But you can't because you're in love with him. You always have been."

I can only nod at the truth of her statement. Tears sting my eyes. "I wish I wasn't."

"How does he feel?"

"That's the thing. He's always pursuing me and being crazy possessive. He even interrupted a date I was on a few weeks ago. Literally pulled the guy away from me and scared him off."

"If you both love each other, why can't you be together?"

"I think he's embarrassed of me."

She shakes her head. "That's nonsense. You're beautiful,

smart, talented, and kind. Just plain perfect. Any man would be lucky to have you. I can't imagine Quincy Abbott has ever said otherwise to you."

I sigh. "He hasn't, but we've always been a secret. He won't love me in public."

"Do you call him out on it?"

"I have. It's all very circular and confusing. In the end, we always get back to the fact that we want different things in life. I eventually want to get married and have kids. He wants neither."

"Ever?"

"That's what he says."

She squeezes my hand. "I don't want you to end up like me, baby. Brokenhearted and never over the man she loved."

I suck in a breath. She's never once mentioned anything like this to me.

My hands start trembling. "Was...was it my father?"

Tears start to fill her eyes before she slowly nods. There's something so impactful about knowing that she loved him. I've always assumed he was another nameless bedfellow. A random Barney. Knowing there was at least some amount of love is a burden off my shoulders that I didn't know ever existed until it was lifted.

"Will you tell me more about him? Please?"

She covers her mouth. "I don't know if I can."

"But I was conceived with love?"

She smiles as if she's remembering. "Yes, baby. So much damn love that I've never truly gotten over him, and it's been nearly thirty years."

"He didn't want me?"

"It wasn't like that. It was...complicated...tragic."

She looks like she wants to say more but instead jumps up and runs into the bathroom sobbing loudly.

I would give anything to know about my father and one day maybe even meet him. To understand why he isn't in my life. But this was a big first step for her. I don't want to push. Perhaps I'll gradually get more information one day soon.

"Fucking hell, the Cougars' coach is sexy as sin. Where have they been hiding him?"

My mother is practically drooling over Dutton Steel. I suppose she's right. He's sexy in an older man kind of way. He looks like Gabe Kapler but significantly more muscular and with much more hair.

Kam elbows Bailey. "He's your type, Bails. He's got old, saggy balls."

Bailey rolls her eyes. "Cut it out. No matter how old, they'd never be as saggy as Cheetah's, and he's only like thirty-one. That guy fricking swallowed two beach balls and they settled just south of his giant ding dong."

Mom raises an eyebrow and asks, "And you've all seen Cheetah's balls?"

We all giggle and nod. I confirm, "We have. It's a long story."

Mom smirks. "I've got one for you, ladies. Why are gingers' balls the most patriotic of them all?"

The four of us shrug.

"They're red, white, and blue."

We all burst out laughing, unable to control ourselves until the game begins and we start to get stares.

Quincy is on the mound for their first playoff game. I know this is his first career playoff start. His team in Houston never made it this far. Being the game-one starter is a big deal. A lot of faith is being put in him. He deserves this. It's been a long time coming.

I swear Layton spends half the game looking at Arizona. It's a good thing because Quincy has been doing his fair share of looking my way.

Mom notices. She leans over and whispers, "He doesn't look like a man who isn't interested. How long have you two been going at it?"

I mentally run the past few weeks in my mind until it occurs to me. We've had sex twice in the past month. Well, more than twice, but it was two occasions. The night he crashed my date was a few weeks before that. I haven't gotten my period since before that date. Oh my god.

MY FREAKOUT IS MOMENTARILY PUT on hold by the fact that Quincy throws a no-hit shutout. It's a rarity in the sport, especially in the playoffs. It's a huge accomplishment.

We're on the field after the game, and Quincy is beaming. I'm so happy to see him like this. All of the newscasters are interviewing him. It's his moment in the sun. He deserves it.

He turns his head and notices me. Giving me a huge smile, he motions for me to come to him. I'm a little surprised, but I walk over.

He throws his arm around me. The newscaster looks a bit shocked. She nods toward me. "Ripley St. James. Did...umm... you enjoy the game?"

I smile. "Of course I did. Quincy threw the best game of his career. I'm so happy for him."

"Oh, are you two...friends?"

Before I can answer, Quincy does. "She's been Arizona's

best friend since they were little kids. Of course we're friends. She was like a second sister to me growing up."

The newscaster nods in realization. I hold back the tears. That fucking hurt. For the briefest of moments, I foolishly thought he was going to admit to something more.

He continues, "I can't wait for their playoffs to start tomorrow. Ripley is the best pitcher in the league. In the world. They're going to win the whole thing. I'm stoked we're off tomorrow so we can go to the game."

I fake smile at the compliment before turning to see Layton pawing at Arizona, loving her publicly without any shame. My heart breaks just a little more knowing I'll never have that with Quincy.

The reporter walks away, and he looks down at me. "Are you okay?"

I swallow back my tears and give a small smile. "I'm fine."

He looks over my head and chuckles. "Your mom is flirting with Dutton Steel."

I turn and see that he's right. Oh hell.

She eventually walks over to us and kisses Quincy on the cheek. "Congratulations. You threw a gem."

He grins. "Thank you, June. It felt great."

She looks at me with a big smile. "I met Dutton. What a doll. I told him about that place Screwballs you mentioned we're going to. He's planning to join us."

I muster yet another fake smile knowing how my mother will shamelessly flirt all night. "Sounds good."

WE ALL WALK into Screwballs together to a loud sea of cheers. The guys are all on cloud nine.

Technically Cheetah was last to walk in and Layton immediately calls him out on it.

Mom leans over. "They still play that silly game?"

I nod. "Yep. All the time."

Cheetah smiles. "I've been waiting to bust this one out. The names of the states utilize twenty-five of the twenty-six letters in the alphabet. Anyone care to guess which poor letter was left out?"

I can see everyone running the states through their minds. After a few silent moments, Cheetah happily says, "I'll give you a hint. He threw the first no-hitter in Cougars playoff history tonight."

We all smile and universally shout, "Q!"

Cheetah nods just as our pitchers of beer arrive. Once we all pour our beers, we hold them up. Cheetah toasts, "To Long Quail Quincy for making history."

Quincy spits out his beer at that name.

Mom asks, "What's with the nickname?"

Cheetah raises an eyebrow. "L.Q. squared? That fucker has the longest quail I've ever seen. I hope he finds a girl who likes it deep."

It takes everything I have not to spit out my own beer. Mom notices and smirks.

Cheetah smiles. "Some women need it like a wide receiver." He side-eyes me as he says it.

Kam narrows her eyes in contemplation. "How is that?"

"Long and deep."

Mom bursts out laughing. "You're funny, Cheetah. I like you."

He winks at her. "And I like you, June."

Dutton places his arm around Mom and looks at her with pure heat. "I like you too, June."

She smiles at him. Arizona looks at me and silently shakes

in laughter. She knows my mom is about to sleep with the famous Dutton Steel. She mouths, "Barney."

I nod.

Everyone is chatting when Layton's phone starts buzzing on the table. He glances down at it and then raises an eyebrow while looking at Cheetah. "Dude, you're calling me right now."

He pulls his phone out of his front pocket. "Ah, shit. Sorry. I keep doing that."

Layton asks, "What? Butt dialing?"

Cheetah smiles. "No, dick dialing."

Layton pinches his eyebrows together. "What's that?"

"When your dick is so big that it dials people from your pocket."

Mom leans over to Kam while staring at Cheetah. "You've tapped that, right?"

Kam smiles. "I sure have."

"Good girl."

Yep, June St. James is in the house.

CHAPTER TWENTY

QUINCY

I'm so amped up over my performance tonight. I appreciate everyone wanting to celebrate, but all I really want to do is get lost in Ripley's body. I tried to proposition her, but she reminded me that we've already had our finale and that her mom is staying with her.

It's nearly one in the morning when everyone leaves to go home. After an hour of tossing and turning, I head over to Ripley's. I know Arizona is staying at Layton's so June can use her bedroom. There's no risk of her being there.

I have a spare key and quietly let myself in. I tiptoe into her bedroom and see her fast asleep, spread out on top of her blankets. The best part? She's wearing my jersey. My heart just about explodes seeing her like that.

As I get closer, I see a file and a bunch of papers laid out over her like she was reading them before falling asleep. I start to clean them up for her when my eye catches a few key phrases. *Dissolution of Marriage* being the biggest and boldest at the top. Looking closer, I realize they're divorce papers with both our names on them.

Why does it fucking hurt so much? I shouldn't care, but I do. On some level, I always knew this was inevitable.

I initially gather the papers and place them on her night table. Then I jam them under several magazines, hoping she'll forget about them. After a few seconds of thought, I decide it's best to rip them up and place the evidence in my pocket for disposal. Yep, that should do the trick.

I then look back at Ripley with her bare, long legs on display. Her perfect profile. Her porcelain skin. A sense of sadness runs through me realizing that one day I'm going to have to watch her walk down the aisle to another man. I look at her covered stomach. One day another man's child will grow inside her. The pain of both of those thoughts is almost too much to bear.

Time is running out for us. She's going to leave town and be out of my life again. This time, I know it will be for good.

For the briefest of moments, I let my mind travel to somewhere I've never once let it go. Could I ever be the man she deserves? Could I ever give her what she needs?

I immediately flashback to my own childhood. The feelings of abandonment. Feeling like I didn't matter. Never seeing a parent in the audience of a school assembly. Never having a parent come to a school art show. Never having a parent at my games. The soul-crushing feeling of loneliness. I vowed to do my best as a brother so Arizona would never feel half of what I felt. I know I succeeded. She wants *normal* things in life. Her pain doesn't run deep like mine. If I've done nothing else good, shielding and practically raising Arizona is the one thing I've done right.

The only thing I know for sure right now is that I need to cherish every moment with Ripley, for each one could be our last. I know I'm on borrowed time with her.

I strip down to my boxers and slip into the bed. I can't help but stare at her beauty. Her hair is wild, and her cherry-red lips seem kiss swollen. I have a moment of panic and look around, but I know no one is here. That's how they get in her sleep. I've never been more familiar with a woman's body than I am with hers.

Not able to help myself, I lean over and start to kiss her. My tongue moves into her mouth before she begins to stir.

Her body stiffens in shock until she realizes what's happening. Once she does, she relaxes, threads her fingers through my hair, and moans into my mouth as she kisses me back.

I pull her body flush to mine and grab her leg over my hip. We kiss and kiss with no sense of urgency. Our familiar tastes and tongues weave in practiced unison. I crave this connection with her. We're two pieces of a puzzle that fit so perfectly together. Physically. Emotionally, I'm the broken round knob on one of those pieces, meaning I'll never fit in with the rest.

After a few minutes, she breaks the kiss and breathlessly whispers, "Hi."

I whisper back, "Hi. I'm sorry, but I needed to be with you tonight. My mind is on overdrive, and I need to feel you."

"We can't—"

"It's not about that. I won't lie and say I don't want

it, I do, but what I want more right now is to be with you after the best night of my life. To share it with you." I sink my nose into her neck. "Let me breathe you in. For one night, let me be close to you. Let me hold you. I promise to behave."

I see her internal battle. Her heart and head want two different things. Eventually she nods. "You have to leave early."

"I know. My alarm is set."

"And you need to keep it in your pants."

"I know."

She lets out a breath as she relaxes into me. Our bodies are still pressed together. I see a small smile form on her lips. "Tonight was incredible. *You* were incredible. I'm so proud of you."

"I've heard other players talk about the adrenaline of the playoffs, but I don't think I ever understood it until tonight. It's a high I've never imagined possible."

She aimlessly runs her fingers through my hair. "I'm glad I was there to see it."

I rub her bare hip. "Me too." I continue staring into her eyes. "I...umm...got the plans back for the house this week."

"And?"

"They're so perfect. Jade is brilliant. I can't wait to break ground. Collin said he knows people in the permitting office and can probably start within a few weeks. He wants to get the shell up before winter hits."

"Wow. You're all in."

"I am. No place has ever felt more like home."

I don't just mean Philly, but I don't say that.

"What about you, Shortcake? Where do you see yourself in five years?"

She shrugs. "I'm not sure. I really like this town, but..." she swallows hard, "you know why I can't stay. I imagine Arizona will live here though. That will be nice for you."

"What makes you say that?"

She rolls her eyes. "They're in love, Quincy. Real, soulmate, storybook love. She's going to marry him one day. You must realize that."

I sigh. I suppose she's right.

She has a dreamy look on her face. "He loves her like every woman in the world wants to be loved. You should be happy for her. For him too."

"How does every woman want to be loved?"

Without any hesitation, she answers, "Fully. Wholeheartedly. Without shame. Like nothing and no one else matters."

I'm contemplating her words when we hear female moans from the other room. I initially wince thinking it's Arizona until I remember June is in there.

Ripley mouths, "What the hell?"

And then we hear a deep male voice. "Oh fuck, June. That's so good."

I smile while trying to contain my laughter. "That's Dutton."

Ripley simply shakes her head. "Leave it to my mother to be in town for less than twelve hours and have the hottest man in her age bracket in her bed."

I pinch my eyebrows together. "Dutton is hot?"

She bites her lip and mock shivers. "Hell yes."

"I don't think he dates much. His wife died a long time ago, but he still loves her and is attached."

She shrugs. "June St. James, everyone. She could make The Pope visit a whore house."

I chuckle before moving a stray strand of hair from her face. "Are you nervous about your game?"

She shakes her head. "Not really. I'm not a nervous person. I play better when I'm relaxed so I try not to allow myself to get too worked up."

"I wish I was like that. I make myself crazy."

"I know you do. You're having the best season of your career. Try to enjoy it. Just a little bit."

"I'm enjoying being here with you."

"We shine in the darkness, you and me."

I know that's a loaded statement. I'm too much of a chickenshit to respond.

We lay in bed and talk for hours about nothing and everything. It's probably the most intimate night of my life.

At some point, I hear her breathing even out. She's fast asleep, nuzzled into my chest.

I fight sleep, not wanting to let go of this moment with her in my arms, but eventually, it finds me.

THE NEXT NIGHT, we're all at the ballpark watching the Anacondas game. Cheetah is up to his usual antics, dancing for the cameras. June is sitting between me and Layton.

She crosses her arms as she eyes him. "You know, Arizona is like a second daughter to me. What are your intentions with her?"

Layton smirks as he looks her in the eyes, and, without an ounce of hesitation, declares, "To love her, to marry her, to have children with her, to grow old with her."

I think back to what Ripley said to me last night about the way he loves my sister. She wasn't wrong. Just a few months ago, Layton was sleeping around with no intention of playing into this notion of happily ever after, yet here we are, just a relatively short time later, and he wears his heart right there on his sleeve. He practically lives for Arizona at this point and doesn't care who knows about it.

June slowly nods. "I can live with that answer. Just don't fuck it up."

He chuckles. "I won't. I promise."

She turns to me and whispers, so no one else can hear, "Speaking of fuckups, what about you and my daughter?"

I didn't know June was aware of anything between Ripley and me. Not having any clue how much she knows, I try to play it cool and respond, "What do you mean?"

"You know damn well what I mean. You popped her cherry all those years ago and you've been dragging her along ever since. She loves you. She always has. If you don't feel the same, you need to let her go. I won't let her waste her life pining after a man who's unattainable."

"You don't know anything about us. Not to be a dick, but I'm fucking thirty-three, June. I don't owe you an explanation."

"I don't care how old you are. You've been jerking my daughter around for over a decade. Shit or get off the pot, Quincy. At a minimum, you must care about her as a person. If you're not looking to see this through, cut her loose. It's not fair to her otherwise."

I briefly close my eyes, tormented by her words.

She gives me a look of surprise. "You *do* love her. I didn't think you did, but I was wrong. It's written all over your face."

Tightening my jaw, I spit out, "I never said that."

"I know you don't want a family and that's the biggest obstacle. I imagine you know nothing of my past, few people do, but I won't see her suffer the same fate. A lifetime of loneliness. Do you want her to end up like me? Hopping from man to man because I can't have the one I truly want. Closing my heart off to the possibility of love so I never have to feel the pain I once felt. Cut her loose. It's time. If you truly love her, give her a fighting chance to find what she's looking for while she's still young."

"I...I can't seem to let go."

"You're a selfish prick. You don't deserve her."

Truer words have never been spoken.

CHAPTER TWENTY-ONE

RIPLEY

After two grueling playoff matchups, the Anacondas have advanced to the championship series against the team from Miami. The Cougars are in the World Series. Philly is electric with excitement. There's already talk about joint victory parades and parties. I hope both teams are able to deliver.

The Cougars play a home game tonight, but we're down in Miami. We're tied at two games apiece in the best-of-five series. Tonight decides everything.

We're up by one run going into the last inning. We secured the first two outs quickly, one via strikeout and one on an amazing diving play by Bailey. I don't have my best stuff tonight. I'm distracted. I'm more than several weeks late for my period at this point, and I'm freaking out. I know I should take a test, but I can't seem to muster up the courage to do it. Uncertainty is better than what I imagine will be my reality.

I walk the next batter, which is fairly unusual for me. Arizona calls a timeout. She walks to the mound. "Everything good? Your rise stopped rising and your curve stopped curving two batters ago."

I sigh. "I know. I feel a little off."

"Are you okay, Rip? You don't seem yourself, and I don't mean the way you're pitching."

"I'm good. I'll get it together."

"It's only the final out in the championship game. Might be a good time to focus."

It's unusual for there to be tension between Arizona and me. I know she's just trying to push me to be my best though. I'd do the same for her.

Just then Coach Billie yells out, "Pound the zone, Ripley!"

Our tension immediately breaks. Arizona smiles at me and mouths, "Pound the zone."

I giggle. "I prefer to be pounded, but I'm on it."

She nods. "Let's finish this shit and go party our asses off. We're in the party capital of the world."

I punch the inside of my glove with authority. "We've got this."

She nods, heads back to home plate, and calls for a drop curve. I throw it dead-on accurate, and Arizona frames it nicely for strike one. Our dugout is going nuts, knowing we're one out away from paydirt. We can all smell victory.

She signals for a rise ball, and I throw it, but the batter doesn't bite, and it's called a ball. Arizona gives me the sign to throw the same pitch again. This time the batter swings and misses for strike two.

My adrenaline is kicked into high gear now. One more strike, and the championship is ours.

Arizona calls for a changeup. I wind up, throw the ball, and the batter swings. She's way ahead of it. She makes minimal contact off the end of her bat and the ball is slowly rolling toward me.

Shit.

I'm a good pitcher. A great pitcher. But I'm not exactly swift of foot. This batter is fast. She's probably going to beat it out for a hit.

But then, out of nowhere, Arizona appears, scoops the ball, turns her body, and fires a bullet to first base.

The next thirty seconds play out in slow motion.

It's a bang-bang play. All eyes turn to the umpire. After a brief moment of hesitation, he punches his fist, signaling the final out.

Arizona's eyes find mine. We both break into huge smiles as she runs and then jumps into my waiting arms, wrapping her legs around me. And then twenty teammates pile on top of us in celebration, causing us to fall to the ground.

Everyone is screaming and crying tears of pure joy.

I'm practically floating in the clouds. My first league championship, and I was able to do it with my best friends. It's such a bummer Quincy and Layton couldn't be here. I'm pretty sure they're playing this on the big screen in the Cougars' stadium. I imagine they're celebrating in their own way.

The next hour is nuts with the trophy presentation and champagne all over. Just in case I'm pregnant, I decide not to drink any. No one notices. We're all pouring it all over each other anyway.

Everyone is talking about partying on South Beach ahead of our morning flight back to Philly. When I get out of the shower, Arizona appears in tears.

I run over to her. "What's wrong?"

She swallows. "It's Layton. There was a collision at home plate tonight. It sounds like he broke his leg. He's in surgery right now."

I gasp. "Oh my god."

She nods. "Reagan Daulton is flying home in her private jet in an hour. I'm going with her. Sorry to miss the celebration."

"Don't worry about it. Go be with him. I'll get all your stuff from the hotel. We'll come by the hospital tomorrow when we get home."

She nods as I help her gather her belongings and see her off.

All I can think of right now is Quincy. This will devastate him. Despite Layton's relationship with Arizona, I've never seen Quincy this close with a teammate. I know Layton's pain will be his pain too. He's going to be emotional.

QUINCY

The mood in the locker room is somber. Layton's injury was horrific to watch. And they fucking kept playing it over and over again on the big screen. In slow motion. His leg snapping in half will haunt my nightmares for life.

No one is speaking the words, but we all know the reality. He'll never play again. Layton Lancaster, a man who will one day be in the Hall of Fame, a man who we all look up to, had his career cut short tonight. My heart is breaking for him.

We ended up losing the game, leaving us one away from elimination. I'll be pitching when we play again in

two days. For now, I'm headed to the hospital with most of the guys on the team.

As soon as I pull out my phone from my locker, I see a text from Ripley.

> Ripley: Are you okay?

> Me: Not really. It was bad. We're headed to the hospital now. Congrats to you guys. They played the last out on the big screen. Everyone went crazy. I'm so proud of you.

> Ripley: Thanks. Arizona is flying home with Reagan right now. I'll be home tomorrow.

I wish more than anything that she was here. I need her.

> Me: Okay. See you then. Enjoy your celebration.

A few hours later, Layton is still unconscious from his surgery. Most of our teammates left, vowing to come back in the morning when he's awake. It's just Cheetah, Trey, Ezra, Tanner, and me. We're all half asleep in Layton's room when Arizona comes bursting through the door.

Tears immediately drip down her cheeks. I run to her and practically catch her before she collapses.

"He's going to be fine, Z. He's strong. The surgery went well."

She sobs, "He'll never play again."

"And if he doesn't, he'll be okay. He's had a long Hall of Fame career. He's one of the best to have ever played the game."

She sniffles as she echoes my earlier sentiment. "My heart breaks for him."

I look into her eyes. I can see the pain in her.

"You truly love him, don't you?"

She stares into my eyes. "More than anything in this world."

The other guys briefly wake up. She kisses each on the cheek. When she gets to Cheetah, he sleepily smiles and mumbles, "Can I have an Australian kiss?"

She crosses her arms. "What's an Australian kiss?"

He smiles. "It's like a French kiss but down under."

She giggles. I punch him in the arm, but not too hard since I know he's just trying to make her feel better.

We hang around for a few hours until he wakes up. After a brief freak out by him over the fact that Arizona is missing her team's celebration, all of us except Arizona are kicked out.

I make my way home in the middle of the night feeling completely depressed about Layton and with an overwhelming feeling of loneliness.

When I step off the elevator, my breath catches. Ripley is sitting on the ground in front of my door with her head tilted at an awkward angle, fast asleep.

I get choked up as my eyes fill with tears. She came back early for me. How many times has this woman known what I needed before I did? One of the million reasons I don't deserve her.

I walk toward my door and notice a blanket covering her. A blanket I recognize from Blanche's couch. I also notice an empty plate of cookies. I smile, realizing that Blanche took care of her.

She blinks her eyes open, sleepily smiles, and breathes, "You're finally home."

I slide down my door, so I'm seated next to her. "I am. I just left the hospital. What are you doing here? You should be partying with your teammates in Miami."

She leans her head on my shoulder. "I figured you'd be emotional. Shortly after Arizona left for the airport, I did too. I needed to make sure you were okay."

I press my lips to her head, taking in her scent. "I'm better now that you're here."

Without any conversation, we both move our hands and intertwine our fingers.

She soothingly rubs her thumb over mine. "How's Layton?"

I blow out a breath. "He's living the nightmare of every ballplayer. Arizona seems to have a soothing influence over him though."

"How was she?"

"Upset when she arrived, but she got it together for him by the time he woke up. I'm starving. Are you hungry?"

She shrugs. "I suppose."

I stand and pull her up. "Come on. I'll feed you."

I grab her suitcase, and we walk inside straight to my kitchen. I open my refrigerator and she giggles at its contents. "Condiments, beer, pickles, and fresh strawberries? Tell me you're a bachelor without telling me you're a bachelor. Except for the fresh strawberries. That's odd."

"I always have fresh strawberries. They remind me of you."

I lift her onto the kitchen island. She screeches when I do. "Stop. You have to pitch in two days. You'll pull a muscle."

I roll my eyes as I retrieve the bowl of strawberries

and situate myself between her legs. I grab a berry and start tracing her lips with it.

"Taste it. There's an Amish farmer's market a few blocks away. They have the best strawberries I've ever had in my life. I go there every week. And you know I cook, we've just been on the road and busy with the playoffs, so I haven't lately."

Her pink tongue slides out and licks around her lips. "Umm. Good."

"That's what you taste like to me." I feed it into her mouth. "Take a bite."

She does, and a little juice dribbles down her chin. I bend forward and slowly lick it off.

"Yum. Definitely what you taste like."

I run my hands up her thighs and move my lips slowly toward hers in case she wants to stop me. But she doesn't.

She threads her fingers through my hair and meets me halfway. Just before our lips meet, she breathes, "Will this feeling ever go away?"

I don't know if it means she wants it to go away or doesn't want it to go away. I'm not sure how I feel about it either, though June's words have been weighing heavy on me. For now, in this moment, I need her, and I think she needs me too.

Our lips meet. Like every time they do, it's a reminder of how incredible it feels to intimately connect with her like this. How soothing it is for me.

My late-night visit with her a few weeks ago was limited to kissing. I don't know if she'll allow more now, but she quickly answers that question, whispering, "Take what you need." It's barely audible, but I'm pretty sure she adds, "One last time."

"What I need is to devour every inch of you."

She squirms on the island as she nods her head. I don't need to touch her to know she wants me every bit as much as I want her.

I make quick work of her shirt and bra, taking in her heavy tits. They suddenly seem bigger, fuller, but it must be my imagination.

I grab another strawberry and circle her nipples with it before lapping them with my tongue. "You taste so good."

She locks her ankles around my waist and rubs herself against my hardened cock. "I need you."

I know the feeling. Nodding my head in agreement, I gently push her back on the kitchen island. "Enjoy the ride, Shortcake."

ABOUT A MINUTE after Ripley leaves in the morning, there's a knock at my door. I wonder if she forgot something. When I open it, I see Blanche.

I smile. "Good morning, Blanche." I look behind her and don't see Thor. "Where's my best buddy? I'll take him for a walk."

I assume she's going to crack a joke about my shirtless state, as she often does, but her face is serious right now. "Good morning. He's taking a nap. I spent some time with your friend last night. I heard her knocking very late and came out to see what the ruckus was about."

"I'm sorry about that. I was at the hospital with a friend, but I saw the blanket and cookies. Thanks for taking care of her while she waited. I'll grab your blanket and plate for you."

She places her hand on my arm. "That's not why I'm here."

"Oh. Okay. What do you need?"

"To talk to you about that sweet girl. The one who loves you with every fiber of her being. The one who I know deep inside you love too. The one who you're going to lose if you don't wake up and smell the roses."

CHAPTER TWENTY-TWO

QUINCY

The past three weeks have been crazy. We lost the World Series in game six. It was heartbreaking. I pitched a decent game, but our team wasn't hitting. I think Layton's injury took the wind out of our sails. He's the leader of this team and was missed. The entire locker room was off without his larger-than-life presence.

I blamed myself for the loss, but my friends and Arizona did their best to keep my spirits up. In the end, I know I had the best season of my career, and I'm proud of that. Perhaps next year will be our year to win it all.

On a happier note, our crew had the best time at the Anacondas' victory parade. With the disappointing end to our season, I'm happy the Philly fans have the Anacondas to celebrate.

We drank, danced, and celebrated with the girls. I was beaming with pride all day for Arizona and Ripley. They were on cloud nine.

Layton had to beg the doctors to let him come in his giant cast. But he was there, beaming every bit as much as I was. Seeing him revel in my sister's success was somehow comforting to me. Ripley was right. They're completely in love. They're going to get married one day.

Arizona eventually had to leave for a two-month international photoshoot she was contractually obligated to attend. Layton is a fucking mess without her. We're all meeting up at Screwballs tonight to try to cheer him up.

I'm sitting in our regular booth when Ripley and Kam walk in. Ripley takes one look at me and then makes a beeline for the bathroom.

Kam slides into the booth. I look at her. "Where did Ripley go?"

"To perform brain surgery. Where do you think? The bathroom."

Cheetah makes a slurping noise. "Damn, Kam bam, you look good enough to drink up tonight."

She pats his hand in a condescending manner. "Are you jealous because my heart is pumping inside me and you're not?"

He chuckles. "You're an endless supply of lines. I love that about you." He leans forward toward her. "I have a few more too. Did you ever wonder why it's called morning wood when it should be called breakfast in bed?"

She leans closer to him. "If men get morning wood, does it mean that women get morning dew?"

They both start laughing hysterically. The rest of us stare at them in bewilderment. They never give it a rest, and they wildly amuse each other.

Before I know it, Ripley is exiting the bathroom and making her way to the table. She's so beautiful. It's like she has an extra glow about her tonight. She takes my breath away.

Besides the parade, I haven't been around her much since the night of Layton's injury. Between Blanche pushing me toward Ripley and June warning me away from her, my mind has been a clusterfuck.

I don't want to hurt her, but I equally can't stomach the thought of being without her. I certainly don't want to be with anyone else. The problem is that I won't deprive her of anything she wants. There will never be a time when I want children. Of that, I'm sure.

I stand to allow her into the booth. She gives me a clearly fake smile. She's hurting. It hurts her to be around me in a group setting. Maybe I'm the one who should be requesting the trade. She's happy in Philly. June called me selfish. She's right. Maybe this is a sacrifice I need to make, not Ripley.

I offer her a drink, but she declines. She seems mad at me. Maybe it's for the best.

Layton eventually wobbles in on his crutches. We're all happy to see him out and about.

One of his former groupies approaches him, but he shows her no interest. She pushes and pushes by trashing my sister. My mouth opens to put her in her place, but Ripley speaks first. "He's not interested. Hit the road. No skanks welcome here."

She turns her vile face toward Ripley and looks her up and down with pure venom. "What are you going to do, fat ass? Sit on m..."

I don't know what comes over me, but her talking like that to Ripley makes me snap. I immediately jump out of my seat and get in the bitch's face. "If you ever talk to her like that again, it will be the last words you utter."

I hear gasps coming from our table.

I turn to the owner who has clearly noticed something going on at our table. He loves our crew and would do anything for us. He knows more than half of his patrons come here hoping to catch a glimpse of us.

I motion for him to kick this whore out, which he immediately does.

Ezra grabs my shirt. "Have a seat, Q. Relax, big bear." His worried eyes encourage me to sit down.

I can't focus on anything or anyone but Ripley. I see her lip quiver ever so slightly.

I sit down next to her. "Are you okay?"

She attempts to mask the hurt I know she's feeling. "I'm fine. It doesn't bother me. I've had comments like that my whole life. I'm used to it."

I can't help but rub her soft face with the backs of my fingers. "It's not fine. No one should talk to you like that. You're beautiful. You're perfect."

She sucks in a breath. Shamefully, I've never shown her any affection in public, and it's clearly taken her off guard.

Her face softens for a moment before it steels. With tears pooling in her eyes, she leans over and whispers, "Don't touch me. We're over."

On some level, I've always known this day was coming. The day she realized how much better she could do.

My face falls as I attempt to whisper back, "I need to talk to you. Now!"

I grab her hand and pull her around the corner. I'm sure everyone at our table is gossiping about our uncharacteristic interaction, but I'm beyond caring anymore. I grit out, "What are you talking about?"

She shoves me away. "Quincy, this hot and cold, back and forth thing we do is over. I'm done with it."

I know she's right, but I don't want to let her go. I want to tell her that I love her. Maybe I could one day be enough for her.

I shake my head vehemently. "You can't just decide we're over. You're my wife."

Her eyes now fully fill with tears. She looks miserable. "I'm not your wife."

"The hell you're not. Check our marriage certificate, Shortcake, you're mine. My. Wife."

"On paper. Not in any of the ways that truly matter. I want a divorce. It's long overdue."

I'm realizing that I don't want to lose her. I'm not ready for it. Am I selfish like June said? Maybe. I'll give her space, but not a divorce. It's the only hold I have over her. "No. I won't give it to you."

Her face and shoulders fall. She's exhausted by us. By me. "Quincy, it's time for us both to move on. We're not really married. We don't live as husband and wife. We both see other people and lead separate lives. No one else except a random justice of the peace even knows we're married. Not our families. Not our friends. No one. It's time."

It's not like I don't know she has the paperwork. I saw it...and destroyed it. But I haven't been served so all hope isn't lost. "Nope. Not happening."

Her face looks pained. "When you hear what I have to say, I promise that you'll want the divorce too."

"Over my dead body will I give you that divorce. Until death do us part."

Her tears get heavier before she says something that

practically makes my head explode. Words I never thought I'd hear a woman utter to me.

"I'm pregnant."

Shock isn't a big enough word to describe what I'm feeling right now. I don't want kids. I can't bring a child into the world. I'm not meant to be a father. It's not my destiny.

I open and close my mouth a few times, but words never find their way out. Suddenly, the whole bar starts spinning. I think I might pass out. Air. I need air.

Like a fucking coward, I turn and make a beeline for the door. Once the cool, fall Philly air hits me, I take long, deep breaths. Over and over.

I stand there for several long minutes, basically in shock. At some point, a leggy blonde, not my usual type, walks over to me. I think I've seen her here a few times before.

"Quincy Abbott? I was hoping to see you here tonight. Want to get out of here?"

I wordlessly nod, simply needing to get away.

BANG. Bang. Bang.

I wake in the morning to a loud, banging noise. My fucking head is throbbing. I have a sudden flashback of a blonde woman and tequila shots. I panic and quickly look to the other side of the bed. It's empty. Phew.

Bang. Bang. Bang.

Who the fuck is that? They need to go away.

I try to remember my evening. I remember doing shots off her body at a bar. I then remember her trying to get me to come home with her. I kept trying to push her away, but she wouldn't listen.

I recall Ezra showing up, dragging me out of the bar, and bringing me home. He made me drink lots of water and then put me to bed. Thank God for Ezra.

Bang. Bang. Bang.

I mumble, "Hold your horses. What's the emergency? I'm coming."

I slowly and shakily get out of bed. Not caring that I'm in boxer briefs, I make my way to the door and open it. There's a policeman standing there. Oh shit, what else did I do last night? Am I forgetting something?

I run my hands through my hair. "What's so important that you need to bang on my door at the ungodly hour of..." I look up at the clock. Noon.

"Mr. Quincy Abbott?"

"Yes."

He hands me an envelope. "You've been served."

Without another word, he turns and walks away.

I quickly open the envelope. It's divorce papers.

CHAPTER TWENTY-THREE

RIPLEY

I've spent the better part of the past few weeks packing up all my belongings and doing my best to tie up loose ends in Philly. I'm moving home for the time being. I need to get out of this town, away from Quincy Abbott.

My mom downsized a few years ago, so I can't live with her once the baby comes, but it will do for a few months as I figure things out. I need my mom right now.

I officially asked the Daultons for a trade. They encouraged me to wait until I was ready to return after the baby is born to make that decision. The baby is due a month before the next season, so it's not like I'll be able to play anyway, certainly not the first month or two.

While Kam and Bailey know I'm moving, I haven't told Arizona since she's on the other side of the world. I want to have this conversation with her in person. I owe her that.

She begged us all to stay here in Philly for Thanksgiving, so that Layton has a nice holiday since he's been so incredibly down without her. I want to give her this one last thing before I throw a wrench into our friendship. She's not coming home for another month. I'll fly back then and talk to her in person about everything that's gone on. *Everything*.

Thanksgiving is at Quincy's. It's going to be hard to see him, but I keep reminding myself that I'm doing it for Arizona.

I haven't seen him since I told him that I'm pregnant. In my mind, I knew how he'd react, but it becoming a reality hit me really hard. Seeing pictures online of him that night partying with another woman was the final nail in the coffin for me. Quincy Abbott is officially in my past. It's more than clear that he wants nothing to do with me or this baby. I've spun my wheels over him for long enough. It's time to change this car's direction.

My mom flew in two days ago to help me finish packing and to fly back with me tomorrow morning.

I look around the apartment with a sense of sadness, knowing I'll never live with Arizona again. I can only hope our friendship survives this. She's so important to me, and I pray I don't lose her. I know I've been less than truthful with her, which will hurt, but hopefully she'll understand and forgive me.

Mom plops down on the couch next to me and lets out a breath. "I think that's everything."

I wordlessly nod.

She rubs my face. "Are you okay, baby?"

I shake my head as tears sting my eyes. "No, I'm not. I hope I will be one day, but it won't be anytime soon."

"Still no word from him?"

"No. It's over. I'll be raising this baby alone. You did it. I'll do it too."

Tears drop down her cheeks. It's very rare for June St. James to cry. "I wanted you to have a better life than mine."

I rub her arm. "I've had a good life, Mom. I know I was unplanned, but I never felt unwanted or unloved by you. I hope to make my child feel as loved as you made me feel."

She gives me a small smile of gratitude.

I shrug. "My father didn't want me, just like Quincy doesn't want our baby. I suppose it's a bit of history repeating itself."

She takes my hand in hers. "Ripley, your father wanted you. Very much."

Tears now fill my eyes. I've never heard this before. "Will... will you finally tell me about him?"

She takes several deep breaths before beginning her story. *Our* story.

"Lucas Beaumont was the most beautiful man you could ever imagine. Both inside and out. You have so much of him in you. He had an innate genuine kindness that I know you got from him. The desire to make other people happy. It's all from him."

Tears drip down my cheeks at hearing the name of my father for the first time in my life and knowing there's some part of him inside me.

"He was a politician and was assigned to oversee the Olympic team. We met about a year before the Olympics, and our affair started shortly thereafter. I say affair because he was married, not happily, but still married. I have a lot of shame over that."

I squeeze her hand, letting her know she has my support, no matter what comes out of her mouth today.

"He was in a marriage of convenience. She came from a wealthy, influential Canadian family. His family all but forced them together for appearances. They lived separate lives privately, but publicly maintained a united front. I fell hard and fast. So did he. So much so that he was willing to leave her, even knowing exactly what the political fallout would be. I was puking my guts out at the Olympics. I thought it was nerves at first, but shortly after, I realized I was pregnant." She smiles as if remembering something. "He was over the moon excited about it."

She grabs my face. "You may have been unplanned, but you were wanted. You were loved. I promise that you were conceived in the purist love there is."

I nod, too choked up for words.

"He told his wife he wanted a divorce, that he was in love with another woman, that she was pregnant, and he intended to marry me."

She takes a deep breath before continuing. "His wife threatened pretty much every nasty thing you can imagine, but he didn't care. We planned to build a life together in Toronto regardless of the damage to his reputation."

"Why didn't you plan to move out of Toronto? Away from the spotlight?"

She visibly swallows, clearly suffering with what's about to come out of her mouth next. "He had two young children with her. A boy and a girl. He couldn't move too far away."

I suck in a breath. "I...I have siblings?"

She nods. "You do."

"What happened? I don't even remember him. I've never seen a picture of us together. Nothing."

Her shoulders shake with sobs, and she briefly closes her eyes. I don't think I've ever seen her look so pained. Eventually, she steels herself to continue our story. "He died in a helicopter crash a week before you were born."

I hug her. "Oh my god. I'm so sorry, Mom."

"A part of me died with him. I never truly got over the loss of my soulmate. That's exactly what he was, my soulmate."

"I've never seen the name Lucas Beaumont on anything.

Why isn't his name on my birth certificate?"

"His wife was a powerful woman. He never told her my name before he died. I couldn't have her finding out. But—"

"She eventually did."

She nods. "Yes. When you were two, she showed up at our apartment. She offered me a huge lump sum of money to move out of the country and agree to never contact her or her children or ever tell anyone who your father was. I refused, but for years she made my life a living hell. She made sure no one would hire me. She had me evicted from every apartment we lived in. Please understand that I was struggling to make ends meet. We moved around from shitty place to shitty place. He was gone. Her money would give us a fresh start. By the time you were five, I would go days without eating because I could only afford food for you. At some point, I gave in and took her money. It enabled me to buy us a nice house in a good neighborhood and give us the fresh start we needed. I was able to get a job and give you the life you deserved."

That explains how we went from small-apartment living to a four-bedroom house when we moved to the US. I suppose I never thought about it at the time, but now I see it.

She continues. "You were already showing signs of being a pitching prodigy. I chose California knowing the weather would be such that you could throw all year round."

"I'm sure my pregnancy brought some of this to the surface, but why now? Why are you telling me now?"

She smiles. "You got his brains too."

"I got your brains. You're no dummy."

She gives me a grateful look.

"His wife passed away a few weeks ago. When your brother and sister were recently going through her old boxes in storage, they came across the private investigator file on us. Apparently, she kept tabs on us for several years after we left. I assume to make sure I wasn't going back on our deal. They had no clue about you. They reached out to me and want to meet you. I told them you know nothing about your father. I'd first have to decide if I wanted to tell you everything about him, and after that, it would be your decision whether you wanted to meet them. I can tell you they seemed sincere on the phone, but I can't be sure."

I'm quiet for a bit. "I think I need to let this settle. I'm a bit of a mess given everything else going on. Let me get through the next few months, and then we'll talk more about it."

"No rush, my love. It's waited twenty-eight years. Whatever makes you comfortable."

Kam bursts through the door with a big smile. "Mama June is back in da house!"

Mom turns and smiles. "Honey Boo Boo is back causing trouble."

I look behind her and don't see Bailey. "Where's Bails?"

"Babysitting. Allegedly. She's probably having her pink fortress attacked. She said she'll meet us later at the group home."

Mom questions, "Group home?"

I nod. "Layton coaches a baseball team of orphaned kids. Arizona coaches with him too. We're going to drop by for an hour and wish them all a happy Thanksgiving. I'll come back here for you afterward, and we'll go to Quincy's together."

"Okay."

Kam looks around and sighs. "I can't believe you're really leaving us. I understand why, but I'm still sad."

I told Kamryn and Bailey everything right after my encounter with Quincy. They saw me in bed crying, and I couldn't deny it anymore.

"It's the right thing to do. I'll visit. Or maybe you can come visit me."

A FEW HOURS LATER, we're walking into Quincy's place. My heart is racing. I saw him briefly at the group home today, but we didn't talk at all.

I can hear several voices in there as we approach his door. I'm glad we won't be alone with him.

He opens the door and starts to open his mouth, but Kam practically punches him in the stomach with a bottle of wine. "Here, dickhead. You can shove this right up your ass. We're only here because we love Arizona. Oh, and thank you for having us."

He nods as if he was expecting it. Staring at me, he says, "Can we talk?"

I shake my head. "There's nothing left to say. Let's just eat and get this over with."

Arizona and Quincy's parents, Paul and Pamela, greet me warmly. When the time comes, I'll tell them about their grandchild. Perhaps they'll want to be in his or her life, even if Quincy won't.

As always, Quincy is cold to his parents throughout the meal, barely acknowledging his father. The whole thing is awkward, but Kam and Cheetah do their best to lighten things up.

As I'm exiting the bathroom after dinner, he pulls me into his bedroom and lets out a breath. "Alone at last."

I cross my arms. "What do you want? I hope this is to hand me signed divorce papers."

His jaw stiffens. "It's not. We need to figure things out."

"There's nothing left to say. I'm super clear on where you stand. I need to put you in my past once and for all. I'm moving home tomorrow."

"Home as in Cali?"

"Yes."

"Where will you live?"

"With my mom for a few months while I figure things out. I've requested a trade. All I ask is that you sign those papers. If you care about me at all, you'll sign them and let me live my life."

He visibly swallows. "Can you give me a minute to digest this? You dropped a bombshell on me."

"You've had three weeks to digest. Five seconds after I told you, you were doing shots off some bimbo's boobs. I have to thank you for that though. It was exactly what I needed to finally let go."

"Is that what you've done? Let go of me?"

I'm trying to be strong, but tears fill my eyes. "I've loved you nearly every minute of my life. Despite your words and your actions telling me we wouldn't ever be anything, I never truly lost hope in our happily ever after—"

"Good."

"Until three weeks ago." I clutch my chest. "You broke my fucking heart. I don't know if I'll ever recover from it, but I want to try. Honestly, Quincy, you're not good enough for me."

He nods. "I know. I've always known that."

I wipe a few tears that have managed to spring free and roll down my cheeks. "If I can love a man who doesn't love me back the way I love you, imagine how hard I could love the man who truly does. I know he's out there."

"I...I...I think I do love you."

"Then I need you to love me enough to finally let me go."

He briefly closes his eyes.

"Like I've told you *many* times before, I want, no, I *deserve*, to find someone who will love me in the light. I know it won't happen anytime soon, but I'll never give up hope of finding the man who wants forever with me. Who loves me openly and proudly."

"That's not—"

I shove my finger into his chest. "Don't fucking insult me with excuses. Relationships are a two-way street. I've always given more than I've received with you. I won't accept that in my life anymore. I don't want to teach our child that it's okay. It's not. It never was. I was too weak to admit it, but not anymore."

He blows out a breath. "Tell me what you need."

"The *only* thing I need from you is to sign those papers. The rest of my needs became inconsequential the moment I found out about our child. That's what parents do. I want nothing to do with you ever again. I'm leaving town tomorrow. I'm only returning for one day when Arizona comes home, so I can tell her everything in person."

"What about money? You need money."

I'm so angry right now. "Money? You think I want money from you? Have you even read those divorce papers? I want absolutely nothing from you ever again. Goodbye, Quincy. Have a good life."

At that, I turn, walk out of the room, grab my mother, and leave Quincy Abbott in my past for good.

QUINCY

"Goodbye, Quincy. Have a good life."

She means it this time. I can tell she does. I've officially broken her.

I want to pull her into my arms and never let go, but I know I'm no good to her as I am right now. So without another word, I let her walk out the door. I've never been in more pain than I am right now. I've never hated myself more.

Everyone eventually leaves until it's just me and my parents. Mom smiles dreamily, oblivious to the obvious evening-long tension. "Layton loves Arizona so much. I can't believe he plans to propose to her someday soon. She finally found the right guy."

Layton pulled my father and I aside to ask for our blessing to propose to her sometime in the near future. My father didn't earn the honor of being asked. I understand that a woman's father is traditionally asked, but he didn't raise her. I did. I more than appreciate that Layton knew enough to ask me too.

She continues, "And it was so sweet that he included you, Quincy."

My anger has been simmering all night. They're clueless, and that comment is my official boiling point. "Well, I fucking raised her, so it makes sense that he'd ask me. What did you do, Dad, show up after she went to sleep at night and leave before she woke up? Quite a fucking father."

My father's smile fades. "What's your problem, Quincy?"

"You're my problem. I'm completely fucked up about marriage and kids because of you. Terrified of making my own wife and child feel as inconsequential as you made me feel. I can't be in a normal relationship because of you."

"I worked hard for this family. Every day and every night of my life."

"I'm more than aware that you worked *every* day and *every* night. So hard that we never saw you."

"How do you think we paid for your Little League and your equipment needs? Your dog and the clothes on your back. Your food and school trips. Money doesn't grow on trees for real people. It takes hard work and dedication."

"I'm a fucking professional baseball player. Don't you think I know about hard work and dedication? Not that you've ever come to see me play. Do you know that I'm probably the only pitcher in the major leagues who didn't spend hours throwing to his father in the backyard? In fact, I've never once thrown a ball with you. Do you even realize how messed up that is?"

"You think you'd be a pitcher if not for me?"

"You had nothing to do with it. Arizona spent hours upon hours with me. My little sister. At seven years old, she should have been having fun with her friends, instead she was crouched down getting bruised while I tried to learn a curveball."

He turns to my mom. "Maybe it's time for us to go."

I shout, "No! I've bottled it all up for years. Arizona always defended you and told me to let things go, but she's not here tonight to defend you. You're going to listen to everything I have to say. You two are so fucking clueless as to the damage you've inflicted. Do you know why Ripley is moving back home?"

They shake their heads.

"Because of me. She loves me. She's always loved me. And I can't love her in return. Not in the way she deserves. All because of you. Because I decided as a little kid that I would never get married and make my wife and kids feel as bad as you made me feel."

Mom's crying now. Dad looks on the verge.

With a trembling lip, Mom manages, "Do you love her?"

I shout, "Of course I fucking love her. I've probably loved her for my entire adult life. She is the only woman I will ever love. And I love her enough to let her and our child walk away because I know it's best for them."

Mom gasps. "Child? What child?"

"Did I forget to mention that?" I ask with a load of sarcasm. "Ripley's pregnant. Enjoy ignoring your grandchild as well as you ignored your children. Take a fucking Uber to the airport in the morning. I don't want to see either of you again. Ever. You ruined my life."

I turn, walk into my bedroom, and slam the door behind me. In some ways that felt good. It was thirty-three years in the making. But the burden hasn't disappeared. The heaviness still weighs on me. The sadness blankets me.

EARLY IN THE MORNING, I hear my front door open and close. I'm glad they left. Good riddance.

A little while later I walk out of my room and into my kitchen to see my father sitting there. My jaw tightens. "I thought you left."

"I sent your mother home. You and I are going on a little trip."

"I'm not going anywhere with you."

"Pack your fucking bags, Quincy. We're going."

CHAPTER TWENTY-FOUR

A MONTH LATER

RIPLEY

Layton looks at me with nothing but concern on his face despite the fact that I'm ruining his reunion with Arizona. "Can I do anything for you?"

I shake my head. "No. I'm so sorry to intrude, but I really need to talk to her."

We're in the back of a limo on our way to the airport. Arizona's plane is due to arrive at any moment.

"Don't worry about it. Take however much time you need. She and I have all the time in the world."

"Thanks, Layton. You're a good guy."

"Of course. Should I take an Uber home, so you two can talk privately?"

I shake my head. "No. I'm sure you already know some of it and you'll hear everything else soon enough. If she's upset, I want you to be there for her. I've kept secrets from my best friend for a long time, and she's going to be hurt. She'll need to lean on you."

He nods in understanding and takes my hand in his. "She loves you, Rip. She'll forgive whatever it is. That's the kind of person she is."

I swallow. "I hope you're right."

We arrive at the airport. The limo pulls right out onto the private airstrip. Just a few minutes later, a small, private plane lands.

With crutches in hand, Layton maneuvers out the door. I stay in the limo. I'm already interrupting their big reunion. I want to at least give them a few minutes of happiness before dropping this bomb on her. Bombs.

When the door opens, Arizona emerges. Even through the tinted windows, I see a huge smile break out on her face when her eyes find Layton. She's so in love with him. Even though I'm a mess, my heart still swells for her and what they share. I know he's her forever.

She practically sprints down the stairs. He's right outside the limo door, so I can hear him laugh. If it wasn't for his leg, she'd leap into his arms.

As she's approaching, he tosses his crutches to the side and holds out his arms. She falls into him, and, without a single word needing to be spoken, their lips meet.

They kiss for several long minutes, like the starved lovers they've been for two months. Neither cares where they are nor who can see them. Their need for each other is palpable.

Her hands move under and up his shirt while his are on her ass.

When they eventually break apart, she breathes, "Hello to you too, superstar."

He lovingly rubs her face. I can see tears falling down his cheeks. "Never leave me again."

"Never."

"I love you so much."

"I love you too. Let's go get into bed and not surface for a week. In fact, we can start in this limo right now."

She reaches for his belt buckle, but he grabs her wrist. "We have company in the limo."

She bends and pokes her head inside before pinching her eyebrows together. "Rip? What are you doing here?"

"I'm so sorry to interrupt, but I'm flying home later today, and I need to talk to you before I go."

Her face falls. "You're leaving? I just got home."

"I know, babe. I'll explain everything."

Once her luggage is packed in the trunk, they slide inside the limo. As it pulls away from the airport, Layton intertwines his fingers with hers. She looks at him. "Do you know what this is about?"

"I have an idea. Let Ripley speak. Hear her out. No matter what, you know she loves you."

Arizona turns to me, worry written all over her gorgeous face.

I take a deep breath. "Let me just get right to it. I'm in love with your brother."

Her chin drops. "With Quincy? Since when?"

"If I'm being honest, since the day I met him when I was five."

She slowly nods as if she's contemplating our past. "I guess I always suspected you had feelings for him, but I'm not sure I realized how deep they ran. I saw it as a childhood crush."

"It started that way, but they've deepened a lot throughout the years. He...umm...he was all my firsts. *All* of them." I give her a look trying to convey just what I mean.

She sinks back into the seat and breathes out, "What? When?"

"The night he was drafted, after you passed out, we kissed. The night before our high school graduation, he and I slept together for the first time."

I see her searching her memory bank for a moment. "The night of our state championship? You slept over after the celebration party where you broke up with Jack."

I nod. "Yes. I broke up with him knowing who I wanted to be my first. When you fell asleep, I went to Quincy's room. The day we all met, he asked me to give him all my firsts. For some reason, that stuck with me, and I wanted to see it through. Between my promise and my crush, I needed it to be Quincy, not Jack, that night."

She blows out a breath. "I suppose part of me is surprised and part isn't. Why are you telling me this now? What's the big deal? That was a long time ago."

"Our physical relationship continued throughout most of my time in Houston. For years, we slept together."

"Oh. I...umm...okay. What about since the move to Philly?"

"Yes. I initially didn't want it to, knowing how strong my feelings are for him, but..." I start to tear as my shoulders fall. "I'm in love with him. I always have been. I can't seem to help myself. In my head I knew I should stay away, but the heart wants what it wants, and my heart has always been with him."

She takes a few breaths. I know she's toggling between being upset with me and wanting to comfort me, eventually saying, "I know you've been secretive. I suppose I understand why. It's not like this is a bad thing. You're my best friend. You're a sister to me. Why would you'd think I'd be upset if you date my brother? I don't understand why it needed to be so secretive." She looks at Layton. "It's not like I'm in a position to judge you for falling for your best friend's sibling."

I swallow. "There's more. I've been keeping a lot from you. Know that it was *so* hard. I hate keeping anything from you. It guts me." I take a breath. "When I first got to Houston, I found out that my dingbat of a mother didn't do what was necessary for me to become a US citizen when I was a kid. I wasn't going to be able to get a work visa in time for that first season and wasn't sure I'd get it at all since I had been here illegally for so long."

She pinches her eyebrows together. "That sucks, but what does this have to do with you and Quincy?"

"He stopped by the morning I found out. After talking things through, he suggested we get married so I could obtain my citizenship."

She lets out a laugh. "Married? That's crazy." Her eyes then widen as realization hits. "You and Quincy were married?"

"*Are* married. We've been married for over six years."

She whispers, "What the fuck?"

"To be clear, we have never lived as a married couple. It's been on paper only. We've both seen other people. That was our understanding. Yes, we also spent time together, but that was physical and completely separate from the marriage."

"Holy shi—"

"And now I'm pregnant. It's his."

Her mouth widens and she covers it with her hand. Tears form in her eyes.

It's silent for several long beats, but when her hand drops from her mouth, a smile finds her lips. "I'm...I'm going to be an aunt?" Her smile widens. "And it's going to be yours *and* Quincy's? This is the greatest thing that's ever happened."

I pinch my eyebrows together in total shock. "You're not angry with me?"

"Rip, I'm experiencing about a thousand different emotions right now, but anger isn't one of them. My brother and my best friend are married and having a baby. This is the best day ever."

She flings herself across the limo and wraps me in a huge hug. "I'm so happy."

Tears of relief stream down my cheeks as I hug her back. Layton the mushball is covered in tears too.

She eventually pulls back. "Omigod. I want to have a huge baby shower. We can have all sorts of baby softball and baseball stuff. And then we can—"

"Arizona, there's more."

"More? What else is there? Is it twins?" Her face is hopeful.

"No, it's not twins. It's actually a baby girl. I just found out."

She screams. "Ahh. So exciting! When are you moving in with him? Don't worry about the apartment. I'm moving in with Layton. I was planning to talk to you about it this week."

"I moved my stuff out already, but I moved it to my mother's."

"Your mother's? In California? I'm so confused. You and Quincy are moving back to Cali?"

I sigh, hating that I'm about to take the wind from her sails. "I've lived there for the past month. I only came here to see you. I'm heading back tonight. It's Quincy. He doesn't want me or the baby. We're getting a divorce. I'm raising her on my own."

Her face immediately falls. "What the fuck do you mean? What did that asshole do?"

"When we first got married, he agreed to it because he said he never wanted a real marriage and was adamant that he was never having kids. This isn't what he wants."

Arizona's face looks like murder. I recognize that look from Quincy. "Tell me exactly what he said."

"We haven't spoken much since I told him about the baby right after you left. That night, he ran out on me and straight into the arms of another woman. The only time we've spoken since then was on Thanksgiving. He doesn't want to be a parent. I think he has a lot more animosity toward your parents than he ever let on. Their constant focus on the business has truly damaged him. It's completely different from you. You accept them for how they are and enjoy whatever they can do, he's venomous about it."

"Let's fucking go over there and kick his ass. He'll realize his mistake. He's being an immature asshole. He doesn't want this. I know he doesn't."

Layton gently grabs her arm for attention. "Quincy is gone."

I look at him in surprise. "What do you mean *gone*?"

He shrugs. "He took off the day after Thanksgiving and hasn't been back since. He told management he'd be out of pocket but would continue his off-season workouts on his own. No one has heard from him. He doesn't return texts and his cell phone goes right to voicemail."

I hope he's okay. I didn't know anything about this. Part of me is surprised that neither Kam nor Bailey mentioned it, but to be fair, I told them I didn't want to know anything about him.

Arizona looks at me with worried eyes. "Are you coming back soon?"

I shake my head. "No, sweetie. I can't be near him anymore. It hurts too much. I've requested a trade. I'm due a month before the season anyway. I doubt playing this year is very likely."

"What about training for the Olympics? Our dream."

I shrug. "I don't know. I'm going to be a single mother. It might not be in the cards for me anymore."

Tears stream down her face as she hugs me. "Oh, Rip, I'm so sorry. He'll get it together at some point. I know he will."

I shake my head. "It's too late for us. He can't undo the damage he's done to me. If a time comes when he wants to be in our daughter's life, the door will always be open, but it's over for him and me."

CHAPTER TWENTY-FIVE

TWO MONTHS LATER

QUINCY

I'm flying to Clearwater, Florida for spring training. I haven't been in Philly for months. I haven't even spoken to my family or teammates. My sister started leaving me nasty texts and voicemails. I sent her one brief text letting her know that I needed time to do some soul-searching and that I would see and talk to her when I was ready.

It didn't deter her in the least. Nasty texts from her were a daily occurrence. Loyal to her best friend through and through. That's Arizona Abbott for you. I love that about her.

The person I've most consistently kept in touch with is June. I asked her not to tell Ripley, but I needed to make sure she was doing okay. June tears into me during every call but at least throws me a bone with a few updates. She said Ripley was sad for a while but seems to be coming out of it, determined to make a nice life for her and our child. *Our* child. I've spent a lot of time wrapping my mind around something I always assumed I never wanted.

I also kept in touch with Collin. My house is almost finished. We made a few last-minute changes, but Collin is incredible and went with the flow. The pictures are amazing. I can't wait to see it in person.

I'm excited to get back into action on the field. I've only thrown a few times this off-season, but I've been working out and am probably in the best shape of my life. I'm ready for our spring training regimen to begin.

I'm hailing a cab at the airport when I see Dutton Steel doing the same. He notices me and smiles. "Quincy Abbott, it's great to see you."

We man hug. "You too, Coach."

He looks at my face. "Shit, you've got a lot of facial hair brewing."

I chuckle as I touch my longer beard. "I haven't shaved in a while. I don't mind it. Want to share a cab to the team hotel?"

"Absolutely."

We get in the cab and begin our journey to the hotel. He asks, "Where have you been the past few months? We haven't seen you around the stadium at all."

"Some traveling. A little...self-development. I have some things going on in my personal life."

He nods. "The woman you once alluded to?"

I nod. "Yes."

"Do you want to talk about it?"

"It's complicated."

He barks out a laugh. "It usually is."

"Do you mind if I ask you a question?"

"You can ask. It doesn't mean I'll answer."

I smile. "Fair enough. If you had to do it all over again, I mean marry your wife even knowing what was coming, would you still see it through?"

Without any hesitation, he replies, "Yes. She was the love of my life. Nothing will ever change that."

"And the fact that your career got cut short; you're good with that decision?"

"I am. My children mean more to me than anything. Baseball is a game. Family is everything. Maybe men are wired a little differently in terms of how much time we consider parenthood before becoming a parent. While I always assumed I'd become a father one day, I didn't sit and dream about it. But once you hold your first child, every priority you've ever had shifts. Every preconceived notion and fear suddenly melts away. And nothing is better than watching the woman you love become a mother."

"Were you ever afraid you'd be a bad father?"

He gives me a knowing smile. "Every single day since I found out that she was pregnant with our first."

"And you were never able to move on from her? Even after all these years?"

He lets out a nervous laugh. "If you asked me this question a year ago, which you sort of did, my answer would be different. I've been talking with a woman lately. It's complicated, but we'll see where it goes."

He seems lighter than the last time we spoke. I'm happy for him.

We continue chatting until we pull up to the hotel. Pitchers and catchers arrive a few days before the rest of the team, so I don't expect many people when I arrive. Because Arizona is...well...Arizona, when I walk inside, she's waiting for me in the lobby with a scowl on her face.

I roll my eyes but can't help the smile on my face. I've missed my sister. "Fucking two minutes. I've been back for two minutes and you're already here?"

I see Layton behind her smirking as Dutton shakes Layton's hand and then makes his way to check-in.

Arizona crosses her arms. "You and I need to chat, bro. You did my best friend dirty, and it's not okay."

I hang my head in shame. "I know I did." I blow out a breath. "Can we go somewhere and talk privately? Somewhere that's not the lobby of a hotel?"

She nods. "Fine. But this conversation is happening, and it's happening right now."

"I know."

She takes Layton's hand, and they follow me.

"I suppose he's coming?"

"He's my husband. Of course he's coming."

I nod. I saw online that they were suddenly married. I feel guilty for missing it, though I think it was a spur-of-the-moment thing and no guests were in attendance.

I check in, and we make our way to my room. When we're in the elevator, she tugs on my beard.

"Your face looks like an unkempt vagina."

Layton shakes in laughter.

I can't help the small smile that creeps out. She loves busting my balls.

I make a spectacle of slowly licking my lips. "Hmm. Thank you."

She scrunches her face. "Eww. It wasn't meant as a compliment."

I wink at her. "I know. Congrats on your wedding. Thanks for the invite."

She doesn't smile as we walk down the hall and into my hotel room. "We had to fucking wait for you to celebrate. We wanted to have a party last month, but selfish Quincy fell off the map, so we still haven't done that."

I slam the door shut. "Selfish? Screw you, Z. You're able to be in a normal relationship and get married because I wasn't selfish. Because I took care of you and shielded you from our shit parents."

Her face softens slightly. "I know you were an amazing big brother. I understand that. But how could you use Ripley, and then treat her this way?"

"I didn't use her. I've always cared about her. I never have and never will feel about another woman the way I feel about her."

Her eyes widen with hope. "Are you in love with her?"

I rub my beard and sigh. "I'd rather have this conversation with her."

She gives me an unimpressed look.

I roll my eyes. She's not going to let up unless I give her answers. "I tried not to be, and I've tried to deny it, but I realized that I am."

Her face lights up. "Then what's the fucking problem?"

"The problem is that I never saw myself as a husband or father."

"Well, now you're both, so stop being a fucking baby and man the fuck up."

"She told you about the marriage?"

"She told me everything. *Everything*. You should be

counting your lucky stars that a woman like Ripley loves you. You don't deserve her."

"That's one thing we can agree on."

She's about to open her mouth again when Layton places his hands on her shoulders and pulls her back to his front. "Sunshine, give him a minute to collect his thoughts before you go on the attack. That was a big admission for him."

I see her physically relax into him as she nods.

I narrow my eyes. "You're the Arizona whisperer."

He smiles and winks at me.

I run my fingers through my hair, which has also gotten longer. "I spent some time with Dad. For the first time in my life, he prioritized me and my needs."

She nods. "I know you spent two weeks away somewhere. Mom didn't know where. She still doesn't. He was tight-lipped."

"We went camping and got a lot of shit off our chests. We yelled, we screamed, we cried, we threw shit, and we fought, both physically and verbally. I don't think he ever understood how deep my resentment went, and I know I never understood him and his actions. Basically, we communicated for the first time in my life."

Her face softens. "What did he say?"

"He explained his unstable childhood to me, moving around a lot due to financial instability."

She pinches her eyebrows together. "Moving around? But Grandpa started Dad's furniture store."

I shake my head. "Remember, he didn't have Dad until he was in his mid-forties. He opened the shop when he was nearly sixty-five. He had only owned it for five years when he passed, and Dad gave up his baseball career to take it over. So for Dad's whole childhood, he had nothing. They moved all over the country. He never lived in one place for more than a year because his father couldn't keep a job and would burn bridges."

"Wow. They never told us anything about that."

I nod. "He said they didn't want us to think poorly of our grandfather. Dad swore if he did nothing else in life, he wanted to work hard to provide his family with a house and stability. He finally admitted that he took it too far, never coming to anything. He has this weird, innate fear of not working. Like the store will fail if he neglects it. When we were kids, he feared that we would lose the house and have to move away. It was his misguided way of ensuring stability for our family. I guess he's as scarred from his childhood as I am from mine."

"How did you two leave things?"

"My head was a mess. I was confused and needed time to consider the things he said to me. I assumed he didn't love us, but that's not the case."

She sighs. "Of course they love us. Can't you just accept them for how they are?"

"I've had years of anger that built and built. I don't think you ever quite grasped how deep it ran for me."

She nods in understanding. She knows I'm right. "Where did you go after he left? That was months ago. No one has seen or heard from you."

I shrug, not ready to admit anything to her. "I traveled a bunch. I needed to figure out where I wanted things to go with Ripley and the baby."

I'm about to continue when my phone rings, and I look down. It's June so I accept the call. "Hi, June."

"Quincy." She sounds frantic. "It's Ripley. Something is wrong. She started vomiting uncontrollably. It was horrific. And then her water broke. I think she went into labor. I'm at the hospital."

"Labor? It's way too early for that. Months too early."

Looking up, I see Arizona's face fall with concern.

I can hear June sobbing as she screams "I don't know what's happening. The nurse said something about pre-eclampsia. There are a million doctors with her. I think something is wrong. They won't tell me anything." She then whispers. "I'm so scared."

"Stay calm. I'm on my way. Keep me updated. Please."

I end the call. My hand is shaking.

Arizona looks at me with concern. "What happened? You're white as a ghost."

"She's...she's in labor."

"What? She can't be. She's only seven months along."

"Something is wrong, Z. I can feel it. I need to get to her. I...I need to get a flight."

She looks at Layton, and they silently communicate something. He nods and starts fiddling on his phone before walking out of the room into the hallway.

She takes my hands in hers. "That was June?"

I wordlessly nod. I think I'm in shock.

"What *exactly* did she say?"

"Something about excessive vomiting, water breaking, pre-eclampsia, and lots of doctors freaking out."

Layton shouts from the hallway, "One hour."

I look at my sister. "What's in an hour?"

"The Daulton jet. That's the fastest way for us to get to Ripley. I know they're down here for spring training. We hitched a ride with them early this morning."

"How do you know what he meant? How did he

know what you meant? You two just had a silent conversation."

She shrugs. "When you love someone, you understand what the other is thinking before the words are even spoken. He knew I was thinking about the jet, and I knew he was answering that silent question."

"Z, I'm scared."

She nods with tears in her eyes. "I know. Me too. We'll be with you the whole time."

"You're coming?"

"Of course."

A FEW HOURS LATER, we're in the air somewhere in the middle of the country. My mind has been racing. I've been googling all the possible causes of pre-eclampsia and early labor in general.

Arizona is fast asleep on Layton's chest and he's caressing her hair lovingly, occasionally kissing the top of her head. Even though I'm a mess right now, I have a brief moment of happiness for my sister for what she and Layton share.

In a quiet voice, so as not to wake her, I say to him, "What's wrong with me that I can't have what you two have?"

In an equally quiet voice, he responds, "Nothing is wrong with you. No more than anyone else. We all have baggage. We just need to choose to set it aside and move forward. I had two choices. Let my past ruin my future or accept this perfect, beautiful woman into my life and be happy. I chose happiness. It wasn't even hard."

"How did you know? How did you know she was the one worth setting your baggage aside for?"

He thinks for several long moments. "That's a loaded question. Trey once said to me that he knew Gemma was the one when the others faded away. He couldn't even see anyone else. I realized that was exactly how I felt. Nothing and no one else in this world matters to me more than her. It forces you to look within yourself. The past, which often haunts you, somehow stops mattering. All you can see is your future, one that only makes sense with her in it. I had no parents—"

"I had no parents."

I see his jaw tic. "No, Quincy, you had and still have parents. Mine were dead. They died in a car crash. I was in the car and didn't get a single scratch, but both of my parents died on impact. I was orphaned as a baby. I'd give anything in the world to have parents like yours, imperfect or not. Maybe your parents didn't give you the picture-perfect childhood you would have liked, but they loved you and were around. They provided for you, you had dinner together, your mom tucked you in at night, and they supported your dreams. Be thankful that they're around to even know what your dreams are. I would kill for that. They were and are there for you in their own way. Grow the fuck up and stop blaming them for all that ails you."

"You don't understand—"

"No, *you* don't understand. You have a good life. You're successful. You get to play fucking baseball for a living. Do you know how many people would kill for that? You have an amazing woman who's madly in love with you. We've both received more than our share of attention from women based on all the wrong reasons. I found one who loves me for all the right ones. So have you, but you're so filled with anger and self-loathing that you won't let her in. You made the arbitrary decision that you didn't want a family as an immature kid. Time to stop being a kid and realize that it's okay to change your mind. I don't know what will happen today, but you might have a child with her, and you might not. Either way, she loves you, and I know deep down you love her too. She's going to need you no matter what."

I run my fingers through my hair. "I know."

"Maybe it's not your time right now, but one day you could have a family with her. You're not some piece of shit, Q. I think you'd be an awesome dad. Look what you did for Arizona. I know you're the reason she views her childhood as a happy one."

"It's hard to explain how I felt as a kid. So fucking insignificant. I don't want to be an absentee parent and make my kid feel that way."

"Then don't. You have a fuck-ton of money, more than most people will ever make in a lifetime. Choose how to live your life."

"Retire, like you? I have no other skills. I don't even have a college degree. Everything I am and do revolves around baseball. Baseball players, coaches, and analysts all travel. A lot."

"You don't have to retire. You don't have to step away from baseball. That's not the only way to make it work. Look at Trey and Gemma and countless other baseball marriages. Quincy, we're lucky. We have a job that only requires us to be *in the office* for half the year. And while some of that time is spent on the road, we're home more than most. You can achieve a good, healthy balance. Being a good spouse and parent isn't about spending every waking moment together, it's about making the most of the time you do have. I don't spend every second of my life with your sister."

I mumble, "It feels like it."

He rolls his eyes. "How do you see your life in the future?"

I sigh. "Alone. That's how I've always seen it. Being an uncle to Arizona's kids is as close as I've ever thought I'd get to little ones."

"Is that what you want or what you've always assumed?"

I lean my head back and am quiet for a few long moments before admitting, "I don't know."

Arizona starts to stir. She blinks her eyes a few times before looking up at Layton and softly kissing his lips.

He looks down at her like she's his everything. Why can't I be like that?

She eventually turns to me. "Any news?"

I shake my head. "Nothing. June isn't answering." I swallow. "I'm terrified."

"Me too. How much longer until we land?"

I look at my watch. "Probably another hour or so. I've been googling what she said. Excessive vomiting is a sign of pre-eclampsia, which can be caused by high blood pressure, which can be caused by stress. Do you think it's my fault? That I caused this to happen to her?"

Arizona shrugs, not fully letting me off the hook. "Who knows why these things happen? There are a million causes, but at this point, the cause doesn't matter. You need to put your selfish shit aside today. This is about Ripley and your baby, not you. I don't know what we're walking into, but you have a wife and maybe a daughter who need you to man the fuck up."

"It's...the baby's a girl?"

She nods. "Yes, she's known for months. If you bothered to call her, you'd know that."

"June didn't mention it."

"That's why you talk to your wife, not her mother."

She's right. Tears find my eyes. "If something happens to Ripley, I'll never forgive myself."

"Don't say that. Ripley is the strongest person I know."

AFTER WHAT FEELS like the longest flight in history, we land in the middle of the night. There's a car waiting to take us to the hospital.

We rush through the hospital doors and up to the maternity floor. The waiting room is empty. There's no sign of June.

I practically sprint to the front desk. A woman in purple scrubs looks at me and smiles. "How can I help you, sir?"

"My wife went into early labor."

"What's her name?"

"Ripley St. James."

She presses a few buttons on the computer before looking up at me with a confused look on her face. "It says here that Ms. St. James is single and the father would not be here for the birth."

"What do you want, a fucking DNA test? I'm a shitty husband. I want to see my fucking wife. Someone needs to tell me what's going on with her."

Arizona grabs my arm. "Relax." She looks at the

nurse. "I believe my name was on Ripley's pre-approved list as her birthing partner. Arizona Abbott Lancaster."

She turns to me. "I had planned to come out for the delivery and help her through it."

I nod, thankful for my amazing sister. The nurse on the other hand...

She looks at the computer. "Yes." She presses more buttons and her face falls. "Oh. Perhaps we should wait for a doctor. Let me page one."

I've fucking had it. I grab her computer screen and turn it around. She fights back, but my eye catches the room number before the screen twists away from me, and I start running.

The woman is yelling after me, but I don't care. I make my way down the hallway with Arizona and Layton following closely behind. I hear shouting, but it's white noise. I just need to get to Ripley.

We finally reach the room number and enter in a frantic rush. I suck in a breath at what I see. Ripley's eyes are closed. She's hooked up to about a thousand steadily beeping machines. They're attached practically everywhere on her body. There's a tube coming out of her mouth. Her skin is white as a ghost. She looks so frail.

This is bad. Really bad.

Arizona immediately starts crying, nearly collapsing, but Layton catches her. He holds her in his arms and looks at me with fear and shock written all over his face.

I mouth, "Get her out of here."

He nods, and they step out. I hear him say, "It's okay. Let's find a doctor. We don't know anything," before his voice fades away.

With shaky hands and a rapidly beating heart, I walk

over to Ripley. She's so pale. I take her hand in mine. It's not soft and warm like always. It's cold. So damn cold.

Tears start streaming down my cheeks as I fall to my knees at her bedside. I kiss her hand over and over. "I'm so sorry I did this to you. I should have been here for you. For our baby. I'm a terrible husband and an even worse man. Please come back to me. I promise to do better."

Nothing. Just stillness.

A sob breaks free from my mouth. I cry in a way I don't think I knew I was capable of. For several minutes, I hold her hand to my face and let go. The pain running through me is so palpable that for a brief moment I think I'm having a heart attack. I can barely breathe. Do I even want to exist in a world without this woman?

Looking at her peaceful face, I know without a doubt that I've loved her as long as she's loved me, I just never fully admitted it to myself. On my knees on the floor of Ripley's hospital room, I make a million promises to God that I will be everything she needs if He brings her back to me.

I gently move the stray strands of her hair away from her face. "You're so special to me. I know I never told you, but I want to tell you now. I...I love you. So damn much."

I kiss the corner of her mouth, unable to reach her full lips because of the tube. I croak out, "Please come back to me so we can have a million more kisses. Your lips are the only lips I've ever wanted on mine. I can't live without them. Without you." My shoulders shake. "I can't do this without you."

I look at Ripley's stomach. There's no evidence of a baby in her body. I know what that must mean. The sense of loss is overwhelming and unbearable. The feelings of guilt threaten to irrevocably break me.

"I failed our daughter. I need you though. Please, Shortcake." I start sobbing again. "Please don't leave me too. I'll give you a million babies if that's what you want. Anything. Just come back to me."

Nothing. I see no signs of her hearing me or anything resembling her being conscious.

I sit there for what seems like hours, kissing her hand, her arm, her face. It doesn't feel like her. I miss my Ripley. *My* Ripley. Why wasn't I here for her?

I have no sense of time, but at some point, Arizona and Layton re-enter the room. I look up with a tear-stained face, noticing a middle-aged woman in a white coat trailing behind them. The woman gives me a somber smile. "Mr. Abbott, I'm Dr. Berger. I operated on your... wife? Ms. St. James is your wife, correct?"

I nod and manage, "Yes. What happened?" I squeeze my eyes shut, unable to face this. When I reopen them, I ask, "Is...is she going to be okay?"

She presses her lips tightly together. "Ms. St. James suffered from a pretty extreme case of pre-eclampsia. Among the worst I've seen. It's a serious blood pressure condition. It can be caused by a variety of things. Considering the information I was given by her mother, my best guess is that it was caused by the severe amount of stress suffered by Ms. St. James throughout her pregnancy."

She says it in a highly judgmental tone. One I completely deserve.

She continues, "It impacted her organs. Her heart, liver, and kidneys were temporarily not operating as they should be. She also lost a lot of blood in her emergency delivery. We had to give her a transfusion. Several transfusions."

Arizona is practically hyperventilating as I hang my head, fearful of what the doctor will say next.

"She's in a medically induced coma to allow her body time to heal from what it went through. If her numbers climb, we should be able to bring her out of it in two or three days."

I swallow. "Is she going to be okay? Please just tell me that."

"I believe so. Her recovery will be slow. She lost a lot of blood, and her body sustained serious trauma. Apparently, she's been suffering headaches and extreme fatigue for a few weeks now but didn't consult her healthcare provider. She should have done so. I think she assumed it was due to a bit of depression she was apparently suffering from."

Trying to put my shame to the side for now, I let out a breath of relief at her prognosis and pledge to myself to do whatever it takes to nurse her back to health. To be here for her like I should have been this whole time. I spent my entire life vowing to never be the absentee person my parents were, and that's exactly what I became. I'm disgusted with myself.

"Thank you. I'd like to be alone with my wife now."

She tilts her head to the side and pinches her eyebrows together. "Don't you want to know about your daughter?"

Tears spill out of my eyes. I know what she's going to say. I don't know that I can bear to hear it.

Arizona walks over to me and takes my hand. She knows too.

"We had to perform an emergency C-Section. She wasn't fully developed yet."

I squeeze Arizona's hand, bracing myself for what she's going to say next.

"It was touch and go for the first few hours, but she's a fighter. She's much bigger than most babies would be at only thirty-two weeks gestation. You and your wife being bigger than average is likely responsible for that." Dr. Berger's lips turn up slightly. "She still has a bit of an uphill battle, and she'll certainly need to spend the next few weeks in our NICU, but she's breathing shockingly well. I'm optimistic."

My mouth opens and closes a few times, words escaping me. Another sob escapes Arizona's lips.

Layton asks the question we've all been wondering. "She's alive?"

The doctor touches her chest. "Oh, heavens, yes. Ms. St. James's mother is with her now, giving her those maternal things premature babies need."

Arizona, covered in tears, wraps her arms around me and rests her head on my shoulder. "Congratulations, Dad."

My eyes widen in realization, and my heart constricts. I'm a father.

The doctor gives a slightly bigger smile. "She's got bright red hair just like her mom. I'm not sure I've ever seen that in a preemie."

"Can...can...can I see her?"

"Of course. She's going to need you, especially given Ms. St. James's condition."

My eyes toggle between Ripley and the door. I don't know what to do.

Noticing, Arizona rubs my arm. "I'll stay with Ripley. Go meet your daughter. Tell my niece that her favorite aunt will be down to see her in a little bit."

Layton motions his head toward the door. "Come on. I'll go with you."

We wordlessly make our way down a floor to the NICU. I have no idea what to expect. Will the baby look like a baby? Will she be connected to machines like Ripley?

My questions are answered when we arrive. I look through the glass to see June. She's wearing some sort of hospital garment that has an opening, so the baby is flush against her body. I catch my first glimpse of the littlest creature I've ever seen in my life.

Tears begin to flow again. I turn and see the same from Layton. He throws his arm around me. "Congrats, man. She's beautiful."

I let out a laugh through my tears. "She looks like an alien."

He smiles through his own tears. "A redheaded alien."

I tap on the glass, and June looks up. She has a mask covering her nose and mouth, but I can tell by her eyes that she's smiling. She turns and says something to the nurse.

The nurse looks at me and walks out of the room. "Mr. St. James?"

I don't bother to correct her. I don't give a shit what they call me right now. I nod. "Can I hold my baby?"

"We need to make sure you're properly sterilized first, but yes. The baby benefits from skin-to-skin contact. I can get you a discreet top that opens in the front if you'd like."

Without any hesitation, I remove my T-shirt.

Layton moans. "Oh, Christ, any excuse to be topless."

I smile at him. "I know it turns you on."

He snort-laughs.

"Oh my god, you're starting to laugh like my sister. You're pathetic, Lancaster."

"I love her laugh."

"You would." I mumble, "So fucking pussy whipped."

He gives a wicked smile and licks his lips. "Umm hmm. I most certainly am."

My face falls and I grumble, "Asshole."

He smiles, loving to rile me up about him and my sister.

After scrubbing me clean and giving me a few instructions, I sit down next to June. She turns to me. "Are you ready to meet your daughter?"

I nod. "What's her name?"

"She doesn't have one yet. It's up to Ripley, and she hasn't met her daughter yet."

She carefully places her in my arms. More like my hands. She's so tiny that she fits in my hands. As soon as I touch her and smell her, my heart just about explodes with this immediate feeling of love and protectiveness. How could I have ever doubted wanting this?

I whisper in her ear, "I love you and promise to always be there for you and your mommy, no matter what."

CHAPTER TWENTY-SIX

QUINCY

Arizona is with the baby, and I'm sitting at Ripley's bedside as I have for the past two days. I refuse to leave, even when they try to kick me out.

Dr. Berger walks in. "How's the patient?"

I shrug. "I think her color is coming back." Her skin is almost back to normal. I see hints of her unique feminine softness and glow.

She nods, flipping through the chart resting at the end of the bed. "Ripley lost a lot of blood. Her counts look fine though. Her organs are finally functioning as they should."

"When will she wake up?"

"She was sedated to give her body what it needed to recover. It's worn off now. It will be soon, I promise."

Dr. Berger checks a few of the machines before placing her hand on my shoulder. "Everything is looking good. Don't worry. You should probably go home and get some rest."

"I'll leave when my wife leaves with me."

She gives me a small smile and then turns and walks out of the room. I'm caressing Ripley's hand with my fingers, promising to love her if she comes back to me. Something I've done about a thousand times over the past two days.

Suddenly her eyelids flutter, and then her eyes start to blink a few times. It takes a few moments, but they eventually focus on me. She attempts to talk but she can't with the tube down her throat. She grabs for it as she begins to freak out.

"Relax, Shortcake. Don't pull it." I press the button above her head. "I just called for the nurse. They said they'd remove it as soon as you woke up."

She nods as she appears to calm down.

I stare at her and kiss her hand. "I love you. I promise to tell you that every day for the rest of my life."

She feels her empty stomach and then frantically looks around the room, no doubt searching for our daughter.

"She's okay, Shortcake. She's beautiful and perfect, just like you, and getting stronger every day."

Her face drips with emotion. I'm sure she wants to see the baby.

"They have to keep her here for a few weeks, closer to your due date, to make sure her lungs and everything else are good. But every day that goes by, she crosses another milestone. She can't wait to meet her mom."

Tears leak out of her eyes, and I wipe them for her.

"Can I get you anything?"

She gingerly pulls her hand from mine. She's so weak and frail right now. I've never seen her like this.

A nurse appears. I turn when she walks in. "She's awake."

The nurse smiles and pokes her head into the hallway. A few seconds later, Dr. Berger returns. "She's awake?"

I nod.

She walks over to the bed and looks down at Ripley. "Ripley, I'm Dr. Berger. Do you remember me?"

Ripley shakes her head.

"I figured. It was a bit crazy when you arrived." She goes on to tell Ripley everything that she told me when I arrived, though this time she starts with the fact that the baby is doing well.

"Ripley, we're going to remove your breathing tube. You're going to gag, and your throat will be very sore. That's normal."

Ripley nods again.

After a few minutes and a little maneuvering, the tube is gone. She tries to talk but she's hoarse. I pour her some water and help guide the straw so she can sip it.

After testing a few of her motor functions, the doctor and nurses are satisfied and leave the room. It's just Ripley and me now.

I try to take her hand again, but she pulls it away, croaking out, "Don't."

I hold my hands up in surrender, not wanting to upset her. "Okay. I'm so sorry, Shortcake. I'm sorry I've been gone. I needed the time to figure things out. To think about if I can be a husband and father. You know I never thought I'd be capable of either. The one thing I came back knowing for sure is that I love you. I will never love anyone the way I love you. If I'm being honest, I was still shaky on the father thing, but now that I've seen our little girl, I'm in love with her too. She's so beautiful. She looks just like you."

She whispers, "Don't call me that," as tears stream down her cheeks. I go to wipe them again, but this time she turns her head.

She reaches and presses the call button again. When the nurse appears, Ripley again can only whisper. "I want to see my baby."

The nurse nods. "Let me check with Dr. Berger."

She then turns and walks out.

"We need to come up with a name, Shor—" I cut myself off, trying to respect her wishes.

She whispers, "I know. I want a name that starts with a K."

"Why?"

She rolls her eyes as if it's obvious. "We're pitchers."

I smile at that. K stands for strikeout in baseball and softball. "Good idea. I'll brainstorm. You focus on getting strong again."

In a crackly voice, she says, "Stay away from me. I just want to see my baby."

Before I can respond, the nurse walks back in with a big smile. "Dr. Berger is okay with it as long as you're in a wheelchair with your IV. Are you ready to meet your little girl?"

Ripley nods and then whispers, "Can I take a shower first? I feel disgusting."

"Not quite yet, but your husband has been keeping you clean. He's taken quite good care of you these past few days. He wouldn't let us do anything, insisting on doing your daily sponge baths."

She snaps her head to me, and I grin. "It was my absolute pleasure."

More tears find her eyes as she sighs and breathes, "Can we please go?"

A wheelchair is brought in. They bring in two male nurses to help move her into it, but I shove them away. "I'll take care of my wife."

I lift her and gently place her in the wheelchair. I roll her down to the NICU. Arizona is in there holding the baby. Her face lights up when she sees Ripley.

After handing the baby to a nurse, Arizona practically sprints out of the NICU to hug Ripley. Her face is again full of tears. "You're awake. Oh thank god."

Ripley simply stares at the baby as tears begin to stream down her cheeks. Arizona wipes them.

I look at Arizona. "Her throat is sore. It's hard for her to talk."

Arizona nods as she rubs Ripley's arm. "She's so beautiful, Rip. Thankfully she looks like you, not vagina face over here." She points my way.

Ripley lets out a hoarse laugh and whispers, "He does look like a vagina."

Arizona nods in agreement. "He's the full package. He looks like a vagina and acts like a dick. He can actually go fuck himself."

Ripley giggles. It's the first big smile I've seen on her face. I truly don't care that it's at my expense.

I roll my eyes. "You're fucking hysterical, Z."

She winks. "Whatever it takes to put a smile on my girl's face. Are you ready to meet your daughter, Rip? She's perfection, but she told me she wants to be a catcher, not a pitcher."

Ripley smiles but shakes her head and croaks, "No way. She's a pitcher."

I wheel her to the sterilization area. "Come on, time for you to meet our redheaded angel."

Ripley gets sterilized and does everything necessary to prepare to hold our daughter. Watching the nurse place her in Ripley's arms for the first time is a moment that will forever be embedded in my mind.

Arizona is there too. All three of us are now crying.

At some point, Ripley asks about her mom. I answer, "I sent her home to sleep. She hasn't gotten any rest in days. She'll be back soon. I texted her to let her know that you're awake."

RIPLEY

Holding my baby for the first time is the most emotion-filled moment of my life. I can't deal with Quincy's hovering yet. I just want to take in my little girl.

When they brought me to the hospital, everyone was so panicked, and I was immediately sedated. I hate that I don't remember her birth. I'm filled with sadness that I didn't have my first moment with her when they took her from my body.

At the nurse's insistence, I'm told to go back to my room to rest. I'm wheeled back by Quincy and Arizona who are bickering, per always. I was surprised to see Quincy at my bedside when I woke. I was more surprised to hear him tell me he loved me over and over when he thought I was asleep and then again when I was awake.

When we get back to my room, Quincy again refuses help

from any staff and places me back in bed. I don't have the strength to fight him. Yet.

At some point, I realize the date. With my throat feeling a bit better, I ask, "Shouldn't you be at spring training right now?"

He and Arizona exchange glances before he turns back to me. "I'm on a family emergency leave of absence."

I nod in understanding. "Are you headed back tonight?"

"No. I'm exactly where I belong. I'll return when you and our daughter can return with me."

I shake my head. "I don't live in Philly anymore."

Before he can respond, Dr. Berger walks in. "There she is. Ripley, you look great. I just heard your voice from the hallway. It sounds like your throat is already doing better."

"That's hardly true." At least the part about me looking great. I look like I was at death's door, which I may very well have been. I certainly feel like it.

"Assuming all goes well, we're going to release you by the end of the week. You'll need to take it easy, but I'm sure you'll be happier to do so at home instead of at this hospital."

I pinch my eyebrows in confusion. "My baby girl will be ready to leave by then?"

"No, but you will be."

"I'm not leaving without my daughter."

She gives me a small smile. "That's not how it works."

Quincy clearly knew this was coming. "Don't worry, I rented a house down the street. We'll be close by."

I shake my head. "I'm not staying with you. I live with my mother. I'll stay with her."

He sighs. "Shortcake," he's never once called me that in front of other people, "your mom lives in a tiny apartment nearly thirty minutes from the hospital. Wouldn't you rather be closer to the baby? Arizona and Layton are staying there too."

Arizona interrupts, "Layton is getting it set up now. It's right down the street. It's perfect for us to be closer to the hospital. Consider it, please, Rip."

I sigh as I see the doctor sneak out. "How big is this place?"

Quincy answers, "Six bedrooms. Your mom is welcome too."

Somehow, he found a damn palace within walking distance of the hospital.

"Fine. Just until the baby comes home, and then we'll be going back to my mom's until I find my own place. I've already started looking. I just thought I had a little more time."

Quincy doesn't look happy, but he says nothing else.

Arizona turns to Quincy. "Why did you call her Shortcake?"

"I've always called her that."

She shakes her head. "I've never heard you call her that."

"I guess it's always been in private. The first time we met, she was carrying a Strawberry Shortcake lunchbox. It started then."

She nods. "Good. I thought it was some dirty thing. I can't believe you two have been bumping uglies in secret for over ten fucking years."

I blow out a long breath. "That's ancient history. All in the past. Arizona, can you help me get cleaned up?"

Quincy shakes his head. "That's my job."

Arizona rolls her eyes. "He wouldn't let me do it when you were unconscious. I think he was perving on you."

Quincy's jaw tightens. "It's not perving when I'm her husband. It's perving if *you* do it, Z."

"No, it's not. I've seen her naked more than you have."

He mutters, "I doubt that."

I've had enough. "Both of you, stop. Quincy, I should have you arrested for what you did. You're not my husband in any way that matters. If you'd sign the damn divorce papers I sent, this nightmare would be behind us. Go be with our baby while you still can. Arizona will help me clean up, and then I'll be back down."

He scowls as he walks out, finally leaving me alone with Arizona. I look at her. "Did he really bathe me?"

She bites her lip. "He went fucking nuts when anyone else tried to touch you."

I lay my head back in disgust. "Ugh."

"Is it that big of a deal? You were sleeping with him for ten years. It's not like he hasn't seen you naked."

Tears fill my eyes. "Yes, Arizona, it is a big deal. It's a violation. We're over. We've been over for a long time. His choice, not mine. Marc has seen you naked thousands of times. Would you be okay if he saw you naked now? If he touched your unconscious body?"

She hangs her head. "Sorry. You're right. I should have done more."

I grab her hand. "I'm sorry. I'm hormonal and emotional. It's not your fault. I can't believe everything that has happened." I give her a small smile. "Now give me a sponge bath, and not the kind you gave Layton when he was in the hospital."

We both giggle. When Layton broke his leg, Arizona played dirty nurse every single day he was in the hospital.

CHAPTER TWENTY-SEVEN

QUINCY

Ripley is coming home today. She cried when they forced her out, fearing being away from our daughter. They told her not to come to the hospital between eight p.m. and eight a.m. because she needs time to physically recover. They're letting June stay with the baby a little later though.

I help her into the house and to the master bedroom. My stuff is in there. She turns to me. "I'm not staying with you."

"I know. I'll move down the hall. What can I do to help before I go?"

"Nothing. I'll have Arizona help me shower. I'm going to cry if I can't wash my nasty hair in the next five minutes."

I sigh. "If you change your mind, I'm the third door down on the left."

I grab my belongings and make my way to one of the other bedrooms.

An hour later, I'm lying in bed listening to music when I see my bedroom door open.

Ripley's gorgeous face pokes through the opening.

I immediately remove my earphones. "Is everything okay?"

Her jaw is tight, but she manages to spit out, "Can you help me deal with the shower? I tried. I can't do it on my own. When I lift my arms, my stitches start pulling."

I jump up from the bed. "Happy to. Where's Z?"

"They've been going at it for nearly an hour with no signs of slowing down. I can't wait any longer."

I wince. "Ugh. I didn't need to hear that."

"I can't believe you haven't heard it. She's so damn loud."

"I've been wearing earphones on purpose."

I help her to the bathroom, gathering everything she needs. I hang a towel on the hook, turn on the water, and wait for it to get warm.

She gingerly sits on the bench so I can take off her shoes and socks. Once I help her up, I start to remove her shirt, but she grabs my wrist. "Don't. Just help me take off my bra. I can't reach around. I'll manage my way through the rest."

I nod as she turns around, and I move my hands up the back of her shirt, unclasping her bra. "Okay, thank you. I've got it from here."

"Are you sure you don't want any more help?"

"I'm positive."

"Can I help you finish getting undressed? It must hurt."

"No. I don't want you to see me like this."

"Are you joking? You just had a baby. You had surgery. And I've already seen you."

"Go, Quincy. Leave me alone."

"Fine."

I walk out of the bathroom and close the door, but I don't go far. I listen at the door just in case she needs me.

After just a few seconds, I hear her start to whimper. That whimper soon turns into sobs.

I'm not sitting out here doing nothing. Walking back in, I see her shirt half off.

"Quincy! I said I want to be alone."

"I know you're upset with me. I know we need to talk. But you're hurting. You could injure yourself if you're not careful. Please, put our stuff aside for a few minutes and let me be here for you in your time of need."

Her voice cracks and her sad eyes find mine. "Please go. Don't you understand? I don't want you to see me like this. This whole thing has been humiliating enough. We don't need to add to it."

"I know how much you want your hair washed. You won't be able to lift your arms to do it. I'm not judging you. Let me help you."

She squeezes her eyes shut as tears saturate her eyelashes.

I remove my clothes, and then carefully remove hers until she's standing in the weirdest underwear I've ever seen. It's mesh and enormous, with a ton of padding between her legs.

I saw it the last time I cleaned her, but I thought it was just for hospital use. I didn't realize she'd come home with it.

Tears stream down her cheeks. I get down on my knees and kiss her stomach before looking up at her.

"Thank you for taking care of our baby for the past seven months. Now it's my turn to take care of both of you."

I place my fingers in the underwear. "I'm going to remove the ugliest underwear ever created."

She lets out a small laugh through her sobs. "I don't know what they are, but I might have nightmares about them moving forward. The hospital gave me dozens of them."

I smile. "I might have nightmares too."

Slowly removing them, I see a little blood in the pad area. She winces.

"Am I hurting you?"

"No I'm cringing that you're seeing all this mess."

"Shortcake, I've fucked you on your period before. I'm not afraid of a little blood."

She mumbles, "You coerced me that time."

"I did no such thing. You jumped my bones. Practically forced *me* into it."

Her mouth widens. "That's not what happened."

"Hmm. We'll agree to disagree."

I discard the hideous underwear and then help her into the shower. She looks around at everything in there and pinches her eyebrows. "How do you know my exact shampoos and soaps?"

"I know what my girl likes. I can neither confirm nor deny that I usually have your shampoo on hand because I need it to get off."

"You sit and smell a bottle of my shampoo while you jerk off?"

"Sometimes I smell it, and sometimes I rub it on my dick when I jerk off."

"You're a freak."

"A freak for you. Now get under the water."

She does. I'm half in and half out, freezing my ass off, but I want to make sure she's taken care of.

Once her hair is fully soaked, I grab the bottle of shampoo. She snatches it from my hands. "I'll do it."

She pours it on her hand, but when she attempts to lift her arm toward her head, she winces.

I scoop the shampoo from her hand. "Let me do it. I'm already in here with you."

Standing behind her, I massage the shampoo into her scalp. She lets out a soft moan, and my semi goes fully erect. I'm standing behind her, so I'm hopeful she won't notice.

She mumbles, "I can't believe you're hard right now."

I guess she noticed.

"If the day ever comes that I don't get hard from your naked body, you should just put me down like a dog. Now stay still so I can properly clean you without ripping your stitches."

I take my sweet time with the shampoo, conditioner, and body wash, making sure every inch of her is clean. I don't know if and when she'll ever let me be naked with her again, so I'm stretching this out to the max.

She turns her head back. "I think my nipples are adequately cleaned. It's been ten straight minutes."

"Oh, I'm...just making sure."

"I officially have the cleanest nipples in the world. It's time to get out. I'm tired. I want to sleep so I can get up early to go be with Kaya."

"Kaya?"

"Yes, I think I want to name her Kaya. It means inner strength."

I nod. "I like it. Kaya." I say it a few times as it sinks in. My daughter's name is Kaya.

"Okay. Let me get out first so I can get your clothes. Don't move. I'll help you do everything."

"I don't have anything with me except those hideous disposable undies. Can I borrow a robe or a T-shirt?"

"You have drawers full of clothes. I went shopping for you."

"You did?"

"Yes. Let me take care of you."

"Fine, but I'll do the pads and mesh underwear. Not you."

"Deal."

I quickly towel off and grab some of the clothes I bought for her. When I return, she's standing there wrapped in a towel. Her curly hair is wild, and the tops of her breasts are peeking out. I can't help but stare at her. "You're beautiful."

She rolls her eyes. "I'm anything but beautiful right now. What do you have for me?"

I hand the set of pajamas to her, and she raises an eyebrow. "Are you kidding me?"

I can't help but smirk. "Quincy Abbott pajamas are all the rage." My face is all over them.

She sighs. "Turn around."

"We just showered together."

"Quincy!"

"Fine, but I'm not leaving. I want to help you into bed."

After a few minutes of her getting dressed and me brushing her hair and teeth for her, I help her into bed, desperate to stay with her but knowing I haven't earned that right yet.

CHAPTER TWENTY-EIGHT

RIPLEY

For the past month, we've lived in this house. We're here at night but spend our days with Kaya. She's getting big and strong. She's already bigger than a full-term baby. They want to keep her one more week to make sure everything is good before releasing her.

We've completely avoided the topic of what will happen once she leaves the hospital. The Cougars' preseason ended, and the regular season just started. Quincy needs to get back to Philly. Poor Arizona and Layton haven't left either. They have a wedding reception to plan and a life to live. I've told them countless times to go home. They said they will when Kaya is out of the hospital.

Quincy hasn't left my side for a single minute. He's made sure every single need of mine and Kaya's is being met. I'm not sure what caused the change in his feelings on parenting, but he does everything for our little girl. Feeding, bathing, changing. Anything they'll allow, he does.

As for me, he's been attending to everything. Physically. Emotionally, I'm not sure I'll ever recover.

My body is healing. I still have a little pain, but it gets better each and every day.

Paul and Pamela have been to the hospital a handful of times. I was happy to see that Quincy was warmer to them. I'm not sure what happened between Thanksgiving and now, but something caused things to thaw a bit.

We're having a late dinner one night with a few bottles of wine. Kaya couldn't breastfeed, so I tried to pump, but my supply dried up without the natural suction of a baby. The good news is that I can drink for the first time in nearly nine months.

Arizona is on Layton's lap as they giggle about something. They have their own little language. They're so cute together.

Quincy places his glass down and looks at me. "I have something to say, and I need you to let me get it out before you jump all over me."

"Oookay."

"I want you to move back to Philly."

"Quin—"

"You promised to let me speak."

"Fine. But I'm not moving again. I'm staying out here, close to my mom."

"I want to be close to you and our daughter. I more than recognize that I made several poor choices when I found out you were pregnant." He runs his hands through his curls. "Hell, I know I've made several poor choices for years when it comes to you, but I love you. I want to be with you."

I shake my head but keep my mouth shut. Arizona and Layton are suddenly very quiet, paying close attention.

"I know you don't trust me, and I understand. I don't deserve your trust, but I want the opportunity to earn it. Just know that I do love you, and I love our daughter too. Every fucking concern I had about myself as a parent went right out the fucking door the first second I saw her and held her. Please don't keep her away from me on the other side of the country. The Anacondas haven't traded you. You had this baby two months ahead of schedule. With a lot of hard work, you can be ready for your season. You can only do that with certain resources and support. My new house is finished. It has a state-of-the-art gym. I've hired a personal trainer to help you get your strength back. I've spoken with your mother. I'm hiring her as your personal pitching coach. I had a pitching tunnel put in the house for you. She's going to stay with us for as long as it takes to get you up to snuff and to help us with Kaya as we manage our busy schedules. The house now has a crib and everything that's needed. All I need is for you to agree to it."

I'm in shock that he did all this. I turn to Arizona, and she gives me a hopeful smile. "Sorry, Rip, but I'm with him on this one. I want my niece near me. I want my best friend on my team again. You love Philly. You love our team. You want your daughter to have her father in her life. It's the best thing for everyone."

Not my heart. Tears find my eyes. I'm torn. I want to be in Philly for every reason in the world other than being around Quincy. How will I ever move on if I'm living with him? But how can I deny him his daughter if he wants to be in her life? How can I do that to her? I would have given anything to have had my father in my life.

He continues, "If, at the end of this season, you decide you want to move back to California, I will either retire or request a trade to a team in this area."

"But you just built the house. I thought you wanted Philly as your forever home."

"You and Kaya are my forever home."

I take a few deep breaths, trying to keep my emotions in check. "I'll agree to this on one condition."

Quincy's face lights up. "Anything."

"Sign the divorce papers."

His face drops.

"If you're serious about being near our daughter, sign them, and I'll come. I'm doing this for her."

Tears fill his eyes. "I don't want to give up on us."

"There is no us, Quincy. You and I are over. Time and time again you chose not to be with me. I loved you so hard for so damn long. I wasted years of my life loving a man who was never willing to love me back. I'm not a toy you can take out and play with and then throw in the closet for days, months, or even years at a time. I'm a real person with real feelings, feelings you've never once considered. On many occasions, I've asked you to love me in the light, not in the dark. You wouldn't give me that. When you walked out on me when I told you I was pregnant, I was devastated. I cried myself to sleep every night until one morning I woke up and swore I'd never let you do that to me again. I've shed too many tears over you, Quincy Abbott. I'll do this for our daughter. I don't want her to grow up without a father like I did. I'll stay with you because I recognize that I'm going to need help and resources these first few months. When my season is over, I'm moving out of your house. We'll figure out a fair custody agreement for Kaya. Your season ends then too. The timing will be right."

He's quiet for several long beats before eventually nodding. "I'll sign them, but I won't give up hope. Ever."

"There's nothing left to hope for." I stand. "If you're serious about our daughter, sign them, and I'll start packing. If not, we'll see you when you get the chance."

I summon every ounce of strength I have to hold my head up and walk out of that room to my bedroom. Laying on the bed, I hug a pillow to my chest and let the tears fall. Why now? I waited years for him to say things like that to me.

A few minutes later, there's a knock at my door. I expect Quincy's voice, but it's Arizona's.

"Can I come in?"

"Of course."

She walks in, lays down, and turns to me. She gently wipes the tears pooled under my eyes. "Don't cry over him. Don't give any man that power over you. You're the best person I know, Rip. Make that vagina-looking, long-haired motherfucker grovel."

I giggle. "Is it pathetic that I think his beard and hair are sexy?"

She scrunches her face. "I think the word you're looking for is crazy, not pathetic."

I blow out a breath. "I've been crying over him for much longer than I'd care to admit."

She tucks my hair behind my ear. "I know. You won't leave the possibility open for it to work out between you two?" She pinches her index finger and thumb close together. "Maybe just a crack in the door?"

The tears start falling from my eyes again. "He's hurt me so many times. You have no idea. I don't know if it's his baggage or some amount of shame about being with me, but —"

She shakes her head. "I don't believe that at all. He's fucked up, but he's been different the past month. He's laser focused on you and Kaya. I've never seen him like this."

"I'm genuinely happy that he wants to be there for her. I didn't think he would. I'll never deny him that."

"I know you won't. It's just...seeing him with you the past

few weeks has been both bizarre and sweet. He loves you, Rip. Of that, I'm sure."

She's quiet for a moment. "I've spent a lot of time thinking about your relationship with him. I can't believe I missed all the signs. The biggest change in you has been your body image. You spent our entire adolescence insecure about your body. While you still don't realize how truly beautiful you are, was he the reason for your uptick in confidence?"

She has a hopeful look on her face.

I nod. "Yes. I don't know how to explain it, especially to his sister. Even the first night we were together, when I was eighteen, he never let me hide my body. He practically worshiped it. He loved everything I hated about myself, but he's never been willing to love *me*. I've asked...I've begged for it. I'm not enough for him. Now we have this child together and suddenly he outwardly loves me? I wanted it for ten years. I think he's transferring his feelings for Kaya to me. I'm thrilled he wants to be in her life, and I'd be lying if I said I'm not enjoying him openly professing his love for me, but why now? If I choose to stay with him, I'll never know if it's for Kaya or me. That's not fair to me."

"I hear what you're saying, but I don't think one has anything to do with the other. I think your pregnancy forced him to finally confront his demons."

"In what way?"

"I'm not completely sure. I know he hasn't been back in Philly since Thanksgiving. The only time I've seen or spoken to him was in the minutes before your mom called to say that you went into labor."

"Where has he been this whole time?"

"He spent time with our dad at first, but then he said he traveled. I don't know where. Maybe he'll share that with you. Just don't close the door completely. You should have seen him in the hospital with you. We assumed on our flight here that the baby was gone. He was beside himself with desperation to get to you. He sat at your bedside, held your hand, and cried. He professed his love for you when he didn't think there was a baby." She rubs my arm. "When I finally saw him again after all these months, I tore into him for how he treated you. He immediately agreed and mentioned wanting to make things right."

"You don't understand. Our whole relationship has been on his terms. I feel like I lost a little of myself. That's not okay. That's not the example I want to set for my daughter. I want a man to love me the way Layton loves you or not at all."

She gives me a soft smile. "He loves me good, doesn't he?"

"Yes, and I hear it every single night. Every. Single. Night."

She giggles.

"Is the guy on Viagra? He fucks you for hours."

She laughs louder. "No drugs needed. It's all him." She rolls to her back and looks up at the ceiling with a dreamy look on her face. "We're definitely insatiable for each other. I keep waiting for it to end, but I think it's getting more intense. I love him so fucking much."

I reach for her hand. "I know you do. And it's the same for him. He doesn't care who knows it. You should have seen him when you were away. He outwardly pined for you. He was incomplete without you. Is it so wrong that I want that too?"

She squeezes my hand. "No, it's not. You deserve nothing less. Let nature take its course. I've seen a different side of Quincy this past month. Just think about giving him a chance."

I WAKE up in the morning to a large envelope that was clearly slipped under my door while I slept. I open it and see the signed divorce papers. I experience a moment of sadness and a moment of relief. I'm not sure which feeling is stronger.

There's a yellow Post-it on the front that reads:

This doesn't mean anything

☑ *get Ripley back to Philly*
☐ *make her mine*

CHAPTER TWENTY-NINE

RIPLEY

As soon as I gave Quincy the go-ahead, there were movers at my mom's apartment packing my belongings and anything Mom wanted to take with her. He won't let me lift a single finger. He even arranged for a doctor to travel with us on the plane in case Kaya has any issues on board.

We're about to land in Philly. Arizona looks at me. "Don't be mad, but we're having a little welcome gathering tomorrow afternoon. It's the only day the Cougars are off. We didn't get to have a baby shower with you delivering so early and my brother being a douchebag. Let us do this for you."

I smile at her. "Thanks, babe. I appreciate it. It will be good to see everyone. It's been a long time."

Quincy narrows his eyes at her. "Yes, thanks for that."

Arizona smiles at him. "You're welcome, Jesus. Are you going to shave and get a haircut, or should we throw you up on the cross?"

Layton and I laugh while the siblings are engaged in a

stare down. Truth be told, I like his beard. I'd be lying if I said a part of me doesn't want to know what it feels like between my legs.

Three Suburbans are waiting for us at the airport. One to take Arizona and Layton to their place, one for mine and Mom's luggage, and one to take me, Quincy, Mom, and Kaya to Quincy's house. I suddenly realize that I don't have a car seat. I have nothing.

Quincy must sense my panic. "Don't worry. I ordered a car with a car seat and have three at the house, one for each of our cars. I researched the best brand on the market."

"My mom and I don't have cars."

He mumbles, "You do now."

"Quincy, what did you do?"

"We're not living in the city anymore. You need a car to get around. I want you in a safe car, so that's what you got. Now either say thank you or be quiet."

I'm silent for a moment before acquiescing. "Thank you. It's a loaner."

He grunts, "Whatever."

I can't help but smile.

He narrows his eyes at me. "What are you smiling at?"

"I missed grumpy Quincy. You've been too nice the past few weeks. It's off-putting."

Arizona giggles as she hugs me. She whispers in my ear, "I'm not the only one who pushes his buttons. Have fun. I'll be over early tomorrow. Love you."

"Love you too."

We strap Kaya in. She mostly slept on the plane but seems wide awake now, tracking all the lights and action around us. Quincy bends down to kiss her, and she grabs onto his beard and squeezes for dear life.

He screams in pain. Mom and I start laughing. Mom pats

his leg. "You know who you look like, Quincy? The fat, funny friend from the movie *The Hangover*."

My laugh deepens, but Quincy appears appalled. "I look *nothing* like him. I'm a foot taller than that guy and have a six-pack."

Mom winks at me. She's messing with him too, but then Quincy pulls up his shirt for her, flashing his washboard abs.

Her eyes bug out of her head, and she shamelessly stares. She leans toward me and not so quietly whispers, "You sure you don't want to tap that again?"

Quincy smirks at me. Oh boy, this living arrangement is going to be interesting.

We begin our journey to the house and eventually pull through a gate and onto the now-paved driveway. I suck in a breath as the house comes into view. "Oh my god, Quincy, it's the most beautiful house I've ever seen."

He breathes out, "Holy shit. This is mine?"

He has a boyish, prideful look on his face. I'm happy for him. I know this has always been a dream of his.

Mom asks, "You haven't seen the house yet, Quincy?"

"Just in photos. It was a shell the last time I saw it."

As we get closer, I notice Collin standing there. Mom mumbles, "Who's the hottie? Is he a gift for me?"

I smile as I shake my head. "No, Mom. He's the contractor, and he's very taken. I've met his significant other. She's gorgeous."

Quincy nods. "Collin and Jade are coming to the party tomorrow afternoon. I hope that's okay."

"Of course. I loved Jade when we met her."

When the car stops, Quincy reaches for Kaya, but I grab his wrist. "Go thank Collin. I've got her." I was only cleared to start lifting things a few days ago. I'm happy to finally be able to do everything for Kaya.

He nods as he walks over and shakes Collin's hand. Mom and I get Kaya out of the car. Collin's face lights up as we approach. "She's beautiful. Congratulations."

"Thank you. You did an amazing job on this house, Collin."

"You haven't even seen it yet. Come inside. I hope you like the furniture. That's not really my area of expertise. Gemma met with the interior decorator a million times until she was satisfied with everything."

Quincy looks at me. "Considering the fact that I wasn't here, and Gemma has such great taste, I asked her to pick everything. And they had a baby last year, so she knows what's needed for a nursery and other childproofing."

I pinch my eyebrows. "You put in a nursery?"

He looks at me like I'm insane. "Of course I put in a nursery. I told you that."

He mentioned a crib, not a full nursery.

Collin hands Quincy a bunch of keys and instructs, "These are just backups. Everything is run through fingerprint or code mechanisms. The temporary code is both of your jersey numbers together, three-four-two-seven. We can set up the fingerprints before I leave, but the audio-visual guy will be out in the morning to walk you through the smart house. Everything, and I mean *everything*, is smart in this house."

We walk in, and all our chins drop. It's modern, huge, and open. Gemma hit it out of the park with the furnishings. It's a true work of art. There's no other way to describe it. A beautiful, perfect work of art that looks like it belongs in a magazine.

The décor and small touches are like nothing I've ever seen. "Oh, Quincy, wow."

I see Quincy struggling with his emotions. He looks completely overwhelmed. I hand Kaya to Mom. Grabbing

Quincy's face in my hands, I pull his forehead to mine. "It's all because of your hard work. You made this happen. This was your dream, and now it's complete. You deserve this. You've earned it. Enjoy it."

He softly rubs my face with his hand. "Dreams change. Mine's not complete yet."

"Because you don't have a dog like Diamond?"

He simply shakes his head as he looks me in the eyes. "Because I don't have you."

I swallow hard before pulling away. After taking a moment to compose myself, I turn to Collin. "Please, show us around."

For the next twenty minutes, Collin gives us the full tour. I didn't know houses could be this incredible, but it's not until we walk into the nursery that tears truly fill my eyes. In my wildest dreams, I could never have imagined a nursery this spectacular for my daughter.

It's filled with colors. The crib is magical. There are tons of toys and stuffed animals everywhere. When I look into the crib, I have to bite my lip to hold back a sob. There's a big Strawberry Shortcake doll sitting there. As I look around, I see a lot of strawberry touches. Hanging artwork, stuffed strawberries, and even more of them painted on the walls. It's the whole theme of the room.

I manage to whisper, "Thank you."

I'm not sure if it's to Quincy, Collin, or the universe, but I say it. Quincy nods. "I'll always take care of my family."

MY ROOM IS next to Quincy's, and my mother's is at the other end of the house. He had a bassinet set up next to my bed so the baby can sleep with me for as long as she needs it. This is my first night alone with her. I'm nervous as hell.

Mom heads to bed early and tells me to wake her if she's needed. I feed and rock Kaya in her room until she's asleep. When she is, I gently place her in the bassinet in my room.

Quincy pokes his head in. "I'm headed to bed. I'm happy to feed her during the night. Just let me know what you need."

"Thanks, Quincy."

He nods.

"I mean for everything. I'm glad we came back with you."

He gives me his small, crooked smile. "Me too, Shortcake."

I have no idea what time it is when I'm awakened by blood-curdling screams, but I physically jump out of bed and pick up Kaya, whose face is red and eyes are watering. "What's the matter, baby girl?"

She screams again.

After changing and feeding her, she's still screaming. I can't get her to stop. I have no idea what to do. Maybe I should wake my mom. Maybe we need to go to the hospital.

Quincy walks in wearing only boxer briefs. His hair is messy. Is it normal to look that good in the middle of the night?

He grumbles, "Is she okay?"

I shrug. "I don't know. I changed and fed her, but she won't stop crying."

He holds out his big hands. "Give her to me."

I hand my red-faced, screaming daughter to him. The second she nuzzles into his chest, she stops crying and lets out a little coo of contentment. Yep, kiddo, I get the appeal.

He winks at me. "The ladies love my touch."

I roll my eyes, and he chuckles as he starts swaying with her in his arms. "Go back to sleep. I've got her. I'll put her down when she dozes off."

"Are you sure?"

"We're a team. Get sleep while you can."

I wake in what must be the early morning hours because the daylight is just breaking through the curtains in my room. I immediately pop up and look into the bassinet. It's empty. I panic until I turn to the other side of my bed.

Quincy is fast asleep with Kaya equally so on his chest. His hand is holding her entire body protectively. I get choked up with emotion at the vision of them together like this. It's quite possibly the most beautiful thing I've ever seen in my life, something I wasn't sure would ever happen. In fact, I was convinced it wouldn't.

I grab my phone and take a picture of their moment, immediately setting it as the wallpaper on my phone.

CHAPTER THIRTY

QUINCY

I was instructed to get Ripley out of the house so Arizona and crew could set up for the party. I made an appointment with a pediatrician to check on Kaya and attend to whatever was needed.

When we return, we walk out back to a sea of cheers and congratulations. The whole back of the house is open to the pool area, which Arizona has decorated in true Arizona fashion. It's a nice spring day. I'm excited to see everyone and have them at my new house, which far exceeded any expectations I had.

I see all of our teammates, plus Blanche, the Daultons, Collin, and Jade.

Kam takes one look at me and crosses her arms. "Holy shit, Quincy, you look like Charles Manson."

Arizona smiles. "I think he looks like a vagina in need of a Brazilian wax."

Cheetah chuckles and asks, "Q, if you cut your lip, do you prefer a tampon or maxi pad to stop the bleeding?"

Everyone laughs...at my expense. As always. I walked in less than sixty seconds ago, and it's already begun.

I narrow my eyes at all of them. "I was last to arrive. How about a random fact?"

They all nod.

"Does anyone know where the term *beard* came from?"

They all look around, no one having any idea.

"It's actually an acronym. B.E.A.R.D. stands for Being Exceptional Among Regular Dudes."

Cheetah shakes his head. "No fucking way."

I nod. "Yep. Look it up."

Kam sighs. "Honestly, Q, it's kind of hot. Frankly, I wouldn't mind riding that beard."

I catch Ripley mumble to herself, "Me too."

I smile down at her, and she widens her eyes as if she didn't intend to say that out loud.

Reagan Daulton interrupts, "As someone whose husband has a beard, I can tell you that the ride is worth the price of admission."

Reagan is basically the boss of almost everyone here. We don't normally see that side of her, though she's always been friendly and casual around us.

The girls all completely and obviously check out her husband, Carter. Reagan gives a knowing smile.

Everyone then spends the next twenty minutes oohing and ahhing over Kaya. I look around. Arizona did a nice job enhancing the natural beauty of my backyard, and Ripley seems happy. That makes me happy.

I lean over to Collin. "Thanks again, man. This place

is amazing. And sorry about the last-minute changes. I did them for Ripley."

He smiles. "I know. I get it." He stares at Jade. "The right woman is worth making a few changes for, right?" He winks at her, and she gives him the universal sign for a blow job.

He laughs.

"I think you're right. Now if I could only get that woman on board, it would be great."

He slaps my back. "The great ones are worth fighting for. Trust me, I know. Be patient."

I nod. "That's the plan."

We sit around all afternoon talking, laughing, and drinking. A few people swim, including Cheetah and Kam who don't keep their hands off each other. I wonder what's gone on between them while I was gone. They've never been this outwardly affectionate.

Everyone has a lot of questions for Reagan and Carter. They're obviously the team owners, but they also own one of the biggest companies in the world, Daulton Holdings. They hear pitches for new business all day long, and everyone seems amused by that.

Kam asks, "What's the craziest business anyone has ever pitched?"

Reagan and Carter look at each other and smile before she turns back. "Secondhand sex toys. It may actually be the dumbest idea ever created. Carter and I couldn't keep straight faces throughout the entire meeting."

Carter nods in agreement. "The two guys who pitched us honestly thought there was a huge market of women wanting to save ten bucks by having a vibrator inside them that's already been inside another woman."

Kam shrugs. "People do it with dicks, why not vibrators too?"

Arizona giggles. "I bet you could come up with some good names for that. Maybe *Buzzed Again. Secondhand Hand.*"

Cheetah's eyes light up. Here we go. "*Vintage Vibrations, Recycled Rectum, Play It Again Plugs.*" He looks at Reagan. "Out of curiosity, what was the name of the company?"

She smirks. "That's the best part. Both of their first names were Richard. The company was named *Double Dicks.*"

I smile. It's fun to be around this crew again. I've missed them.

At some point, the party naturally splits into men and women. I see the girls all laughing in the far corner. I'm holding Kaya, who has a bottle in her mouth.

Trey nods my way as his own child sleeps on him. "Fatherhood looks good on you, Q."

I smile. "Thanks. I can't believe how much I love this little thing."

Cheetah sips his drink. "There was always some tension between you and Ripley, but I don't think any of us realized exactly what was happening."

I sigh. "Yep, I was an asshole."

Cheetah lets out a laugh. "No news there. Are you two together?"

I shake my head. "She doesn't want any part of me right now, but I'm breaking her down. One day soon, she'll be mine again. For good."

RIPLEY

I'm sitting with all the women as I watch Quincy across the pool where he's feeding Kaya. He's such a natural with her.

Kam breaks my thoughts. "Now that we know you've been fucking Quincy on the down-low for a decade, how about some details about Mr. Size Sixteen Feet?"

I can't help but giggle, though Arizona moans in disgust. My eyes move to Blanche with caution.

She scoffs. "Oh please, as if I haven't been wondering the same thing for over a year."

Everyone starts laughing. I turn to Arizona. "Sorry, babe." Turning back to the group, I admit, "He's...umm... proportionate. *Very* proportionate."

Blanche mumbles, "I knew it."

Arizona makes a gagging noise. "Ugh. Gross."

Blanche laughs before turning to Jade and examining the can in her hand. "What are you drinking, dear?"

I look closer at the can. What the hell? It can't be.

With a straight face, Jade answers, "Pussy Juice. It's a natural energy drink. Want some, Blanche?" The can actually has the word pussy written on it.

Blanche raises an eyebrow. "Darling, I haven't sipped from those waters since Kennedy was president. But if you're offering..."

She now wiggles those eyebrows, and we all burst into laughter. I love Blanche.

Jade shakes her head. "You're funny, Blanche. You remind me of my new grandmother. Do you know Glinda Windsor?"

Blanche lets out a laugh. "That old coot? I certainly do. She's a good friend of mine. You must be Amanda's daughter. Your mother married Beckett recently. Glinda adores your mom."

Jade nods. "Yep. They're besties."

"Glinda is dating that younger man now." She glances at Quincy and smiles. "She succeeded where I failed. Ripley stole Quincy from me."

I shake my head. "I don't want him. He's all yours, Blanche."

She pats my hand. "No, sweetie. Trust me, he's all yours."

AFTER A FUN AFTERNOON of being reunited with our friends, I bathe and feed Kaya. I'm now trying to get her to go to bed. She doesn't seem to want to cooperate.

Quincy walks in, again in boxer briefs that leave little to the imagination, and grabs her from me. "Go take a shower or a relaxing bath. I've got her."

"Are you sure?"

He nods. "My best girl and I might dance a little."

I throw my hair up in a messy bun and take a very quick shower just in case I'm needed.

When I get out, I wrap a towel around myself and listen at the door. I hear music and Quincy's voice.

I'm unable to make out what he's saying, so I open the door a crack and peek through. I see him dancing with her and talking to her. He's singing, but it's not to the words to the song. "You're a beautiful girl just like your mommy. I need you to be a good girl for me, so I can focus on winning back your mommy. I promise I'm going to try as hard as I can. I love her, and I love you. Neither of you are ever leaving me. We're going to be a family. I promise."

My eyes fill with tears. I must sniffle because his head snaps up toward me. He simply smiles and holds out his free arm. "Come dance with us."

Without any regard for my own emotional well-being, I walk over to them and let him hold me. It's been so long since he's touched me like this.

I wrap my arms around them both and sink my head into his chest. His scent is as familiar to me as my own. I inhale and then feel every muscle in my body relax.

The three of us sway for at least two songs, but I'm not truly sure how long it goes on. I'm completely lost in this euphoric feeling, never wanting it to end.

As one of the songs ends, I look up at him, and he looks down at me. Without any other words, our lips find the other's. It's as if my progress over the past few months hasn't happened. My mind goes right back to where it's always been. With Quincy.

Just as the kiss is about to deepen, Kaya stirs, and I jump back. "Sorry."

He looks down at me in a way that threatens to break me. "Don't ever apologize for kissing me."

I need space. I turn away and mumble, "I need to go get dressed. I'll be back in a minute."

CHAPTER THIRTY-ONE

QUINCY

I'm awakened in the middle of the night to Ripley rubbing herself against me. Hells yes. Finally we're getting somewhere.

I look down and her eyes are closed. She's not totally with it. I think she's asleep. Should I wake her?

She's really going to town on my leg. I flex and move it a little to try to give her what she needs. Her hands move across my bare chest, and she mumbles, "Quincy."

At least I know she's thinking of me while she's doing this in her sleep.

Kaya fell asleep on my chest again. Ripley was already sleeping, so I placed Kaya in the bassinet. I should have gone back to my room, but I didn't want to. I slid into bed with Ripley, as I've done most nights since we got back, needing to hold her. And now, in her sleep, she's humping my leg.

Even through her shorts, her heat and wetness coat

my bare thigh. I feel slightly guilty knowing she's not conscious right now, but I didn't start this, she did. I'm an innocent bystander.

Her hips gyrate, and she mumbles my name over and over until she starts moaning and shaking. Even in her sleep, her neck flushes when she comes. So sexy.

Her eyes eventually blink open and then widen. She looks down, noticing her legs wrapped around my thigh. A bit out of breath, she asks, "What just happened?"

I bite back my smile as best as I can. "I'm pretty sure you had a wet dream...and used me." I can't stop my smile from breaking free. "I feel dirty."

She blows out a breath. "Shit. I had them constantly when I was pregnant. Something about the extra blood flow to the area. But I haven't had any since I gave birth."

"Fuck, I didn't know that about pregnancy. That's so hot. I haven't had a wet dream in nearly twenty years. You're so lucky."

She rolls her eyes. "Yes, I got to carry a baby, ruin my body, go through labor, be sliced in half, and nearly die, but hey, I got a few wet dreams out of it, so it's worthwhile."

I chuckle. "Point taken."

"I'm sorry. I didn't know what I was doing. I've obviously been sleeping alone throughout the pregnancy."

I'm not sure that was obvious, but I'm happy to hear it.

She starts to pull away, but I hold her to me, desperate for contact. "Don't go yet."

She makes no attempt to move but breathes, "Quincy, we can't."

I rub my hand up her thigh and feel goosebumps spread across her skin. I still affect her.

I run my lips over her cheeks. "Why can't we? It's obvious we're meant to be together."

"I've told you why."

I sigh as I pull my head back a bit. "I've been thinking. We've gone about this the wrong way. We've done everything in the wrong order, putting the cart before the horse. We've never been on a proper date. Let's start from the beginning. I want to take you out on a date."

I see a small smile form on her lips. "Are you asking me out?"

I emphatically nod. "Yes, I am."

"We're divorced with a child."

I rub her arm. "We can start over. No one writes our script but us. I refuse to believe it's too late for our happily ever after. I want to go on a date with you. Our first date. I want to pick you up and take you out to dinner."

In an accusatory tone, she asks, "In public? Somewhere people will see us?"

We've never once done that before. Have I mentioned that I'm a dick?

"Of course. We have night games all week and then a short road trip. I have a day off when we get back. Ripley St. James, will you go out with me next Monday night?"

She chews on her lower lip for a while. A long while. She looks up at the ceiling. "God help me. I'm a glutton for punishment." Turning her eyes back toward mine, she nonchalantly says, "Fine, I'll go. Just so you know, I don't put out on the first date."

I rub my fingertips over her neck in the way I know

drives her mad. Her eyes flutter and her whole body trembles. She loves my hands on her neck.

I stare deeply into her eyes. "I've gone over six months without sex. I'll wait as long as it takes. Forever if it means having you one more time."

She pinches her eyebrows together. "What do you mean you haven't had sex in over six months?"

"Ripley, you're not hearing me. You're not listening to what I've been saying to you for the past several weeks. I love you. I only want you. Since the moment you moved to Philly nearly a year ago, I haven't looked at or touched another woman."

I see the shock on her face as that sinks in. For a moment I'm annoyed, but then I realize that I brought this on myself. She has no reason to suspect I'd be loyal to her. Once again, I'm a dick.

She keeps it playful though. "No woman likes a guy who tells her he loves her on the first date. That's clingy and creepy. I don't know if I want to go out with a guy like that."

I smirk. "We're not on the date yet. I promise not to say it on Monday. I'll be a perfect gentleman."

She lets out a laugh. "You're a lot of things, Quincy Abbott, but a gentleman isn't one of them."

That hurts. I'm going to show her exactly how gentlemanly I can be. "Is it yes or no?"

She nods. "Okay, I'll go out with you. Mostly for amusement. I just need to check with my mom about staying with Kaya. You better be a gentleman."

"Me? You just dry-humped my leg...for the third time in our lives. You *really* like my leg. You better keep your hands off me this Monday. I don't put out on the first date either."

She giggles. "Have you ever been on a first date?"

"Hmm." I suppose I haven't. "No."

"You're thirty-four. Why not?"

I twirl her hair on my finger. "I was waiting for the right woman to come along."

Her face turns serious as she whispers, "I've been here the whole time."

I whisper back, "I was too fucked up to see it."

"You're not anymore?"

I shake my head. "No. I finally know what I want."

"What's that?"

"You."

RIPLEY

We've settled into a bit of a groove over the past week. Quincy spends time with Kaya all morning while I work out with a trainer, attempting to get myself back into game shape. His home gym is as nice as our stadium gym.

I'm already on my second trainer though. The first guy was young and attractive. Quincy walked into the gym while the trainer's hands were on my hips. He immediately kicked him out and hired a woman to work with me. Her name is Sophia, and she's been kicking my ass every day. She'll have me ready to go in no time.

After we all have lunch together, Quincy heads to the ballpark, and Kaya goes down for a nap. Mom and I go to the tunnel Quincy had built so I can practice my pitching. Arizona has been catching for me so my mom can focus on my mechanics. It's been nice working with Mom again. We haven't done this in years. To this day, I've never had a better pitching coach than her. I wonder if the Anacondas would consider hiring her. I wonder if she would ever consider living here.

We watch the Cougars games on television at night. I haven't brought Kaya to a game yet. We'll wait another month or so for that. Even though she's healthy, we still want to be cautious about her being out in public.

When Quincy gets home, whether Kaya's awake or not, he usually wakes her, feeds her, and dances with her. No matter where he starts the night, I always wake up with him in my bed. Each night, we get a little more handsy.

Quincy is now on his road trip. He constantly FaceTimes me so he can see Kaya. I think he's already struggling being away from her. *From us.*

I'm finishing up pitching for the day. Mom heads upstairs for a shower, leaving Arizona and me alone.

I'm feeding Kaya, looking into her gorgeous little face.

Arizona practically melts at us. "You're such a natural with her."

"You should see your brother with her. He's totally smitten. Can't get enough of this little one. When he dances with her every night, I just about lose it. It's so sweet."

"How are things with you two?"

I shrug. "I'm not sure. He's been a hundred percent devoted to us. He does and says all the right things, but, honestly, I'm still on guard with him."

She nods. "That makes sense."

"He asked me out on a date for when he gets back into town."

She gives me a huge smile. "That's great. Where are you going?"

"I don't know anything. He said I can be casual." I blow out a breath. "I'm so confused about him. He's completely different than he was during our entire pseudo-relationship. He's very...outwardly into me. He was never like that. It was purely booty calls."

"You would just have sex and leave?"

"No, not quite. Remember, we were always friends. We'd have sex, and then we'd talk and laugh for hours until we fell asleep. And then usually have sex again in the morning before heading out on our respective ways."

She raises an eyebrow. "You were basically in a relationship."

I shake my head. "No, we weren't. We never once went out for a meal. We never told another soul. Everything was behind closed doors. And now he throws around the L-word like it's no big deal. We called things off in Houston because I told him I loved him in the heat of passion one morning. Actually, it was the morning you called to tell us you were engaged to Marc."

She thinks for a moment. "I called him, and then I called you. You were together?"

I smile. "Each of us heard both conversations. You should have seen Quincy's face when you started telling me about how Marc proposed while you were fucking. It was priceless."

She lets out a laugh. "That's hysterical." Her face softens. "What exactly happened between you two?"

"After years of our booty calls, I was caught up in a passionate moment and blurted out that I was in love with him. He completely lost his shit, so I kicked him out, for good. I was so far gone for him at that point, but when he rejected me, it was the end of my rope. I couldn't continue to pretend we were nothing but physical. It was time for me to protect my heart and try to move on. I didn't see him for months after that day, not until your wedding stuff."

"Oh, Rip. I'm so sorry. I wish I had known. I wish I could have been there for you."

"I know. The whole situation was messed up. At times, he acted like he cared about me, and then we would equally have times when I wasn't sure he gave me a second thought. And now he casually tells me he loves me every single day. He's given me whiplash for years. I'm afraid this is one turn of the head, and the other turn will come when he freaks out like he did that day."

She gives me a compassionate look. "I can't give you answers or guarantees. I can only tell you that my brother has grown up a lot in the past few months. I don't know what he did when he was missing for all that time, but whatever it was gave him some inner peace and direction as to what he wants in life. Has he mentioned where he went to you?"

"No. He pushes his way into my bed every night, but most of our conversations are about Kaya. We haven't gotten deep yet. I'm not sure I can. I've always had this need to help him, but I'm done with that. I need to help myself."

"Do you want to be with him, Rip? I know what he's put you through, and he's an asshole for it, but in the end, do you want him?"

I blow out a long breath. "That's a loaded question. I won't lie to you and tell you that it wasn't always my dream. It was. But I can't let him hurt me again. Ever. He has to earn my trust. He needs to open up to me. One misstep, and I'm out the door."

"My fingers are crossed that he behaves. It's so weird that only a few months ago I had no idea about you two, and now I want it to work more than anything."

I sigh. "We'll see. Enough about my drama. How are things with your *husband*? I can't believe you're married."

She leans back on the sofa with a dreamy look on her face. "Honestly? I feel like I'm living in a fantasy."

"You are. He dresses as Captain America and fucks you

senseless." Arizona has a thing for Captain America. Layton indulges her and dresses up like him sometimes in the bedroom.

She giggles. "He does that too, but it's so much more. I feel so utterly loved by him. He never leaves room for any doubts. I love how happy he always is to simply see me."

"Is it so wrong that I want the same? That I won't settle for less than that?"

She shakes her head. "You deserve nothing less."

LATER THAT NIGHT, I'm holding Kaya while watching Quincy's game. He's pitching tonight. His stride is a little off. His curveball usually has much more movement. He must be a little rusty. I love watching him play though. I always have.

Mom walks downstairs in a dress with a full face of makeup and perfect hair. "Wow, Mom, you look great."

"Thanks. I have a date."

"Who with?"

"Some guy I met at the grocery store this week. He was sweet. I figured I'd have dinner with him and see where it goes." She glances at the television. "I was watching upstairs. His curve isn't moving as much as it normally does. I think he needs to stride more."

"I agree." Kaya fusses a bit, so I switch positions. Nothing seems to keep her satisfied for long tonight. "I don't know how you did it alone, Mom. I have you, Quincy, Arizona, and basically bottomless resources, and it's still hard. I can't imagine what it must have been like for you to have a newborn all alone with limited money."

She gives me a small smile. "It wasn't easy. I hope you

realize how fortunate you are to have Quincy. I know you two have things to work through, but he does love you, Ripley. I was certainly skeptical at first, but he's made his intentions clear. He's truly stepped up since she was born."

"I know but it's complicated."

"It's not. You love each other. You have some baggage, as does every relationship, but the feelings are real. Besides, a man who walks around shirtless all the time and looks as good as he does while doing so isn't easy to find. I think he's trying to entice *you*, but it's working on *me*."

I giggle. "He's always done that. I think he has a higher-than-normal body temperature."

"In all seriousness, the feelings between you two are very real. Don't lose sight of that trying to stand on principle. Love is love. Did you know that he called me every single day from Thanksgiving until the day you gave birth just to check on you?"

I sit up. "What? You never told me that."

"He asked me not to. And frankly, I wasn't a fan of his at the time. But you and Kaya were never far from his thoughts. I've had a broken heart for nearly thirty years. It's no fun and it's very lonely. You can make him work for it, but at some point, accept his love. I know you love him. You always have."

"Why have you never considered moving on from my father? There was never *anyone* for you?"

"Could you easily move on from Quincy?"

I'm silent for a moment as I consider that. I've never been able to move on, but thirty years is a long time. "Why the revolving door of men? Were you ever open to meeting someone special?"

"Unfortunately, my broken heart never healed. I drown myself in pleasure to numb the pain. I don't want the same thing for you. I'm not proud of how I cope. I suppose I'm lucky that I still garner male attention because it's not like I take the time to let anyone get to know me. My looks won't last forever. And then I'll truly be alone."

I roll my eyes. "You're beautiful, Mom. Your looks aren't remotely fading. If anything, you're more beautiful now than ever."

"So are you, Ripley. Everyone around you sees it except you. Both inside and out. I know you have some misguided notions of being undeserving of a man like Quincy. If anything, it's the opposite. He's the lucky one."

"Thanks, Mom."

"I love you."

"Love you too."

She starts to leave, but I stop her. "Mom?"

She turns around. "Yes?"

"Maybe it's time for you to open yourself up to the possibility of more too."

She has a weird look on her face, almost as if she's considering it. "Maybe you're right."

"Speaking of being open to scary things, will you give me the contact information for my brother and sister? I think I want to reach out. It's time."

She's told me a handful of times in the past several months that they keep calling her about getting together. I haven't been emotionally ready for it, but I think I am now.

Tears sting her eyes, but she nods. "Of course."

THE COUGARS FLEW into Philly after their night game, and Quincy arrived home in the middle of the night. I heard him open my door, remove his clothes, check in on Kaya in her bassinet, give her a kiss, and then slide in behind me in bed.

I pretended to be asleep, but he pulled my body into his and kissed my back over and over, telling me how much he missed me and loves me. My mind is a complete and total mess over him. He's never been this outwardly affectionate.

I think of what Arizona said about how happy Layton always is to see her. That's certainly how Quincy is making me feel right now.

I keep replaying my mom's words repeatedly in my head. But I'm afraid. Afraid of the hurt he's inflicted on me in the past. Afraid this is too good to be true.

CHAPTER THIRTY-TWO

RIPLEY

It's finally Monday. I don't know why I'm nervous. Perhaps it's because Quincy and I have never been on a date before. All those years, and never once have we done something as simple and ordinary as going out for dinner, just the two of us.

I'm putting the final touches on my makeup when the doorbell rings. That's odd. Quincy has a gate at the end of the long driveway. We always know if someone is coming, and no one called up to the house. It must be someone with the code.

I run down to open the door and see Quincy standing there in jeans, a white T-shirt, and a dark blazer, holding two bouquets of red roses. *Fuck, he's hot.*

"Good evening, Ms. St. James. I'm here for our date." He hands me one of the bouquets. "These are for you because... I'm a gentleman."

I can't help but smile as I take them. "Thank you. They're beautiful." I inhale the fragrant scent before nodding toward the other bouquet. "Do you have another date later, *gentleman*?"

He shakes his head. "Nope. I'm a one-woman kind of man. I prefer redheaded pitchers. It's my understanding that you have a beautiful daughter who might feel jealous of her mom getting flowers and not her. I didn't want her to feel left out."

"I'm sure she'll be thrilled given that she's not even three months old."

"Nonetheless, I hear she's a stunner like her mom."

My mom appears out of nowhere and grabs the flowers. "I'll take care of these. You two kids have fun. Stay out as late as you want. Kaya and I have our own date tonight." She smiles down at my baby sleeping in her arms. "Don't we, baby girl?"

Mom practically shoves me out the door. Quincy chuckles as he takes my hand, another thing he's rarely done.

After opening the car door for me, we're on our way. I turn to him. "You pitched well this past week considering you haven't thrown in a while."

He didn't pitch many innings. He has to build back his stamina after not pitching much for the past few months.

He shrugs. "Three innings is a good start. My curve isn't moving as much as it normally does, but that's to be expected."

"Your stride isn't as long. Work on that. It will help with the spin."

He smiles.

I look at him. "What?"

"I forgot how fun it is that you know the game so well. You're exactly right. That's what our pitching coach said to me. How's it going for you? It must be nice to be throwing again."

"My stomach was cut in half. I feel weak and my speed is down, but the muscle memory is still there. It's nice working with my mom again. Despite some of her...shenanigans when I was a kid, she's always been a great coach."

365

"She's a great mom too. She just took a leave from her teaching job and moved across the country to help us. That's very special."

"I know. You're right. Did I tell you that she finally told me a little bit about my dad?"

He shakes his head. "No. What did you learn?"

"It wasn't what I thought. He wasn't just a nameless, faceless man in her sea of many. She loved him. He died before I was born, but they were in love. It made me happy to hear that."

He squeezes my hand. "That's amazing."

I nod. "I know. And he had two other kids. I have a brother and sister."

He blows out a breath. "Wow. Have you met them?"

I shake my head. "No. They reached out to my mom about meeting me. I wasn't in the right headspace at the time." I quietly add, "With you and the baby."

He squeezes my hand again. "I'm sorry for how I reacted when I found out you were pregnant. I think I was in shock."

"I don't understand what's changed for you. You're a different person from the Quincy I've known."

"We'll talk inside. We're just about there."

We pull onto a small, one-way city street. I see a restaurant that clearly serves pizza. "Is this the place you told me about?"

He has a huge smile on his handsome face. "Yep. You have to reserve your dough in advance. It's the best pizza I've ever had, and you know that means a lot coming from me. I can't wait for you to taste it."

We walk in, and the owners seem to know him. A few patrons ask for photos and autographs, per normal when Quincy goes anywhere in public. Two or three even recognize me and ask for the same. While we're always happy to indulge fans, some of them are simply taking pictures of Quincy and me without our permission as we walk through the restaurant hand in hand. He doesn't seem bothered by it.

I whisper, "I think people are photographing us."

He shrugs. "Who cares? Let them take their pictures and post them. I have nothing to hide."

I swallow down my emotions. He has no idea how much that means to me.

We're shown to a booth big enough for four people, but Quincy sits on the same side as me and pulls me close. I'm confused by this shift in him. Loving, sweet, affectionate Quincy is new to me.

The waitress, in a thick Philly accent, asks us what we want, the only options being pizza or pizza. I leave it to Quincy to pick our toppings.

He pours our wine and holds up his glass. "I know we've taken a weird road, but we've managed to create the most perfect baby girl. Well, you did almost all the work, so thank you for taking such good care of her. She's changed my life for the better. You both have."

Tears fill my eyes as I clink my glass with his. "Quincy, you're not supposed to make your dates cry, at least not at the beginning of the date."

He smiles. "You know I'm new at this. I'll do my best to only make you cry at the end of the night."

I giggle. "Thank you."

"You're welcome."

After a few sips of wine, I ask what I've been dying to ask since Arizona told me about Quincy's disappearing act. "Tell me where you went after Thanksgiving. Tell me what's gone on for you to change your tune about me. About us. I need to understand it."

He briefly brings his lips together in a thin line as if it's hard for him to talk about. "I finally had it out with my father after you left on Thanksgiving."

"I think it was long overdue."

He nods as he lets out a long breath. "I should probably go back to the beginning. As you know, I spent my whole life drilling into my head that I didn't want a family, but even before you told me about the pregnancy, I was starting to question things. You know full well I simply couldn't let you go."

"I suppose."

"Are you sure you're ready for this? I'm about to lay a lot on you, but I want total transparency. It's part of my healing, and I think it's what you and I need. It's heavy, and it took me a long time to come to terms with it all myself."

I nod. "Tell me. I want to understand what's going on in your head."

"Since the minute I saw you up on that ladder when you were sixteen, something shifted in me. And then when you fully gave yourself to me two years later, there was never a chance of going back. Any women I've been with since were faceless and nameless. A poor substitute for the woman I couldn't get out of my mind. And then this marriage with benefits thing fell in my lap. It was the perfect solution. We could be together but not in a way that frightened me. It was a good few years. A great few years. And then you told me you loved me. I've spent a lot of time thinking about my behavior. I realized that I freaked out because I felt it too but never wanted to let myself go there. I was immature and mistreated you, and I'll forever be regretful about that."

Tears fall freely from my eyes. I whisper, "Quincy." Him admitting all this to me is a big deal.

He takes my hands in his. "Let me continue."

I nod for him to do so. I'm so choked up with emotion, I don't think I could speak if I wanted to.

"I moved to Philly thinking the distance would help rid me of the feelings I had for you. It didn't. And then, a few months later, you were back in my life, in my bed. I realized I couldn't exist without you. I was honestly thinking about taking a small step in that direction, talking to you about giving us a chance at real dating, but then the baby thing happened, and I was spooked. I'd rather not be a father than be a bad one. After Thanksgiving, my father and I spent a few weeks alone together. I still can't get over him taking a few weeks off work for me. We had our come-to-Jesus moment. We yelled and screamed. We got it all off our chests. I told him everything I'd bottled up for thirty-three years. It felt good. Great. He helped me understand why he is the way he is. I assumed it was because he didn't care—"

"He cares."

"I know that now. Though misguided, he wanted to give us the stable life he never had and sorely craved growing up. And then...and then...I went to rehab."

My eyes widen in shock. I don't even try to hide it.

"Rehab? For what?"

"I'm not sure rehab is the right term. More of a therapeutic retreat program. I was depressed. There's no other way to see it. You're the only person who knows this. I told Arizona I was traveling the world to get my head together. I don't owe anyone but you an explanation. I did it for you and me, no one else."

He rubs my face. "I want to be a better man. The kind who deserves a woman like you. The kind who can find a way to be a good father despite spending a lifetime insisting I'd never be one. It was time for me to seek professional counseling to help me cope with some of the issues I've been struggling with for so long."

He runs his hands through his hair in typical Quincy-like fashion before he takes my hands in his again. "I want to be honest with you but don't want to freak you out."

"You can say anything to me."

He nods. "My counselor helped me realize that I've been in love with you for thirteen years but was too chicken shit to act on it. That I never let myself be truly happy, so I never let myself go there mentally. My heart was feeling one thing, and I was too fucked up to accept what was right in front of me all along."

"Why didn't you come to me after that?"

"My retreat finished the day before I was scheduled to be in Clearwater. Honestly, I still wasn't sure what I was going to be capable of. I thought I had a few more months before I needed to do anything. The team had a West Coast road trip scheduled for the beginning of the season. My plan was to talk to you then. I had no way of knowing you'd go into labor two months early. But when you did, it hit me like a ton of bricks. Everything my therapist said to me came into color. The feelings inside me suddenly became clear. I want to be happy. *You* make me happy. I'm in love with you. I can't and won't do life without you and our baby girl."

Tears now fall from his eyes. "I thought I had lost you, and if I did, I don't think I could have kept on going. I had already assumed the baby was gone, and of course I felt sad and guilty, but I hadn't met her yet. It was different. Thinking you were gone too was soul crushing, Shortcake. It changed everything for me in the blink of an eye. I—"

Not able to take another minute without it, I crash my mouth onto his. His soft lips immediately embrace mine. Our tongues taste each other for the first time in what feels like forever. His longer beard is rubbing my face in the best way possible.

His hands squeeze my hips and mine grip his shirt. I think I see a few flashes go off, but if he doesn't care, neither do I. There never has been and never will be a time in my life when I don't love this man. My imperfectly perfect man.

The waitress popping her gum causes us to break apart. "Yous lovebirds ready fa some pizza?"

Our lips are no longer together, but our faces are still close. Quincy wordlessly nods and she leaves the pizzas at our table. We simply stare at each other.

He whispers, "Are we going to be okay? You and me?"

I whisper back, "I don't know. I hope so."

I'm finally realizing it was never about me. All this time, I thought he had some amount of shame about being with me, but that's not what it was. It's always been about him and his personal struggles. I want to believe everything he's saying to me right now, but there's still a small part of me that can't go all in.

I run my fingers through his sexy beard. "Thank you for sharing with me. I know it's not easy for you. Let's put the heavy stuff aside for now." I grab a slice. "I need to try the pizza that has pizza snob Quincy Abbott so enamored."

He smiles as he reaches for his own slice, and we both take our first bites.

We talk and laugh throughout dinner. It's just like our pillow talk in Houston. As much as I missed my lover Quincy, I've missed my friend Quincy just as much. And he was right. This is the best pizza I've ever had in my life.

When we get back to the house, he stops us at the front door. "Can I have a kiss goodnight?"

I smile. "A goodnight kiss? You know you're going to end up sneaking into my bed."

He feigns shock. "I'm merely watching over you and our daughter."

I shake my head. "Just remember, I don't put out on the first date."

Taking me into his arms, he breathes, "I don't want to mess things up this time. I want to take it slow on the physical too. We already know we're compatible, more than compatible, on that front. You need to know how serious I am about this. I want to date you. I want to court you."

"Court me? What century are we in?" Insecurity starts to creep in. "You don't want me?"

He takes my hand and rubs it over his severely hardened denim-covered dick. "Trust me, Shortcake, I want you. That will never be an issue. Our relationship beforehand was purely physical. Now I need more than that with you. I want to give you everything you deserve."

"I guess you'll be sleeping in your bed for the first time ever tonight?" I joke. He hasn't spent a full night in his bed since we've been here.

"I didn't say that. It doesn't mean I can't hold you. I sneak in not so you'll dry hump my leg, but because I'm happier when you're in my arms. I'm happier when I can breathe you in all night. I'm committed to my happiness. *Our* happiness."

My mouth drops a bit at the stranger before me. "You went from a cold, grumpy, never expressing a feeling asshole to a smooth, swoony, mushy teddy bear."

He chuckles. "I have an example to set for my daughter. I read that women model appropriate behavior for all men in their lives from their fathers. I'm going to treat you the way I will one day want a man to treat her. Like a princess."

"You read all this?"

He nods. "Yes, when I was alone in my room at night during the retreat, I read all kinds of parenting books. For both boys and girls since I didn't know what we were having, but I always suspected it was a girl. That's what I was hoping for."

I lean into him. "I think I'll take my kiss now."

He smirks as his lips meet mine for a disappointingly short, sweet kiss.

When we walk inside the house, it's shockingly quiet. I scoff. "Of course she slept while we were gone. She'll be wide awake crying all night."

He smiles. "Don't speak unkindly of my little princess."

"My mom must have gone to bed. I'm going to grab the baby monitor from her room, so Kaya doesn't wake her up during the night."

I make my way up the giant staircase. Assuming my mother is asleep, I quietly open her bedroom door...to her naked body riding an equally naked man like she's a rodeo queen.

His hands are on her boobs, and she's moaning something unintelligible. Looking closely, I realize it's Dutton Steel. I'm not sure if I'm more shocked to walk in on my mother having sex, which was not a rare occurrence when I was growing up, or the fact that she's sleeping with the same man for the second time, something I've never once seen.

I gasp and they both turn their heads and slow their actions. I cover my mouth. "I...I...oh my god!"

Quincy must hear my words of shock and runs to the room likely thinking something is wrong. Unlike me, he just barges in and stops short at the scene before him. He belts out, "Holy fuck!" before quickly turning around and speed walking out of the room.

I'm frozen for a moment until I tiptoe, as if my presence isn't known, to her night table. I grab the monitor. Like an idiot, I decide it's a good time to explain my obvious actions, "I just came for the monitor. I didn't want her to wake you during the night."

Mom shamelessly smiles at my clear discomfort. "Goodbye,

Ripley. I'm a little busy right now. Can we chat more about this later?"

I'm temporarily frozen in place again. "Oh...umm...yes. Later. We'll talk later. Bye."

Still with a big smile, likely at my severe embarrassment, Mom waves goodbye.

I sprint out the door and make my way to the other end of the hallway where Quincy is waiting. As soon as we see each other, we start laughing hysterically. I shrug. "At least someone in this house is getting laid."

He shakes his head. "I can never unsee that. It's permanently imprinted in my brain."

"I wish I could tell you it's the first time that's happened to me. It's not. It happened dozens of times when I was a teen. Though never with the same guy twice. I wonder if she really likes him."

"Wouldn't that be something? Dutton mentioned to me a few months ago that he had interest in a woman for the first time since his wife. I wonder if he was referencing your mom."

I smile at that possibility.

KAYA BARELY SLEPT LAST NIGHT, wailing through most of it. Quincy and I are finally sleeping in the early morning hours when my phone starts ringing. I can't move. Quincy's big body is wrapped around mine like a glove.

I mumble, "Quincy. Phone."

He mumbles back, "Tell them to go away. So fucking tired."

"Let me get it before it wakes the monster."

"I'm too exhausted to chastise you for calling our daughter

a monster."

"Can we agree to calling her the *Exorcist* baby?"

I feel him smile into my neck. "Yes. It's better than the word monster, and, after the excessive middle of the night vomiting, it makes perfect sense."

He releases me enough for me to reach for my phone. It's Arizona. I accept without realizing it's a FaceTime call.

I immediately see her smiling face. "Is that my brother who you're wearing like a second skin?" She sarcastically adds, "Shocking that he's topless."

I whisper, "Shh. The *Exorcist* baby is sleeping. And no, it's Chris Hemsworth. I bumped into him last night and ditched your brother. You know I'm a sucker for the superhero Thor, though not quite as much as you are for Captain America."

Quincy's eyes narrow "I'm hotter than Thor."

"Blanche's dog, Thor? Definitely. The superhero?" I shrug. "Hmm, I'm not sure."

I giggle while he tickles my side and mumbles, "Very funny."

I roll my eyes at the obvious resemblance. "You look like him. Why do you think I have a thing for Thor in the first place?"

Arizona gasps. "That's why? Ugh. I'll never look at Chris Hemsworth the same again. He's forever tainted."

"Big, muscular, sexy man. Longer blond hair. Blue eyes. You seriously never added two and two together to get four? It's no wonder I had to do your math homework all the time."

"Listen, fucker, do you want to know why I called so early in the morning?"

I'm giggling again. I think I'm so tired that I'm losing my mind.

"Is it morning? The spawn of Satan had us up all night."

"It's early, but it's morning. Anyway, pictures of you two

out last night are all over the internet. There's even a video of you kissing. I guess it went well."

I whisper, "Your brother wouldn't put out, but it was fine."

He tickles me again. "You're not funny, Shortcake."

I still get chills that he's now calling me that in front of other people.

I turn back to the phone. "I suppose I'm not surprised. We saw people pointing their phones at us."

She nods. "The headlines are kind of cute. Most are something like *Pitch Perfect* or *Mound of Love*. They mention a budding relationship between the two best pitchers in town."

I twist my lips. "At least it's not *Beauty and the Beast*."

Arizona nods. "It wouldn't surprise me if they called Q a beast. He's looking like one these days with his animalistic face."

"I meant me."

"I know what you meant, and you're nuts. Every man on the planet has a thing for hot redheads. They all want to know if the carpet matches the drapes. I'm giving an interview later where I'm going to confirm that they do for you."

Arizona and I both start laughing. Quincy opens one eye. "Why are you looking at my wife's carpet?"

I elbow him. "Ex-wife. And she's seen me naked as much as you have."

"I certainly hope not in the same way I have."

Arizona smiles. "As entertaining as your weird foreplay is, I'm going to go wake my husband up by polishing his helmet." She suggestively licks her lips.

Quincy scrunches his face. "Ugh. TMI."

Arizona giggles as she ends the call. As soon as she does, Quincy gets out of bed and pulls me with him. I whine, "What are you doing?"

He's got a firm hold on my arm as he growls, "Come with me."

We walk into the bathroom and stand in front of the mirror, him behind me, his front to my back.

"Look at yourself. What do you see?"

"A woman who didn't sleep last night." I've got bags under my eyes and my curly hair is extra unruly this morning. I didn't fully remove my makeup, so I've got the whole raccoon thing working for me too.

"Wrong. Try again."

"Quincy, we've already played this little game. Several years ago."

"Apparently you didn't learn last time. Let's play again. What do you see?"

"A woman who needs to lose baby weight plus another forty pounds."

He makes a buzzer noise. "Ehhh. Wrong. You're going to learn just how sexy and beautiful you are."

He once again rips my T-shirt straight down the middle, leaving me in my panties.

"Stop ripping my shirts." I try to reach for something to cover me, but he pins my wrists behind my back with one of his giant hands. I'm completely exposed.

With his other hand, he grabs my chin to make sure I'm looking into the mirror. "This is the most beautiful face in the world. I see it in every single fantasy I have." He thrusts his hard dick into my behind. "It causes me to wake up with this every morning of my life because I dream of being back inside you. Every. Damn. Morning. The simple thought of your wet pussy sliding over me drives my dick crazy."

He drops his fingers down from my chin and cups one of my breasts. "These cause him to leak. They're so soft and full, with perfect nipples I miss sucking." He pinches my nipple.

As if on cue, those nipples immediately harden at his touch and his words.

His hand moves over my flabby stomach. I cringe.

"You housed our angel daughter here. You took care of her when I was nowhere to be found."

I mumble, "She's no angel."

He chuckles. "You're both my angels."

His hands move down to my thighs. "And these—"

"What could you possibly have to say that's positive about my thighs?"

"They represent strength. These are the reason you're the best pitcher in the world. The reason your teams win championships over and over again. The reason you and Arizona will eventually be Olympic champions. These will one day be gold medal-winning thighs, and I love nothing more than grabbing onto them while I pound deep inside your body. One day in the future, I'm going to fuck you while you wear nothing but that gold medal."

He turns me around and pushes me until I'm sitting on the vanity, positioning himself between my legs.

Our bare chests meet and his dick presses against my center. They're separated only by the thin layers of my panties and his boxers. I can feel every hard inch of him.

He leans over and whispers in my ear. "There's a reason you're the only woman who has ever truly done it for me." He pushes his dick hard to my center. "I never want to hear you doubt it again. Are we clear?"

I'm so turned on right now that I can only nod. I don't have to look down to know that my body is flushing at his words and actions.

He kisses down my neck, knowing what I'm thinking. "Not yet, but soon." He then kisses my forehead and walks out of the bathroom, leaving me a wet, panting, exposed mess.

CHAPTER THIRTY-THREE

ONE MONTH LATER

RIPLEY

"Great practice, ladies. No one works harder than the Anacondas." Coach Billie places her hand in the middle of our circle, and we all follow suit. "Hard anacondas on three. One, two, three!"

We all smile and shout, "Hard anacondas!"

Coach Billie is constantly trying to come up with Anacondas cheers, but they all end up being unintentionally sexual. We all giggle as she seems blissfully unaware.

I noticed two of the owners watching practice, Reagan Daulton and Beckett Windsor. Beckett's daughter, Andie, was also watching. She's about eight years old and comes to almost every game. She's a huge fan. Sitting with her is Tanner Montgomery's daughter, Harper, equally adorable and also a huge Anacondas fan.

As soon as practice is over, Harper sprints out and jumps into Bailey's waiting arms. Kam leans over and whispers to Arizona and me, "Is it just me, or is Beckett Windsor super-hot for an old dude?"

I nod. "He's, like, my mom's age, but he's so fucking sexy. He's jacked." He's tall, broad, and muscular with dirty blond hair. "He looks like the actor who plays Jack Reacher."

Kam moans, "Yes! Totally. Yum."

Arizona smiles. "He's hot, but he's not available. I met his new wife. She's gorgeous. They just had twins last year."

Kam bites her lip. "Lucky kids. I'd love to call him daddy."

We giggle.

Kam looks behind them. "Speaking of daddies, there's Bailey's *daddy*, Tanner. He must be here to pick up Harper." She mumbles, "Or maybe bang my sister."

I shake my head. "What's with all the hot older dudes around here?"

Just then, Reagan motions our way. I assume it's for Arizona since they have a bit of a friendship, but she shakes her head indicating it's for me. I wonder what she wants.

I walk over and she smiles. Reagan Daulton is a blonde-haired, blue-eyed stunner, a few years older than us. She's always dressed in designer pantsuits that hug her perfect figure like they were custom made for her. They probably are.

"How are you feeling, Ripley?"

"I feel great. I've been working out with a trainer every morning and pitching with my mother every afternoon. I wasn't expecting to be ready for the beginning of the season, but the early delivery seems to have helped in that regard."

"Great. Is it safe to assume that you're not thinking about a trade anymore?"

"Definitely not this season. I don't know yet about future

seasons." I bite my lip. "I'm hopeful about staying here, but I don't want to overpromise."

She nods. "I understand. I didn't realize your mother was still out here. She's a former Olympian and longtime coach, right?"

I nod. "Yes. She's the best. She taught me everything I know. She's out here to help with the baby at least through our seasons. It's hard with Quincy and I both having demanding schedules."

"Does she have any interest in coaching this team? I'd be crazy not to consider someone with her experience and talent level."

I can't deny that I was thinking the same thing.

"I imagine she'd be interested. I'd certainly like it. It's just a matter of childcare."

She nods. "We can help with that. Let's try to get your mom out to practice tomorrow morning."

"Will do. Quincy is around then. It won't be an issue."

Quincy has a game tonight, and I'm home with Kaya. The past month has been special. He's done exactly what he said he was going to do. He's courting me.

We've gone out together, we've stayed in together, we've spent time with our daughter together, and we stay up late talking and reconnecting every single night that he's not on the road. While there's been some kissing and roaming hands, we haven't been intimate. I'm still a little on guard with him, and he doesn't push at all.

Despite my hesitancy, I can't deny that I've fallen in love

with Quincy Abbott all over again. I swore I wouldn't let him back in, but the simple fact is that I love him and always will.

He chose not to address the publicity surrounding our relationship. It's the one thing giving me pause. I will always have those insecure moments where I fear he's ashamed to be with me. But I'm focused on my upcoming season and our happy little family. I also have a date set next week to meet my brother and sister. They're coming into town.

Despite my encouraging them to go out, my friends said they're happy to come over to Quincy's house tonight to hang out with me and Kaya. I've barely seen my baby today. I've missed her.

We plan to have takeout and watch terrible reality television.

We're sitting in the family room eating Chinese food when Arizona looks at me nervously. "So...how's it going with you and my brother?"

I'm leaning back on the sofa with Kaya sleeping on my chest as I twirl my fingers through her growing, curly hair. I love it.

I look at Arizona. "You want me to shoot straight?"

Her face turns worried. "Yes. What's the matter? Did he fuck up again?"

"He didn't fuck up. Just the opposite. He's completely devoted himself to us."

"Then what's the problem?"

"I still don't trust him with my heart. I'm waiting for an inevitable Quincy freakout. I can't bring myself to be physical with him, because if I do, I don't think I'll ever recover if he walks away again."

Kam shakes her head. "You've been sleeping in the same bed for weeks, and you still haven't cleaned the cobwebs in the womb room?"

I giggle. "Do you know every single slang phrase for sex?"

She nods. "It's better than the one Cruz...err...Cheetah, used last week. He said he wanted to take the skinboat to tuna town. I've never heard that one before."

We all smile. I ask, "What's the latest with you two? You seem very touchy-feely when you're together."

"Nah-ah. No deflection. Back to the lack of cream in your doughnut hole."

Arizona winces. "Ew. Don't talk about my brother's cream. That's weird."

Kam rolls her eyes. "Says the woman whose doughnut hole is overflowing with superstar cream."

Arizona smiles. "It certainly is." She shivers. "Just when I think it can't possibly get any hotter, he rocks my world."

I sigh. "Ugh. I hate you. I can't even troll the Bermuda Triangle myself because he's in my bed."

Kam smirks. "What? When was your last orgasm?"

I shrug. "Sometimes I have wet dreams. I had them all the time when I was pregnant. A few since."

Kam narrows her eyes. "Define *all the time*."

"A handful each week. I read it has something to do with increased blood flow." They all look shocked. "Quincy was surprised by it too. I think it's one of those little-known pregnancy facts that no one talks about."

Kam mumbles, "Maybe I should get pregnant."

I turn to Bailey. "What about you, Bails? What's the latest in your love life?"

She sighs. "I've definitely been having my batter dipped by a corn dog." She mumbles, "A big fudging corn dog." She gasps, covering her mouth. "Oh my god, I'm starting to sound like my sister. Hell has frozen over."

We all giggle as Mom walks in with a huge smile. "I love hearing you girls laugh."

Kam looks up at her. "Mama June, did you have wet dreams when you were pregnant with Ripley?"

A small smile forms on her lips. "Almost daily. It's the best part of pregnancy."

I nod. "I told you so."

Kam shakes her head in disbelief. "They should advertise this more than they do. I think more people would be into getting pregnant if they knew."

Mom giggles before asking me, "Do you want me to put Kaya to bed?"

I look down at her sleeping soundly on my chest. "No, it's okay. She's content, and I missed her today. I want to hold her. Let's not poke the bear."

"Alright, I'll head up to my room. I don't want to disturb your fun."

Kam shakes her head. "You're not disturbing us, Mama June. Bailey was just about to tell us what it's like being with a man closer to your age."

Mom smiles as if she's remembering something. "I used to like older men too. Ripley's father was older. Now I don't like my men much older than me. I don't want a man with saggy balls who needs Viagra to make me come."

I shake my head. "Thanks for the overshare, Mom. How old was my father when you were with him?"

"Hmm. Let's see. I was twenty, so that would have made him thirty-five."

Kam wiggles her eyebrows. "Ooh. Fifteen years. Does that sound familiar, Bails?"

Bailey rolls her eyes.

I see Mom starting to leave the room but stop her. "Actually, Mom, we were just about to watch a reality show. We're split on which one we're watching. You can be the deciding vote."

She nods. "Which shows? I don't watch much reality TV."

I answer, "I want to watch *Love Is Blind*."

"What's that?"

"A bunch of men and women date with a wall between them. For weeks. Then they propose, then they meet in person, then they decide if they want to get married."

She scrunches her face. "That sounds ridiculous. Who would get engaged without having sex first, let alone not having even seen them? If you're not physically compatible, what's the point?"

Kam nods. "It *is* stupid, and I agree. I want to watch *Too Hot to Handle*. They take the twenty most attractive, horniest people on the planet and tell them they can't have sex. They pay them to not have sex for a few weeks, and those dumb fuckers can't manage to do it. It's hysterical."

Mom smiles. "That sounds much more fun."

LATER THAT NIGHT, I hear Quincy walk in from his game just as I'm finishing my shower. He rushes into my bathroom, not considering that I'm naked in the shower. "Where's Kaya? She's not in the bassinet."

Turning off the shower, I answer, "I thought it was time for her to try the crib tonight." I point to the monitor. "I've been listening. She's out cold. And do you mind? I'm showering."

As if it's just occurring to him that I'm naked, his eyes slowly drink in my body.

He immediately walks my way and opens the shower door with a towel in hand. "Allow me to dry you."

He begins slowly running the towel down my body. I swear I almost have an orgasm from it. I'm starved for his touch.

He only dries my legs before standing to his full height and handing me the towel. "Your towel, princess."

He's so tempting. I know my body is flushing. It always does when he's nearby.

He's being patient and letting me control the pace of things, but a little animalistic Quincy wouldn't be unwelcome right now.

He's still standing close to me and I'm still naked. I can see the bulge in his sweatpants. I'm aching for it.

He rubs my cheek with the backs of his fingers. He breathes, "Can I kiss you?"

I wordlessly nod.

Uncaring that I'm getting his clothes all wet, he pins me to the tiled wall of the shower and proceeds to kiss the shit out of me. I can feel every hard ridge of his body against my soft one.

His thumbs brush across my hardened nipples before he begins to pinch and twist them in the way he knows I like.

His cock, though covered, is pushing hard against my center. Oh god, it feels good.

I swear the way he pinches my nipples is a direct line to my clit, which is throbbing. That, coupled with the pressure of his dick, has me quickly ascending the ladder toward ecstasy.

I wrap one leg around him and shamelessly grind myself over his thick length.

Maybe I should be embarrassed that this is doing it for me, but I don't care right now. I'm starved for it. For him.

I take in his scent and taste, my favorite things in the world. He pinches and pushes just the right amount. My face scrunches and my legs go numb as I orgasm on a long moan, releasing a small amount of the pent-up frustration I've had.

As I come down, he pulls his lips away just a fraction. I can still feel his breath in my mouth. "That's the fourth time you've come on my lap. Next time, it will be with me inside you."

"I do want you, Quincy. I'm still scared though. My heart couldn't take another rejection from you."

He nods. "However long it takes for you to trust me, but I promise you can. I'll never let you down again."

He pulls away a few inches. His eyes widen in horror as his fingers gently trace my face and neck. "My beard has you all red. Did I hurt you?"

I shake my head. "No."

He rubs his beard. "I think maybe it's time for me to shave this. I don't want to hurt you, and the guys are giving me so much shit. Vagina Jesus is my new nickname. I think I much prefer Long Quail Quincy."

I gasp. "Don't you dare shave. I've been fantasizing about it for weeks. Not until I get to feel it between my legs at least once."

That gets his attention. He squeezes his eyes shut as if in pain.

After opening them, he traces his fingertips over the tops of my breasts. "Is that what you want, Shortcake? My face between your legs."

I nod. Or maybe I moan. I don't know at this point. What I do know is, despite the fact that I came seconds ago, the thought of that beard between my legs is mighty appealing.

He pulls me out of the shower, picks me up, and places me on the vanity next to the sink. He rakes his eyes over me before spreading my legs wide.

"Are you wet? Did coming on my covered dick make you extra wet?"

I nod.

"I'll need to see for myself."

By all means. Have at it. I spread my legs wider in invitation.

He smiles as he slips two fingers inside me. As soon as he does, he bites his lip. "You're very naughty. And very greedy."

I breathe, "Punish me."

He pulls his fingers out and takes my hand in his. This time he slips both of our fingers inside me. Fuck, I'm so wet. "Can you feel it? Can you feel what I do to your body?"

"Yes." I squirm, desperate for him. "Please."

He pulls them out and sucks them both into his mouth. "Hmm. I've missed your taste."

"There's an overflowing buffet of it waiting for you."

His shoulders shake in laughter as he drops down to his knees. He kisses up my inner thigh. I'm officially loving the feeling of his beard running up toward my center. I've been dreaming about how it would feel between my legs. Just a little higher.

He continues moving in the right direction. He's almost there. Please lick through me. I'll do anything for it.

He parts my lips, and just as he's bending to lick, there's a blood-curdling scream from the baby monitor.

I tilt my head back. "Noooo!"

Quincy stands and smiles. "Raincheck. I'll deal with the other princess."

As I get dressed for bed, I listen on the monitor to him talking to her as he tries to rock her back to sleep. I must drift off at some point.

I assume with Kaya in her room for the first time, Quincy will sleep in his own bed, but in my sleepy state, I feel him slip into mine and pull my body to his. It feels good. It feels right.

CHAPTER THIRTY-FOUR

RIPLEY

The Cougars have a day game today and I'm bringing Kaya for the first time. Quincy is pitching. I'm so excited for her to see her daddy play, even though she won't see much.

It's an especially big day because tonight I'm meeting my brother and sister for the first time. I'm both nervous and thrilled.

I've got Kaya strapped to my chest in a baby carrier. The press doesn't know that Quincy and I have a child. I have no idea how he plans on handling this, but he wanted her to come, and I'm letting him dictate the dialogue.

I'm sitting with Arizona, Kam, Bailey, and Mom as we walk down to our seats just behind the Cougars' dugout. I've missed being at the ballpark. I love it here. The energy in Philly is so much better than it was in Houston. They live for the Cougars.

We're greeted by a small sea of applause. Winning the championship last season has more than ingratiated us with

Philly fans. We're asked to pose for pictures and sign autographs by several fans before we finally make our way to our seats.

Layton is in the dugout with the team. He works with the catchers as a part-time coach when he's not working with the Anacondas. He nonetheless takes every opportunity possible to steal a glance at Arizona.

As soon as the Cougars take the field, Quincy's eyes immediately search for us. His genuine smile when he finds us makes my heart melt.

I lift Kaya's little hand to wave at him, and he waves back. Arizona wraps her arm around my shoulders and squeezes me. "You two are going to be okay. I can feel it."

I pinch my lips together. "We'll see."

Kam harumphs, and I turn to her. "What's up?"

She nods toward the screen, which has some sort of Amazon ad running. "Have you ever noticed that the arrow under the Amazon logo looks like a penis?"

My mouth widens. "Oh my god. It totally does. I'll never look at it the same. You've ruined Amazon for me. Every time an Amazon truck goes by, I will only see a penis."

Bailey examines it closely. "You're right, but it's a crooked penis."

Kam nods. "Totally. It's like a boomerwang. I wonder if guys like that have to fuck you from around the corner." She thrusts her hips at a diagonal angle.

We all giggle. Arizona asks, "Have you guys ever had sex with a man who has a crooked penis?"

I smile. "I had one once. Honestly? It felt kind of cool. It rubs differently." I wiggle my eyebrows. "As long as it's in the right spot. I wouldn't want it all the time, but it was a fun change of pace, so to speak."

Naturally, my mother feels the need to chime in. "I've had

plenty, and I agree. As long as they know how to use it properly, it's a good time. I don't think I'd buy it for the long run, but an occasional sideways tickle is nice."

Kam giggles. "I love you, Mama June. Our mother is so prim and proper. I'm not sure she's ever had sex. Our family dinners were so boring." She turns to me. "Yours must have been the best."

Mom and I smile at each other. We did have fun dinners together. Our family might have been small, but she was always there, and we did a lot of laughing.

Kam continues, "Our mom was like Kris Kardashian, a true momager. She was a psycho when we were modeling."

Bailey enthusiastically nods. "She was. She's the reason I hate modeling. Speaking of which, what's the latest with you and that lingerie company, Rip?"

"I canceled the second campaign when I found out I was pregnant. They called about giving it another go, but I don't know. My body hasn't recovered fully."

Mom rubs my back. "You look great. I didn't know they called again. You should do it."

I scrunch my nose. "We'll see."

I haven't mentioned it to Quincy. He was pissed as hell last year when I didn't invite him to the set. He'll probably want me to do this. I need to think about whether I'm comfortable with my post-baby body.

Quincy ends up throwing a complete game shutout, his first complete game of the season. He's being interviewed on the field after the game while we wait around.

Arizona is on the field with Layton while they unashamedly grope each other. At some point, Quincy motions for me to join him on the field. He probably wants Kaya.

I walk their way and Quincy smiles at me before turning

his head back to the reporter. "The Anacondas' season starts next week. They're going for a second championship. Ripley is the one you should be speaking to, not me."

The reporter eyeballs me curiously, toggling her eyes between the two of us before eventually speaking into her microphone. "Are the rumors that you two have recently started dating true? There have been pictures of you out and about."

Quincy shakes his head. "No, we didn't recently start dating." He's denying that there's something between us. All my fears were warranted. Sadness immediately engulfs me.

I turn to walk away, not wanting to cry on camera, but he pulls me close to him and kisses me softly on the lips before admitting, "We've had an on-and-off relationship for years. This is our daughter, Kaya. And maybe if I stop being a bonehead, this beautiful woman will be mine again. For good." He looks me in the eyes. "These two ladies are my world."

The reporter looks stunned. She can't possibly be more stunned than I am.

Mom and I are on the way back to the house from the ballpark. Quincy has a few team obligations before he returns home, and I'm in a little bit of a rush because of my brother and sister coming over.

I think those comments from him were the final thing I needed to truly let him in.

"Mom, will you keep the monitor in your room tonight?"

She smiles. "Does this mean what I think it means?"

I bite my lip. "Maybe."

"Use protection this time."

I roll my eyes. "We used protection last time."

"Use better protection."

I choose not to inform her that Quincy came so long and hard that he overflowed the condom. That's the only explanation I can come up with for my pregnancy.

"I had an IUD put back in at my six-week checkup. I should be fine."

"Need me to put a box of condoms in your bathroom again?"

I let out a laugh. "That was so embarrassing. And then you handed one to Jack in front of everyone."

She giggles. "I guess it was a bit much."

"You think?"

We arrive home, and Mom takes Kaya upstairs for a bath and bed so I can quickly shower. I'm so nervous about meeting them.

At exactly the agreed-upon time, I get the signal that someone is at the front gate and press the button to open it for them.

Mom walks down the stairs. "They're here?"

I nod.

"Kaya is asleep. I think the fresh air got to her. Do you want me to stay upstairs or join you?"

I hold my hand for her, and she takes it. "I need you here."

The doorbell rings, and I swallow nervously. I take a breath and then open it. Mom takes one look at them and lets out an audible sob.

I rub her back. "Mom, are you okay?"

She turns her head. "I'm sorry." She looks at the man I assume is my brother. "You look exactly like your father. Maybe a little smaller, but the resemblance is uncanny. I guess you're about the age he was when I knew him."

The man smiles and holds out his hand to me. In French-accented English, he says, "I'm Pierre. This is my...our sister, Colette."

Pierre has red hair. It's a darker shade of red like mine. I assumed my hair color was from my mother, who happens to be a shade lighter than Pierre and me. He also has blue eyes. He's tall, maybe an inch or two taller than me. I still look more like my mom, but Pierre and I clearly resemble each other. It's weird.

I shake his hand and smile. "I'm Ripley. It's nice to meet you."

I turn to Colette and hold out my hand. She has darker hair and eyes. She's much shorter than the rest of us. We don't look alike at all.

She gives me a small smile. Also in heavily French-accented English, she says, "Nice to meet you. May we come inside? It's very hot here."

"I'm sorry, of course. This is a little crazy for me. Please come in." I motion for them to do so.

Colette looks around. "You have a beautiful home."

"It belongs to a friend, but thank you." I motion toward the living room. "Why don't we go in there and get to know each other."

We all walk toward the living room and sit as we exchange a few normal get-to-know-you questions before I ask, "How long have you two known about me?"

Colette answers, "Our mother passed last year. We were going through some of her belongings as well as those of our father. We barely remember him, but it appears as though my mother held onto many of his things."

I feel Mom stiffen next to me and squeeze her hand.

Colette notices but continues, "It was only then, in some paperwork, that we found out our father had another child. We were brought up to revere him, so knowing he had an extramarital affair and a bastard child was devastating to us—"

Pierre warns, "Colette, we've discussed this. It's not Ripley's fault."

Colette gives my mother a death stare, grits her teeth, and nods. "Yes, you are right. I apologize, Ripley."

I'll give her that one small outburst, but if she looks at my mother like that again, I'm going to ask them to leave. "I'm sure it wasn't easy. Go on."

"That's when we learned of your existence."

Just then, the front door opens. Quincy walks in and takes us all in. "I'm sorry I'm late." He holds out his hand. "I'm Quincy Abbott. It's nice to meet you both."

They shake his hand and give their names before he sits down next to me.

Colette asks, "And what is your relationship to Ripley?"

"I'm her husband."

"Ex-husband," I correct.

Quincy mumbles, "For the time being."

I add, "Quincy and I share a daughter."

Pierre gives a genuine smile. "We have a niece? How lovely."

I slowly nod as I just now realize that's the case. "I suppose you do. She's only three months old. She had a long day and is passed out upstairs."

Quincy intertwines his fingers through mine and asks, "What did I miss?"

I answer, "Colette was telling me how they only recently learned of my existence after their mother passed. I'm sorry we got interrupted. Please continue, Colette."

"Very well. It appears as though my father made some provision for you before he passed. I assume my mother had no idea or she would have seen to it that you received the money years ago."

I feel my mother stiffen again. I'm guessing his wife knew but decided to keep the money from me. It doesn't matter now. And it's certainly not their fault.

Colette reaches into her purse. "We'd like to make sure you receive what you're owed." She pulls out some papers and then hands them to me. "I'll need you to sign these, and a check will be issued."

I look down at what appears to be a contract, but it's in French. I do see a dollar figure and gasp. It's about five times what I make in a year.

She continues, "We'd like to get this settled before we return home. Pierre has some business in Philadelphia. We will be here for three more days."

Quincy grabs the papers. "I'll have our attorney look at it, and we'll get back to you as soon as we can."

I shake my head. "Is that really necessary? They came all this way."

Mom grabs my arms. "I think Quincy's right. Just because it's in French, and, frankly, my French is a little rusty at this point. It can't hurt to know what you're signing."

Colette appears annoyed. "Very well." She stands. "We are staying at the Four Seasons downtown. Contact us after you've reviewed everything."

Before I can answer, Quincy does. "We will."

Pierre and Colette sort of abruptly leave. I can't deny that I'm disappointed. This felt like a business meeting, not a reunion of long-lost siblings. I didn't even get the opportunity to ask them if they were married with kids. To ask them anything personal.

As if sensing my thoughts, Quincy rubs my back. "I'm sorry. I doubt that was what you were hoping for tonight."

I shake my head. "It wasn't."

He pulls me into his arms and whispers into my head, "Not everyone is as genuine and perfect as you. Just one of the many things I love about you."

Mom grabs the monitor. "I'm going to hold onto this tonight. You two sleep...or whatever."

She quickly exits the room and disappears up the steps.

Quincy looks down at me. "What was that about?"

I look up and give him a small smile. "I told her I want you all to myself tonight. No interruptions from the demon princess."

He chuckles before his eyes widen as realization hits. "Really?"

I nod. "Really. Thank you for today."

"You want to have sex with me because I threw a shutout?"

I giggle. "No, you jerk. You went public with our relationship today. It meant a lot to me."

"If I knew that's all it took, I would have done it months ago." He whispers, "Years ago."

I slide my hand down his arm until it rests in his large hand. With a small tug, I say, "Take me to bed."

He looks down at me with concern. "Are you sure? I know meeting them was hard, and the way they handled it can't be easy for you. We can do this another time."

"I'm sure, Quincy. I need your hands on my body tonight."

We walk in silence up the stairs, but when I start to turn into my room, he tugs my hand. "Can we go into my...our room tonight? I know it's not our first time, but it feels like it is. I want to make love to you for the first time in there. I'm hopeful it's the first of many."

I nod and we walk into the giant master suite. I've honestly only been in here a handful of times. It's a beautiful room with an oversized California King bed. The multiple windows overlook the city skyline that we can just make out. It has a fireplace, a sitting area, and even a desk.

There are two giant walk-in closets. He's left one empty. The same goes for the second vanity in the bathroom. He says they're for me if and when I'm ready.

I start toward the bed, but he pulls me into his arms. "Dance with me first."

"There's no music."

He fiddles on his phone and suddenly "You've Lost That Loving Feeling" starts playing.

I smile. "I thought you hated this song and this movie."

"But you love them, and I love you." He gives me his crooked smirk. "Don't ever tell anyone."

I giggle as he pulls my body flush to his as we move to the slow beat. We're silently swaying together for the first half of the song.

His hands move up my sides and back, while mine roam his neck and hair. After giving me a soft kiss, he rubs my face with the backs of his fingers and stares at me with an intensity that's almost too much to bear. I've wanted Quincy Abbott to look at me this way my entire life. I've wished for it countless times, and now it's here.

He then looks pained for a moment before saying, "I have to admit something to you."

A sense of dread washes over me. This is the moment he's going to pull the rug out from under me. Some part of me has been waiting for this, knowing it was coming. The past few months have been too good to be true. Today was too good to be true.

He tilts his head to the side. "You think I'm going to blow things up right now, don't you?"

He steps away, looking hurt.

I blow out a breath. "I'm sorry. I fear you freaking out and taking off. I'm trying to get past it, but your history doesn't help."

He nods in understanding. "I'm trying to be everything you want. Everything you need."

I nod as my voice cracks a bit. "I know you are."

"At some point, you'll have to trust me, trust us, if we're going to have a chance."

"You're right." I fall back into his arms. "Tell me what you were going to say."

He swallows as he pulls me close again. "I was going to admit to you that I haven't kissed another woman since we got married. Barely any since our first night in bed, but zero since we got married."

"I don't understand. You've been with plenty of women."

"But I couldn't bring myself to kiss any of them. It was too intimate. They weren't you. You saved your firsts for me. I saved my kisses for you."

My heart feels like it might explode from this revelation. Tears fill my eyes. I've waited for this moment my whole life. I never truly believed it would come, but it has. I'm not a young girl dreaming anymore. Quincy Abbott, the love of my life, loves me back. He's finally mine.

I bury my face in his neck, taking him in. I can't help the sob that escapes my throat at the enormity of the moment. There's nothing left standing in our way.

I look up into his blue eyes. "Make love to me."

His lips immediately capture mine. Knowing that he's saved his kisses for me makes this one all the more special. Quincy Abbott could kiss anyone in the world he wants, but he's only giving them to me. For years, only me.

We kiss like we've been fighting for this and we're finally crossing that finish line. That's exactly what it is. It's ownership. It's desire. It's love.

We begin moving our hands all over each other, both aching for closeness. With one hand, he grabs onto my hair and the other, my ass, sending waves of pleasure to every part of my body.

My hands can't touch enough of him. He's so hard and manly. Everywhere. Every inch of this beautiful man is perfection.

I can't help but grind against him. One of us moans. I'm not sure who. Maybe it was both of us.

With his hand on the back of my head, he pulls my hair, exposing my neck to him. He scrapes his teeth over my chin and down my neck before licking his way back up.

We feverishly claw at each other's clothes until they're nothing but a pile on the floor. His eyes take me in. There was a time when this made me self-conscious and uncomfortable. I couldn't bear to expose myself to him. That time is long gone because the way he's looking at me right now tells me everything I need to know. He's attracted to me. He wants me. He loves me. I'll never doubt it again.

I can't help but take in his beauty. Pure masculinity oozes from him. He's long all over, from his hands to his feet, from his arms to his legs, to the long, perfect cock of his that reaches so deep inside me.

He stalks at me, forcing me to walk backward toward the bed. I fall back onto the cool, silky sheets as he stands between my legs. His eyes and hands slowly move up my leg, his gaze and touch conveying so much reverence.

He pushes me back until there's room for both of us, but before he positions himself on top of me, he bends and slowly licks through me. My nipples immediately tighten at the sensation. His fingers move up to tweak them while his tongue continues lapping at me.

I love his tongue, and the feeling of his beard between my

legs is ecstasy, but I ache for him to fill me. It's been so long since he did, and suddenly, I need it more than I need anything.

As if sensing it, he looks up at me and cups my center. "You're so wet for me. Do you need my cock to fill up this pussy?" He squeezes it harder. "My pussy."

I love the new, sweet Quincy, I really do. But I miss my dirty-talking dream man. Shivers work through my body at his words. He smirks, knowing exactly what it does to me.

He licks his lower lip. "I thought so."

He crawls on the bed and nibbles, licks, and sucks his way up my body.

"Quincy, please. I want you inside me."

He closes his eyes. "You have no idea how many times I've thought of you like this. On *our* bed. Naked. Spread wide open. Begging for me to fill you again."

"Stop talking about it. Just do it."

He smiles. "So impatient."

"It's been eight months," I whine. "Give me everything."

His hips finally meet mine, nuzzling between my legs. My body begins to tremble in anticipation. But he doesn't enter me. Not yet.

His lips find mine again for a toe-curling kiss. He begins to slide his cock through me but not into me. His long, hard, veiny cock rubs across my most sensitive region. My body involuntarily jerks each time he passes my clit.

He manages to stay in control, all while devouring me with his tongue. I, on the other hand, am losing it.

He works his way to my ear. "I love watching you lose control. I love how much you need it. Need me. I'm going to bury myself so deep inside you, you'll be feeling me for days. Tell me how badly you want my cock."

"So bad. Please."

I wrap my legs around him and grind my hips. I might come from this. His touch and his words have me so close.

He knows exactly what I need to give me the final push. His hand moves up to my throat. I can feel my eyes flutter.

"Oh god."

"No, it's Quincy."

And then he squeezes my throat, and I come so fucking hard that I practically lose consciousness. Years of longing physically pour out of me.

He's cursing, probably in shock at how hard I'm coming, but I can't make out any words because I'm floating in outer space. I don't know if I screamed or moaned. Probably both. I may have purred for all I know.

He waits until my eyes find their focus again. When they do, he stares into them as he finally begins to enter me. It's not fast and it's not slow, but he keeps moving until he's buried to the hilt. That's a lot of inches inside me. I feel so full.

This time it's him who moans. My stomach muscles clench at the intensity of the feeling of having him inside me again after so long.

He laces his fingers through mine and begins long, deep thrusts. I tilt my hips up, wanting every bit of him I can handle.

It feels different from all the other times we've been together. We've always had great sex, but knowing he loves me is making it so much more intense.

One of his hands moves down and grabs my breast. "These tits. So pink. So full. So perfect." He sucks a nipple into his mouth, and my back arches.

I love the feel of his hard body rubbing against my soft one as his big body pummels into mine.

Before I realize what's happening, he flips us over so I'm on top, but he's sitting up. His movements are slow as he pushes my hair away from my face and mouths, "I love you," before picking up his pace again.

I may be on top, but I'm not controlling this. I wrap my arms and legs around him and enjoy the ride. I roll my hips, but my dominant man is in full control.

He mumbles into my neck, "Can you feel how perfectly we fit together? How deep you can take me? How deep you need me?"

I breathe, "Yes. Only you. Only you can take me there."

That seems to embolden him to take things up yet another notch as he pushes as deep inside me as physically possible, hitting the spot he knows well. The spot that only a man like Quincy Abbott can reach.

His hands are on my hips, gripping me, bruising me. I love it.

I bend my head forward and involuntarily bite the space in between his neck and shoulder. His body spasms.

He grabs my hair with one hand and wraps the other around my neck, pistoning into me at an inhuman pace.

"Oh fuck, I feel you squeezing me. You're about to orgasm. Do you want me to fill you up with my come? To show you who will forever own your body?"

"Yes. I want it. Give it to me."

"Let go. Now!"

Because Quincy Abbott always has and always will control my body, it listens, and I begin to convulse as another giant orgasm works its way through me.

As soon as it does, he gives me four more hard pumps before he groans and spills himself inside me for the first time. On purpose.

He breathlessly falls back, taking me with him. His gorgeous face is covered in sweat. "Holy shit."

I nod into his chest, equally out of breath. "Yep. Let's hope

IUDs work better than condoms against your super sperm."

He chuckles. "I'm good either way."

I lift my head. "Are you fucking nuts?"

He smiles. "Now that the can of worms has been opened, I'm a little addicted to it. I want you pregnant with my babies all the time. And I'm not missing a minute of it ever again."

I rest my cheek on his chest, listening to his heart beating hard and fast. "I only let my husbands impregnate me. You're my ex-husband."

He rubs my face and lifts my chin. "Hopefully not for long."

"Relax there, Henry the Eighth."

He smiles. "How many wives did he have?"

"Six, you dope. That's why the musical about his ex-wives is called *Six*."

"Hmm. That actually makes a lot of sense."

He squeezes me. "This feels right, doesn't it?"

"I wouldn't have gone here again if it didn't. We have a little girl to consider now."

"I promise I'll never let either of you down again. I will always love and protect you."

I look up at him. "I love you, Quincy. I've loved you every day of my life."

"And you've always shown it to me. Now it's my turn to show it to you."

QUINCY

I wake in the morning with Ripley's naked body pressed to mine. My eyes are closed, but I take in her scent. I want this every morning for the rest of my life, and I'm willing to fight anyone who threatens that, even the shady fuckers who claim to be her siblings. Something is off with those two, and I intend to find out what it is.

I begin kissing her neck. She stirs and turns around in my arms before smiling sleepily. "It wasn't a dream."

"It was sort of a wet dream, wasn't it? You would know better than I would."

She giggles. "It was *much* better than that."

I nod. "It was. Should we relieve your mom?"

She shakes her head. "Just a little longer. I've waited a lifetime for this."

Because I can't help myself, I move my lips to hers for a kiss, one she immediately deepens. I must be in love because I'd rather have a morning breath kiss from Ripley than a minty fresh one from anyone else.

Before I realize what's happening, my bedroom door flies open. "Hey, vagina face, have you seen Rip...oh my god, this is weird. I mean, I'm happy, but it's still weird. It's also kind of gross."

Ripley moans, "Oh please. How many times have I walked in on you and Layton naked in the morning? Or listened to you and the Energizer Bunny going at it for hours. You deserve a little payback."

Layton pops his head in. "Did I hear my name?"

I roll my eyes. "I'm so thrilled there's a party in my bedroom this morning. Thanks for knocking."

Arizona smiles at me. "Relax, killer. Don't shit your pants over this...at least, not again."

Ripley laughs. She knows the story. The one that never seems to die.

Arizona looks back at Layton. "Ripley was just complaining about your...longevity."

He turns his head to me. "Are you a two-pump chump, Q?"

Before I can answer, Ripley does. "Definitely not. And even if he were, they'd be *very* long pumps."

She and Arizona both giggle. What the hell is wrong with these two?

June then walks in holding Kaya.

I sigh. "I don't recall a *welcome everyone* sign on my bedroom door."

She scrunches her face. "Sorry. Kaya is being a little fussy this morning. I think she wants you guys."

I hold out my hands. "Give me my girl."

June hands her to me, and Kaya immediately proceeds to tug on my beard with the strength of a professional weightlifter.

I scream out in pain.

Arizona laughs hysterically. "Oh my god, even little Kaya hates your beard. Time to shave, ZZ Top."

Ripley shakes her head. "Nope. The beard stays." She smiles. "Don't knock it till you try it. Until you *feel* it."

Arizona rubs her fingers over Layton's face. "Hmm. Maybe we need to give that a go."

He grabs her ass and kisses her hard. "Do you have any complaints?"

She smiles into his mouth. "Not a single one."

He nods. "That's what I thought."

I grimace. "Take your nauseating PDA downstairs so we can get dressed."

She walks over and grabs Kaya. "I want my niece. I'll feed her while you do your thing."

She winks on her way out. "Take your time."

And we do.

CHAPTER THIRTY-FIVE

QUINCY

After a nice breakfast with Arizona and Layton, Ripley leaves for a long walk with Kaya. Normally I would go with them, but I want some time alone with June. I told Ripley that I needed to do extra stretching for the game today.

June is in the gym working out, as she does every day. I decide it's time for me to do the same.

June St. James has always been a bit of a contradiction. She's an extremely attractive woman. Ripley very much resembles her...outwardly. Inwardly, June plays her cards close to her chest whereas Ripley doesn't. I've known June since I was ten, but I don't truly *know* her at all. You only see what she wants you to see.

Teenage boys and every grown man in our hometown used to froth at the mouth for her. Hell, she probably went out with every one of the single men at some point.

She was a teacher at the high school. My friends

fawning over her was a daily occurrence. I wasn't in high school at the same time as Ripley, but I can't imagine it was easy for her.

June slept around, never caring about her reputation or whether it impacted her daughter. She was, however, always there for Ripley, coaching every single team Arizona and Ripley played on until they left for college. She spent countless hours with them, helping to make them into the all-American players they both became.

I walk in and see her. She's in tiny spandex shorts and a sports bra, her standard workout uniform. Her straight, red hair is pulled into a ponytail. She looks up when she hears me walk in. "You didn't go for a walk with them?"

I shake my head. "Not today. I need to get in a little workout and stretch a few tight muscles."

We move about in comfortable silence for a bit until I break it. "Can I be blunt with you, June?"

She smiles. "If you're going to ask for her hand in marriage, you're a little late for that."

I let out a laugh. "No, not that. Though she'll marry me again one day."

She gives me one small nod. "I know."

"What makes you so sure?"

"She's always been in love with you. Even as a little girl, you walked on water to her. I'm just happy to see you finally returning the sentiment. I didn't believe you ever would."

"I've always loved her. I just didn't think I could give her what she wanted. But I want to try."

"I'm happy to hear it. Ripley is my everything. I don't want her to struggle like I did." She places the free weights she's been using onto the ground and stands tall. "What is it you have to say to me, Quincy?"

"I want to know more about her father's family."

Her face falls. "What do you mean?"

"Something is off with the story she told me and those people that were here yesterday. Don't bullshit me, June. I refuse to let anyone hurt her."

She blows out a breath. "What has she told you?"

"That you had an affair with an affluent, older, married man. You loved him. He was prepared to leave his wife for you but died before Ripley was even born. His wife paid you off to go away, and you used that money to move to our neighborhood when you did."

She nods. "That's all true." She swallows. "His wife's family was more than just affluent. They were and still are one of the most powerful in Canada. We're talking about real, old-school money. She feared me upsetting the applecart. Because of her long reach, no one would employ me, no one would house me, and I couldn't even find a lawyer that would represent me to assert paternity against his estate. I didn't care about it for me, but I did for Ripley. She was owed that money. Lucas promised to always take care of her. At the time, I had a small amount of notoriety in Canada because of the Olympics. Before I was pregnant, I did a bit of modeling to make ends meet, but that well dried up when I fell pregnant. I'm pretty sure she also had a hand in the sudden ending of my offers. I eventually became desperate. I set my pride aside and began banging on her door until she finally offered me a fresh start to disappear."

Tears begin streaming from her eyes. "I know Ripley was entitled to more, way more, but I had no means to get it for her. I signed away my rights for a relatively small bite." She hangs her head. "I'm ashamed and feel like I failed her, but I was so desperate, Quincy. You have no idea what it's like to be unsure how you're going to feed your child."

She looks around at our luxurious surroundings. "I'm grateful to you that Kaya and Ripley will never know the same struggles I endured."

"I will always provide, but Ripley doesn't *need* me to provide. She's strong and capable of doing it on her own. You raised an incredible woman."

She hangs her head. "You're right, but trust me when I tell you that it's easier this way. It's not just the money, Quincy. It's you. She loves you to her core. Do you think I want her to be the brokenhearted town tramp that I was? Someone who has to numb themselves in random men to feel alive? When she came to live with me when she was pregnant, that's what I feared. She said she was ready to move on from you, but she, like me, would never be able to. Loving you is as natural as breathing to her. God help you if you hurt her again. I don't have many resources, but I'll use every single one to rain holy hell down on you."

I can't help but give a small smile, loving how much she loves Ripley. "I don't want to hurt her again. I'm trying to be a better man for both of them."

She nods. "I know you are."

"Tell me about the Canadian Bonnie and Clyde."

She shrugs. "I don't know much. I put that part of my life behind me when we moved. Their mother passed, and they claim to have just found out about Ripley. They said they needed to meet with her urgently, but I told them I wouldn't pressure Ripley. It had to be on her timeline. They called me every few days, mostly Colette, which I didn't relay to Ripley because I wanted it on her terms. I don't owe those two shit. Only my daughter concerns me. It was up to her if and when she wanted to meet them. She said she did, and I arranged it."

"I think their French fucking contract is bullshit."

"I agree. There's something off with it. They were all business. They're hiding something."

"I sent it to my lawyer this morning, but I think I'll do a little research of my own."

I **WALK OUT** of the shower and into the locker room after our game. Layton still hangs around and is here tonight. He's standing there talking to Cheetah, Ezra, and Trey when I approach them.

"Have you guys ever seen the movie *The Town*?"

They all nod. Who hasn't seen that movie? It's incredible.

"You know that scene when Ben Affleck's character tells Jeremy Renner's character something along the lines of, *I need your help. You can't ever ask me any questions about it, but we're gonna fuck up some people.* And then Jeremy Renner's response is simply, *whose car are we taking, yours or mine?*"

Cheetah lets out a laugh. "Hell yes. Best fucking scene ever."

I nod. "Agree. I need some of that energy from you guys tonight."

Layton, Ezra, and Trey all simply nod. Cheetah channels his best Boston accent, and mimics the movie line, "Whose car we takin'? Yours or mine?"

I've never in my life had a group of friends like this. I'm almost choked up with emotion over it, but I'm too focused on the task at hand to let it get the better of me.

IT'S JUST AFTER MIDNIGHT. I told Ripley I was having a beer with the team at Screwballs after our night game. She didn't question it because she doesn't have a deceitful bone in her body, so it wouldn't occur to her to think that I was lying, but I could tell she was disappointed. I would have preferred we spend the night together too, but this is important.

We all walk into the fancy hotel wearing nondescript baseball hats to partially cover our faces. We don't want to be recognized, though it's not easy. Everyone in Philly knows us. Five big guys walking into a hotel forces people to take notice, so we split up. I'm with Layton in one corner while Ezra and Trey are in another corner.

I couldn't get the room number when I called, but Cheetah has a way about him, so I sent him up to the desk in the lobby to charm it from the hotel clerk.

We're all in our respective spots, watching from afar as he approaches the desk. We can't hear them, but within a minute, it appears as though the younger woman is laughing and blushing. I turn to Layton, and he smiles. "Fucking Cheetah and his flirting."

I poke my head out a drop more to see if I can hear what he's saying when I bump into a scantily clad blonde woman. I grab her arm, so she doesn't fall over. "I'm so sorry, ma'am. I didn't see you there."

Her face lights up as she secures her footing. "Oh my god. You're Quincy Abbott. The pitcher."

Shit.

I nod. "I am. I'm sorry about bumping into you, but I'm actually in the middle of something right now."

She rubs her hand on my arm, ignoring my obvious attempt to get rid of her. "When you're finished, why don't we get a drink?" She licks her lips. "And maybe grab a room if you don't have one already."

I remove her skanky hand from my arm. "Thank you for the offer, but I'm not interested. Have a good night."

Her smile fades and her eyes narrow slightly before she finally walks away.

I turn back to Layton. He scrunches his face. "I think she's a streetwalker."

"Who uses that term for hookers?"

"Would you prefer a lady of the night?"

"No, call her what she is. A prostitute or hooker."

"What's the difference between the two?"

I shrug. "Probably about a hundred bucks."

He chuckles. "My grandmother used to call them trollops. I'll stick with that."

I can't help but roll my eyes and smile.

A few minutes later, Cheetah returns to us in the darker corner where we've hidden since the hooker incident. "They're in two different suites on the top floor. You can't just press an elevator button to get there. You need a secure pass to get up to that level."

I mumble, "Damn it. How are we going to get up there?"

Cheetah gives us one of his huge smiles and holds up a key card. "No woman can resist my charms."

Layton shakes his head in disbelief. "What did you say to her?"

"I can't reveal every trick in my bag, but I did tell her that I'm like Domino's Pizza. If you don't come in thirty minutes, the next one is free."

I scrunch my face. "Ugh. I can't believe that shit works."

He holds up the key card again. "Every damn time."

Cheetah grabs my shirt, "Quick, hide behind that plant. Someone is coming."

The three of us quickly move behind a large potted plant. I poke my head out but don't see anyone. "Who's coming?"

Cheetah chuckles. "No one. I just wanted to see if you'd do it. This is like an episode of *The A-Team*. I loved that show when I was a kid. I feel like Hannibal." He was the leader and brains of the operation.

I shake my head. "If anyone is like Hannibal, it's me. You're like the quirky, funny, weird sidekick, Murdock."

Layton tilts his head to the side. "Does that make me Mr. T?" He was the actor who portrayed the brute muscle of the crew.

I shake my head. "No way. You're Faceman, the good-looking fucker who always uses his charms to help them."

Cheetah's chin drops. "We just used my fucking charms to get this key. I'm Faceman. Let Layton be the weird, quirky fucker. I don't want to be him. He never got laid."

Layton scrunches his face. "I want to be Mr. T. He was a badass. I need gold chains and a mohawk to complete the look. What was his character's name? I can't remember."

Cheetah gasps in astonishment. "Only one of the greatest characters in TV history. B.A. Baracus."

Layton enthusiastically nods. "Oh right. I'm definitely him." He flexes his muscles. "He was jacked."

I sigh. "Can we cut this stupid conversation short and get back to the mission?"

Cheetah nods. "As long as we can agree that I'm Faceman. I want to be called that for the rest of the night."

I roll my eyes. "Fine, Faceman. Let's go."

I motion for Trey and Ezra to meet us at the elevator, and they do. The five of us ride up together. Cheetah explains to Trey and Ezra that they need to call him Faceman for the rest of the evening, which starts a whole fucking conversation about their characters in our fictitious A-Team. Why did I bring these morons?

Because they're my brothers and they came without even asking why.

We step off the elevator. Layton starts giving hand signals. None of us know what they mean. I growl, "Just talk. No one can hear us."

He shakes his head. "You're a terrible spy. What if the enemy is listening?"

"What enemy? You don't even know why we're here."

He twists his lips. "Hmm. True."

I point to Ezra and Trey. "You two stand watch by the elevators. We're going in."

Trey whines, "Why do you guys get to do the fun stuff? We want to come."

I respond, "You have a wife and kid at home. Stand watch and stay out of the line of fire."

Layton furrows his brow. "I have a wife too."

"Ugh. Don't remind me that you're married to my sister. I'm still in denial."

He smiles. "She's so hot. And so sexy. You know what she did to me the other day?"

Before I can grab him by the shirt, Cheetah stands between us. "Relax, Q. He's fucking with you. Layton, stop riling him up."

Layton chuckles. "But it's so fun."

Cheetah tries to contain his smile. "It *is* fun, but he doesn't need to know about your wife's sexy pink nipples."

My eyes widen. "What the fuck? Why do you know that?"

Cheetah winks.

Before I can kill both of them, we hear a noise at the end of the hallway. We all turn to see one of the doors opening. I warn everyone to stay still as a flannel-pants-clad Pierre walks out, and we all hold our breath as if it makes us invisible.

Worst. Spies. Ever.

He simply places a tray of food on the floor of the hallway and turns back into his room. We all breathe again when his door closes with a loud thud.

I breathe out, "Phew."

Trey asks, "Who's the ginger?"

"Don't worry about it."

Cheetah asks, "What do you call a sexy woman with a redheaded man?"

I shrug. "What?"

"A hostage."

I roll my eyes. "You realize I might have a redheaded son one day, right?"

"Whoops. As long as he looks like Ripley, I'm sure he'll be fine."

I motion with my hand, "Let's go, you moron."

We walk down the hallway and I knock on his door.

In Pierre's deep French accent, we hear, "Who is it?"

I respond in an unnecessarily high-pitched voice, "Room service."

He answers, "I left my tray in the hallway."

"I need you to sign for it, sir."

I can hear him scoff before he begins to open the door. As soon as he opens it a crack, I push my way through and grab him by the neck, pushing him against the nearest wall.

His eyes practically pop out of his head. He's a big guy, but I have a few inches and a lot of muscle on him.

I can faintly hear Cheetah and Layton freaking out about what I'm doing, but I zone them out.

I growl, "Don't fuck with me, Pierre. I want the truth. Do you understand?"

He vehemently nods.

"What's your angle? I know you don't give a shit about forming a relationship with Ripley."

He tries to speak but he can't because my hand is around his neck. I move it and pin him with my forearm across his chest.

He takes a few labored breaths. What a pussy.

I grit out, "Answer me."

"It's...it's Colette. It was all her idea." Like I said, what a pussy. "Ripley is entitled to much more than what we offered her. Our father left her significant money. My mother buried the paperwork. Colette wants her to sign away her rights."

I'm not surprised their "magnanimous" offer wasn't

that. Based on what June told me about their wealth, I had a feeling it was something along these lines.

"How much is the estate worth?" I push his chest hard. "Don't bullshit me."

When he gives us the number, our eyeballs just about bulge out of our heads. I hate how this ends for Ripley. No matter what, she doesn't get the relationship with her brother and sister that she wants. She doesn't care about the money. It's the family she desires.

I'll be her fucking family now.

WHEN I ARRIVE HOME in the middle of the night, the house is quiet. I tiptoe upstairs and open the door to Ripley's room. The bed is empty.

Opening the door to my room, I see her asleep in my bed. My body fills with both happiness and relief. She's really come back to me.

I peel back the blankets to see her naked. I remove all my clothes, slide in behind her, and pull her close.

She stirs and then turns in my arms. Her eyes blink open.

I move her hair out of her face. "I'm sorry. I didn't mean to wake you."

She sleepily smiles as she snuggles her body as close as possible to mine. "I'm glad you did. Did you have fun with the guys?"

"I missed you. How was the princess?"

"She shit straight through her clothes and up her entire back. I swear it was more than she weighs. I don't know how something so little can produce so much."

I chuckle.

"I bathed her, and then she did it again."

"Hmm. Sorry I missed the fun. Did your mom help?"

"Apparently, she was meeting up with Dutton after the game, and I don't think she came home. I've never known her to see the same man multiple times. I think she really likes him. Maybe this is her second chance."

"Perhaps it is." I look down at her body. "I like you waiting naked for me in our bed." I nudge my hard-on into her stomach for added effect.

"I like you coming home to me."

I slip my cock between her uppermost thighs and through her slippery flesh. "Always so wet for me, Shortcake. Do you want me inside you?"

She bites her lower lip and nods.

I pull her top leg over me, circling her entrance with my tip. "Grab me and take what you need."

She reaches down and wraps her fingers around my cock. I love the feeling of her soft hands on me. She pumps it a few times before guiding it into her. As soon as I'm fully inside her, her eyes flutter and she breathes, "Quincy."

"I'm here. Forever."

CHAPTER THIRTY-SIX

RIPLEY

G iven the fact that we were up most of the night going at it, Quincy told me to sleep in while he spent some time with Kaya. He has a day game today, so he needs to leave for the ballpark earlier than normal.

He brings her into our bedroom when it's time for him to go. He has a huge smile on his handsome face. "She's rolling all over the place. According to my book, it's early for that."

I roll my eyes. "You and your books."

"It's a big milestone, and she's ahead of the curve. Definitely a little athlete." He holds his nose to hers and in his softest voice, coos, "Are you going to be a pitcher like your mommy? She's the best in the world. I want you to be just like her when you grow up. We're going to sit and watch Mommy at the Olympics in a few years."

I moan. "Ahh. Pressure. What if I don't make the team?"

He gives me an incredulous look. "You and Arizona will be

the starting battery in the gold medal game. Mark my words. I have zero doubts. I can't wait to watch."

"You'll be in season during the Olympics."

"They'll either give me a leave of absence or I'll retire, but there's zero chance of me missing that. You two have been talking about it for nearly twenty-five years. Nothing and no one will keep me away."

He smiles as if talking of retirement is no big deal.

"You're just hitting your stride. I'm not letting you retire."

"Priorities change. I won't be my father."

I start to talk but he holds up his hands. "I get it. He was doing what he thought was best. Blah, blah, blah. It's still not the kind of family man I want to be. I've spoken with Layton. We may have a few ideas on companies we'd like to invest in. Things that will better secure our financial future without necessitating me being on the road as much once I retire." He rubs his nose with Kaya's again. "I don't want to miss any milestones for our little prodigy."

"Prodigy? She shits herself and rolls. Let's hold off on the prodigy talk."

He chuckles as he covers Kaya's ears. "Drown out the negativity, princess. You're a prodigy, just like your mommy."

Kaya then proceeds to grab his beard again and pulls on it for dear life.

QUINCY LEFT FOR THE BALLPARK, and I'm in the kitchen feeding Kaya when Mom returns home. I lift an eyebrow. "Hmm, those look a lot like the clothes you were wearing when you left last night."

A small smile finds her lips. It's a different kind of smile for her. It's almost shy. Very unlike June St. James.

"Oh, Mom, you really like him, don't you?"

She blushes. I've never once in my life seen her blush over a man.

She sits down at the table. "I suppose I have to admit that I do. He's just so...incredible. He's sweet, smart, attentive—"

"And sexy as all hell."

She nods enthusiastically. "God, yes. So sexy. He makes me lose my mind. He's very alpha in bed. And he has this finale move where he—"

I hold my hands up. "Okay, okay. Enough. I don't need to hear that."

She giggles.

"Did you two go out or straight to his house for the main event?"

"We had one drink at that Screwballs place we went to with you last year."

"Oh, I think Quincy was there with the guys. Did you see him?"

"No, I didn't see him or his crew, but we were only there for a short while. We were...anxious to get back to his place."

"That's odd. I think they went there right after the game."

She shrugs and then bites her lip nervously.

"Is something else on your mind, Mom?"

"You're thinking of settling down in Philly permanently, right?"

"I haven't thought past this season, but I suppose things are headed in that direction."

"What would you think if I were to move out here too? Not here in this house, but here in Philly."

"I'd love that. Did things work out with Reagan Daulton?"

I know she and Mom spoke about her coming on staff for the Anacondas.

"Yes, but I told her I wanted to talk to you before making the commitment."

"Obviously I want you as the pitching coach."

She smiles. "You do?"

"Of course, Mom."

"Okay. I'll need to find another job as well. Coaching the Anacondas won't be enough. I wish it was, I love coaching more than anything, but perhaps I can find another teaching job to make ends meet. Tell me if it's too much. I don't want to be overbearing and intrusive in your life."

I grab her hand. "You're fine. I'm more than happy to have you here. You're the best coach I've ever had. And you'll get to be near Kaya. If you're not living with us, where will you plan to live?"

She bites her lip nervously again. "That's the thing. Dutton asked me to move in with him."

I'm in shock. "Really?"

Her eyes light up with excitement. "Yes. It's just so unexpected. He's unexpected. I know he feels the same. He's barely dated since his wife passed. But we've discussed it, and we want to give it a go. I'm fifty years old and have never lived with a man in my entire life. I don't know if this old dog can learn new tricks."

I hadn't considered that fact. She deserves this. I rub her arm. "I think it's great. I'm truly happy for you. I didn't realize you two were so serious."

She fixes her hair nervously. These are unchartered waters for her. "We had this instant connection when I was here last year. I haven't felt something like that since...since..."

"My father."

She nods. "Yes, your father. And then I did something I've

never done. I talked. Every single day when I was back in California, Dutton and I spoke on the phone for hours."

I wrack my brain. I suppose I was out of it those months I lived with her back in Cali, but I do remember her on the phone in her room at night. It's also just now occurring to me that she didn't bring any men home during my time with her.

"What about that guy from the grocery store you went out with a few weeks ago?"

She sighs. "I was freaked out about Dutton, so I agreed to that date. Five minutes into it, I realized my mistake and took an Uber to Dutton's house. I don't know how to do this, Ripley. I've never let myself feel, not since your father."

"Well, if he makes you happy, why the fuck not?"

She smiles and slowly nods. "You're right. Why the fuck not? He does make me happy."

"When are you thinking of moving? No rush. It's nice having you here."

"We'll wait until after this season. You and Quincy need me for Kaya."

"I don't want to hold you back."

She waves her hand dismissively. "You're not. It's for the best. I want to make sure we're truly solid before I take a big step like this. You know it's a big deal for me."

"Yes, I do."

AFTER MOM GOES UPSTAIRS to shower, Kaya is wildly amused in her bouncy seat while I begin aimlessly surfing the internet on my iPad. I usually look at TMZ or one of the other gossip sites because they love to photograph Arizona and Layton. It used to be bullshit stories and innuendo, but now that they're married, that nonsense has died down. It's just photos of them out and about. They're huge stars who happen to be incredibly beautiful. The camera loves them.

I'm flipping through when a familiar figure flashes on the screen. It's definitely Quincy. Even though his face is covered with a hat, I'd know his body anywhere. I click on it to see him with his hands on the arms of an attractive blonde woman. One with a perfect body, a lot different than mine. The caption reads, *Quincy Abbott and Unknown Woman Seen at Upscale Philly Hotel*.

This must be an old picture, but as I zoom in, I realize that he's wearing the clothes he wore last night. My mom mentioning him not being at Screwballs suddenly hits me.

Tears fill my eyes. Can this be true?

I think back to when he came home. I don't remember a foreign smell on him. He immediately pulled my body to his and we made love.

I refuse to believe this is true. I'm not sure what explanation there could be, but there must be one.

We're not kids anymore. We're not playing games. We have a child together. Every single thing he's said and done since Kaya was born tells me he and I are the real deal this time around.

He asked me to trust him. To trust *us*. I'm going to choose to do that. The Ripley of old would crumble into a sea of self-doubt right now. Mature, confident Ripley is going to stay and have a conversation. I'm choosing to believe in our love.

MOM WATCHED Kaya during my softball practice, and now Kaya, Mom, and I are spending some time in the pool this afternoon. There's a big television out there, so we can watch the Cougars' game. Quincy isn't pitching today.

I've been running through my head how I want to approach things when he gets home. I'm going to be an adult and have a direct conversation with him. I'm going to give him the chance to explain himself and whatever he tells me, I'll believe. Despite all of our shit through the years, Quincy has never lied to me.

About thirty minutes after the game is over, I receive a text from him.

Quincy: Something came up. I won't be home for a few more hours. Kiss Kaya for me.

My stomach drops. What is going on?

QUINCY

I pull into my garage, tears filling my eyes as they have for most of the past few hours. How am I going to tell Ripley? She's going to be devastated. I'm devastated.

I look at the clock. It's after ten. Kaya will be asleep. I'm sad I won't see her, but this is going to be a difficult night, and it's better off she not see us this way. I hope June has made herself scarce. I look at her spot in the garage. Her car is gone. Good.

Not seeing any signs of Ripley downstairs, I immediately make my way upstairs. She's not in any of the bedrooms though. Where is she?

I walk back downstairs and notice that the giant glass-paneled doors leading to the pool are open. She must be out back.

I walk through them and see her sitting in the hot

tub. There's a glass of wine and her iPad next to her on the ledge. She's got her arms spread out and her hair is pulled into a messy bun. She looks exactly like she did the first night we kissed. So perfect. So beautiful. I'm truly the luckiest man on the planet. I can't believe it took me so long to get here, but the hard journey was worth the end result. Ripley St. James is mine and I'm hers.

Her eyes are closed but as soon as I get closer, they open and gaze at me. I notice that they're red. She's been crying. Maybe she already knows.

"Shortcake? Are you okay?"

Her head tilts to the side as she examines me. "Have you been crying?"

I nod.

She squeezes her eyes shut and more tears spill out of them.

"What's wrong?" I ask.

She croaks out, "You tell me."

I want to hold her when I tell her this. I sit down and remove my shoes. I'm about to remove my clothes when she lets out a sob.

Not caring about my clothes anymore, I immediately slip into the hot tub, still wearing them, and take her into my arms.

She starts sobbing uncontrollably. I rub her hair. "I'm so sorry. How did you hear?"

She whimpers, "It's on all the gossip sites. I don't understand why."

Huh? "Blanche passing is on the gossip sites?"

She pulls back with a shocked look on her face. "What? Blanche died?"

"Yes, baby. That's where I've been. Her son left me a

voicemail. He said she left us something and needed me to come to her place as soon as I got the message."

Her face scrunches and her sobs get louder. I hold her close. "I know. It's so sad. I feel like she had more life to live."

She cries, "She did."

"I didn't realize her age. I always assumed her to be in her mid-seventies. She was nearly ninety. She was in amazing shape for her age."

Ripley nods as she continues to sob.

We cry in each other's arms for several minutes until she pulls away and whimpers, "What did her son say? What did he want with you?"

I give her a small smile. "Blanche wanted us, as in both of us, to take Thor. She left a sweet note about our relationship and how we reminded her of her and her husband."

She looks behind me, and I shake my head to answer her silent question. "He's not here. He's staying with a friend of theirs. I told her son I needed to check with you first. He's a big dog, and I didn't know how you'd feel about him with Kaya. Her safety comes first."

She nods in understanding, her big blue eyes searching mine. I wipe her tears with my thumb. "If you didn't know about Blanche, why were you crying before I got home?"

She reaches over and flicks open the iPad screen. My jaw clenches at what I see. It's a photo of me with that hooker from last night.

I rub her face, and she briefly closes her eyes. "Shortcake, you don't believe this do you? We've fought so hard for so many years. Do you honestly think I'd trash it for some two-dollar hooker? I asked you to trust in us. To trust me."

She shakes her head. "I saw it this morning right after you left. Even though it was clearly taken last night—I recognized the clothes—and you told me you were having drinks with the guys, I just knew in my heart there was some reasonable explanation. But then you didn't come home tonight. I can't lie and say that I didn't start to let the doubts creep in a little bit."

I zoom in on the bottom right corner of the photo. "Tell me what you see there."

She looks closely and squints her eyes. "Is that Layton's wedding band?" His left arm is in the photo.

I nod. "It is."

"Where were you guys?"

I blow out a breath. "We were at the Four Seasons."

It takes a second, but I see it in her face the moment it registers. "That's where Pierre and Colette are staying."

"It is. I'm sorry, but I had a bad feeling about them when they came here. I went to confront them."

"Who's this woman? It's not Colette."

"Some hooker who propositioned me. I immediately sent her away. You can ask Layton. He heard the whole thing."

"I don't need to. I believe you. I knew there had to be some reasonable explanation. I do trust you."

"Good. I'll never hurt you—again."

"Deep inside, I knew that. What happened with Pierre and Colette?"

I swallow. "We went to Pierre's room and I...massaged a bit of a confession from him."

She sighs. "What did you do to him?"

I wave my hand dismissively. "Nothing to

permanently harm him, but he admitted something to me. Your father left you money."

"I know. They told me."

"Not those pennies."

"Pennies? It's more than I'll make in the next five years."

"Trust me, it's pennies. Colette was trying to get you to sign away your rights. Your father left you a fortune. He took care of you every bit as much as he took care of them."

I give her the number and her chin drops. "Holy shit."

I nod but tears fill her eyes again. "What's wrong?"

"I don't care about the money. It's my mom. She needlessly suffered for such a long time. If I was given this when he died, things would have been easier for her."

"I had the same thought. My initial instinct was to tell them to shove their money up their asses. Then I was thinking you should take it and donate it all to Layton's group home or some other worthy charity. While I still believe you should donate a lot of it, I think you should also open a softball academy for your mom. Consider all the young girls that will benefit from it. Teaching softball to them is her passion. She's obviously very good at it. We can find space near her apartment and build her whatever she needs. You can also buy her a bigger place if she wants one."

She smiles widely. "Mom is planning to move to Philly. Into Dutton's house."

Now it's my chin that drops. "For real?"

She giggles. "Yes. Apparently they've been talking for nearly a year. She's really into him. Let's do it. Let's build it here. My whole team will pitch in. It will feel good to pay my mom back for all the sacrifices she made for me. She'll get to pursue her passion."

"I love it. I told Pierre he had forty-eight hours to fix the situation or you'd pursue twenty-nine years of interest on your share of the money. You should expect a *very* big check, Ms. St. James."

She runs her fingers through my hair. "Thanks for looking out for me."

"Always. I'm sorry about Pierre and Colette being assholes."

"I had already realized after I met with them that a real relationship wasn't happening. Honestly, I wasn't that upset."

"I know you were excited at the prospect of having a bigger family."

She softly kisses my lips. "I already have my family. You and Kaya are my family now. Arizona is my sister in all the ways that truly matter."

"That better not make me your brother."

She smiles. "I definitely don't think brotherly things about you." She wraps her arms around my neck. "You and Kaya are my everything."

I turn us around so I'm seated on the hot tub bench and she's straddling me. Grinning, I say, "This is exactly how we started."

"Thirteen years ago. It's been a long journey, but I feel like the circle is complete. I think we're finally where we belong. I love you, Quincy. I loved you that night and every single night since."

I nuzzle her cheek with my nose. "I did too, I was just too stupid to realize it. I'll never take your love for granted again."

She nods as her lips find mine. First brushing over them and then latching on in her unique way.

Before it deepens, I break the kiss and mumble into her mouth, "There are too many clothes between us, just like that night."

Her eyes light up. "Don't you dare come in your pants again."

I chuckle. "I still can't believe you knew."

I pull off my sweatshirt while she slides down my sweatpants and boxer briefs before re-straddling my lap. I slip down the straps of the top of her turquoise bathing suit until her full tits fall free. They're so sexy and perfect, just like her.

Reaching for her glass of wine, I pour some of it over her chest before grabbing her tits with my hands. Squeezing them together, I alternate between her nipples, circling them with my tongue, licking off the wine.

She moans in delight as she runs her fingers through my hair. I've missed the way she worships and tugs at my hair. I know it turns her on.

My eyes glance sideways as I catch a mirror-like reflection of us in one of the large, folded glass doors. Without removing my hands, I release her nipple and motion my head in that direction. "Look at us, Shortcake."

She turns her gorgeous face and takes in the same reflection. The corners of her mouth turn up. "We look pretty good together, Abbott."

I blow out a breath and shout into the night sky, "Finally, she admits it."

She giggles as we continue to take in our reflection. She's topless on my lap with her hair up and her curls falling forward. Her fingers are in my hair. The steam from the hot tub is in the air around us. It's very erotic looking.

Her nipples pebble as the pace of her breathing intensifies. My cock leaks from the tip. Neither of us want to tear our eyes away from the scene before us.

I rub my thumb over her soft cheek. "You are so damn beautiful. I love you so much."

She turns her eyes back to mine. I see tears in her eyes again, but this time they're happy tears, not sad. Emotional tears. Tears of two people who fought and clawed for thirteen long years to get to this point.

"Shortcake, I want you to watch us while I make love to you. I want you to see how perfectly our bodies work together, how exquisite your face is when you come."

She momentarily hesitates before standing in the hot tub and then putting on a bit of a show for me while slowly sliding her bathing suit down and off her curvy body. I love seeing her confident and carefree like this. It's got my cock begging to be buried in her.

In all her naked glory, she stands, sits on the ledge of the hot tub, leans back on her hands, and spreads her legs in invitation for me.

"You want my mouth first, sweetheart?"

She motions her head toward the reflective glass and gives me a look that can best be described as vixen-like as she scrapes her teeth along her lower lip. "Yes. I want to watch it."

I run my finger up her calf and thigh. "You want to watch while I devour your pussy?"

She nods and breathes, "Make me come, Quincy."

I happily push her legs as wide as they can go. We can both see her full pink pussy in the glass now. "Look how beautiful you are." I run my finger through her slippery flesh and then suck it into my mouth. Closing my eyes in bliss, I murmur, "And so damn tasty."

She moans, "Quincy, please. I need your mouth."

Slowly licking my way up her long legs, I bite, suck, and nibble until she's squirming. I run my beard along her inner thighs. Her eyes roll back in her head. Yep, beard stays. It's worth all the harassment to see this look on her face.

I lick until I'm above her pussy and over the beautiful evidence of childbirth scarring her lower abdomen, thanking her for the greatest gift I've ever been given.

She doesn't even flinch. I love that.

I finally work my way down to her pussy, stare into it, and lick my lips in anticipation. "You're dripping for me."

She wordlessly nods as I grab her curvy hips with bruising strength and smash my face into her.

She yells out, "Oh fuck, that beard. You're never allowed to shave."

I smile as I alternate between kissing, sucking, and licking everything she's offering. Eventually, I penetrate her opening with my tongue all while circling her clit with my nose.

She yells out and then grabs my hair and begins tugging at it. Her hips gyrate while I fuck her as deep as I can with my tongue.

When my thumb meets her clit, her whole body jerks. "Oh, fuuuuuck."

I work her over with my thumb and tongue until her whole body starts to shake. She pulls my hair with the force of an army. Her back arches.

I command, "Look at yourself. Watch as you come."

Her eyes pop open and she stares at our reflection. She pants, "Oh god, that's so hot."

I see the moment it tips her over the edge. Her legs begin to flutter. Her moans escalate, and she fills my mouth with her sweet come.

I slurp and lick her juices until her orgasm fades away. She collapses back. Her body is limp and sated, her chest rising and falling at a rapid pace.

Standing on the bench of the hot tub, I lean over my goddess, capturing her mouth in a bruising kiss. It reawakens her. She grabs my face and tastes herself on my tongue.

I lift her arms and pull her until we're both resubmerged in the warm, inviting water of the hot tub.

I break the kiss and turn her so that her back is to my front. I want us to both watch what we're about to do.

"Keep your eyes open. I want you to see how good we look when I fuck you." My cock rubs through her pussy. Even in the unforgiving water, her juices coat me. "Can you feel how hard you make me? Only you. Only ever you. I need you. Always."

I latch onto her neck as my cock continues running through her, knowing what the teasing does to her body.

She places my hands on her tits. "I love your big hands. Touch me. Everywhere."

She then reaches down, lifts her body, and maneuvers my tip to her entrance. She slides down as I thrust forward into her with a loud grunt. "I love your warmth. The way you grip my cock so tight."

The water is hot, but our bodies are hotter. I grab her sexy, round hips as I push into her over and over again.

She reaches up behind her to grab my hair, pushing her tits above the water line, bouncing wildly to the rhythm of my thrusts. I mumble into her neck. "Look at you. Look at us. Your luscious tits moving as I fuck you. Tell me if you've ever seen anything more beautiful than this."

She stares at our reflection. Our eyes meet in the glass. Hers are filled with nothing but lust. Nothing has ever felt so right.

We're two pieces of a puzzle that finally fit together. I'm no longer that broken piece that will never find its fit. She's fixed me. Her love fixed me.

Our eyes remain fixated on our reflection in the glass throughout the duration. It's beyond erotic and intimate.

I swivel my hips while her grip on my hair tightens. "You're so close, Shortcake. I want you to come all over my dick, and then I'm going to pump you so full of my come it will be dripping out of you for days."

I grab her throat with one hand. She drinks in the image. "Oh my god."

Her eyes flutter, and her pussy clenches around me. "You feel too damn perfect. That's it. Come. Now."

My name flows out of her mouth on a loud scream. We find our releases together as if it's the most natural thing in the world.

I lean back with her in my arms, still buried inside her as we both return from the euphoric state we've been in.

She turns her head and nuzzles my beard with her nose. "I think your tongue is longer than most penises."

I chuckle. "I think your pillow talk is top-notch."

I feel her giggle into my face.

We sit there silently for a while, neither of us in any rush to move. I feel more peace than I've ever felt, knowing this will be my reality for the rest of my life.

What I feel, maybe for the first time in my life, is true happiness. Ripley makes me happy.

Her head rests back on my shoulder as we continue to silently enjoy this moment. She eventually breaks the silence. "I think we should take Thor."

"Are you sure? He's huge. I don't want Kaya accidentally getting hurt."

"He's a gentle giant. He's so much like Diamond, who did nothing but protect you and Arizona. Thor could be that for her." She rubs her fingers through my beard. "I remember it being your dream. Your own big house with a dog like Diamond. Doesn't it feel like fate? I love Blanche even more for gifting this to you."

"To us. She was highly specific that he was only to come to a home we share."

She smiles. "Even in death, she's trying to push us together. The old slickster."

"She adored you. She and I had several conversations about you, both before and after your move to Philly."

"Before?"

"Yes. I've been conflicted over my feelings for you for a long time. I wanted you but didn't know if I could give you what you wanted."

"You give me so much, Quincy."

I pull her tight. "Promise me you'll stay. Even when our seasons are over. I want this. Us. Permanently."

She swallows before softly kissing me. "I want that too. It's all I've ever wanted."

"Me too, Shortcake." I blow out a breath. "Okay. I'll pick up Thor early in the morning before you leave for practice. I want you here. If you think it's too much for Kaya, we'll find him another home."

She smiles into my face. "I can't wait."

I HAVE Thor in my car. He keeps licking my ear from the back seat. "Buddy, I need you to protect our girls when I'm not home, not swallow them whole."

He lets out a short bark.

"I'll take that as a yes."

We pull in through my gate, and I see Ripley sitting on the front steps with Kaya in her arms. She holds up Kaya's little arm and waves at us. I love the thought of coming home to them waiting for me.

I turn back. "I know you're a big boy. I am too. You've got to be extra careful with the ladies when you're big. You never want to hurt them."

Bark.

"I feel like you really hear me, Thor."

Bark.

"Good talk. Let's go meet your sister and your new mommy."

I open his door but keep his leash tight to me. I'm terrified he'll accidentally hurt Kaya.

Ripley shouts out, "Let him go. If you act crazy, he'll be crazy. Let him sniff and explore her."

She's so calm about this. I blow out a breath. "Here goes nothing."

I unclasp his leash. He immediately barrels toward Ripley and Kaya. Oh god.

He stops short just as his nose meets Kaya's. They both tilt their heads and carefully examine each other. She's not afraid of him and he hasn't eaten her for breakfast. I suppose that's a good start.

Ripley doesn't flinch, allowing them to explore one

another. Theoretically, you never want to pull a kid from a dog unless you know it's dangerous. That's easier said than done with a dog Thor's size.

Kaya reaches out and squeezes his nose.

He then proceeds to lick her entire face in one fell swoop. And she begins giggling. Uncontrollably. Deep, hard belly laughs. I've never heard her laugh like this. It's the cutest thing I've ever seen.

Ripley and I smile at each other, knowing everything is going to be okay.

CHAPTER THIRTY-SEVEN

RIPLEY

Today is our first game of the season. When I found out I was pregnant, I never thought I'd be able to play today. What a crazy year it's been.

I'm on my way to the stadium with a big smile on my face. Yesterday I did a photoshoot for plus-sized lingerie. With the money I've received from my father's estate, I didn't *need* to do it. I *wanted* to do it.

At his absolute insistence, since he missed my first session last season, Quincy came with me. The entire day has been replaying over and over again in my mind.

"Quincy, I need to get out there."

His hands slide into my silk robe. As soon as his skin touches mine, my body ignites. Again.

He grumbles in my ear, "You look so sexy. I'm about to explode. I need to be inside you."

He presses his body to mine and takes my lips with his. I can't help but run my fingers through his hair as I kiss him back. He's so fucking hot. And he's mine.

Michel clears his throat. "Mr. Abbott, once again, you are ruining her lipstick. We're already delayed due to your inability to maintain control."

Quincy sighs. "My cock might explode watching you do this."

I giggle. "At least you're not being photographed with a wet spot, which is what's about to happen to me."

His eyes lustfully move down my body, taking in the red lace bra, panties, and garters that I'm wearing. "Red suits you, Shortcake. Be sure to bring this outfit home tonight."

I catch a quick glance at myself in the mirror. I do look good. The outfit is beautiful, and my makeup is perfection. They've got my curls styled in a sexy way. I'm proud of how I look, and my man is making me feel even better about it. I don't think there's ever been a time in my life where I've felt as good about myself as I do right now.

Michel fixes my lipstick for the tenth time, and we finally make our way out of the dressing room and into the studio. A middle-aged man with a camera around his neck throws his hands in the air. In French-accented English, he shouts, "Finally. Ballplayers are the worst." He eyes Quincy. "With Abbotts being the most difficult of them all."

Quincy raises an eyebrow, but the man simply smiles at him. "I'm Francois. I've photographed your sister in the past."

I can't help but be excited. "I've heard of you. You photographed their Sports Illustrated cover last year."

He enthusiastically nods. "I did, and they, too, couldn't keep their hands off each other. I expect better behavior from you two."

Quincy winks. "Unlikely. My wife is hot."

"Ex-wife," I correct.

He mumbles, "We'll see about that."

Francois smiles at me. "Tu es belle." You are beautiful.

I smile in gratitude, remembering a little bit of French.

I step on a green carpet area with a green screen. I learned last time that they can practically superimpose any backdrop they want. The wonders of modern technology.

The photo session begins, and Francois snaps away. This doesn't come naturally to me, but I'm doing my best to channel my inner sex goddess. The bulge in Quincy's pants and his twitching fingers only serve to embolden me further.

They've got me holding my glove and a softball all while wearing the lingerie. It's kind of a ridiculous combination, but it's not my shoot to run. They're paying me an insane amount of money to do it. I'm their puppet for the next few hours.

After a while, Francois tells me that he's changing cameras and to have a sip of water as he does so. As soon as his assistant takes one step in my direction with a bottle, Quincy snatches it away from him and walks my way.

He stalks at me before unscrewing the top, slipping in a straw, and handing me the bottle for a sip.

"Let's get out of here. I want you."

Before I can bother to respond, Francois shouts, "No, no, no. I know where this is headed. Step away from le belle femme."

An idea occurs to me. "Francois, Quincy is wearing the brand underneath his clothes." I know he wears their boxer briefs. "Why don't we do this together? I can't imagine they'll be upset to have Quincy Abbott model the brand."

I make eye contact with the company representative standing in the wings. There's no way he'll pass up on this.

Francois turns to him, and he enthusiastically nods.

Quincy gives me his crooked smile. "Was this your plan all along?"

I bite my lip. "Maybe." Placing the glove and ball down, I run my hands up his chest. "Let's show Layton and Arizona that they're not the only hot ticket in town."

Quincy's blue eyes light up. "I like the way you think, Shortcake. Undress me."

I nod toward Francois, letting him know he should start shooting, which he immediately does. I slowly remove Quincy's T-shirt before running my hands down his chest and abs until they reach his belt buckle.

I'm aware of flashes going off, but I'm lost in the lust of this moment. I can feel my body flushing with desire.

Once his jeans are removed, Quincy stands in front of me in nothing but his boxer briefs, a smile, and a giant boner.

I can't help but giggle. "You better keep your back to the camera, Abbott."

He nods as he slowly kisses his way down my body until he's on his knees in front of me, kissing my hips and stomach over and over again. An assistant hands me my glove and a softball again.

I take in the scene before me. The teenage Ripley would laugh at this, never believing it could be my reality. I'm modeling sexy lingerie. My forever dream man is on his knees in front of me, worshiping my body. All while dozens of people run around fiddling with lighting, taking photos, and making this day just plain perfect.

Francois showed us some of the photos on his computer before we left for the day. I couldn't get over them. I've never felt sexier or more desired.

And the way Quincy attacked me when we got home. I can't help but audibly moan at the memories of our evening. He was like an animal.

I arrive at the stadium and head to the locker room. We're all getting dressed in our uniforms just ahead of taking the field.

I'm washing my hands in the bathroom when I hear excessive vomiting in one of the toilet stalls.

A few seconds later, Arizona walks out of the stall while

wiping her lips. I look at her. "Are you okay?"

She nods. "I'm fine."

"I haven't puked like that since I was preg—" And then it occurs to me. My eyes widen. "Are you?"

The corners of her mouth raise ever so slightly as she slowly nods. "I think so. We started trying like one minute ago. I didn't think it would happen this quickly. I haven't taken a test yet, but it seems pretty obvious." She grabs her boobs. "My tits grew like three sizes overnight. And they're so fucking sensitive."

I shake my head and smile. "Damn baseball players and their super sperm."

She laughs. "Truth."

I wrap my arms around her. "Congratulations. Our kids will be close in age. I'm so happy."

She hugs me back. "Me too. I hope it's a girl and they're besties, just like you and me."

I can't seem to let go of her. "I love you."

She squeezes me tight. "I love you too."

Kam walks into the bathroom tucking in her Anacondas jersey but stops short when she sees us. "It's bad enough you're fucking her brother, Rip, but Arizona too?"

We giggle as we pull apart. I shake my head at Kam. "Is your mind always in the gutter?"

Before she can answer, Bailey walks in buckling her belt and answers, "Yes, it is."

We all laugh until Coach Billie pops her head around the corner. "Time to stick it to them, ladies."

We all smile at yet another inadvertent sexual innuendo from her. Kam lifts an eyebrow and thrusts her hips a few times. "Yes, let's stick it to them. Hard. Long. Deep."

Coach Billie smiles and cheerily shouts, "That's the spirit, Kam!"

QUINCY IS THROWING out the ceremonial first pitch today. He's tossing it to Layton. Even though Quincy is on Kaya duty, Mom is holding her for this in our dugout. She's now a coach on the staff.

He asked me to walk out to the mound with him, which I do. Arizona, Trey, Cheetah, and Ezra are all standing next to Layton as he crouches down into the traditional catcher's position to receive the pitch, all smiling like idiots. I wonder what they're all doing here. This is bizarre.

The announcer introduces Quincy to a wild sea of applause. It's a sellout crowd of over twenty-five thousand. That's almost unheard of in softball. Our Philly fans are out in full force tonight.

I take in my man. He looks so handsome in athletic shorts and my Anacondas jersey. His hair is a little shorter than it was, and he trimmed his beard, but he's keeping it longer than he used to knowing how much I enjoy it. *Thoroughly* enjoy it.

He winks at me and then winds up to throw the pitch but doesn't throw anything. Swiveling around, he smiles at me before putting on sunglasses and bringing a suddenly appearing microphone to his lips. He begins singing into it, "You never close your eyes anymore when I kiss your liiiips..." the opening line to "You've Lost That Loving Feeling."

Before I know it, the rest of the guys are standing next to him in sunglasses, each singing the next few lines until they all belt out the chorus together, with Quincy smiling in the middle of them. It's basically exactly how it was performed in the movie *Top Gun*. They clearly practiced for this.

They serenade me and run through about half the song with the crowd going absolutely wild. Quincy, looking so fucking perfect and handsome, hands the microphone to one of the guys and then drops down on one knee.

Twenty-five thousand people gasp, me included. He takes my hand in his. "You once asked me to love you in the light, Shortcake. Well, there are about ten thousand lights on us now, twenty-five thousand pairs of eyes on us in person, and millions more watching from home. As much as I also *love* to love you in the dark," he wiggles his eyebrows up and down, "I promise to always love you in the light too. You're the mother of my child, the love of my life, and my soulmate. Our whole lives you've given and given. Now it's my time to give to you." He opens a maroon velvet ring box. I don't even notice the ring at first, simply staring into his deep blue eyes. "Ripley St. James, will you marry me?" He mumbles, "Again."

Cheetah coughs, "Don't do it," which he says too close to the microphone. Everyone in the stands hears him and starts laughing.

Quincy smiles. "Fun fact, pitchers who embarrass themselves for the women they love are twice as good in bed as centerfielders." He side-eyes Cheetah.

I'm quiet, not in contemplation, but in shock. A woman in the crowd screams out, "If you don't say yes, I will."

Everyone laughs, including Quincy and me. He shrugs. "It looks like I have other offers. What do you say, Shortcake? Want to make an honest man out of me?"

I'm beyond choked up with emotion. After a brief pause, I can only manage a nod, which sets the entire crowd off into cheers. Quincy stands and raises his arms in triumph before slipping the ring onto my finger.

He pulls me into his arms. In front of millions of viewers, and millions more who will undoubtedly watch this on replays, Quincy Abbott, the man I've loved my entire life, unashamedly gifts me the greatest kiss that has ever been.

EPILOGUE

THREE YEARS LATER

RIPLEY

I puke my guts out in the locker room bathroom for the third day in a row. I mumble to myself in my best deep Quincy voice, "Get your IUD out now. It takes a few months. We want to start trying right after the Olympics. I'll use a condom." Quincy Abbott and his damn condom-repellant super sperm.

I haven't taken a test, but I have zero doubt that I'm pregnant. I'm late, and this is exactly how I felt when I was pregnant with Kaya.

Somehow, I'm pregnant at the Olympics, just like my mother was with me. This kid better be well-behaved. After Kaya, we're owed a good one. That child is the devil incarnate, getting into trouble at every turn, with Thor being her willing accomplice in most of it.

I haven't told Quincy about the likely pregnancy yet, wanting to find a perfect time to do so.

I flush the toilet just as I hear a puking noise in the stall next to me. As I'm washing my hands, Arizona walks out. She wipes her mouth and freezes as she sees me. It's a bit of déjà vu.

I narrow my eyes at her. "Are you—"

At the same time, she asks, "Are you—"

We both nod and then start laughing. "I'm pretty sure I am. I haven't taken a test, but I know."

She smiles. "We found out two weeks ago. We were going to start trying right after the Olympics, but I guess you can't plan these things."

"Us too. How did we get through our teen years without ending up on an episode of *Teen Mom*?"

Laughing, she answers, "Yep. Wow. Pregnant together." She squeezes my hand. "This is going to be so much fun."

"It is. I hope my kid is just like...Ryan."

She giggles. Arizona and Layton's daughter, Ryan, is significantly easier than Kaya. She's like a mini adult. I have no doubt she's sitting calmly in the stands with Layton while Kaya is running around like a lunatic, driving Quincy nuts as he chases her.

We walk out of the dugout and onto the field with our hands locked together and tears in our eyes. I turn my head to my best friend. My sister. Technically my sister-in-law, but she's always been a sister to me. "This is the day we've dreamed about together for twenty-seven years. The gold medal game of the Olympics."

She shakes her head in disbelief, looking down at her USA Softball jersey. "I can't believe this is real."

"It is." I blow out a breath. "We have one more game to win."

She pulls me into her arms. "I love you so much, Rip. I wouldn't be here without you."

I squeeze her back. "Neither of us would be here without the other. Every day for twenty-seven years, we've pushed each other to be better."

She nods. "Let's fucking do this."

"Fuck yes."

As we run out onto the field, I see my mom in the front row, wearing my jersey. Mom smiles as she points to the USA on her jersey. Her running joke for years about switching from a Canadian to a USA jersey for me runs through my mind.

In the row behind her are Layton, Ryan, my in-laws, and two empty seats. I toggle my eyes around until I see Quincy chasing Kaya up and down the stairs. I can't help but giggle. I've done that plenty of times at Quincy's games.

Quincy is still playing ball. He thinks he has a few years left in him, and I agree. Because his wife is in the Olympics, the team agreed to a one-week leave of absence for him to be here. They were able to work things out so that he's only missing one start. He threatened retirement if they didn't allow it.

The Anacondas' season ended a few weeks ago with our fourth straight championship. All the league owners agreed to an earlier season this year with so many of us being on the Olympic team.

IT'S TIED at zero going into the sixth inning. I'm exhausted. The grueling schedule and the pregnancy are catching up with me.

Arizona knows me well. "Six more outs. Muscle up. You've got this."

I nod. "Doing the best I can. I need the bats to come alive."

As a pitcher, I haven't batted since middle school. My job is to focus on pitching. I leave it to my teammates to provide the offense.

She nods. "I'll take care of business."

I know she will. She's never let me down in twenty-seven years.

After a seeing-eye single up the middle, our left fielder goes all out for a humpback liner down the line, and it gets by her. The run scores. Shit. We're down by one going into the bottom of the sixth.

Arizona leads off the half-inning with a bunt single. We're standing in the dugout cheering for her. Kam is up now. I see the coach give Arizona the sign to steal. That's ballsy and risky, but no one is faster than Arizona Abbott. I love it.

Kam watches the first pitch and Arizona takes off. She dives headfirst into second base just ahead of the tag. We're all going nuts as she expertly wipes the dirt off her uniform.

Kam executes a perfect sacrifice bunt, sending Arizona to third base. We have to plate this run, so we can at least tie the game.

The next batter steps into the box. We need a hit, a sacrifice fly, or a weak groundball to the right side. Either would score her. She *has* to put the ball in play though.

Unfortunately, she strikes out. We've got two outs now. The only way to bring in Arizona now is if the next batter gets a hit.

Bailey is up. She had a long road to get back into playing shape. I'm so happy she's here. I'm truly happy I get to experience this with all my best friends, but now that we've gotten this far, I can smell the gold medal. It's something my mother wasn't able to accomplish. I want to do this for her as much as I want it for me. And, of course, for all the budding softball players around the world who look up to us.

Bails watches the first two pitches, one being a called strike and one being a ball. She looks cool as a cucumber in there.

Digging her cleats into the dirt, she takes a small practice swing. She gets set for the pitch. We all watch as the pitcher releases the ball. It comes in...and *bam*! It's a rocket over the left field wall. *Way* over the left field wall.

We all start jumping up and down screaming in excitement. Bailey is holding her hands on her helmet in shock as she practically dances around the bases. The crowd is going nuts. We all greet her at home plate, jumping on top of her.

I'm so happy for her. What an epic moment.

After the next batter grounds out, we head to the seventh inning. Three more outs until paydirt. Until we get to fulfill our lifetime goal of winning a gold medal.

Arizona fist-bumps me. "Let's finish this bitch so we can celebrate." She mumbles, "With non-alcoholic beverages."

I giggle as I make my way to the mound. Mom gives me our universal sign to stick with my rise ball and curveball. Always coaching me, even when she's not.

Mom now runs the biggest softball facility on the East Coast. She's turned a small warehouse operation into a successful business that has a mile-long waiting list. She has instructors, strength and conditioning trainers, and several hitting and pitching tunnels. You name it, she does it. Both the Cougars and Anacondas help out when they can. It also gives some of the lesser-known players on the Anacondas a place to work in the off-season. Arizona, Kam, and I are the faces of the team, and we get endorsement offers, but most others don't. I love that they don't have to take odd jobs to make ends meet. They get to work with the next generation of softball players.

Dutton couldn't be here because of the Cougars' schedule, but he and my mom are still going strong. His kids have become like siblings to me. I may not have gained Pierre and Colette Beaumont, but I gained Anderson and Sage Steel.

I see Quincy now sitting next to his dad. Their relationship has grown so much in the past few years. Paul and Pamela make much more of an effort to spend time with Kaya and Ryan, constantly flying back and forth. They're considering retiring and moving to Philly to be near the grandkids. I love Quincy's changed attitude toward them. He's doing his best to understand them, and in turn, they're devoting more time to all of us.

As for Quincy and me, we've never been stronger. My husband has lived up to every promise he made me, showering me with more love, affection, and respect than I could have ever dreamed possible. I'm living my fantasy life.

Kaya is sitting on his lap with a giant lollipop. Oh man, that might keep her still for a bit, but we're going to pay for it later. Her big red curls are more wild than usual. Quincy can't manage them quite as well on his own, but I certainly never mention it.

He whispers something in Kaya's ear, and she giggles. For a man who didn't think he was cut out to be a father, he's just about the best one I've ever seen. I think he's managed to achieve a good balance. While he does have to travel for road games, when he's home, he's truly with us. Kaya wants for absolutely nothing in the father department.

We make eye contact, and he mouths, "Love you," as I make my way to the mound, possibly for the last time.

I subtly blow him a kiss before getting back to the business at hand. I strike out the first two batters. The atmosphere here is electric. We can all smell the gold medal.

Arizona gives me the signal for an outside curveball. I nod and secure the proper grip on the ball. The second I release it, I realize that it's not going to hit the target. It's going to catch too much plate.

The batter swings and connects hard. It's a shot into the five-six hole. Crap. That's going to be a hit.

But it's not.

Kamryn *fucking* Hart dives and stops the ball from going into the outfield. She gets up on her knees and fires a damn missile to first base.

It's a bang-bang play. All eyes are on the umpire. As if it's in slow motion, he lifts his right fist and signals that she's out.

Arizona and I immediately make eye contact. I think we're in shock that this happened. We did it. The moment we've dreamed of since we were little girls playing in the park together.

She then takes off in a dead sprint toward me with her hands raised in the air and the bigger-than-life Arizona smile. She leaps into my arms, and I catch her.

"We did it, Rip!"

I laugh as the rest of our teammates pile on top of us in celebration.

Once the madness dies down, Arizona heads straight for Layton and Ryan. I'll find Quincy and Kaya in a minute, but there's one stop I need to make first.

I walk toward June St. James, whose face is covered in tears. She holds out her arms for me and I fall into them, my tears matching hers.

I whisper, "Thank you, Mom. I wouldn't be here without you."

"You did it. I'm so proud of you."

"*We* did it."

I look up and see Quincy anxiously waiting for me. I pull away from Mom and move toward my husband, who kisses the shit out of me. He has a tendency to do that quite often.

I mumble into his mouth, "I've missed you this week."

We had to stay in the Olympic Village. No spouses allowed. It's been a long week without him. I missed him so much.

He mumbles back, "Congrats on achieving your dream. I can't wait to achieve mine. I'm going to do you tonight with you wearing nothing but your gold medal."

I smile as my body shivers in anticipation. "Can we do it on the field?"

He gives me his sexy crooked smile and subtly nods.

I see that Arizona brought Ryan onto the field, so I reach for Kaya. I notice lollipop bits stuck in her hair. Quincy chuckles. "Your kid is a handful."

I pull him close to me again until his ear is by my lips. "We've got another one on the way."

His eyes meet mine and his whole face lights up. "You are?"

I nod. "*We* are. I'm almost certain."

"I'm not missing a single day this time."

I smile. "I know."

Kaya and Ryan run around the field with the team in celebration. Happy and carefree. I see Quincy and Layton snapping a million pictures. I hope the girls will one day truly cherish this memory.

I'm posing for pictures when I see Kaya pick up my glove and Ryan pick up Arizona's. Kaya winds up and fires a pitch at Ryan. Oh my god. She threw it hard. She's going to hurt Ryan. But Ryan catches it and then they imitate mine and Arizona's exact celebration, with Ryan jumping into Kaya's arms.

Arizona and I smile at each other. And the cycle begins again.

THE END

Want to know how they "celebrate" Ripley's gold medal? For the extended epilogue, scan below:

ACKNOWLEDGMENTS

To Ripley and Quincy: You fuckers made me cry. A lot. I loved being back in this world again. Softball has been a part of my life since I was a child. I love bringing women's sports to romance novels. About damn time.

To the Queen, TL Swan: This amazing journey would never have begun if not for you and your selfless decision to help hundreds of women. This crazy and unexpected new path in my life has brought me so much happiness. I owe it all to you. Please know that I try every single day to pay it forward. Getting to meet you in person was the icing on top. It's amazing when your mentor is even better in person.

To Lakshmi, Thorunn, Mindy, and Brittany: Thank you for being the best beta bitches a girl could ever hope for. You all drop everything in your lives when I call (see video). I hope I'll be able to repay you someday. Perhaps Lakshmi's chef can make us all a meal one day.

To Jade Dollston, Carolina Jax, and L.A. Ferro: You are my bookish besties. Our daily texts are my lifeline. I love the support we have for each other. I REALLY love that we are doing a project together. Book Boyfriend Builders for life!

To My OG Beta Readers Stacey and Fun Sherry: Thank you for being there for me since day one. You've been my biggest and hottest cheerleaders every single step of the way.

To The B!tch Squad Members: Every single day I marvel that you all support me and my books the way you do. Every single post and word of encouragement is beyond appreciated. My goal is to meet all of you in person one day.

To Chrisandra and K.B. Designs: **Chrisandra**: Thank you for making me feel illiterate. That's what makes you such a great editor. **Kristin**: Thank you for helping this artistically challenged woman. Thank you for creating covers with specific instructions from me like, "Do what you think is best."

To My Family: I truly feel bad for you. An immature mother and wife can't be easy. To my daughters, thank you for tolerating me (ish). Thank you for telling everyone you know that your mom writes sex books. I appreciate that by the time you were each six, you were more mature than me. To my handsome husband, thank you for your blind support. You never question my sanity, which can't be easy. But let's face it, you do reap the benefits of the fact that I write sex scenes all day long. Every single male main character has a little of you in him (only the good stuff - wink wink).

ABOUT THE AUTHOR

AK Landow lives in the USA with her husband, three daughters, one dog, and one cat (who was chosen because his name is Trevor). She enjoys reading, now writing, drinking copious amounts of vodka, and laughing. She's thrilled to have this new avenue to channel her perverted sense of humor. She is also of the belief that Beth Dutton is the greatest fictional character ever created.

AKLandowAuthor.com

ALSO BY AK LANDOW

City of Sisterly Love Series

Knight: Book 1 Darian and Jackson

Dr. Harley: Book 2 Harley and Brody

Cass: Book 3 Cassandra and Trevor

Daulton: Book 4 Reagan and Carter

About Last Knight: Book 5 Melissa and Declan

Love Always, Scott: Prequel Novella Darian and Scott

Quiet Knight: Novella Jess and Hayden

Belles of Broad Street Series

Conflicting Ventures: Book 1 Skylar and Lance

Indecent Ventures: Book 2 Jade and Collin

Unexpected Ventures: Book 3 Beth and Dominic

Enchanted Ventures: Book 4 Amanda and Beckett

Extra Innings Series

Double Play: Arizona and Layton

CurveBall: Ripley and Quincy

Payoff Pitch: Bailey and Tanner

Off Season: Kamryn and Cheetah

Faking the Book Boyfriend: Gemma and Trey (Being published as part of the Book Boyfriend Builders collaboration)

Signed Books: aklandowauthor.com